When her boyfriend backs out [of their] trek through Asia at the last m[inute, she] doesn't quite realize what she's gotten herself into by going solo . . .

"I'll be skinny and brown. I'll wear little sarongs and tiny vests, and I'll stand around looking lovely and thinking deep thoughts. Tom will beg me to go back to him but I will have met someone intriguing and devoted, and I will look sorrowfully upon Tom and tell him not to dwell on what might have been. I'll tell him that it could all have been so different if he'd joined me on the spiritual and physical journey, but that now I have left him far, far behind. Perhaps I will have tales of soul-searching: 'I spent six months on a beach in Thailand staring into the depths of my self—it wasn't a pretty sight'; 'I sat in a slum in Calcutta with rats running around my feet and cockroaches in my hair, and I suddenly realized what true happiness was'; 'It wasn't until I'd lived in the monastery for three months that I truly felt free from the shackles of The West.' Yes, the year itself will be a small price to pay. I'll grit my teeth, and it will pass, and then I'll get to go home again.

"In anticipation of how ill I will get in Asia, I consume everything in the plane lunch, including the chocolate, and two bottles of wine."

EMILY BARR has written columns and travel pieces for London's *Observer* and *The Guardian*. *Backpack* is her first novel. After traveling around Asia for a year, she has settled back down in England.

BACKPACK

Emily Barr

A PLUME BOOK

PLUME
Published by the Penguin Group
Penguin Putnam Inc., 375 Hudson Street,
New York, New York 10014, U.S.A.
Penguin Books Ltd, 80 Strand,
London WC2R 0RL, England
Penguin Books Australia Ltd, Ringwood,
Victoria, Australia
Penguin Books Canada Ltd, 10 Alcorn Avenue,
Toronto, Ontario, Canada M4V 3B2
Penguin Books (N.Z.) Ltd, 182–190 Wairau Road,
Auckland 10, New Zealand

Penguin Books Ltd, Registered Offices:
Harmondsworth, Middlesex, England

Published by Plume, a member of Penguin Putnam Inc.
First published in Great Britain in slightly different form by Headline Publishing.

First Plume Printing, January, 2002
10 9 8 7 6 5 4 3 2 1

 REGISTERED TRADEMARK—MARCA REGISTRADA

LIBRARY OF CONGRESS CATALOGING-IN-PUBLICATION DATA:

Barr, Emily.
    Backpack / Emily Barr.
       p.   cm.
    ISBN 0-452-28293-4
       1. British—Asia—Fiction. 2. Inheritance and succession—Fiction.
    3. Young women—Fiction. 4. Asia—Fiction. I. Title.
    PR6102.A77 B3 2002
    823'.92—dc21   2001036716

Printed in the United States of America

To James, with love

BACKPACK

CHAPTER 1

On the day we buried my mother, I deduce, I have poisoned myself with alcohol and drugs, and woken up in the hospital. I console myself with the knowledge that it's what she would have wanted.

This must be a hospital, mustn't it? I'm in a single bed, strapped in tightly by sheets. I can't move, any more than my mother can. I'm in my own coffin. Nothing is particularly sore except for my stomach. I feel sick, but I haven't got a discernible injury. One of my legs feels bruised, and I am suddenly scared that it's a phantom pain on an amputated limb, but there is a leggy bump under the sheet. I think I'm intact. I have a blinding headache, and I feel fuzzy, much more so than on a normal New Year's Day.

This place smells of disinfectant, but not in a reassuring way. Half disinfectant, half sick. I'm attached to a machine. It must be a hospital. This is alarming. The only thing I want to do is to burst into tears. I try to remember why. I should be happy. I force myself to be happy. It's only the comedown that's making me sad. I was happy last night. I was relieved.

I don't think I even made it to midnight. What a way to greet the year: passing out and probably forcing some doctor to inspect the contents of my stomach as the clock struck twelve. I wish I was at home, nursing this monstrous hangover. Mum was ill; I'm not. I don't want to lie here and do nothing. I can get up and go. That's all I need to do. I'll get up in a minute and find my clothes.

I have a hazy memory of being in an ambulance—a quick flash of lying down, driving fast, drifting. Someone with me, trying to make me sick. Shouting at me to wake up. I couldn't do it. I went back to sleep. Now I feel, appropriately, like death. I will get up in a minute—I have to—but I'll just have a rest first. I've always wanted to go in an ambulance. I'm half-heartedly cross not to have been awake enough to appreciate it. I suppose most people aren't. A broken leg or something would be the optimum ambulance experience.

Cars swerving out of the way, me storming through the red lights, lots of people concentrating only on me, and all because I took a line too many of coke, or had one too many vodkas, or both. I can't believe I missed that.

I often feel like I do now, but not so dramatically. I know if I drank enough water and juice and coffee, and filled up on carbohydrates, I'd be all right by tonight. I need a full English breakfast at the café. The very thought makes me heave. I wonder how to call a nurse; I don't think I've got much of a voice.

I can't remember how, exactly, I got into this stupid state. I know yesterday was the funeral. I certainly didn't collapse then. I made a supreme effort to be as dignified as possible, and I think I carried it off extremely well, though it appears that the dignity didn't last until the sun set. That's unfair, it probably did, since that would have been at about 3 p.m. but not much beyond.

It was a hypocritical service at the church in Hampstead, an establishment I happen to know Mum last attended on Christmas Eve twelve years ago, and then she only went to get a glug of Communion alcohol. "Ghastly!" she exclaimed on her return. She banned us both from attending in future. God lost her soul by serving bad wine. He must be gutted.

Yesterday, the ban lifted, I sat in the front pew, smelling the old musty smells, and I rejoiced. I sang the hymns I'd chosen for her: Lord of all hopefulness, Jerusalem, All things bright and beautiful. These are the hymns you know if you don't go to church. I sang them loudly, discarding my self-consciousness. I was glad she was dead. Glad for her, glad for me, and glad for the fact that my boyfriend, who left me three weeks ago, came back to comfort me. Tom sat next to me, looking suitably sombre. His presence beside me electrified me. Tom always dominates any space he's in. He is a big man, and in the past few years his waist-line has taken on a life of its own. The same thing has happened to all his friends. Boys don't have to care when their lifestyle catches up with them. Girls do. Life isn't fair.

His dark hair and rosy cheeks had been shampooed and scrubbed respectively. He looked sensitive and full of regret. But he was still my Tom, and he still knew Mum. His solemnity, like mine, was just for show. Together, we looked handsome, and that knowledge bolstered me further. God knows what I must look now, in a hospital gown and crinkly knickers.

Yesterday, I was wearing a black scoop-necked dress I bought months ago in New York with the funeral in mind, a black fur coat that I'd taken from the back of Mum's wardrobe, and killer heels, with deep red lipstick. I enjoyed the bimbo-widow look. Tom, who never wears a suit, was wearing a black one he'd had made in Hong Kong, years ago when he was lithe. He couldn't have done the jacket up if he'd tried. His hair was shining. He looked completely unlike his normal, dishevelled self, and I loved him for doing that for me. My brother Will was on my other side, and I was proud of him too. He looks like Mum did in her hey-day: tall and blond and striking. The same as me really. The vicar talked about her for a little bit, which was risible. He didn't know her. She didn't know him, and if she had she wouldn't have liked him. He said she had "touched the lives of those around her," which must be the catch-all, bottom-of-the-barrel citation. He must have to bury unrepentant infidels all the time. I bet they outnumber the faithful.

Oh God, here we go. I grab a strange, kidney-shaped plastic container beside my bed just in time to vomit into it. A radioactive green liquid comes out. This should make me feel better, but it doesn't. I try to remember that my underlying state is happiness, but for now the nausea has penetrated all other feelings, and grown there, like cancer. Where is Tom? Where is Will? Where is my scoop-necked dress?

I can picture the burial, and it is unreal, like a film. It was, of course, freezing, though I was snug in my dead minks. The sky was slatey, the grass was that bright green it goes just before it rains (a toned down version of my sick). Towards the end it began to drizzle. There were very few people. Dad was there, and Lola had made sure he brought a child with him, lest he should enjoy being alone for a moment and leave her. Poor Briony was standing, three years old and bewildered, at the burial of a woman whose name may not be mentioned in their house. She behaved admirably. A few of Mum's horrible family had turned up. She was always coy about why exactly she never saw them and they never sent more than a terse card at Christmas. I know the reason, now. They were all beautifully dressed, rich, so-called Christians from the country—the kind of people who not only go hunting, but host the hunt ball and rub foxy gristle on their children's faces—and looked satisfied to see her finally lowered into the ground. I hated them all.

Will skulked at the back, where they had to turn and stare if they wanted a quick look at him. He had the air of someone furtively having a fag, but of course he wasn't. He was just hiding from the people he's always wanted to meet.

I remember Tom behaving appallingly. While all the ashes to ashes stuff was going on, and I knew it was my moment to be sad, the only one I was allowed, and I was feeling dull and empty instead, he started moving his arm down my back, slowly, until he was stroking my bottom highly inappropriately. I found this horribly funny. Mum would have too, but only because of all her relatives, and her ex-husband, standing around looking pompous and hypocritical, like Prince Philip at Diana's funeral. I tried hard not to laugh, but it got worse and worse. Tom was straight-faced. How dare he? That was my mother, in that box. It seemed so stupid. Mother in the box. Jack in the box. I felt a huge snort of hysteria coming, and whipped out my orphan's handkerchief in time to bury my face in it and pretend to cry. My hair was blowing everywhere. I pictured us all in a long shot from far, far away. Maybe an aerial shot. We were archetypal mourners, yet I don't think there was a single person there who was genuinely pained that she was dead. I couldn't believe it had finally happened. Will was sad, but that was only because he hadn't met her. Nothing surprises me now about my family. They are too bizarre to make up. Still, it probably makes me more interesting than someone who had a boring old crappy normal childhood.

I am becoming agitated. I really want to cry, but I mustn't start or I might not stop. My tummy hurts. Being here is intolerable. I should be at home with Will and Tom, watching telly and making resolutions. I don't like being ignored. I find a button with a picture of a "toilet" lady on it, and press it. I want someone to take away my green sick, apart from anything else, and bring me a glass of water. There is no discernible sound, and nothing happens. I bet everyone's hungover. Perhaps all the nurses have called in sick. I wish the curtains weren't drawn round my bed. There are noises in the ward, but I don't seem to have the energy to get up and have a look, or, indeed, to whisper for a passer-by. Hospitals are full of farting, shouting men, and I don't want to invite one, inadvertently, into my boudoir.

Will pissed me off when he phoned, last week, the day after I found her on the floor. When I picked up the phone, he said, "Hello, who's that?" I hate people who ring you up, forcing you to stop whatever you were doing and answer the phone, and then demand to know your name. They could be anyone. They have to tell you their name before you tell them yours; that's the rule. So I said, "More to the point, who's that?" He said his name was William and he needed to speak to Anne. I told him he couldn't. Then he said that, although I didn't know him, he was my brother. I'm still shocked. I wish I'd known I had a big brother. I'd have made Mum see him. As it was, he was writing asking to see her, and she was saying she couldn't face the trauma. She was so weak, that woman.

I have a niggling feeling when I think of Will now. I hope I didn't say the wrong thing to him yesterday, because the wrong thing could be completely, disastrously wrong. I don't expect I did.

After the service, all the strangers stomped around my home as if it was a village hall or a pub. They complained that there was no toilet paper left, and asked where we kept the bottle-opener. Everyone was there, except for the one person who had barely stirred from her comfy chair for fifteen years. Now, that was strange. We'd got loads of nibbles in from Waitrose. It cost me a fortune but, I reasoned, I don't need to worry about money now. I thought we'd have masses of food left over, but we didn't. The mean relatives not only ate everything I'd bought, they also found Mum's store of chocolate treats. She certainly doesn't need them. Tom and Kate and I had a secret stash of vodka, which they didn't find. We made everyone else drink the cheapest wine in the shop. I owed Mum that much.

I think the vodka is where the day's drinking began, but I wasn't necking them back, just keeping my courage up. Cunningly, we had them laced with Coke, and all the oldsters thought we were on soft drinks. One lecherous relative bought into the whole "innocent kids" act and slipped me a fiver, presumably unaware that I'm £50,000 richer now. I stumbled a bit in my amusement, and grabbed the table to stay upright. I wandered off, found Briony painting my old Tiny Tears with nail varnish in my bedroom, and gave her the money.

"Buy a nice toy," I suggested. "Something that makes a big loud noise."

"A BIG LOUD NOISE!" she agreed enthusiastically. "I'll buy it with money.'"

"Like a trumpet," I told her. I don't know why I bother, she's hardly going to be visiting the shops on her own. She seemed keen on the trumpet, so maybe she'll nag until she gets one.

At one stage I was sitting on the stairs with Tom, drinking a very strong "Coke" and watching in amusement as the horse-faced wankers who'd disowned Mum for having the misfortune to get pregnant at sixteen nosed around her house. Thank God we'd had the professionals in to clean up. They'd have loved it if it had been as encrusted as she liked it. It was her Miss Havisham house.

"Do you promise to be nice to me now?" I pestered Tom. He always gets annoyed when I talk like this and I only do it by accident, when I'm drunk. I forestalled his protest, however, with my killer punch. "I'm an orphan now, you see.'"

Unfortunately, my father was within earshot. "You are not a bloody orphan!" he hissed furiously, trying not to attract anyone's attention, and thus attracting more. Tom laughed loudly. Dad was livid.

"Not technically," I conceded, taking Tom's hand for moral support. "I just mean, I half am. More than half really, I've never lived with you."

"You've got me and you've got your stepmother," he said. "That's as many parents as most people get. You are twenty-seven, you know. You're not a child."

I glared, and downed the rest of my vodka. My father is a twat, and he doesn't even know it. I was dying to tell him many, many things, but it would just have delighted the onlookers, who ignored Mum for thirty-two years and then flocked in from the country to nose around her house.

Sniffling a little, I remind myself sternly of my position on Mum, from which I am not allowed to deviate. It is as follows: she messed up my life when she was alive, so now that she's dead I'm not allowed to mope around. I've got to see that the sun starts shining right now. It is symbolic that we buried her on New Year's Eve. I hope it is less symbolic that I woke up to greet my new life in a crappy hospital with yellow paint peeling off the walls. Me, the sad drunks, and the cute children with leukaemia, tragically hospitalised over the holiday period. If I tip my head even slightly, I can feel everything inside it washing around. It is agony. I shall make a resolution. By this time next year I will have radically changed my life. Tom will have realised that his future is with me. I want us to go travelling. Somewhere hot, to start new lives and have fun, and not be stressed.

"That is a splendid coat!" exclaimed an arse-faced woman, nodding towards my fur, which I had hung up conspicuously, savouring the glamour. Even though she was just saying it as an excuse to stand around me waiting to see if I continued arguing with Dad, I do agree with her. I shall tell everyone except these wankers that it's fake. And I'll never see this lot again. "You know," she continued, "I rather think I remember Anne in this. Lucinda gave it to her when she had the, um, embarrassment." She looked significantly at William.

Will, meanwhile, was shifting from foot to foot while an elderly man, possibly my grandfather (yes, that is how close my family is) talked at him.

"She never even told us!" the old git was explaining. "We just noticed one day. She took that coat off, and there it was, clear as day. Threw her out, of course. Not impressed with bastards. She never did make anything of herself."

Will's expression is murderous. I wonder whether this fat old twat knows he's talking to the bastard. I think he probably does. Will probably wishes he'd just stayed an orphan, like me. I can't wait to get to know him properly. We'll look after each other, form a new, non-dysfunctional family.

The curtains part and a woman ambles in. She's not a nurse. Next to this lady I am fragrance itself. She's wearing a hospital nightie which gapes open so I can see her knickers. She's quite old and clearly confused, as she first walks all the way over to my bed and then starts climbing into it.

"My bed!" I rasp crossly. My mouth is dry. These are the first words I've uttered. She ignores me, so I haul myself into a sitting position (ouch), untucking sheets as I do so, and push her back. She sits down abruptly on the floor, still looking glazed. I would call a nurse, but I can't seem to get the impetus. I leave her sitting there, and snuggle back down, and try to remember how I came to this. After the house, memories are fuzzy.

There is a scene of impossible glamour. I am in a gorgeous bar with Tom and Will and Kate and Guy. It is dark outside, but it's early. Everyone is wearing black and grey and deep red, the colour of my lipstick and of my second favourite coat, which I am now wearing (I wouldn't take a fur into Soho). It is very squashed but we don't mind. We are actually sitting on the floor, at my instigation, but we are still the epitome of cool. I am sipping elegantly at a glass of vodka. Outside it is cold, but nobody minds that, because we have come together into this warmth to escape the climate. People smile and talk. I look at my dearly beloved boyfriend, who is cradling me in his strong arms, and I look at my brother. I don't really know him but I love him. Kate is my best friend. She's beautiful. I've always envied her Asian blood. One Indian grandmother, it seems, is all it takes, and you end up with a year-round tan, huge dark eyes, and glossy hair. Kate's lifestyle will never catch up with her, but I can't resent that. I love her.

Guy is saying that he's going to be looking for a new flatmate soon. I rouse myself sufficiently to ask if it can be me. I realise I can leave the Hampstead house forever, now. We will sell it. I will live here in Soho with the beautiful people. I look at Guy, waiting for his answer. He always claims his hair is "sandy," but we all know ginger when we see it. He's shorter than me—shorter even than Kate. He knows how to party, and he's horribly untidy. We'll be good flatmates.

"Can't see why not!" he replies.

I feel loved and wanted. Outside, there are no homeless people, only smiling, lovely people. At the bar I decide to buy a whole bottle of vodka to stop myself having to go back again. I wonder why I've never done that before.

"My mother has died and I'm happy," I announce, beatifically, to the barman.

I repeat it when I get back to the others. It is my little haiku.

"That is a fucking horrible way to be talking," Will bursts out after I say it for the fourth time. "Even if you felt that you should never bloody say it." I remember that I must ask Will about what his life was like in between being adopted and meeting me last week. I've been meaning to ask him but I always forget.

"With respect, mate," says Tom in his mock-Cockney, "you don't know how hard the past few years have been for Tans. Make allowances, yeah?"

Everyone loves me. I am happy indeed.

Then I am walking around in the cold with Will. I don't know where Tom and Guy and Kate went. This frightens me a little, but I keep talking. I hear my voice, but I don't know what it is saying. "The thing with working in the media is, you mix with the sort of creative people you might not meet elsewhere and that means you live a different kind of life. I think I live quite a bohemian life, and that has to be a good thing for me as a person . . ." and so on, and on. I must have had some coke. One of the others must have given it to me. Will stops me talking.

"Tansy," he says. "Tell me about our mother. Tell me what she was like. Please. You're the only connection to her."

Urgh. This is the last conversation I want to have. We have reached some park gates. It's Regent's Park. I think I'll climb over.

"You don't want to know," I tell him. "Come on." I start trying to climb the gates. William pulls me back.

"For fuck's sake. Come back here and tell me. Of course I want to know."

"She was a terrible woman. She was drunk all the time, and she never admitted she had a problem. But she's gone now." I found a little package in my pocket. "Why don't we have some more coke? I will anyway."

"Come and sit down," says Will, "and talk to me." So I do.

All I have after that is a flash of the interior of the ambulance, and a niggling bad feeling. I'll have to ask Will, try and get him to tell me whether I said anything I shouldn't have said. Will I be able to ask him in such a way that if I haven't told him, it won't matter? I will when I'm sober, I expect. I can be a clever girl sometimes.

I have the thick feeling in my head that comes from coke. I have the throbbing that comes from alcohol. I have the shakes and the misery that always follow such happiness. I have an old woman sitting on the floor by my bed. I want to see a doctor, yet I don't want to, because I know they'll tell me off. But I have the perfect excuse for using the National Health Service's resources to clean me up after my self-indulgent excess. I can pretend, convincingly, that I was so upset about Mum that I had to seek oblivion. I can present it as a halfway suicide attempt. They'll never know that I'm glad she's dead and it was just normal high spirits. I think I'm going to be sick again, and there's no other receptacle. I untuck acres of sheets, and get out of bed, on the side where the woman isn't. I wobble alarmingly. I quite like the perverse aesthetics of this regulation gown. I remind myself of *One Flew Over the Cuckoo's Nest,* or maybe a Channel 5 drama about anorexia, not that I'd be a convincing anorexic. Perhaps I'm one of those girls who gets sent to a mental ward by her cruel family who don't understand her and make her have a lobotomy, and I'm battling bravely to get out, while learning about life from the other inmates who really are mad. Dad may not think I'm an orphan, but I do. I'm a sick orphan. These paper knickers are classic. I feel dizzy. And extremely sick. I stumble.

Within moments, I'm back in bed, and the smelly old lady has gone, and my curtains have been opened to reveal that I'm on a mixed ward—gross—and that I am by far the youngest, prettiest person here. What a bunch of shuffling, hacking losers.

"What happened?" I ask the nurse who accomplished all this, assuming poor-little-orphan persona.

"What do you think happened?" she snaps as she fills in some charts. "You took an overdose, didn't you?"

"Did you pump my stomach?"

"Not personally, no."

"It was my mother's funeral."

"We know. Your brother explained. You were lucky to have someone responsible to look after you."

"Well, I haven't got my mother anymore, have I?" I say sharply, and look at her with eyes that are as big and as hurt as I can make them. She doesn't know any different.

A bit later, a doctor fills me in. "You could have died," she says. "Do you know that? We're not here to preach, but hard drugs are extremely dangerous, and I think you should perhaps consider some treatment for your dependency."

"That's just silly," I tell her. "I've never done this before. My mother just died. I won't do it again. I'm not dependent—it was a one-off. I'm sorry for wasting your time." I am being as nice, and contrite, as I possibly can. I think she's just staying and chatting to me because I'm so much more wholesome than the other people, with their papery skin and their sunken eyes. Normally an insult such as "dependency" would have me bristling, but today I can't be bothered. She says I can go home this evening. Because I'm fine, you see.

I'm happy now. My worries have vanished. As I sit in my rumpled bed with tears streaming down my cheeks, I know, for the first time in my life, that I'm going to be uncomplicatedly happy. I'm going to go somewhere hot with Tom, to get away from arse-faced people and the National Health, and we'll have adventures. My new life will begin very, very soon indeed.

CHAPTER
2

Ignoring them, I press my face to the window to see the last of England. Through the double glass, it is unimpressive, and I am furious. Dawn is breaking, in an insignificant way. Sky, runway and grass are grey. In the distance, an area of cloud is silvery grey: this is the advent of the day. If you didn't know, you'd never realise. The airport buildings are ugly and I am leaving. It's been a disappointing year, it's winter again, and, entirely against my better judgement, I am going away. Good riddance, I say silently. Goodbye, Gatwick, goodbye, London, goodbye, job. Goodbye, friends and enemies alike. Everybody in my life is equal now; everybody, significant or not, is left behind. I'm on my own. Fuck you, Tom. Fuck you for doing this to me.

Behind me, the cabin is full of people who hate me. I can hear the man next door talking. "Did you hear what she just said?" he asks his neighbour on the other side. "Actually, I wouldn't like to repeat it."

The plane sets off along the runway. At first it just drives like a car, and then the experience is transformed as we get faster and faster, and louder and louder, and the wheels leave the ground. Gatwick is surrounded by fields, which grow smaller as we ascend, and then wisps of cloud appear next to my window, and a moment later, everything is covered. All I can see is lumpy cloud stretching out forever.

That's it, then. For some reason, I have left the country. For a while back there, I thought I wouldn't make it. I heard my name on what the airline woman claimed was the third time they'd called it. "Final call for passenger Harris, flying to Singapore," a woman read, in a slurred and echoey way. "Please proceed immediately to gate fifty-four where your plane is about to depart."

I had been drinking coffee and reading the paper, for two hours. My corner of the café was resolutely unwelcoming; my most hostile "go away" vibes, as well as my bags all over the other chairs, had kept everyone from my table. I had read the paper from cover to cover. I had not dwelt on my imminent departure from my native shores, or my recent departure from my dear flat, or, above all, the fact that that arsehole had abandoned me. I hadn't even thought about how my old life, or Tom's sex life, would continue without me. Above all, I had not seriously considered returning home and going back to bed. This had taken a considerably concentrated spell of reading the finance news, and now it was eight twenty-three. The plane was taking off at eight-thirty. Normally I am first at the gate, leaving plenty of time for the last-minute upgrades that never happen, and then for reading the inflight magazine and trying to work out which movies we're going to get. Perhaps I didn't really want to go today, but I knew that if I missed this flight, boarding pass in hand, I'd end up getting up in the middle of the night tomorrow and doing it all again. Anyway, I had decided to go. Backing out now would be pathetic. It would be meek. It would mean I was dominated by men. It was never a serious option.

The time to back out would have been three weeks ago, immediately after backing in. I couldn't countenance the idea of missing the plane, of being back in bed and, sheepishly, being discovered when Guy came in to snoop through my stuff, for no other reason than because my subconscious had kept me reading an article about IRAs.

Outside, it was still dark, which I think had lulled me. I could see a few dark shapes of planes looming, scary in the dullness of the dawn. In the terminal, the artificial light made the people in their casual travelling clothes look grotesque. A family gallumphed by, their faces bright white, their features hideously pronounced. They were wearing coordinated purple sweatsuits. Only in England, I muttered to myself. And Wales, I added hastily. And maybe Scotland as well. Take me to Asia. In Asia they have style.

I knew that the only way I was going to reach the plane in the next seven minutes was by moving faster than anyone else in the building. I abandoned the paper and half of my third cafetiere of coffee, and I slipped off my heels and ran like hell. Snotty children and disabled people blocked my way at every turn. I shoved everyone aside equally rudely, old, young and ugly alike. I might well have toppled an old woman right over but didn't have time to look back; there was certainly a small commotion behind me. I tore along the moving walkway, which bounced up and down alarmingly. I shouted "Excuse me!" at the top of my voice, and leaped over suitcases. My tights laddered, even though they were expensive ones from Harvey Nicks. I knew I should have trimmed my toenails. I saw a little car, with some bags on the back, and rushed over to it, breathless. I jumped into the back and got the breath together to say, "Gate fifty-four," but the boy who was driving (pink, spotty face) said he wasn't a taxi and went in the opposite direction, compelling me to leap off again. This, despite the fact that he had no people on board.

"Cunt!" I yelled at him. Not very poetic, but I was under a lot of stress. A pair of pre-pubescent boys, lagging behind their parents, sniggered. The adults glared.

As I approached the gate, things became eerily silent. Chairs were empty, and a bored woman strolled around half-heartedly hoovering. An Asian man was moving a cordon, and closing a door. He saw me—heard my pounding feet first, no doubt—and held it open, while another woman appeared from nowhere and pushed me down the walkway. I ended up in the arms of an orange lady with leathery skin, who bundled me down the aisle. Every door slammed shut behind me.

I was hot and sweaty and red in the face, with my shoes in my hand and my big toe peeping out, its nail a fashionable burgundy. Every single passenger looked up, looked away again quickly, and smiled and murmured as I passed. In business class, the pampered folk sipped disdainfully at their champagne. I wished I could take a seat among them. There were plenty of spare ones. I did ask for an upgrade, but when the man saw my backpack he practically laughed in my face. Through the curtain, in economy, it looked just as bad as I'd expected. Jammed in. Everybody was uncomfortable, waiting for their free alcohol to make them feel better. I shuffled past a badly dressed family I'd noticed earlier, and looked at them with pity. How can they be going to Asia? They must be changing planes and carrying on to Australia. In fact, they could even be Australian. The man looked up at me. He was wearing tracksuit bottoms that, I am sure, sagged around his bum when he stood up. "Don't worry, love," he said. "You made it by the skin of your arse!" And then he laughed long and hard, and his wife joined in. So much for my stylish exit from England.

We have levelled out at what I think is thirty thousand feet. The orange lady reappears, pushing a trolley. She looks at me with narrowed eyes, but she has to serve me because I am indirectly paying her salary.

"Bloody Mary, please," I tell her, remembering, belatedly, to smile. Bloody Marys are the best plane drinks, because the tomato juice cancels the dehydrating alcohol, and also because they're harder to make, which shows the cabin crew who's boss, and irritates people further back who are gagging for their free booze. Serves them right for all laughing at me. Baldie pretends not to notice when the stewardess holds my drink out for him to pass it to me, so I reach across, and Mrs. Orange looks at my hand, which, annoyingly, is shaking.

It shouldn't be shaking. It must be the exercise and stress of nearly missing the plane, as well as the singularly objectionable people with whom I am now confined. Not to mention all the coffee. When the orange lady escorted me to row 23, I was furious to see this bald man in my window seat. He looked up, embarrassed, and started to pick up his stuff—he appeared to have moved in comprehensively, with his paper in the seat pocket, his blanket tucked in, and his shoes off. The plane started to taxi.

"Just sit here for now," said Mrs. Orange, pushing me to his horrible middle seat.

"No I won't," I announced. "This is my seat, and I booked it two weeks ago especially for take-off."

"Then you should have got here on time," she told me firmly. The bitch.

I wasn't giving up my window seat because a bald man couldn't be bothered to put his shoes on. I was still the centre of attention, and I didn't care at all. Meekness is grossly overrated; you can almost always get what you want by being brazen (as for inheriting the earth, serves them right). If people dislike you enough they'll do anything to make you go away. After a brief stand-off, Baldie sighed and moved, looking around at the audience and rolling his eyes. Mrs. Orange stalked off because she had to stand at the front and do the actions. My seat was still warm. From his bum. Horrible.

I didn't watch the safety stuff, apart from my favourite bit, the emergency exit. It reminds me of the cartoon *Aladdin*, when Robin Williams (in a rare burst of funniness, possibly because he's a cartoon genie so you can't see his smug face) points out the exits from the magic carpet: "The emergency exits are located here, here, here, here, here and here." My half-sister Jessica fell off the sofa laughing at that a couple of years ago, at the age of seven, and the memory of her stupid hilarity always makes me smile. It didn't particularly make me smile today but it took my mind off the fact that I am leaving everything I know, without a travelling partner. I wondered how Jess will have changed, next time I see her.

When they got to the bit about mobile phones, I remembered that mine was switched on, and retrieved it from my pocket, where it had been bruising my hip. I decided there was time for a quick call, and dialled the office.

"I won't be coming in today," I told my secretary.

"Oh?" she said, and I could hear the distant sound of typing. "Will we be seeing you tomorrow, do you think?"

"No, I don't think so," I said, and that was as far as I got. The orange woman was by my side, having abandoned the pseudo-falling oxygen mask to attend to me. She leant across and took the phone from my hand.

"I was resigning from my job," I said.

"And I don't care," she replied. "You know you're not allowed to use a mobile on the aeroplane. I'll look after it for you."

"Where are you?" asked the phone in a tiny little voice.

The audience was loving this, in a snide way. I was the one-woman inflight entertainment, and we hadn't even taken off yet. By now the plane had taxied to the end of the runway, so Mrs. Orange held on to my phone and flounced off to sit on her stupid jump seat.

"For fuck's sake," I said. I had been planning a dignified and enigmatic exit, and now it was comprehensively ruined.

"You could have been speaking to the Queen, love, and it wouldn't have made any difference," said the bald man, taking it upon himself to assume I was talking to him, which I wasn't. "She could have been resigning as lady-in-waiting!" he added to the woman on his other side. "It interferes with the radio signals," he added, back to me again.

"I know," I said, and turned to the window. Grey grey grey.

"So why do it?" he persisted, speaking loudly for the benefit of the neighbours.

"Fuck off, you cunt," I said, for his ears only, and turned back to watch the take-off. And then we were gone.

As I reach across Baldie for my drink, I can see Mrs. Orange taking in the fact that I am trembling and concluding that I am scared of flying. She smiles, now, with a modicum of faux-warmth, and hands me an extra little bottle of vodka, which I stow in the back of the seat in front. I have a look around inside, in case Baldie has left a copy of *Playboy* or anything else I can embarrass him with.

"Are you going to be all right?" she asks. She has mentally switched to the "passengers with fear of flying" lesson.

"I expect so," I tell her, and smile a little fake smile in the hope that she will keep slipping me alcohol without my having to ask for it. She probably used to be quite pretty before she toasted herself and bleached her hair to straw. I wonder what her boyfriend would be like. He probably wears a fringed suede jacket and tight trousers, and he'll be at least fifty, with tough skin as well. Matching leather. I wonder whether she ever shags the passengers. Only the desperate ones, I imagine. Perhaps she and this bald git will get it together later.

I see him looking at my shaking hand.

"Parkinson's," I tell him.

The thing is, I'm not scared of flying. I love flying. It makes me happier than almost everything. It is unlikely, but it works. Mum used to spend the rare flights she ever took concentrating on keeping the plane aloft with her willpower, but I hand over that responsibility to science. Science, I know, will be better at it than Mother ever was, and even she never caused more than a little turbulence when her concentration lapsed. Quite apart from that, flying is the only time when responsible adults get to sit down, read, watch films, sleep a bit, and have meals brought con-

tinuously, with free alcohol on tap even in the morning. If they're
sick, there's not only a bag, there's also someone who has to take
it away with a smile. Someone whose job it is to attend to your
comforts and needs. I'm surprised people don't enjoy flying more.
It's not just a way of getting somewhere, it's a time to let go, for
once, and let somebody else take charge.

Today, however, I appear to be in a bit of a state. Anyone
would be, I suppose, with this much alcohol and this many drugs
coursing around their veins, and after so active a night. My heart
is still thumping from the stimulants. I had a last going-away
party with my friends last night. We ate a Thai curry that I made
Guy get, and we drank lots of wine, and I'd got the drugs in specially, and afterwards, when everyone had gone home, I let Tom
stay the night, partly for old times' sakes and partly because I have
no idea when I'll next get to have sex. After freezing him completely for three weeks, I needed his comforting familiarity. I still
love him, and I thought I might have an outside chance of changing his mind.

It didn't work. An hour after going to bed I crept up again, and
took my bulging backpack from the cupboard, and went outside
to wait for the taxi. Tom and Guy had both said they'd get up to
say goodbye, but when the moment came, I just wanted to go. I
phoned Will on the way, because he was the person I most wanted
to say goodbye to.

I look back on the life that I'm leaving and the unexpected way
I'm leaving it. The crunch came on Sunday, three and a half weeks
ago. I was in my flat, in a dressing gown I'd nicked from a hotel
in France, in the middle of the afternoon. Tom and I were fighting, but I wasn't unduly worried because I knew we were actually
doing it, going travelling in Asia, in less than a month. Meanwhile
we were trading half-invented accusations and damning character
assessments, almost mechanically.

"You think you're so fucking hot just because you're good-
looking," I told him. "You think that means you can treat me

however you want. You're just a spoilt brat, and you have no idea how people are meant to relate to each other, and it's all because you're insecure. By the way, you're getting *really* fat."

"So I'm spoilt *and* insecure?" he asked. "Well, at least I'm not sick enough to use my bloody mother as an excuse for everything when I didn't even care when she died."

"You don't understand anything."

"Well, in that case you'll be glad to hear that you won't have to put up with me much longer. I'm not coming away with you."

"You fucking are." This, I thought, was a particularly mean new tactic. I was occupied with where to go. I couldn't storm out, as I wasn't dressed because we'd been having sex all afternoon. The flat was so tiny that I couldn't slam a door without knocking something over. A window would probably fly open. A three-room flat above a porn emporium, which you share with Guy, is not a good place to argue. This hypothesis has been frequently tested, especially in the past month.

Tom came over to me and put his hands on my shoulders.

"Tans," he said, "I've been meaning to tell you this for a while, but the moment has never been right. I've cancelled my ticket, and got the money back, and I've arranged to stay on at work. I'm not coming. Really."

I was stunned. I stared at him, trying to work out if he meant it. He continued, "It was always your thing, going away. My heart was never in it but I went along with it because it meant so much to you. I never thought you'd actually do it. Now we can't seem to talk to each other for ten minutes without screaming, and I think you'll have a better time on your own."

"But it'll be different when we're travelling." I was amazed. "That's the whole point. That's why it doesn't matter that we're fighting now. When we go away, everything'll be all right." I said this clearly, explaining the obvious to a child.

"No it won't, Tans."

I suddenly realised what he'd done. "You fucking bastard!" I screamed. I looked around for something to throw at him. "You've tricked me! You never ever intended to go, but you let me buy my ticket—you just wanted to get rid of me. You devious fucking arsehole. You've engineered it all to be shot of me. Well, you fuck right off. I'm never ever speaking to you again. Have a horrible life."

He wanted to stay and talk, but I wouldn't have any of it. I wouldn't even look at him.

After he left, I got the bottle of wine out of the fridge and managed, through my tears, to open it. I poured it into a pint glass, put on my skiing socks for comfort, and picked up the phone. My world had collapsed.

"Go anyway," advised Kate firmly. "You should have got out of that relationship ages ago. This could be the best thing that ever happened to you."

"Don't you think he's a horrible bastard? Isn't it the nastiest trick you've ever heard?"

"I don't think Tom's a bad human being, but yes, he's horrible for you and an awful boyfriend to you. You're not thinking of staying behind, are you?"

I nodded and grunted, and reached for the fridge, where I found an aluminium carton of cold noodles.

"You are, aren't you? Don't. Look at yourself, Tans. You're miserable. You need to stop drinking so much and cut down on the charlie. You need to get away from London. Not that I won't miss you terribly."

I paused to execute an enormous swallow. "Stop drinking?" We always drank.

"Not completely. Just stop losing control."

"I do not lose control. It's not my fault."

"Yes you do. Tom takes advantage of that. You should dump him, for good. Your relationship is no good for either of you. I mean, you can drink for fun, sure. Just try to stay in charge. Whether it's your fault or not, it's your responsibility. I mean, look at your mother."

"Don't you dare compare me to her!"

So my best friend was abandoning me too. For the rest of the afternoon, I industriously devoted myself to the task of blotting out sorrows and shame as effectively as possible, by drowning them, snorting them, drowning them again just to be sure they weren't holding their collective breath, and writing them down. I decided I wouldn't go. I decided I had to. I didn't know what I wanted. I hoped I might wake up in hospital again. In a state that weirdly combined the anaesthesia of alcohol with the hyperactivity of cocaine, and with last night's remnants still swooshing round my bloodstream, I picked up the newspaper and flicked through, reading the headlines and nothing else. I had no attention span—it had been bred out of me by a job in which I had to read every paper every day, listen to the headlines, get to grips with a story just enough to pass it on, and then forget it. My social life was similarly a series of quick, cheap highs. My life was crap, Tom had walked out on me in a way that was, finally, unambiguous. My best friend thought I was out of control. Life was hopeless. The only person who might support me was Will, and he was in Scotland. I chucked down the paper and picked up another section, crying tears of self-pity.

"It's not my fault," I said angrily as I leafed through the travel supplement. "It's not my fault, it's not my fault." I wondered whether Guy had any drugs in his room. I hoped he'd come home soon and sort me out. There was a travel feature about Vietnam. I didn't know whether to read it or not. Vietnam was our first stop. I could recite our fantasy itinerary in my sleep: Vietnam, Laos, Thailand, Malaysia, Singapore. Fly to Delhi. Go and see the Dalai Lama. Hang out in India. Fly home from Bombay. I knew nothing of any of those places. It was Tom's project, and all he'd been doing was finding obscure locations for my banishment. Sending me away for a fucking year.

I called Will. "It's not fair, Will," I complained. "What shall I do? I can't go on my own."

"Why can't you?" he demanded. "Of course you can. You want to travel, don't you? You've got the money, you've got the ticket, you've lost that deadbeat which is the best news I've heard all week—I think he's gay anyway. Go. For Christ's sake, I can't believe you're even considering not going."

"Do you want to see the back of me as well?" I demanded petulantly.

"Sis, you can be a silly girl sometimes. I want what's best for you. So does Kate."

I was distraught. "I'm scared!" I wailed. "I want someone to look after me."

Some part of me was waking up and was displeased with what it was observing. Some little unaddled part was looking on coolly and wondering how it had come to this. Wondering who this pissed girl was, drinking herself into oblivion, refusing to accept responsibility for her actions, and heading, as though on purpose, straight, and with admirable singlemindedness, down a path to destruction thoughtfully cleared for her by her mother. That part of me knew there was only one option.

From my cooler, airborne perspective, however, I don't think that existence was so bad. I don't think it merited this drastic action. It didn't compare to Will's situation, for instance. I know who my parents are, or were. I've never had to worry about money. I've never been shunted between foster homes and I've never slept on the street except for the time Kate and I slept in the park when we were fourteen to see what it was like. No, my life was fine. I was simply suffering from Paradise Syndrome.

That was a bad afternoon. It isn't like I was always like that. The next day, supported by Kate and Guy, I decided to go, mainly because if I stayed, Tom would have me exactly where he wanted me. I phoned everyone I knew asking if they wanted to come with me, and hoping they'd advise me to stay, but they did neither. Every single person thought I should go on my own. So much for friends. I thought Tom was going to change his mind, but he didn't. He just said, "Hey, cool. You'll have a better time on your own." I walked away from him and, for the first time, I forced myself not to look back. Not for a while, anyway.

The orange woman is strolling down the aisle. I call her over.

"Yes, could I have another Bloody Mary?" I ask her. Then I remember, belatedly, to smile and try to ingratiate myself. "Please?" I add. She is expressionless. Her skin clashes criminally with her red uniform. This airline should never have employed her.

The further I get into the unknown, the better London looks. Going away has, admittedly, been exceptional for my social life. For the past fortnight I have had dinner out every single night, and not only have I not paid once, I have also not put on any weight because of the rushing around I've had to do the rest of the time. People were remarkably nice, once they knew I was leaving. They bought drinks, gave me drugs, and told me secrets which made my own eventful life look like a Blue Peter summer picnic. Trevor, I learned, has closet heterosexual tendencies, while Miles, in the office, has snogged Amanda, the best journalist in the office, three times, even though Amanda's married and Miles is engaged. He doesn't seem to find a conflict between the repeated groping and the fact that he is shortly to promise eternal fidelity to his girlfriend, whom I've only met once and who seemed a bit of a drip; an earth-inheritor if ever there was one. Amanda, meanwhile, didn't know I knew and kept on about wedded bliss and how I must find myself a husband while I was away. "It's not just that there's someone to cuddle up to in bed," she explained drunkenly, "it's the companionship, it's someone there you can tell anything to."

"Anything?" I asked her.

"Yes, everything. Honestly, Tansy, you've no idea what it's like."

I managed never to get so wasted that I let her know I knew. Normally I can't keep a secret when I'm drunk.

They make surprisingly good Bloody Marys on planes. I wish

they still did peanuts, though. These biscuity things are a waste of time. If people are so feeble as to be allergic to nuts, they shouldn't be going to Asia.

Tom will have woken up by now and found me gone. I think the fact that I left without waking him means that I win not only that particular game, but also the set and the match. With any luck he'll feel like a loser, the one left behind while I jet off to the sun.

I found it hard, when I got up, to work out what was my heart pounding with excitement, and what was the coke. I think it was mainly coke. My travelling outfit was out neatly on the chair—black trousers, Ghost vest top for when I get there, with a cardigan for now, and my fur coat for leaving London in December. I had to wear tights—now ruined—under the trousers because it was so cold I could write my name on the inside of the window. The flat is usually warm because it's so small, and when it's cold indoors I know it's going to be freezing outside. Specially at night. My room was all packed up with boxes—my dear tiny boxroom—and my pictures were off the walls. It didn't look like my room at all. In fact, it isn't my room now. Dad'll collect my boxes this afternoon, and Guy's friend Mo will move in next week. So it's not my room and I don't live in Soho. I'm a nomad, a traveller, a tourist. I can't stand the word "backpacker." I'll never be one of them.

I crept down the stairs for the last time. Out on the street, life was still going on regardless. A bloke was pissing in our doorway, and just avoided splashing my shoes. "Yer a fuckwit," I told him, still the inner-city dweller. I have long discovered that the only way to get through to the wasted people is to be—or act—wasted oneself. There were the usual Soho sounds of vomit and laughter. A prostitute tried to steal my cab, but she was no match for me. Not with her spindly little track-marked arms and her junkie confusion. One push and she was gone. I got my bags—my big backpack and massively oversized hand luggage—into the boot. The driver held the back door open for me.

The streetlamps lit up patches of Dickensian fog, and I could see my breath.

"There you go, love," he said, and I got in and huddled up, smiling. Only here, I thought, would you find a cabbie with a Romanian Cockney accent. I tried not to look back. Once we turned off Old Compton Street, I explained to him what to do.

"You have to get me to Gatwick by six," I told him, "and don't speak until we get there unless it's a real emergency. OK?" The joy of Soho, I have long thought, is that you can be as rude or as weird as you want, and there's always someone worse.

"Keep on your hair," he muttered, and I snuggled into myself, a blonde, urbane adventuress, going away while everyone else is either going home, or about to get up, or both (in which case they are bound for a crappy day at work). I watched the houses, all alike, pass by, with their curtains closed, their inhabitants sleeping, as London got grimmer and grimmer until we reached the airport.

Will wished me good luck again when I phoned from the taxi. He sounded quite touched that I'd called, even though I woke him up. Since the funeral, his life's been transformed. He's got a flat in Edinburgh which he rents with the money Mum left him, and as a result of that he's got a job. He's got me as family, and I've got him. He's being coy about it, but I think he's seeing a woman as well. An authentic rags to riches story.

"Take care, then, sis," he said. I love being sis—my fond, ironic name. "If anyone gives you any hassle, I'll come out there and do them."

I hoped someone might phone me, but they didn't. Who would call, anyway, at six in the morning? (Tom? No). Dad did phone, at the least convenient moment, when I was in the check-in queue, claiming he'd tried to ring last night but it was engaged all the time. Either that's true or it was a safe bet of a lie. He was up with Archie, he said, so he'd thought he'd give me a bell now. He held the phone to the baby's ear, and Archie allegedly said goodbye. He sounded quite cross about it. Archie is the youngest of Dad's dynasty, for the moment, and I am the eldest. Perhaps that means we should have a special bond.

"You've packed then?" Dad supposed sleepily.

"I'm at the airport," I reminded him, "and anyway, I did most of it last week."

"Of course, you would have done," he said. Then he trailed off pathetically. My father is crap, absolutely laughably hopeless. Archie started crying.

"Just like my mother." I finished his train of thought for him. Just like she used to be, years and years ago. Archie screamed at this point. Dad always claims that his new family don't like being reminded of the fact that he had a family before, but what he really means is that Lola doesn't like anyone to remember that he was married when she met him, and indeed when they conceived Jessica. The children don't care at all. Though Archie now appears to have developed a sudden sensitivity, just to spite me. I can't say I feel any bond with Archie, or indeed with any babies. They're no fun until they can talk (even I admit it's fun teaching someone to say "bollocks," as I did with Jessica). They also appear to do nothing for Lola, but it doesn't stop her dropping one about every six months and handing it over to an au pair. She must be crazy to trust my father with an au pair in the house.

There are no babies on this plane, which is something. I can hear my neighbour's conversation with the woman next to him, and count myself extremely lucky to be offensive enough to be spared.

"Going to Singapore, are you?" he begins. "Well, I go often, and the thing *I* have noticed"—emphasising the "I" as though that proved it really was interesting—"is that although it is often considered the most, quote, *civilised* unquote of Asia's cities, it is mightily foreign. For example, you should stay out of the Indian quarter, where you might as well be in India itself—very much a case of hold on to your moneybelt. There's Little China. That speaks for itself. It is, quite literally, a little version of China. And you can't visit the city without going for a cocktail at Raffles. Now, I really insist on that . . ." On and on he drones. The woman on the other side of him, who probably lives in Singapore, is clearly bored.

I look to the window, and discover that it is still cloudy all around, which is disappointing. The world should be spread out below me by now. At this rate I'll need my fur after all.

This plane is full of people fleeing from Christmas at home, so desperate to escape the festivities that they trust a metal box to fly. They want an interesting New Year. One where they don't find themselves at a party full of their enemies, or standing on the pavement in the rain and realising it's ten past twelve, or indeed in hospital. My last New Year swiftly became a standing joke among all my friends.

I try to imagine this New Year, in a month. My challenge is to find something to do, and some people to do it with, by then. Tom and I were going to head for the countryside in the north of Vietnam, and do a bit of walking. At least, that's what we said we were going to do. We never would have done, really. Neither of us is strong on voluntary exercise. I imagine we would have been more likely to settle in a bar somewhere, and order champagne. I hope you can get champagne in Vietnam. It won't be much of a New Year if you can't.

I will meet people, I'm sure I will. I'll meet soulmates, other people like me. Whereas these people, my fellow flyers-away with the lack of style sense, will escape for a few weeks, and then, unlike me, they'll go back, smugly, to Britain in January, showing off their tans and complaining about the weather. Back to their stressful jobs and families, to drink too much, take too many drugs, work too hard and plan the next holiday. Most of these sorry people will either be staying in Singapore or flying on to unimaginative places like Australia. I bet I'm the only one flying on to Saigon.

I call the orange woman over and ask for neat vodka. She smiles patronisingly. "You sad and pathetic loser," say her eyes. "Certainly, madam," says her mouth.

It occurs to me that I like drinking, taking drugs, and working hard. I appear to have overlooked this fact lately. I've got into this dramatic situation because I wanted to make things work with Tom, and now I've lost him and I'm here anyway. I'm livid that nobody stopped me.

The person in front, who has dandruff, reclines his seat and crushes my knees. I wedge my knees firmly into the small of his back and wriggle them around a bit. It becomes a battle of wills, but I get bored and recline my own seat instead to see the film. I feel someone's knees there, and hear a loud, male Australian voice saying, "Why do I always sit behind the arsehole?" I turn round and smile. "Sorry, darl," he says politely. I flick him a finger so quickly that he'll wonder whether he imagined it.

The movie is *Doctor Dolittle,* and I cannot bear to watch it, even ironically. I try to read, but can't concentrate. Instead I put my Walkman on to shut out the dreadful surroundings, and concentrate on how enlightened this trip will make me. There was enormous social mileage in going away alone; there will be more still in coming back having done it. I will be able to do yoga, to meditate without getting bored, to say, weakly, "Just a cup of hot water for me, please," when everyone else is having espressos.

Above all, I'll be skinny and brown. I'll wear little sarongs and tiny vests, and I'll stand around looking lovely and thinking deep thoughts. Tom will beg me to go back to him but I will have met someone intriguing and devoted, and I will look sorrowfully upon Tom and tell him not to dwell on what might have been. I'll tell him that it could all have been so different if he'd joined me on the spiritual and physical journey, but that now I have left him far, far behind. Perhaps I will have tales of soul-searching: "I spent six months on a beach in Thailand staring into the depths of my self—it wasn't a pretty sight"; "I sat in a slum in Calcutta with rats running around my feet and cockroaches in my hair, and I suddenly realised what true happiness was"; "It wasn't until I'd lived in the monastery for three months that I truly felt free from the shackles of The West." Yes, the year itself will be a small price to pay. I'll grit my teeth, and it will pass, and then I'll get to go home again.

In anticipation of how ill I will get in Asia, I consume everything in the plane lunch, including the chocolate, and two bottles of wine.

On the screen, Eddie Murphy is having a conversation with a hamster. I am glad to have left in the bleak midwinter. London has been unbearable: bitingly cold, dark grey, and grumpy, with "Have yourself a merry little Christmas" playing in shops. I am on the way to Vietnam. I will be there tonight. This is a good thing. The beginning of my new, calm, Buddhist persona. Are they Buddhists in Vietnam? I don't think they're peaceful enough. I will become a belligerent Buddhist.

Baldie is asleep with his mouth open, exhausted by a bout of staring sidelong at my tits and picking his nose. His carefully tucked-in blanket has slipped off, revealing that his waistband is too high, bisecting his paunch. The woman next to him has wisely moved seats on some flimsy pretext or other. Here I am, leading the travelling life, rubbing shoulders with the kind of people I wouldn't speak to at home. He makes me feel sick. In Asia, however, people will be beautiful, and the other westerners will be similar to myself. High-powered, professionally successful, but open-minded and sickened by the materialism of their lives. I'm not sickened at all, actually. I like materialism. I am a material girl.

I open my little bag, which I wore under my cardigan so no one could count it as hand luggage. Time to touch up my lipstick. I've only brought three with me: an understated brown, a deep red evening colour, and, my normal colour, pale-ish pink. I figured I can easily pick up some more at duty free. I've also got a novel to read, a diary which I must try to remember to write so I can look back on it when I'm old (otherwise I'll forget I was alive at all, like the woman in the ward last year), hairspray, hairbrush and body spray. It was hellish having to pack so light.

In between fitful bursts of sleeping, I ponder my alarming situation. Although I've told everyone I'm staying away for a year, I don't have to. If travelling proves to be boring or slummy, or if I can't find anyone to talk to, or get malaria, then I can go back. I'll stay with Will, and I won't see my friends until such time as it would have been acceptable to decide that London really is the best place in the world, and give up on the rest of it. Meanwhile, I have a connecting flight to Vietnam in 90 minutes. Vietnam is a chic destination. I imagine it to be war ravaged yet laid back. I can make it amply clear that I am British and not American, thus not in any way responsible for horrible drawn-out deaths, napalm, birth defects *et al.* Nor am I French, so I am also not responsible for colonial atrocities. I am glad I'm going somewhere that, although comprehensively screwed, has not been screwed by the British. We're not that bad, really.

I disappear into sleep, which feels as fluffy and soft as the clouds that remain beneath the window.

Waking fuzzily, I have a minor panic as I realise I am late for work. Then I remember, and imagine, with pride, the office this morning. Probably at this very moment.

"Where's Tansy?" asks somebody, someone who doesn't know me very well. Let's say for now that it's Sarah because she hasn't been there long.

"Oh, she's gone," says Miles-the-unfaithful. Paul, who is leaving as well, looks envious, because he's still working out his contract. He made such a big thing about leaving, and he's only going to another paper.

"She'll be in the air right now," he calculates. A hush descends on our corner, the funky corner, and they all wish it was them.

33

Ha. My desk sits empty and tidy, reproaching them for their staid lives.

I snooze again.

When we land in Singapore, Baldie smiles a wary, I-forgive-you goodbye. I forgive you because I lust after you. Or because I don't know if you were joking about the Parkinson's. He is one of the deluded people who leap to their feet the moment the wheels touch the runway and start getting their bags down, so they can queue in the aisle for ten minutes. He chucks down my coat.

"You won't be needing this!" he exclaims.

"Oh, I'm not staying in Singapore," I tell him, being enigmatic.

"Oh no?" he says, lips flopping fishily. "Where then?"

I try to think of somewhere intriguing yet cold. "Tibet," I say, in a moment of inspiration.

"Tibet?" He looks surprised. "It'll be far too cold!" He can't think of anything else to say (no tourist tips to offer), so he begins to shuffle with the queue, even though we haven't reached the gate yet. People are just squashing up closer to each other to foster the illusion that they are progressing off the plane. Before he squeezes right away from me, I call over to him.

"Everybody else is probably too polite to tell you this," I say loudly, "but I think it's only fair to let you know that you have a significant body odour problem."

The person behind him eases out of the crush and sits back down. A few people look at me on his behalf, with disgust, but the man himself doesn't look back. His whole head goes deep red. I feel slightly better. My hangover is beginning to disperse. The next one hasn't kicked in.

CHAPTER
3

Within seconds, the children push me to snapping point, and I shove them away, with both hands, as roughly as I can. Given that I am five times their size, they don't stand a chance. The boy topples into the gutter, and the girl staggers, reaches to check the baby's still there, and retains her balance. That surprised them. That will teach them to put their grimy little hands all over my brand new Irish linen blouse.

They look disappointed. "Too right," I tell them. "There's more where that came from."

With no shred of pride or dignity, they begin their mantra again. "Hello, please, hello, please," they mutter, looking imploring with their big brown eyes but keeping a safe distance. As if. As if I am going to discover a well of pity and suddenly hand over the cash now. The baby on the girl's back doesn't look bothered at all. Its eyes are dull. I don't rate its chances.

Vietnam is disgusting. At least, this quarter of its capital is. I keep thinking it's a joke; I keep expecting to turn a corner and find the real Vietnam, the one everyone else has been to. The interesting one in the guidebooks. The one where I walk around like a model, fanning myself gently, strolling into ancient temples and learning about inner peace. The real Vietnam is scented with frangipani and huge tropical flowers. This one stinks. Animals, vegetables, and probably people are rotting everywhere. I don't mind the heat so much, but I do object to the overpowering vapours of stale piss. It smells like the gents at King's Cross station. But I am outside. This is meant to be fresh air. The sky is grey and dripping with moisture, like a sponge. There is no sunshine, and no breeze. I can hardly breathe. All the smells are trapped. They should clean the city up if they're trying to attract tourists.

I read about the beggars in the Rough Guide, and I know that you shouldn't give to children because it stops them learning trades and makes them dependent on a life of tugging people's brand new blouses. That is a happy coincidence for me, because I wouldn't give to them anyway. I don't believe in it. I believe in people helping themselves. I have suffered for my money (although not as directly as those kids) and I don't feel I owe it to anyone just because they wipe their pooey fingers on me and ask for it. So I am resolute about these imploring little people. I can't let the fact that we are strongly on their territory, and that many pairs of eyes are watching our encounter, affect me.

I can make out ten grimy fingers on my blouse. White is, aesthetically, a good colour for these surroundings, it gleams against the grime, so I'm also wearing a short cream skirt and strappy sandals. Grime, however, does not look so good against the white. These kids have ruined my Asia-wear. Maybe my throwing them across the street has saved someone else's. I leave them behind, still mumbling "please" at me, and walk on, a swagger in my step, with a surge of elation. I'd like to see them hold out so well on my territory. Round one to me.

At breakfast, I loitered because I knew it was going to be like this. Suddenly finding oneself in an extremely strange country, with no friends, and for no apparent reason, takes some getting used to. Contrary to my romantic assumptions (linen curtains fluttering in the breeze, baskets of croissants, respectful natives), the dining room was grimy and sticky, with minimal light struggling through a smeared window. The dusty plastic flowers on the wall made it worse. Every time I speared a piece of egg with my bent tin fork, the table wobbled and rattled so loudly that the waiter came crashing out of the kitchen, abandoning his foul-smelling frying task, to see why I wanted him.

"Can I help you, Mr. Brown?" he said every time. I think he learnt his English from a book.

"My name," I said clearly, "is not Mr. Brown, it is Ms. Harris. And you can help me by getting a table with legs the same length." It was lost on him, but the people at the other table, a midget Australian couple, guffawed as though they were sharing a dining room with Monty Python. I looked at them. They really were tiny. If they'd sat on each other's shoulders they'd have struggled to reach my height.

"Occasional tables, eh?" I tried, riding the comedic wave. "What are they the rest of the time?"

The girl, blonde and bespectacled, didn't chuckle at that. "No, they're always tables," she explained, and conversation abruptly halted. To hide my embarrassment, I pretended to be completely absorbed in the Rough Guide, a pretence I kept up for ten minutes. Fuck this, I thought. Tom and I used to use the occasional table line frequently. It was an in-joke, funny precisely because it wasn't. Other people don't think it's funny. There's no reason why they should. I know this now.

I had a fuzzy head from drinking on the plane. I was tired, and I felt sick. I didn't eat last night so I can't even blame it on Vietnamese food. I was mildly interested to discover from my pretend flicking through the book that Vietnam actually won the Vietnam War. The way they go on about it, I'd assumed it was a Gulf-style all-American triumph.

I couldn't help listening with half an ear to the Australians' conversation. There was no other sound except scraping. I noticed they had a book called *The Tibetan Book of Living and Dying* placed ostentatiously on the table. It did not impress me.

"I said to him, you want to go to Bondi, mate, not Nimbin," confided the bloke, who had the chiselled face of Robert Carlyle. "I said, you do realise Nimbin isn't even on the bloody coast! That took the wind out of his sails."

"Heaps of people want to go to Australia! It really makes me see how lucky we are. Maybe it really is the best country, like they say." She cradled her coffee cup as she spoke, but she never drank a thing.

"It's like the Buddha says, isn't it? You only know your home after you've been away from it. I'm certainly finding that."

I have never wanted to go to Australia, but I wouldn't mind being there now. Eventually they forced their conversation upon me.

"You just arrived?" asked the girl.

I sighed, and put the book down. "Yess!" I replied, Basil Fawlty style.

"Where from?" asked Mr. Carlyle.

"London."

"Just started travelling?"

"Yess!"

"Alone?"

"Not through choice."

"Wow," breathed the girl. "I really admire women who can do that. It's so brave! I don't think I could do it. I'd be scared. Aren't you scared?" She looked like an earnest schoolgirl. I wondered whether they had sex. Neither of them looked ready for it, but on the other hand they were clearly suited to each other.

"No," I told her firmly. I hated them. Surely I am not the only single woman traveller in Asia? That would make me the bravest girl in the world, which seems unlikely.

"I'm Ally, by the way," she added, "and this is Andy."

"Tansy," I said reluctantly.

"Tamsin?"

"No. Tansy. T-A-N-S-Y." I know there's more of this to come. An entire year of it, in fact.

"Have you had any hassle yet?" asked Andy, hopefully.

"No. I haven't been out. I only came from the airport late last night." It wasn't really late, but I couldn't bring myself to go out and I wasn't telling these two that I spent the evening drinking the minibar dry on my balcony, looking down at the cesspit below.

"You might find," said Andy portentously, "that the men here think you're a porn star or a prostitute. You see, that's probably the only image they have of western women, and because you're on your own, they'll think you're available. You should have come away with a bloke."

"Cheers." I raised my cup of coffee to him.

"Andy!" admonished Ally, who looked about ten. No one would mistake her for a porn star.

"What?"

"Don't scare her. She'll be fine, probably. Hey, Candy, do you want to meet up with us tonight? We're going out. We'll be around here at about eight if you'd like to hook up."

I couldn't imagine anything worse, but I nodded weakly, so I can keep it as a fallback position. "If you can't find me, just assume I've been sold to a brothel, and go without me."

They nodded seriously.

"OK, mate," agreed Andy.

Several pairs of eyes are staring suspiciously from across the street. A young man calls, "Excuse me, sir!" I ignore him, keep my eyes down as if I am on the Tube at rush hour, and retreat into my own world. I am walking fast, away from the trouble. I'm fine. I'm in Saigon and I'm fine. I hurry round a corner, straight into a woman with a pointy hat and milkmaid baskets full of bits of hairy meat.

"For Christ's sake," I scream. There are splats of blood and gristle on my shirt. The woman squeals accusingly, and we glare with equal venom. I could win the Turner Prize with this shirt. It is a piece of performance art fashioned from linen, dirt, shit, and blood, and that's only after one block. To give the woman credit, she swiftly recovers her equilibrium, smiles, and reaches out her begging hand to me, yabbering.

I postpone the morning's scheduled discovery of beauty and inner peace. I need to find the westerners' district, which, according to my book, is a few streets away. This part of town is so horrible that I can't really believe there is a mecca for travellers on hand. Although the last people I want to hang out with are backpackers, with their stupid dreadlocks and "Ooh, if it's Tuesday this must be Thailand" pretentiousness, I think I'd rather be with them than with anyone else. More than anyone local. There is clearly no common ground. I can't stop myself cursing the fucker who dropped me in this. If it wasn't for him I would not be here. But here I am. If I am going to the travellers' ghetto, I reason, that means that my hypothetical soulmates will want to go there too. Which means I'll meet like-minded people, and soon. I am not the bravest person in the world, no doubt about that; therefore, there are other women here alone, and therefore I will meet them. All I need to do is find someone else like me, and I'll be able to keep going.

On top of everything, I am now on my guard against being taken for a porn star. If anyone tries to grope me I'll knee his balls so hard they'll come out of his mouth. It won't be the first time I've been mistaken for a lady of ill repute. The flat above us in Soho was inhabited by two girls whose card by the door read "top Models, Second floor"; it's amazing how many men can't count to two. The first time, I was terrified. I'd moved in, two days before, exhausted from sorting out all Mum's stuff and selling the house. I was knackered, and a bit depressed (though still basically happy), because Will had taken his share of the money and gone to Scotland. I wanted him to settle in London now he could afford to, but he said he couldn't take the pace of life. Nevertheless it was a new start for me, and the world was full of possibilities.

Tom and I had already started planning this trip. Or so I thought. I bet he already knew.

I'd unpacked a few boxes, and put things in their places, and I was sitting on the sofa knocking back champagne—a present from Will—when there was a rap at the door. I leapt up, glad that I had visitors, and flung the door open, glass in hand.

A middle-aged man in a shiny suit looked me up and down. I could smell the whisky on his breath.

"Model, hey?" he said, and stepped into the flat.

"What?" I asked.

"Champagne as well. I'm impressed. I'm very impressed." He walked right up to me and stood so close I could smell his after-shave, his drink, and his sweat. He had brown hair in a bowl cut.

"What are you doing?" I managed to demand. "Get out of my flat."

"Playing hard to get, are we?" He shoved his body up against me, and I felt the pressure of his erection on my stomach.

This, luckily, jolted me to my senses, and I kneed him in the balls and shouted, "Get the fuck out of my home. I'm dialling nine nine nine, you pervert."

"Christ!" he bellowed. "You put the bloody card up, didn't you?"

The "top Models" begged us not to call the police. They ended up putting cards with arrows on them all the way up the stairs, coaxing the drunken fuckwits past our front door. After that, it happened about once a month. I forced myself to see it as part of the appealing grittiness of living in Soho. No one, I told my friends, ever comes to your door intending to pay you for sex in Hampstead. The ones we did get were the really drunken, stupid ones, who could neither count to two nor read, and they could generally be toppled back down the stairs with a gentle nudge.

To give the men of Vietnam their due, they haven't threatened me yet, and I've been out for ten minutes. The trouble now appears to be crossing this strange road. I have never seen anything like it. A quick analysis reveals that the biggest vehicle takes priority, and that, while comparatively big, I am not a vehicle. The very few cars storm down the road, with bikes scattering from their path. Cars beat motorbikes, which beat passenger bikes ("cyclos" apparently), which beat normal bikes. Everything beats pedestrians. I will never cross the road. To make it worse, I am being shadowed by two men with cyclos, who want me to pay them to take me somewhere. I don't trust them. I'm hardly going to climb on a bike with a strange man and be whisked away into a life of sexual slavery.

Far away, across a sea of fast-moving machinery, a green man lights up. This makes no difference whatsoever to the flow of traffic. I can't even tell which side of the road they're meant to drive on here; they seem to be weaving around each other wherever there's a space. I don't know what to do. I wish I was with Tom. He'd get on the bike without even thinking about it, and I'd squeeze on his lap. Will would walk straight out and let them avoid him, and I'd run, shrieking, with him. Kate would giggle with me.

But, on my own, what would I do? I don't know. For the moment, I wait for a gap in the traffic. It is a futile approach, and I am drenched with sweat.

"Where you go?" asks one of the cyclo men, as if our encounter was just beginning. "Kim Café?"

I ignore him. He has asked the same question six times.

"Sinh Café?"

Nope.

"I take you there. No money. Then I take you to War Museum, Reunification Palace, Art Museum, everywhere in Ho Chi Minh. OK, yes. What is your country?"

"Fuck off," I shout. "Leave me alone. It's not fair. I don't need you. If you don't go away, I'll call the police. I told you before, I'm walking."

He smiles a gruesome grin (call the police! what am I on

about?). The second driver is hovering. I glare at them both. This glare has felled mightier people than these two, but they are oblivious to its power. I take occasional steps out into the road, but am driven back in terror, hair blowing, when I see the traffic bearing down on me. An old woman stops and peers at me, then reaches up a wizened hand to touch my hair, before shuffling on.

Was Tom always planning to desert me? Does he hate women so much that he hatched this evil plan to pay me back, because I symbolise female-kind, stretching back to Eve? No, I think it was personal. The good thing is, he's never cared much about anyone else, either. Not even himself. He's forever wallowing in crises of his own imagining. It used to amuse me. I had the strangest family ever invented, and spent my entire sentient life looking after the very person who should have been looking after me, but I was generally fine and happy. Tom, on the other hand, whose family could not have been more secure and traditional, was forever miserable. He called his angst "passion." I called it self-indulgence. He used to tell me I wasn't "passionate enough." The lowest he ever stooped was to claim "You don't understand what it's like, being a Pisces." Well, I'm passionate enough now. Passionate with hatred. I am positively Piscean in my passion. I am consumed by it. I shouldn't be here! Not on my own. It is a huge mistake, and the mistake was trusting bloody Thomas. He is going to regret this. You see? I have entirely forgotten about my mother and my loss, and am obsessed with a man. Does that make me heartless? I think it just makes me unsentimental and realistic. I'm sure everyone feels like this really but doesn't dare admit it.

In Kim Café, shaky after my petrifying yet inevitable ride as a cyclo passenger, I am amused to realise that I find the sight of three hulking Germans, clad in stripey dungarees and rectangular glasses, to be reassuring. I sit next to them with a little smile. They ignore me. In fact, everyone ignores me. I order coffee. Nearby, I see a woman and two blonde children, all three of whom look far happier than I feel. I try to imagine any of my little siblings out here. They wouldn't know what to do with themselves. No toys, no Teletubbies, no computer games. No playroom. Nothing. I suppose the blonde children are seeing a different culture, but I think the only effect this will have is to make them appreciate what they've got at home.

When I was about seven, and the parents were still married but in crisis, Mum collected me from school one day and took me for "a drink in a shop," which was my favourite treat, and increasingly hers as well. The drinks involved were different, a distinction I did not appreciate at the time. We trotted off to one of the Hampstead teashops, and while I sucked my sticky Fanta through a straw, and stroked the velvet on the chair, and swung my legs, Mum downed a glass of wine (it was the early days when she did it in public) and took a deep breath.

"Darling?" she said. "How would you like it if you and I went away?"

I nodded. "Where to?"

"Well, it's quite exciting. To Kathmandu. Do you know where Kathmandu is?" Of course I didn't. "It's in a country called Nepal. Which is next to India. They have a different kind of life there. They live outside a lot, and there are mountains."

"Is it by the sea?"

"No, but there are lakes. Sometimes we'll go to the mountains in the snow. Mount Everest is there."

"Is Daddy coming?"

"No, because Daddy's got to work. We'll go away for six months, and Daddy will come out and visit us, and then Mummy will get better, because I haven't been very well, and we'll come home to Daddy and we'll be a family again forever and ever, and perhaps we'll have a brother or sister for you."

I thought about it all. "Do they have Tiswas? Can I still go to ballet?"

"You can practise your ballet. And they have other things.

We'll find out what there is when we get there. Do you know what else, you won't have to go to school! We'll wear different clothes, called saris, and you'll meet lots of other children."

"When will we get the baby?"

It never happened, of course. I nagged her intermittently. I told Lisa, my best friend. Lisa told everyone else. Everyone else told Miss Taylor, Miss Taylor asked me if it was true, and I asked Mum again. This time she didn't seem so certain.

"Maybe, darling," she said quietly, so that Dad wouldn't hear. By this stage they had staked out the house, so she got the sitting room and her comfy chair (in which she was frequently stationed even then), and Dad got the kitchen and the big pine table. He used to work there, listen to Mum, and never speak. He must have been monitoring her trips to the drinks cupboard. I would trot between the two of them, but I spent more time with Mum because she was more fun.

"But when?" I demanded. "We have to go, we just have to—you promised! And everyone knows! And I'm not going to go to school, I'm going to Mount Everest! I can't wait, Mum, please can we go? Because if we don't go where are we going to get the baby?"

At this, Dad came and stood on the threshold.

"Anne," he said sadly. "What have you been telling her?"

She looked angry. "Nothing!" she exclaimed.

"Tansy," he said. "What did Mummy tell you?"

But I knew not to tell him. I couldn't tell tales with Mum in the very room, so I went upstairs. She must have been joking, all along.

I've had a vague yearning for Kathmandu ever since. In my mind it is a world of ballet practise up a mountain in a sari, a world of freedom, other children, and baby brothers. I'll be there next year. It will be my second to last stop, the one before India. I don't know if they really do wear saris there, or if Mum was speaking vaguely of the subcontinent. I don't plan to wear one myself, unless by then I have been transformed into the kind of self-conscious "traveller" who doesn't realise what an arse they look. Like the people in this café, for example. The girls in particular have a tangible aura of self-conscious casualness. Look at me, they seem to be saying, I can adapt to a different culture. I look good in these wanky clothes, and with these stupid beaded plaits in my hair. You, they say silently to me, are not one of us. You are wearing proper, well-made fashionable clothes which the local people here would kill for. We despise such imperialism. Therefore we will ignore you but will give you snide sideways glances from time to time.

I'd love to know whether I'd have liked Kathmandu at seven, or whether it would have been as disillusioning as Vietnam is now. The café is as grotty as the dining room was. Since this city is so squalid and depressing, contrary to everyone's expectations, there should be some camaraderie, a kind of Blitz spirit. I thought I would be welcomed into the international community of travellers. I sip my coffee, even though the caffeine jitters are the last thing I need. I fiddle with the condensed milk, stirring clockwise and anticlockwise. I flick half-heartedly through the guidebook again. From time to time I scan the room with little "So, here we are then!" smiles, but even the children don't acknowledge me. Backpackers in London charge around the streets bellowing, being sick on each other's shoes. They don't look like an exclusive brotherhood then; more like the dregs of society. Tom and I used to misdirect them when they were looking for Covent Garden, just for fun.

I realise it's time to start smoking. I haven't smoked for three and a half years. I buy a silly lighter with Mickey Mouse engraved on it from one of the millions of vendors who constantly pester the clientele.

"Is belonging GI Joe," lies a smiling young woman as she pockets enough money to move into the Sheraton with her entire family for a week. I hold it away from me, certain that it'll blow up in my face. It doesn't. It just produces a pathetic flame. I ask the Germans for a fag. One of them pushes the packet to me without breaking off from his incomprehensible conversation, and, indeed, without looking at me.

I want to scream, "I don't like you! I'm not interested in you!" They think I want to hear their travelling tales, but I don't. They think I want to join their little cliques, stampeding around the world trampling on local people and demanding pancakes and Nescafe. I don't. I don't care if they get malaria next week. I just object to being frozen out by pathetic losers exercising the slight power they still possess. This is what happens when you let yourself be vulnerable.

"He was from County Galway," an Irish girl is saying, behind me. "He knew Brendan O'Leary, you know, from school, and he was gorgeous. Well, he said, will we be going down to Ko Phi Phi with him, so I had to change my flight . . ."

"Ah, but it was worth it, wasn't it?"

They may be involved in conversation about shagging other Irish people, but I can feel their eyes in my back. I can feel their condescension. I hate them, too. I have to keep myself going because nobody else is going to do it. I'm on my own. And I know who to blame. At a corner table, a freaky-looking young man grins at me. He has bushy hair in a ponytail and a big beard. He is tall and wiry, as if his joints were on springs. He is a genuine weirdo. He signals to me to join him. Happily, I am not quite that desperate.

I take a motorbike taxi to the museums, which seriously upsets the cyclo driver who brought me here. It's fast and scary and it takes my mind off my pathetic plight. I start off hanging on to the guy's waist—this, after all, is how you ride a motorbike—but realise in no time that people are staring more than before. The Vietnamese women perch elegantly on the back of bikes, with their arms full of babies, or cows' heads, using some innate ability to balance. I realise I'm probably acting like a harlot. I wish I'd worn trousers. I shift round and hold on to the back of the seat with one hand, and grip my thigh with the other, adding a sweaty palm print to the day's trophies. The air is so thick that I feel we are cutting a hole through it as we drive. I remember how to lean, and I like the minimal breeze in my sweaty hair. The city smells to high heaven, and every time I open my eyes I see that I am almost dying under someone's random wheels.

If I'd known Asia would be like this I'd have gone to America. If I'd been planning the trip on my own, I'd have gone to America. It was that bastard who wanted to go to bloody Asia. I hate Asia. The two of us sat in the pub after work, with a whole stack of Lonely Planets I'd got by phoning the press office and pretending I was writing a big feature about how great they are. I had the USA, New York and California guides out, and the rest in a plastic bag on the floor, and I kicked off my shoes, and opened one at the map.

"I thought we could fly into New York," I began, "and get a car and perhaps go right across the deserts and everything, and then spend a month or two on the West Coast." I sipped my beer and traced Route 66 with my finger. "You like America—you're always on about it." I beamed. A happy Tom meant a happy me.

He picked up my bag from under the table and started shuffling through the rest of the books. "Here we go." He found the one he wanted. "If we're going travelling we might as well do it properly." I pulled it out of his hand and looked at the cover with a sinking heart. It was called *South East Asia on a Shoestring*.

If Tom had left me alone, if he hadn't come back to me when Mum died, I'd be chilling in Manhattan right now, wearing my best clothes and sipping skinny latte. I would be discovering my inner self, without discomfort or rudeness. People would love my accent. I thought India might be a cesspit of poverty-stricken people trying every trick in the book to rip me off, which is why we left it till last. Vietnam is next door but one to Thailand, and is therefore meant to be westerner-friendly. But it isn't, and I shouldn't be here alone. It's not fair.

I am so cross that I resort to conversation with Pong, my aptly named driver.

"Were you born in Saigon?" I shout, over the racket of the engine. I quite like the way my hair flies out in the wind. This could be a *Vogue* picture, if it wasn't for the smell.

"Yes, born. You born?" Disconcertingly, he turns round to speak to me, taking his eyes entirely off the murderous road.

"In London."

"London-girl, you like marry?" he asks slyly.

"What?" I think he just proposed. I am amazed and, perhaps, a tiny bit amused. So he does think I'm up for it.

"You like marry wa!" he clarifies defensively.

"I'm sorry," I tell him primly, "I don't understand what you're saying." I am planning my escape, in case he really does think I'm gagging for a shag or, worse, a wedding. I weigh twice as much as he does. I'll lean suddenly, and when the bike tips I'll leap off gracefully, and run away. I really wish I'd worn trousers. He frowns over his shoulder. "You speak English?"

"Yes."

"So you no smoke?"

Oh. Marry-wa indeed. I've read about this trade in the guide-book.

"No thanks. Have you got any cocaine?"

"Cocaine, no! You joking! Is very bad drug."

"Yes," I say firmly. "I was joking." Bugger. I don't speak to him for the rest of the journey, and he keeps his eyes on the road. I sense vibes of disapproval from his back. Even the bloody driver thinks I'm a degenerate.

At the War Museum I sit in the shade of a scrawny tree, between a tank and a helicopter, and wonder what's happening in the world I left behind. My friends, at least, probably think I'm assuming languid attitudes and meeting intriguing strangers like Jane March in *The Lover*. I attempt a languid attitude, but a couple of Chinese tourists gape at me. Exhibit H: Languid Western

Harlot. I wonder what Mum would think of me doing this. Having the strength that she never had, to go away and travel. No one would really call Vietnam part of the hippy trail, but it's closer than Hampstead. I wouldn't contemplate travelling anywhere with a child. It was quite strong of her even to consider it, back when she had some life in her. Tears are welling, but they mustn't. Don't be weak.

The museum itself is horrible and one-sided. I am amused to discover that its name has been changed, for tourism's sake, from the "American War Crimes Museum" to the more poetic and tactful "Museum of the Remnants of War." I am so edgy from the world outside that the meticulous documentation of atrocities actually calms me. I make a lengthy perusal of photos of war crimes, maps, and some spectacular malformed foetuses in jars. I never even knew exactly what Agent Orange was (I might even have assumed it was a person, *Reservoir Dogs* style). Now I wear the expression and the aura of one who is contrite and on the right side, particularly when I notice any locals. I am surprised that these people welcome westerners at all, considering we fucked their country so comprehensively. I am not surprised that they hate us.

I feel like an old grey dishcloth. It is still night at home. When my friends wake up, it will only be their second day without me. I might still be being missed. I hope I am. I hope that Tom remembers he could be in glamorous Vietnam, his personal choice of starting country. I hope he wonders whether I'm meeting handsome travellers. He's never going to know that the sum total of interest in me from my fellow travellers has come from two mini-Australians and a freak. I know Will will be thinking of me. At work they'll still think of me. Eventually someone else will get my desk and then they'll forget me. I will be no one. Invisible in Vietnam to all but the beggars and the dealers of the wrong drug. Out of sight and out of mind in London. Adrift, nowhere. I wonder how much filthy watery atmosphere has gone in through my pores today, and polluted my body. It's the opposite of a cleansing steam bath.

An Asian child is playing picturesquely in a big gun. I am tormenting myself with what could have been if Pong sold my drug of choice. I need it now; this is exactly the situation for it. If I knew Saigon, I'd go to the right part of town and buy a gramme. I would share it around, of course, though chance would be a fine thing, and enjoy a day's happiness. Come night time, I would ease the downer with enough Valium to ensure a calm night's sleep, and in the morning I would be balanced. I don't know where to start here, and I wouldn't trust anything a local sold me anyway. I am annoyed to realise that I could have brought some with me. They hardly even looked at me at customs.

I try not to picture Tom and me, exploring Saigon together. Wrinkling our noses cutely at the smells, ignoring the beggars, laughing at the backpackers. Together, we would be high-class travellers. We would seek out the real Vietnam. The fragrant, scenic Vietnam beneath this jarring exterior. Even though he's not with me now, I must pretend he is, and get through like that. I'll survive abroad by thinking of Tom. This separation makes me more certain than ever that, long-term, he is the man for me. He wouldn't keep coming back to me if we weren't meant to be together, would he? He can sense it as well. That doesn't make me any less angry. My fury is bubbling, but it will get me nowhere. We wouldn't argue here, just as I suspected; I was right and he was wrong, and that fact makes no difference whatsoever.

A young, thin Vietnamese man approaches me, and opens his mouth to speak.

"No!" I yell.

He starts, and backs away. He is looking at me as if I am unhinged. He could well be right.

CHAPTER
4

The music is atrocious, the air is sweaty, and everyone smells of beer. I love it here. The Spice Girls are entertaining the ragged hordes with a heartfelt rendition of "Who do you think you are?" which booms blurrily over a bad sound system. It's not exactly a clubbing anthem, but it probably goes down well with backpackers, who have no taste and like things to remind them of home. The room is packed, and we have to push people aside to get near the bar. Everyone is wearing faux naive backpacking gear: little vest tops and combat pants for the girls; shorts and "Beer Lao" T-shirts for the boys. There are few exceptions. The Vietnamese prostitutes, who are poorer than anyone else in the room, look breathtaking in silky minidresses; the older men are in uniform cream linen, like parodies of ex-pats; and I am wearing my black Ghost dress. I don't see why I shouldn't dress up. I like dressing up, even if it lumps me in with the hookers. That is a reflection on everyone else, not on me.

The dripping walls are decorated with murals of war scenes. The ceiling fans form the swooshing blades of painted helicopters.

"Postmodernism gone mad!" I exclaim.

Ally follows my gaze. "Oh yeah," she agrees. "S'pose."

"Why call a club Apocalypse Now anyway?" I ask. "Don't they know what it's about?"

"Good business, I guess. I'm having a G and T. I'm sick of the Asian beer. What'll you have?"

"Asian beer sounds good, whatever kind you recommend."

Andy is happy. "Good girl," he says, "I'll get you a Tiger. Arrrgggh!" and he vanishes into the crowd, clawing a tiger's claw. Ally and I fight our way out to a courtyard, which is also packed but which has a faint whiff of air to it. A fat man with white hair is snogging an Asian girl of about sixteen.

"Urgh," I say.

"You never know." Ally is conspiratorial. "When we were in Chiang Mai we were like, oh my God, gross, it's a white guy with a prostitute, and it turned out they'd been married for like fifteen years. The Asian women just look really young."

I study the pair in question. "They're not married. If they were married they wouldn't come here to snog. And the woman wouldn't pay that prostitute tax." This club has an admission charge for Vietnamese but not for westerners.

"Off to the loo!" Ally shrills, clutching herself like a toddler. She vanishes abruptly.

I survey the scene. I like it a lot, now I've got friends. I feel superior to these people again. I wouldn't even mind speaking to some of them. There are two unmistakable Americans standing next to me. Both are wearing long shorts, vest tops and backwards baseball caps. One has a bizarrely shaved goatee, which extends in five little lines to his chin. The other has long straggling hair. They are Beavis and Butthead. I smile at them. Beavis, with the facial hair, shifts over to me.

"Yo!" he offers.

"Hello," I say primly.

"How you doing?" he asks.

"Fine, thanks." We contemplate the courtyard for a while. I notice that the freak from the café is nearby, towering over everyone else. He is, not surprisingly, on his own. He's drinking a Tiger beer as well, and smiling to himself. He sees me looking at him and gives me a little wave. He has such a funny manner that I think he must be Latvian or something. Beavis and I chat in a bored way. I wonder how long it'll be before Andy comes over with the drinks, or Ally empties her bladder.

"Do you feel awkward, as an American in Vietnam?" I ask.

"No, man, we don't because we believe in peace, and we love the Vietnamese people. It's not, like, us who burnt the babies. I was on the demos." He smiles nostalgically. "Hey, hey, LBJ, how many kids did you kill today? Did you go to the War Museum? Well, I'm in one of the photos, no joke. You know, the photos of the demos in Washington."

I am baffled. "So how old are you?"

"How old d'you think?"

"I would have said thirty-five, tops, but clearly I would have been wrong."

He is triumphant. "Fifty-eight!" he exclaims.

"That's crap. It must be crap."

"Straight up. I'm psyched to be in Vietnam. Should have been here way back when, but we burnt our cards."

"How old's your friend?"

"Seventy-two. No, just kidding. He's a youngster. He's forty-nine."

Butthead sidles into the conversation. "It's a pleasure to meet you, Tammy," he affirms. "Tell me, Tammy, are you interested in eternal youth?"

I really hope the others get back soon. "You two clearly are."

"We have the elixir, and we'd like to share it with you."

"I do not make a habit of sharing the elixirs of strange men," I tell him icily.

"Yeah, but seriously, we have the herbal tonic which will activate the de-ageing process. Provided you follow the spiritual guidelines, you too can look like we do!"

Butthead clasps my arm. "We'll give you the spiritual help that you need," he says softly.

Back indoors, I am trying to work out why the atmosphere is so different from clubs at home, aside from the liberal sprinkling of certifiable madmen. Partly, I suppose, it's because people are away from their normal gangs of friends, so they've got something to prove. Then I realise: it's alcohol-fuelled. There aren't any drugs here. At least, they're not readily available. This place is full of young Europeans, freed from all responsibility, who are drinking. This seems like a recipe for disaster. The Brits among them are used to packing in as much beer as possible before closing time, and then having a fight. They need some pills to mellow them out. Drugs would send everyone away, calmly, to their own planet. As it is, this is like a football crowd, and I am uneasy. I have nothing against alcohol—nothing at all—but in a situation like this I'd love a line of coke. Really love one.

I have survived one full day away from everything and everyone that is dear to me (not to mention the fuckwit who dumped me in this random city). I have a drink in my hand, and I am hot, on a December night. I am getting plenty of looks. I don't think they're all coming from people who think I'm a hooker. I have established, today, that I don't like backpackers and they don't like me, but I quite like the Australians. I don't like Saigon, but that makes me realise how much I love London. I haven't yet met my soulmate, but I'm happy to wait a brief time for that. I can't expect that on my first day.

All, in fact, is in place for a reasonable night (a great triumph, under the circumstances), but for the acceleration of my consuming craving for coke. It is, of course, possible that this is the one place in town where a reliable gramme, or at least a poor-quality E, can be purchased. I need it. I can imagine it. I try to ignore it, but I can't.

"Have you been to London?" I ask the Australians, shifting my weight from foot to foot and trying to concentrate.

"You bet!" shouts Andy. His accent doesn't go with his moody, sensitive looks at all. "We spent six months there. Loved it! Great city!"

"Did you live in Earl's Court?" I've always thought it good that so many visitors get to stay in Earl's Court which, even though it's grim, is lovely and central (if not quite as central as my darling Soho).

"You're joking, eh?" he laughs. "Earl's bloody Court! We're not rich! We stayed in a houseshare in Upminster. Seven Aussies, three Kiwis, and a South African. I tell you, we had some rages."

"We did," confirms Ally. "The house had three bedrooms. Our first two months we slept in the bathroom!"

"What do you do if someone wants a wee in the night?"

"You duck! No, you make them go in the garden. As long as they avoid the tent. Two of the Kiwis lived in a tent, you see."

"It's if they want a shit or a barf you're in trouble," explains Andy.

"It sounds grim."

"It was the best."

Oh God, this is what you have to be like to be a traveller. I'm not a backpacker. I'm not even a traveller. I'm a tourist, if that. I want my charlie. I want my Tom.

"So where in London are you from?" asks Andy.

"I grew up in Hampstead," I tell him, "but I lived in Soho, until yesterday."

"Wish we'd known you when we went to London, eh!" He treats "eh" as though it were not only a word in its own right, but the most important word in the sentence. "Do you have a job, or are you one of those little rich girls? What are they called? Spoons?"

"Sloanes. And no, I'm not. I work, I mean I used to, for a newspaper. I used to work really hard, actually. I got too stressed, and I came away at the last minute, really, on the spur of the mo-ment." I am surprised at the way I can present myself to these people any way I want. I can say I worked hard, or I didn't work hard (and I'm not even sure which would be true). I can say I had to leave my stressful life behind, painting the trip as a self-finding mission of one who has seen through what the "developed" world has to offer, or as the temporary distraction of a thrill seeker let down by a bastard man at the last minute.

Ally is nodding understandingly. "I worked for Channel Seven in Sydney," she says. "I know what you mean about the stress. Mind you, we only work to save up to go travelling."

"So if you're not a spoon," probes Andy, swaying into a lager lout who's stumbling past with a local woman on his arm, "how long did it take you to save the money to come away? You said you came on the spur of the moment."

"I had some savings," I say, stalling. I might as well tell him the truth. "Actually, it wasn't my savings because I've always spent more than I've earned. I inherited some money last year."

He is triumphant. "See!" he exclaims. "I knew you were posh! Good luck to you, that's what I say. That woulda been a bit of luck, then!"

"Not really," I tell him. "I inherited it from my mother. She died, you see." I smile to try to let him know it's all right. They both look stricken. I know I have to be brave.

Before anyone says anything, a short, spotty youth in his early twenties taps me on the shoulder. I turn round, and when I see him, I know what's coming. I decide I'll defuse the tension by letting him down rudely.

"Are you English, by any chance?" he asks, in a Manchester accent.

"Yes," I say, and turn back to Ally.

"We're so sorry," she says. "Andy didn't mean anything."

"What a drongo," adds Andy, hitting himself on the forehead.

The Manchester lad puts his arm round my shoulder. I shake him off. "Me and my mates," he shouts, "were just saying, it's funny, because at home you would be really gorgeous and you'd never give us the time of day, but here, you don't look fit at all. Not next to the Vietnamese women. So we were just saying, we wouldn't give you one, not even if you were begging for it." He looks at me, waiting for a response.

Ally turns on him. "Why don't you go fuck your grand-mother's sheep, arsehole?" she demands.

The lad just stands there leering.

"Beat it, mate," says Andy, looking menacing. He becomes thuglike and scares the boy away.

They turn to me.

"Just ignore that," advises Ally.

I am distraught—far more so than I should be, considering I've just been insulted by a wanker who looks like he should be sitting in a doorway under a holey blanket, saying "Spare any change, please?" with a scrawny dog on a string at his side. In fact, he looks like the boy on Dean Street who liked to call me a fuck-ing bitch, and I never used to mind him. I would just explain that I had a job and a home, and that I was, therefore, the winner and he was the loser. This, I would tell him, made his aggression to-wards me entirely understandable. Then I would walk off laugh-ing, just as I should now. Will witnessed an interchange once, and was horrified, but I explained that it was just a joke.

I mumble, "Excuse me," and run to the loo. I knock back my drink as I go, and put the empty bottle on a table. Things are blurry, and I walk into a few people en route. A hand steadies me at one point, when I stumble. I look round, and see the Freak, smiling at me.

"Are you all right?" he asks. He's Yorkshire, not Latvian.

"Yes."

"You don't look it." He really looks very odd indeed. "What's your name?"

"Tansy," I mutter, waiting for the naff approximation.

"Tansy?" he asks. "Like the herb? Like Topsy and Tim's friend?"

"Yes!" I am impressed, for the first time today. "Do you know where I can get some coke?" Please say yes, I think. Please be as good at drugs as you are at names.

He looks surprised. "At the bar . . ." He realises. "Oh, right, sorry," he says. "No, I wouldn't have a clue. You could try the cyclo blokes but I wouldn't risk it. They might report you."

I force a smile. Tears are escaping now. "Thanks anyway," I tell him and hurry on.

"Well, I'm Max," he calls after me. "Can I get you a drink?" I pause. Why not? He's friendly, even if he does look like a demented Jesus. Right down to the sandals, I notice. He is a parody of all the other people in the club. I'll take him over to meet the others.

"I'll have a beer," I say, forcing a smile. "Tiger!" I do the claw that Andy did. "Back in a minute."

The loos are a stinking hellhole, and that seems appropriate.

CHAPTER
5

From: K.Jones@Herald.co.uk
To: Tansy Harris
Subject: miss saigon

darling—I can't believe you've really gone. how was the journey? what
was at the end of it? this place is empty and sad without you.
everyone wanders the corridors, lost and baffled, muttering "where is
she?" particularly me.

I cheered myself up the other day by buying a beautiful pink silk dress
for jenny's wedding. I wish you could see it. I don't dare put it on, but
prefer to stroke it reverently. I'll freeze in it. the weather here is
shocking. today it has barely got light.

where are you now? in saigon? is it beautiful? I want to hear all your
adventures. it seems so weird that one minute you were here,
planning to go travelling (just like everyone is always planning to go
travelling), and the next minute you've really done it. let me know how
things are going. I will then pass the news to your jealous friends.
there was a backpacker who got murdered recently, a girl from Devon
(Clare something, I think) who looked really like you. it gave me a bit
of a shock. they're looking for a Canadian guy. please do take care.
are you travelling with people?

the wedding's this weekend, so once again I am being forced into church. don't know why I keep having to "worship" someone or something I don't believe in at all. god, eh? can't, it appears, live without him. I imagine they're not too hot on holy communion over where you are for which I hope, young lady, you are grateful.

anyway, tell me everything. I miss you lots and love you lots, and wish I'd had the balls to do what you've done. Go, girl.

masses of love

k xxxxx

PS before you ask—no, I haven't seen Tom and nor have I wanted to. Will called the other day, sounding well. he'd just started his job and sounds like a different person.

From: TomD@aol.com
To: TansyHarris@hotmail.com
Subject: none

so you've actually gone? I have to say this surprises me. are you in fact hiding out at your dad's? the joys of the email address, the potential for deception . . .

life is continuing without you, somehow. cheers for not waking me. I would like to stress, you must do whatever you want while you're away, take any opportunity that presents itself, have a great time and don't restrain yourself from doing anything on my account. OK? whatever has happened between us before and might happen in the future, right now you're independent. which makes me feel a bit odd but I know it was my decision to have things that way. do you still hate me?

am off to the pub this evening. meeting the boys. stamford bridge on sat, obviously, as we're playing utd. if we can do this one we'll be over the moon as it'll give us top spot, and while at this stage in the season that doesn't necessarily mean anything and there's still everything to play for, it'll be a fantastic morale booster. anyway I shall keep you informed (I know you must be on tenterhooks).

funnily enough, I miss you and am on tenderhooks. wondering whether I should have come after all . . . how would you feel if I took a holiday in thailand?? I hope asia knows what's hit it. take care out there . . . avoid the axe murderer.

much love

tom xxx

From: Roger.Harris@btinternet.com
To: Tansyharris@hotmail.com
Subject: SAFE ARRIVAL?

DEAR TANSY

I TRUST YOU HAVE ARRIVED SAFELY AND ARE ENJOYING YOURSELF STOP ALL CONTINUES AS NORMAL HERE STOP FAMILY VERY EXCITED ABOUT CHRISTMAS STOP TRY TO CALL US ON THE DAY. PLEASE NOTIFY RE: YOUR SAFETY. BEST

FROM EVERYONE. LOVE, DAD

To: Tansyharris@hotmail.com
From: WMarchmont@hotmail.com
Subject: hi

Hi, "Sis"

You know that job I went for? Well, I got it! Which is why I am now writing to you on email. I have set up this account so my emails to you won't show up on the company computer—I'm getting clever already. My boss thinks I'm working and my back is to the wall so no one can see that I am writing to my little sis, off having adventures in sunnier climbs instead. My job entails organising the housing at this charity, we house homeless people like I used to be. In fact I have already met some of my old friends like Mick for instance, who was very surprised to see me in this capacity I can tell you.

I like the work. It feels good to be doing something useful, and to come back to my flat every evening after maybe having a drink with some colleagues, and just to be living a normal life. I am also studying for an English exam as I know my grammar leaves something to be desired still. It frustrates me a lot. I wish I'd had the proper education you did. And I am learning to type by practising a lot. It has already taken me forever to type these few lines.

I hope this finds you well. What is Vietnam like? Is it like the movies? Rambo! Please tell me all your news. I have got a world map to trace your progress so you must tell me every little place you go to and I will add it on. My work mates are interested in my little travelling sister. I liked it when they asked about my family; and for the first time in my life I could say I have got one. Even if it consists of just one person.

Look after yourself Tans and keep in touch. I'm looking forward to seeing you in a year. Hope you're not too hot where you are. Don't get ill and remember the malaria tablets. You wouldn't believe how many people don't take them apparently.

With love from,

Your brother, William.

To: Tansyharris@hotmail.com
From: OHare@Herald.co.uk
Subject: absence

Tansy

It has been brought to my attention that you have left the newspaper
before the end of your contract. Although we were all aware that you
were planning to depart these shores, I would like to make it clear that
walking out with two months to go is not responsible behaviour, as it
leaves others in the lurch. This, I have to tell you, may seriously affect
your chances of re-employment on your return.

Having said that, I wish you all the best on your travels.

Regards,

Tim.

From: Stuart Higgins
To: Tansy Harris
Subject: WHAT HAVE YOU DONE TO ME?????

Tans, how are you doing? Where are you? I'm sitting at my boss's
desk, hoping he doesn't come back from lunch till I've written this. I
don't have email at my own desk, in fact they've only just given me a
phone as you know very well.

This is a cross email I'm afraid. How could you do that to me? How
could you leave, when we used to have so much fun in the flat? That
bitch Mo moved in three days ago, into your room, and I'm now
wondering whether to move out myself. I might come and join you,
you see. Because she has not got off to a good start. She turned up
with millions of boxes, and put her stuff all over the place—New Age
things in the bathroom, a few crystals, lots of plants that were already
half dead and are now fully so. She complained cos there was still

some of your stuff around the place, and she went through the fridge throwing out some of my most treasured friends ie that cheese, which was almost ready to hold a conversation. I told her it was penicillin, but she told me not to be stupid, penicillin comes in pills, and then she stared at me and sniggered to herself as if she was so clever. I remembered how you used to say that a dignified silence is the best way to deal with wankers, so I shut up. Later she told me v. seriously that she wants to change her name to Venus because she identifies with it more, so I think I get the last laugh even if she doesn't know it.

Anyway, then the real trouble started, the next morning. I suppose I hadn't realised that, since she has a "proper job," i.e. she works at an ad agency (proper job my arse, I can hear you saying) she'd be getting up too. I started on my well-oiled, out-the-house-in-half-an-hour routine, only at every stage there she was. Went to the bathroom: door locked, girly soap smells exuding. Went to make some coffee: espresso machine dirty and flung in the sink with cereal bowl on top of it. Went back to my room and decided to have a shower later, but she only bloody walked in while I was dressing to ask whether there was a compost bucket for coffee grounds and could we get one. I said Soho was one big compost bucket but she gave me that look again.

All the time, Tans, I was thinking of the way you'd sit at the table in your dressing gown and I'd make our coffee, and you'd just sit and read the paper while I did all my stuff. I wish you were still here. Please come back or I'll have to come and get you. There was a "backpacker murder" in the paper the other day, in somewhere called "Mumbai." I think it's in India, near Goa and Bombay. You're going there. Please take care. You see, you'd be better off back home with me.

By the way, you didn't wake me before you left like you were meant to. I had a little present I was going to give you. Tell me an address and I'll post it.

Missing you, hoping you'll come home soon, keeping your room reserved for you, and thinking about your adventures. Hoping you can still remember who I am. The short guy you used to live with in peace and harmony. top Models send their love.

Much love

Guy x

From: Amanda.Evans@Herald.co.uk
To: Tansy Harris
Subject: Bon voyage

Hey, Tans

How's it going? You must be having an amazing time. Lucky old you. You're so lucky, having all that freedom. I fear the days I could have done that are at an end: don't tell anyone (I'm telling you this because you're so far away) but I've just discovered I'm four months pregnant, not that I'd want to get rid of it anyway I think, but I couldn't now. I know, I should be happy, being married and everything. And sometimes I am happy about it and sometimes I'm not. It's just come as a bit of a surprise, Tans, and I don't want to tell anyone here as that would make it official somehow and I think if I can ignore it for a bit that'll give me time to come to terms.

Look at me, the one with all the gossip, harbouring my own secret. To be honest, I haven't even told Paul yet. I know he'll be happy because he's been going on about kids almost since I met him, and he'll tell everyone and start wanting to move house and make me sit down with my feet up. I'm a bit worried as well because during the four months of blissful ignorance I didn't behave like a "pregnant lady": I drank and took things, you know, I mean you of all people know because you were there too. Specially at your leaving party. I shudder to think what that might have done and don't dare mention it to the doctor for fear of being severely told off and the implication that I'd killed someone.

God, I don't know why I'm telling you all this, Tansy. We're not best friends, are we, although I like you v. much and have always suspected that beneath that brash and moody exterior lurks a heart of gold or at least bronze. I wouldn't dream of telling anyone else in the office. The awful truth is that, at a time like this when I need a best friend, I realise just how much I've neglected my old friends from uni etc. You've done the best thing, chucking it all in, believe me.

Please write back. Must go now as the trolley's here and people will suspect if I don't rush over to it. Have fun and please do me a favour and appreciate your freedom on my behalf.

Best love

Amanda.

From: Roger Harris
To: Tansy Harris
Subject: hello

Hello tansy this is jessica here. I'm sitting in dad's office writing to you to say have a nice time and I hope you're not too cold because its very cold here. Mummy says its warm wear you are but I don't believe her because Ive got the electrick blacnet on my bed. Archie is crying very much and marianne has to take him out in the pram all the time. mummy says she is tired of babys. I brought the britney album with my pocket money and i asked father Christmas for nsync. do you like nsync. I hope so.

love from jessicaXXXXXXX

From: Tansyharris@hotmail.com
To: Amanda.evans@Herald.co.uk
Subject: Don't worry

amanda—sorry I haven't written sooner but have only just checked my email. DON'T WORRY about anything. first of all I promise I won't tell anyone. second of all I know from my evil stepmother's many pregnancies that unborn babies (or should I say foetuses, don't want to start sounding like the anti-abortion nutters) are hardy things. lola drank and smoked throughout and had four perfect kiddies, in the physical sense at least. I think in the early stages it tends to be all or nothing, so if anything had damaged it, it would only have been a cluster of cells and that would have knocked it out altogether, which plainly hasn't happened. however, I am no expert and you absolutely must talk to a doctor. they won't mind—it's not their place to mind and anyway, you didn't know you were pregnant so nobody is going to judge you.

you poor, poor thing. I wish I was there to give you a big hug. amanda, if you haven't done so already you have to tell paul. he's bound to have noticed a change in you since you found out and he's probably worried about you. please tell him. he's your husband, and you're having his baby. you need support, not just from me here in the middle of bloody vietnam but from the person who's pledged to look after you forever.

take care, and tell me if there's anything I can do from here. you're bound to be feeling weird with all those hormones. soon you'll settle down and feel happy, I promise. it'll be ok. now go to the trolley and get a twix (kingsize—remember you're eating for 2) and keep in touch. vietnam is cool. a total culture shock, but I'm enjoying myself.

loads of love,

tansy xxx

BACKPACK

From: Tansy Harris
To: William Marchmont

Good morning, "bruv"

congratulations on getting that job. it's fantastic news. I'm so proud of
you, getting your life together like that. and studying as well—and here
I am loafing around in Asia. you put me to shame. it must be
absolutely bloody freezing in scotland right now. is it nice and
christmassy? will you be there for New Year's? from time to time I
think about all the parties I'm missing, but that's the point of going
away really, isn't it? I could do with some cheery company at the
moment.

vietnam is strangely like the movies, in some ways. the shadow of the
war is everywhere, despite saigon's strenuous efforts to modernise
and become like the west. I fear it has a long way to go yet. I'm now in
a little town called Hoi An, halfway up the country. Sweet place—my
favourite so far. asia is a weird place to be, and I don't really know
what I'm doing here. I feel quite lost, although I wouldn't tell that to
most people. I know I have to be honest with you. I fear I am coping
with a completely different life rather less well than you are. Isn't it
strange how both our lives have changed so dramatically since mum?
my travelling seems self-indulgent (although now I'm doing it it feels
more self-torture, self-punishment) next to you.

Next country, as you know, is laos. I can't imagine it. Hadn't even
heard of it.

Take care of yourself and write back soon. I'll write whenever I can,
wherever they have the internet. What's your flat like?

lots of love

tansy. xx

From: Tansy Harris
To: Tom
Subject: Good morning (from) vietnam

morning

having an excellent time, thankyou. vietnam is weird and wonderful, inhabited by downtrodden yet resilient people who hate us but, with their wily oriental ways, don't admit it and instead make a show of friendliness.

you'll be pleased to know I've become a proper backpacker and have adopted appropriate dress of tie-dye t-shirts, patterned trousers and sandals. I may soon get a yin/yang tattoo. in fact I'm quite glad you didn't come. this is my little adventure. I now know for certain that I've done the right thing.

nothing, of course, can compare to the excitement of being at stamford bridge. missing you a little (oh, all right, a lot)—you can only have a holiday in thailand if you do it when I'm there. march?

just think of the sunshine. It is truly glorious.

see you soon I hope

lots of love, t x

From: Tansy Harris
To: Roger Harris
Subject: Re: SAFE ARRIVAL?

Dad, for God's sake of course I'm all right. In fact I'm fine, having an interesting time. People are very friendly and it feels much safer than London. I've had many adventures already. Do not start worrying, at this stage, about my safety.

I'll call on Xmas day if I can. not sure where I'll be so if you don't hear from me, don't worry—I'll call as soon as I can. have a good day if I don't speak to you (and if I do).

how is everybody? don't forget I gave you the children's Xmas presents.

send love to Jess, Briony, Jake and Archie and to Lola. Tell Jess I'll write back to her soon.

Love

Tansy

PS can't work out if you're joking or not with your weird style. email is not a telegram. but you know that.

From Tansy Harris@hotmail.com
To: Tim O'Hare@Herald.co.uk
Subject: because I wanted to

Tim—thanks for your email. I can't really explain my walking out like that (although I know you are aware of my family traumas of the past year) other than because I was faced with a sudden urge to leave the paper, the country, and everything. Now I'm in Vietnam I do regret being so abrupt.

Sorry about that.

Best wishes

Tansy

From: TansyHarris@hotmail.com
To: K.Jones@Herald.co.uk
Subject: Good morning from Vietnam

hi darling

and THAT is why you're my best friend.

I don't feel ballsy. I feel rather pathetic. this morning i woke up in a smelly windowless room, to the overwhelming smell of drains. I'd been bitten in the night because the mossie net had a huge hole in it. I spent most of the night wondering if I'll get used to rugged lifestyle, and concluded I won't. I'm in a place called hoi an—a bizarre yet pleasing town where every shop is a tailor's, and all are keen to make you cutprice designer-esque clothes. now, I'm on my way to pick up brown faux-armani suit I ordered yesterday. weirdly, I'm even writing this in a tailor's, which has an Internet terminal. it is infuriatingly slow, and surrounded by rolls of cotton and sample garments. the shop people are ignoring me for now, but I know the moment I finish emailing, they'll pounce and try to sell me a flouncy prom dress, on top of charging 2000 dong a minute for the computer (yes, the currency really is called dong). I hadn't expected people here to be quite so avaricious. westerners keep walking past and staring—a huge blonde person working (so it appears) in this little shack. feeling awkward and out of place is nothing strange for me these days. poor me. I know people say they're jealous, but they don't mean it. if they did, they'd be here themselves.

how are you? how is life continuing over there? happy hope. can't imagine how cold it must be—here it is meltingly hot, but humid too. the fellow backpackers froze me out at first—they could tell, I think, that I'm not one of them. I hate a lot of them. they have this stupid "we're so cool" attitude. we know better, don't we, darling? they reinforce their stereotype with great enthusiasm. I met a hilarious bloke in saigon, who looked the part but turned out to be sweet. but he was the exception, I'm afraid.

I wouldn't say this to anyone else, but I'm furiously jealous of you being at home in our old life, and I don't know for the life of me what I'm doing here. Have you got any nice relatives in India who'd take me in and feed me aloo gobi for a year? Vietnam is a hellhole of a country, frankly. it's almost comical how horrible it is. I keep expecting to stumble across the "real" Vietnam, but it's just a smelly cesspit. it's so much worse than home. it seems stupid to come to an undeveloped country when you have the good fortune to live in a developed one. by the way, I am a long long way from India which I believe is where that girl got killed—almost as far, in fact, as you are, so nobody's to worry about me. I read on the bbc website that she'd had a chewed pen forced into her hand. do they reckon he was trying to make her write something? weird, but no more of a danger to me than to you, or anyone else. and I am currently travelling with two minute (my-newt not minnit) australians, so I'm not alone anyway. and I have yet to meet a single canadian.

I shall still be in 'Nam for Christmas. in fact my big challenge is to find somewhere to spend it that isn't an anticlimax. I want to get away from it all. you know why. my ozzie buddies are keen on going walking north of hanoi so I might do that. they've got a friend who they reckon is in hanoi too, and who might join us. a pathetic xmas party, really, compared to the ones at home. not least because it seems that organising it will be entirely up to me as I'm not stoned.

went on a trip to the mekong delta the other day, 2 days long, with a minibus full of westerners. the mekong delta was centre of much guerrilla warfare in the olden days. today the food is crap, and the locals, when you stray away from the air-con bus and protective guide, are terrifying. in the market a man with 3rd degree napalm burns all over his face came and stood in front of us (me and the australians, ally and andy) and blocked our path until we gave him some money. he had a little collection bucket balanced on the stumps where his hands should have been. he probably never had hands to start with: that is agent orange for you, the agent of birth defects. a woman in the market refused to sell us any fruit. that I found especially spooky as normally they're falling over each other to part you from your cash.

other people on the trip were hugely depressing. there was a large english contingent, very much the duke of edinburgh crowd, all keen, wearing navy blue fleeces and sensible shoes. urgh most of them were just out for a few weeks for hardy little holidays. there were a couple of germans who I ignored (I know you would expect no less) and the little ozzie folk. they tend to smoke a lot of grass, which as you know isn't my cup of tea. it became a bit dull. they'd stumble out of bed in the morning and skin up, and spend the rest of the day giggling and staring out of the window, and reading me extracts from a Tibetan buddhism book. they've run out of grass now, and gone back to normal, which is good.

I miss the charlie far far more than I'd expected. this seems strange as it's not like we were at it every day. not quite. still there is plenty of alcohol here to compensate. no wine. but I'm craving a proper high— that is, the combination of drink and drugs. I don't suppose you'd post me some? no, I suppose not.

must go now as the dong are mounting up and the hotel in saigon cleaned me out completely by charging western prices on the minibar: the bill ended up being $155 for two nights. I threw a tantrum but with zero effect. take care, let me know how you're doing, and write soon.

buckets of love

t x

74

CHAPTER
6

I lean on the windowsill, too tired to do anything but look at Hanoi spread below me. The houses are grey and shoved together any old how. Far away to the left, there are huge, shiny office buildings that look incongruously western. On a roof below, I can already see the scrawny rooster that will wake me at 4 a.m. with a premature proclamation of the break of day. In the distance, I think I can see the glint of the lake, and in the foreground there is definitely the sound of a train. From this distance, the masses of people are aesthetically pleasing in their pointed hats, rather than alarming. It's chilly, which I appreciate, because the shitty smells don't drift so far in the cold. I have a good perspective on Hanoi: six floors up in the sky, safely out of interaction's way. I am an observer, and not a part of it.

It's not a bad view for a crappy hotel, and I speak as a recently qualified expert. I close the window and shiver. I will go shopping for warm clothes later. I will also take all my dirty clothes to the hotel laundry. For now, I tip everything from my rucksack onto the floor; as soon as I've had a sleep, I'll sort it out. I am trying to be upbeat today. Hanoi is better than Saigon: it is smaller, more manageable, and less rude. I say all this with confidence; all I've seen is what whipped by during the cyclo ride from the Romantic Darling Café, which apparently doubles as a bus terminal, to this, the Victory Hotel (they don't like to miss an opportunity to rub in the fact that they won). I was much more interested in hanging on to my backpack than watching the sights go by. I was more pleased that the ancient bus hadn't crashed than enthused about the possibilities of another bloody city. Everything I know about Hanoi, I have gleaned from the guidebook.

I left Ally and Andy in Hué last night, in a violent thunderstorm. They are coming here by train, travelling the luxurious way. Hué seemed like a nothingy sort of place to me, and although we trailed wetly around some nominally interesting sights, like the gorgeously named Forbidden Purple Palace (stormed in the war and the movies), everything was in ruins, and I wasn't really in the mood for any of it. Overnight, I covered a huge chunk of Vietnam, which can only be good. Now it remains to be seen whether I'll manage to meet up with Ally and Andy again, here at the Victory, as arranged. They might seize the opportunity and lose me, too polite to tell me they don't want to travel with me anymore. In which case I'm no further on than I was when I started. Maybe this is what travelling's all about: starting afresh, over and over again. It is an exhausting thought. I think that people who spend ages on the road must be people who are scared to have proper friendships, who are too insecure to put down roots, but who want to reinvent themselves, safe with strangers, year after year after year.

I think that the most authentic traveller I've met so far has been Max, back on my first day in Vietnam. He certainly looked every inch the backpacker. I was amazed when he turned out to be charming. He didn't show off, he didn't name-drop places, and he seemed genuinely concerned for my well-being. In my terror at being in Asia, and alone, I drank so much, so quickly, that I could barely stand up. While Ally and Andy joined me in my drunken laughter, Max took me outside like a naughty child. He paid for my cyclo in advance, lifted me into it, and sent me home. I don't recall the journey. Outside the hotel, the driver, too, suf-

fered an amnesia attack, and insisted that I pay all over again. I ar-
gued. His fellow drivers slunk across the road to back him up. I
was so drunk and so furious that I took a five dollar note (three
dollars more than he wanted), ripped it in quarters, and threw it
on the sticky pavement. As I waited for someone to let me into
the hotel, I watched my tormentor kneeling and picking up the
pieces. He looked right at me, and I looked right back. I hate you.
I hate you, too.

Yes, he was a good traveller, Max. I'll never see him again.

I can't keep my eyes open. Last night's bus must have been an
old Soviet one, or similar, which was handed to Vietnam because
it was too fucked even for Russia. I would not have been at all surprised if we'd gone over a huge pothole and the whole thing had
disintegrated into its component parts. There would have been
twenty passengers sitting in the road, in a pile of twisted metal.
The seat cushions (such as they were) would have come off the
metal backs. The rear-view mirror, had there been such a thing,
would have fallen apart. Every screw would have come out. It
would have been a heap of spare parts, and nothing else. The fellow passengers, all westerners, were perfectly pleasant. One of
them, a Finnish bloke, flew in from Bombay last week, where he
stayed in the same guesthouse as the girl who got murdered. He
banged on and on about it. It was fascinating, in a morbid kind
of way. He said it was a Virgin Atlantic pen she was holding.
Everyone's got one of those. I used to chew on them all the time.
He said authoritatively that the bloke (because killers always are
blokes—women should run the world) was trying to make her
write something. He even claimed to have seen the suspicious
Canadian. He quite liked the sound of his own voice and we were
a captive audience. There was nothing else to do.

Luckily there were few enough of us to give some passengers,
including me, two seats to "stretch out" on, or at least to uncurl a
fraction. I was frozen, having packed precisely nothing for the
eventuality of an Asian cold snap. My cashmere funnel-neck from

Nicole Fahri is the only thing that's even got long sleeves. I wish I hadn't sent my fur home. It would be perfect. I cuddled into myself, and waited for morning. I felt as though I was awake all night, listening to the wail of passing horns, and flying up in the air and crashing back down on my seat, regularly. It must have toned some muscles. At one stage I woke up from a nightmare I couldn't quite remember. I didn't even know I'd been asleep.

I am owed a night's sleep, and I can feel it overwhelming me. I snuggle into bed, fully clothed. The sheets are surprisingly crisp and pleasant. When I've had a nap, I'll go out and check my emails. I know I shouldn't be thinking about Tom, but I can't help it. I haven't seen anyone who even slightly makes me want to have a fling. I am determined to get him back, and certain that I will manage it. I constantly imagine us on a paradise island, chilling together in the sun, and being happy. It is my Romantic Darling dream. Is it, I wonder, more mature and enlightened to survive my travelling by thinking of delights that I am earning for the future (karma, as Ally would insist), rather than having Tom as an imaginary friend, with me, in my head, all the time? Maybe this is a pathetic kind of progress.

I'm not cut out for this life, but sometimes I wonder whether I might be adapting to it. At least, I'm not in crisis any longer. I've been away from home for four weeks, minus a day. I need to extend my visa. This trip has been longer than a normal holiday, now. Every day has been a little bit easier. I've met people I can talk to. I've talked to people I hated on sight. I've stayed in greasy hovels and been ripped off by infuriating bastards on a daily basis. Every day I feel more certain that I can survive this accidental travelling experience. Enjoying it is a different matter, of course, but I think I can get through it.

Today I have achieved a milestone of sorts. I have now travelled almost the length of Vietnam on my own. I have, at least, covered the distance between its two main cities. I should have been keeping a diary, and I haven't at all, largely because I didn't want to write "I wish I was at home with Tom" every single day. I wouldn't have liked my grandchildren reading it after I died and saying, "Granny was a bit pathetic, wasn't she? But at least she loved Grandpa." There is, of course, another milestone, a rather more serious one, coming up next week. I am trying not to think about it. It is, however, an important time, and I think I will need to read a diary documenting all this, to remind myself that I did such a crazy journey. Travelling in Asia will probably turn out to be the maddest thing I ever do—a weird time of aberration, away from my lovely life. I'll need to remember it when I'm old and crap, like that woman in the hospital last year. If I manage to get the trekking organised, I'm going to take my funky little notebook with me, and I'm going to write in it every day, however tired I am. I want a record of being here, on the anniversary of Mum's death. I want to show Mum that I can do things. Now that she's not here.

Kate gave me the notebook as a leaving present at my party. And now it's here. I bet that when it started its little life on a shelf at Harvey Nicks along with all the other identical pink plastic-covered notebooks it never imagined it would be the one to go to Vietnam. Me too, little notebook, me too. I never thought I'd be the one either. How did we get so far from London? It arrived in my hand in Soho House, which would have been a perfectly normal and unsurprising place for it to find itself, and now it's in 'Nam, as shocked as I am.

God, I hope I manage to get away from all this for Christmas. As far as I can tell, all we need to do is to get a train and a bus to a place called Sapa eight hours north of here, by the Chinese border, and then hire a trekking guide. It shouldn't be beyond me to sort that out. I desperately want to be nowhere near anything western. I'm not sure about going with Ally and Andy. They're perfectly pleasant company, but they must be getting bored of me by now. They must be craving time on their own. They decided to come here by train, and the more I think about it, the more certain I am that it was a way of getting away from me. I left them a note at the hotel reception, saying they could share with me if they wanted to. I hope they do. I will pay the bill. I have no qualms about buying friends.

Company would be good. I feel that it's incredibly important to be with the right sort of people next week. I wish I could be with Will.

I need to go walking, to get skinny. I think that so far I've put on at least half a stone as a result of lurching from one meal to the next and doing no exercise at all. Trekking in the countryside would be like a super-rigorous health farm. I suppose you have time to think while you walk, but at least the exercise endorphins will be swamping my brain. Maybe the result will be happy thoughts of Mother, though I can't imagine what they would be.

For some reason, she is becoming linked in my mind with the girl, Clare, who was murdered. Maybe it's because they both died horribly. I expect the girl was killed by a local, probably for money. It's very Eurocentric to assume—as, apparently, it is being assumed—that it was the work of a sick western pervert. Just because people said she'd been hanging out with a Canadian man, and then they couldn't trace him. It doesn't make him guilty. Asians aren't all childlike and innocent, I can vouch for that. There was that Japanese child the other year who killed his fellow students, and cut their heads off and left things in their mouths, and I'm sure there have been sick Indian killers. The very fact that it's happened so far away from me gives me a pleasant frisson. I like the fact that, to most of the people at home, Vietnam and India are practically next door. To them, I am in the thick of things, sitting next to the murderer on the bus. Whereas I know that it's far more likely that I'll die in the tangled wreckage of that bus than at the hands of any human being. I suppose I'd rather dwell on the distant killing than on the mundanity of Mother, who will soon not have been alive this time last year.

I am just about warm enough. I'm so sleepy. I wish Mum

would get out of my head. She's been there more and more lately. Perhaps this is what it means to be haunted. Perhaps ghosts aren't troubled souls in themselves but souls whose memory troubles the people who are left behind. Ghosts don't exist, they're in the mind. I've known that all along, I think, but I didn't realise how literal and mundane being haunted really was. Every time I'm on my own, with no distractions (and that is just about all the time, these days), then sooner or later there's the sinking recognition. Oh. There you are. Come in, pull up a comfy chair, and make yourself at home in my conscious mind. Close the door to the subconscious on your way.

I wish I'd brought Teddy with me. Something from home, to cuddle up to. The next best thing to Tom. It can't have been my fault, what Mum did to herself, because she started it when I was so tiny. Perhaps if I'd been a better child it could have been different. It had been going on for all my life when it ended. It wasn't my fault. It can't have been. Sometimes I wonder if Will thinks it was my fault, if it must have been in some way avoidable. He wasn't there to stop her. I was the one on the scene. I tried to make her go to AA, but she never got anywhere near admitting she needed to. When Victoria, who was one of my friends at university, got anorexia, I saw exactly the same thing. She'd make sure everyone knew how fat she thought she was, and how little she ate, and how she despised people with "huge arses," but nothing anyone said would make her eat more, because she didn't want to get better. She enjoyed being skinny as a pipe-cleaner person, and that was that. She thrived on the attention. She looked like a concentration camp victim by the time I walked away from her, and I haven't seen her since. I don't even know if she's alive. "You're exactly like my mother," I told her, once. She laughed coldly. "I'm nothing like your mother," she said flatly. I didn't ask why, because I knew what the answer would be: mother was fat.

I was glad I abandoned Vicky. There was nothing anyone could do for her. I suppose I walked away from Mother as well, in the end, and left her to her fate. In fact, I more than walked away. She deserved it, too. But Vicky was just a person whose path had happened to cross mine. Mother gave birth to me. I should not have given up on her.

As I sleep, Mother, Vicky and poor murdered Clare come together in my head and become one person. They are one victim. One focus of attention. Two-thirds manipulative bitch, and one-third blonde-haired girl about whom I know nothing. Two-thirds dead, one-third maybe dead. Two-thirds young and pretty, one-third monstrous and puffy and saggy. As I sleep, they pursue me, a three-headed monster. I didn't kill Clare, but someone did. I didn't kill Vicky. I didn't keep my mother alive. I rejoiced when she was dead, and she knows that and she is coming after me. She's coming to get me.

Vicky and Clare will help her. They chase me onto a rickety old bus, and we lurch through a city that is sometimes London, sometimes Saigon, about to crash at any moment. They are going to torture me, like the man tortured Clare. He put a pen in her hand and strangled her. They give me the pen. I have to write "My fault." I shout for Will. My brother, save me.

I jolt awake, but I don't dare open my eyes. The sheets are twisted all over the place. I have to catch my breath. There is someone in the room. I can feel it. I forget what is real and what is a dream. Is it Mother in the room? Is it the three of them?

Ally and Andy must have arrived, and got the key from reception. I can hear footsteps walking around. It sounds like only one person. The springs on the other bed creak, as someone sits down. I can't open my eyes yet. My heart is still thumping. I think it's Mum in the room. I think of the way I tipped my dirty washing all over the floor. The room is strewn with my knickers, and tampons, and bras and everything.

The person has gone very quiet. I can just hear them breathing. I open my eyes a fraction. The person shifts a little. I look at them.

It's a man. A bloke of about my age, dressed in scruffy clothes like a backpacker. He is sitting in my bedroom, and he has seen all my stuff all over the floor, and he's looking right at me. The door was locked. The hotel is almost empty. How did he get in? Will anyone hear me scream?

I am wide awake. I am definitely not dreaming. I shout, as loudly as I can. It sounds hollow and silly. He flinches. He must be the Canadian.

"Shh," he says. "I know who you are. There's no need to shout."

He has a pen in his hand.

CHAPTER
7

This is real. I don't know why he isn't getting on with it. This is his optimum murder moment, but he is staring at me, without moving. I don't doubt that he is here to get me, that he has come from Bombay. I hate the pathetic sound that comes from my mouth. I should be shouting the place down, but what emerges is a self-conscious yelp. I am not a good victim. I'm not brave.

He sits beside me and fiddles with his pen. It isn't an airline pen. It's just a normal Biro, slightly chewed. He looks at me.

"Hey, you're all right," he says. "What's the problem, yeah?" His calm is sinister. It's not a Canadian accent. It's Australian. Near enough.

"Fuck off!" I shout "Go away! Someone'll come and help me, you know." I look towards the door, planning my route out. The door is open. Ally is standing on the threshold, looking concerned. Thank God. I am delighted, and relieved, to see her. She is, for all practical purposes, the best friend I've got.

"Ally!" I exclaim. "Thank fuck for that."

"Hey, guys!" She doesn't seem very distraught about the fact that I am being assaulted. "What's the problem? Mike?"

My would-be assailant shrugs. "Search me. I think she was having a nightmare."

"Tansy? Are you OK?"

"You *know* him?"

"Sure. You remember I told you we were trying to hook up with our friend? We just met him at the station. He said he'd come up and say hey to you. He wanted to talk to you. What's wrong?"

"Why has he got that pen? He scared me." I can't look at him.

Ally looks stern. For such a small person, she can be surprisingly intimidating. "Mike, did you knock?"

"He did not! I just woke up and he was sitting on my bed!"

"Mike, you fucking drongo."

He looks sheepish. "Sorry, mate. They gave me their key while they finished checking in. They're coming to share your room. I thought it must be a dorm." He shows me the key, then extends his hand. "I'm Mike. Pleased to meet you. I hear you're sorting a trek. I'd like to come. I'm sure we'll get along just fine."

By Christmas Eve we almost are getting along fine. We have walked for several days, and I have stopped worrying about what I look like, whether I can keep up with the others, and the anniversary of my mother's death. I haven't told anyone about that. I don't want them asking if I'm all right all the time.

In the evening, I sit by myself, by the fire. I won't be phoning anyone to wish them a Merry Christmas. Father Christmas will not be visiting me, tonight. I can't even check my seasonal emails of goodwill. In the background, there is the vague and out-of-place drone of a television. They have a telly here but they don't have a phone. A phone would be a day's walk away, at least. I'm not even sleeping in a bed tonight. They don't have beds here. We're all going to bed down on blankets on top of straw by the fire. I love the idea. I can't wait to tell people at home. I am spending Christmas with new friends. That's tenuous, actually. New acquaintances. I am spending Christmas with Australians. I would never have predicted that. I seem to have met an awful lot more Australians than Vietnamese.

I stare hard into the flames. I remember my mother telling me that you can see whatever you want to see in firelight. I look for Tom, but I can't persuade the fire to form him. I scan the room, just in case. The television is speaking English. It's going to be the news headlines soon. I don't know how a television penetrated the wilds of the far north of Vietnam, but I don't want to know about the rest of the world. I'd love to see Tom walking through the door, coming in from the freezing muddy cold outside. There's no way he'd come all the way here to look for me, but the optimistic part of me has been hoping, all along, that he would surprise me for Christmas. He might, I hoped, see how wrong he had been to send me off alone, and track me down to comfort me through the anniversary.

I sent him a studied, casual email before we left Hanoi. I furnished him with place names and dates, under the cover of a feigned enthusiasm for this Christmas adventure. I made sure that the guesthouse man in Sapa, our starting point, knew what my name was and where we were going. All the same, Tom would never find me here, even if he did try. The question is academic because he won't try.

I don't allow myself to dwell on the events of a year ago. I didn't have a Christmas then, and I'm not having one now. When I opened the door, I knew what I'd find. She'd been spiralling downwards for days, and this time I hadn't had the energy to force her out of it. I was exhausted, drunk, and angry. I lingered in the pub for as long as I could, talking loudly about anything that came into my head and refusing to let anyone leave. Eventually, though, pubs shut, and people go home. No one would go clubbing with me because it was Christmas Eve, and we'd have been hard pushed, anyway, to find an acceptable club that was open. I sat on the Northern Line, reading a three-day-old copy of the *News of the World*. I walked home from the station, listening to the clopping of my heels on the pavement, and concentrating on what I'd do if someone attacked me. I awarded marks out of ten to the Christmas trees in the windows. I looked up in the sky for Father Christmas and his sleigh. I directed my thoughts in every direction but the obvious one. I turned my key in the door and listened. It was quiet, and dark, and there was a funny smell. I thought about going straight to bed and leaving it all until morning. But I knew. So I switched the sitting room light on, and it shone too brightly, lighting up every corner of the room. It lit the pictures on the mantelpiece. It lit the dust in the corners. It lit the droopy plants. And it lit the body of a fat, pickled woman, lying, face down, like a beached whale, on the rug in front of an electric fire which was singeing her hair.

I'm proud of the fact that I've organised this trip, and brought four people away with me. I've even found and employed a guide, a cheerful woman called Hong who knows the path, and bribes us with sweets when we get tired. She wears running shoes with holes in, and threadbare leggings, and she's the only one who never falls over. She cooks all our meals. We love her. Hong's here for the money, but everybody else is escaping something; they must be.

The fifth member of our group is a young Australian called Carrie. She's short and stocky, with cropped brown hair and a disconcerting habit of farting silently, apparently assuming no one notices. Some people have an innate sense of style, whereas others do not. I think I do, and I know that Carrie does not. But I'm probably being unfair. She's only twenty, and I have never seen anyone more desperate for friends. Ally took us all to the hotel café, after Mike scared me, so we could supposedly have a coffee and make friends. Mike could never be mistaken for anything other than an Australian. He has blond ringlets and big muscly arms. He even surfs. I sulked and refused to catch his eye, while he was too friendly to be trustworthy. The only other person there was wearing combat pants and reading *The Tibetan Book of Living and Dying*. Carrie's bag still had a "Cabin baggage approved" label on it.

"Where have you come from?" Ally asked her, kindly. I was forcibly reminded of my first meeting with the two of them. They do a good line in befriending the lost.

She looked delighted. "Europe," she replied, and looked around at our surroundings, miming bafflement at her sudden immersion in Asia.

"What, Europe airport?" I wasn't feeling kind. I don't think I'm a kind person.

"Yeah, I think so."

"Where did you go in Europe?" Andy took over being friendly, while Ally kicked me under the table and frowned.

"England," said Carrie. "Ireland, Scotland, France, Germany, Spain, Italy, Prague, Belgium, Holland, Amsterdam. I think there might've been some more."

"Holland *and* Amsterdam?" I was impressed.

"You bet!"

"Do you speak those languages?" I remember Ally and Andy admitting that they never made it further afield than Brighton in their college years. All they remembered of Brighton was smoking under the angel statue. They were very surprised when I mentioned it was a seaside town. "Well, your sea is different from our ocean. Not a surprise that we didn't notice it," Andy reasoned.

"Languages—yeah, right!" Carrie laughed. "I hardly would. The guide takes care of all that."

It emerged that the Australians who don't live in overcrowded squalor for two years see Europe from hop-on, hop-off buses. There is a guide on board who handles the foreign talking, delivers them to the doors of their hostels, escorts them safely past any culture to the nearest drinking establishment, and scoops them up in the morning. I asked what she thought of Paris.

"It had a really massive Aussie bar," she said, after a moment's thought. "I think that was Paris. The people were bastards on the way back to the hotel—shouted at us in foreign. There was a big pylon kind of thing."

"That's Paris," I confirmed. "Did you go to the Louvre?"

"Of course! We were there twenty-four hours! Mind you, it was more a hole in the ground than a proper toilet."

"I hate the fucking French," Mike interjected.

"Don't be racist," I told him.

"I'm not racist. They're just arseholes."

"I'm French." I said this on the spur of the moment to shut him up. I was still smouldering with humiliation.

"No, you're English, aren't you, Tammy?" asked Carrie.

"Half French. My mother was French."

"No way." Mike didn't believe me.

" 'Fraid so."

Carrie has now "done" Europe, and ticked it off her list. I find this fascinating and chilling in equal parts. I have a horrible feeling that my view of Vietnam is as distorted as this. In fact, it must be.

I peer into the flames, trying to make out Tom's face in there. I can't see him, but I can see Mum in every flicker, every flame, every ember. Typical. I look up. Ally is looking over at me. She has a familiar expression on her face. This is how people arrange their features when they wish to convey "sympathy." She's sweet. She doesn't even know it's the anniversary. She's just being generally nice, which is probably more than I deserve. It still surprises me that I think of her as an equal, when she looks so young and so unpolished.

"Coming to see the news?" she asks, when I catch her eye. She walks over and puts her hand on my shoulder. "Come on, it's the BBC."

"Have they got a satellite dish?" This village is populated by about twenty people. No beds, but, it seems, satellite TV.

"Looks like."

"That's grotesque."

"Hong says they get money from having us staying, and that was the first thing they bought. It is a bit dodgy, I guess."

Andy joins us. "Yeah, but who are we to say that? How can we love our telly and then say these people shouldn't be allowed it? Just because we want to come and stay with nice backwards cave people. They're entitled to progress, doncha think?"

"It's complicated, isn't it?" I thought travelling would be straightforward. I don't want the TV to be here, but if I wasn't here, the television wouldn't be. Nothing is as well defined as it should be. Increasingly, I am sure that backpackers have no reason to be smug. Even though this reinforces my prejudices, it doesn't make me happy.

The villagers are seated on rows of chairs, staring at the magic box. I know they don't speak English, and yet they are all fascinated. I watch the people watching the screen. They are beautiful, tribal people, and they are entirely transfixed. The picture is blurred and crappy, and I think it's a story set somewhere in the Third World. Then I listen to what's being said.

At first I think it's an update on the first story. Maybe the killer has been caught. Then I realise it's something different. A different woman. She's also British, and also blonde. She's travelling alone, and she's been murdered. She had, the reporter says, a pack of Charles and Diana playing cards in her hand.

I look at Mike. He grimaces. The firelight makes him look scary, but I know—of course I know—that it wasn't him. It can't have been, now. She was killed in Delhi. I'm probably the only one among us who hasn't been to Delhi. It's on my itinerary.

Her photo appears on the screen, slightly out of focus. She's got messy blonde hair, and she's wearing a fleece. She's leaning towards the camera, smiling broadly, with a bottle of water in her hand. A few of the local people look surprised. They turn round and stare at me. They don't know the girl on the telly is dead. They think it's me.

The chances of these people ever setting eyes on that woman are minuscule. About the same as their ever meeting me, and yet here they are, seeing us both. They are entranced by the very fact of television without feeling any need to know what's being said, who it is in the picture. Before long they'll be watching *The Simpsons* and *Days of Our Lives*, and America will have won the war, after all.

We try to talk about other things. If anything, the slight potential danger to western travellers enhances our enjoyment of our situation. We know it won't happen to us. It's like a rollercoaster: a sanitised thrill. We know people at home will be thinking of us. We like that. It is, of course, dreadful for that girl, Joanne, and her parents. But bad things happen every day, everywhere.

Mike offers me his beer. I take a swig straight from the bottle.

"Cheers," I tell him, handing it back.

"Hey, no worries. Merry Christmas."

"You too."

"Beats being at home."

"It certainly does." I look at him sideways. I wonder what propelled him all the way here. "Christmas in Australia can't be up to much," I probe. "It must be too hot to be properly Christmassy. Or do you celebrate it on June the twenty-fifth? I forget."

"Pardon me, but that sounds like colonial bullshit to me. Like, it would have been snowing in Bethlehem? In bloody Israel? The Middle East? Reckon not."

"It probably gets cold in Israel," I guess. "Although admittedly snow might be quite unlikely. In any case, I celebrate a pagan winter festival. I'm not a Christian."

"How come you were stoked to be sleeping on straw like the baby Jesus, huh?"

"It's *romantic*. That's all. A girl's allowed a little romance in her life, isn't she? There's fuck all else round here."

The wet air clings to me. I expect to put my hand in my pocket and bring out a handful of fog. It would be squishy and bouncy, and I'd throw it around; bounce it off a tree. The countryside is green and luscious. Everything is covered in a fine layer of moisture. Even me. Particularly me. We walk through mist. We tiptoe along the muddy edges of rice paddies, taking care not to slip as the options would be to fall to the right into a submerged terrace, or to fall left down a sharp drop into a submerged terrace. We trudge up hills. We slide down them. Hong hands out sugar boosts, and we carry on. I amuse myself, in my head, all day long. I feel a bit strange. I'm probably being affected by the absence of fumes, something I have inhaled daily all my life. I'm free. I can do things like this whenever I want, now, and there is never again going to be somebody sitting at home, resenting me, demanding everything, and pretending not to drink. Never again, for the rest of my life.

After dinner, I peel my socks off and hope no one can smell my feet. I don't realise Mike is talking to me.

"So, Tamsin," he says. I don't respond. He says it again, and on the third time I look up with a start, jolted from a solemn consideration of whether it would be better to burst a blister using an earring, or to leave it.

"Sorry," I say. "What?" I've given up correcting anyone's approximation of my name. I just accept it as a flattering bonus when someone bothers to get it right. It's only the English speakers who get it wrong.

"I was just going to say, did you think you'd be sleeping like this, on the floor with strangers, when you set off backpacking?"

I lower my foot to the ground. "I'm not backpacking!" I tell him. I have standards to uphold.

He looks confused. "Sorry, mate, I thought you said you were away for a year? Are you just on holiday?"

"No. But I'm not a backpacker."

"How come?"

"I really hate the word. I hate the word backpack—it's a rucksack, that's its name. And apart from that, why do I have to be labelled by the kind of bag I've got? When I've been away before, no one's tried to call me a suitcaser. I haven't been suitcasing. I'm not a handbagger when I'm in London."

Andy wanders over. "You're not a suitcase. You're a headcase."

"No I'm not, I'm just not willing to conform. I don't like the image that goes with the backpacker. The smug, self-righteous git. I'm sorry, but I just happen to be away from my own country for a while, for various reasons. I'm not one of the herd."

"Oooh," Mike laughs. "Lady Di!"

Carrie looks up. "It was Princess Di actually."

"Well, she started off as Lady Di," says Mike, reasonably. "We all remember that, when we were kids. Prince Charles and Lady Di. And that's what Tansy's like. She even looks like her."

"I do not!"

"You do, too. She was tall, you're tall. She had blondish hair, so have you. She was posh, you're posh. She married the King, and you're a surefire bet to do something like that."

"Watch out, Prince William!" cackles Andy. "Can we come to the royal wedding?"

"Fuck off!" I slam my glass down and stare at them all. "She is dead, you know. I'm not."

"Lady Di!" Mike taunts. "Lady Diana Spencer!"

"Christ!" I say, looking around for an ally, and finding none. Ally's gone outside to take photos of the children. "Just because you come from a nation of convicts—the dregs of our society, shipped away across the world because we don't want you—it doesn't mean you have to come at me with this inverted snobbery."

"As it happens, my family are descended from the governors," Mike informs me.

"So are mine," Carrie adds hastily.

Andy grins. "Convicts and proud of it. I think my ancestors stole an apple."

I didn't have a Christmas, last year. I switched off the fire first of all, and tried to fan away the worst of the smell. The I looked at her. I knew I should call the police. I'd been thinking about this day for years. Not this particular Christmas, but the inevitable day when she would die. And I'd been thinking about it particularly keenly over the preceding week, because it had become clear that, finally, something was going to happen.

I always imagined I'd feel happy, and, it turned out, I did. I felt happy because I forced myself to feel happy. I sat in her chair, and picked up her vodka bottle and her lipstick-smeared glass, and poured myself a generous measure. I held it up towards her—cheers—and downed it in one. I was trembling as I picked up the phone. I called Kate, and then I called the police, and then I called Tom. They all came to see me, as soon as they could. A week later, Will came too, and I found I had some sort of family after all.

When the police had gone, and she was safely in the mortuary, I had a look around the house to see if she'd gotten me a present.

I hadn't gotten her one either.

CHAPTER
8

From: Tom
To: Tansy
Subject: None

fuck, xmas and new year do this to me every year. have overindulged
again, and need a holiday. I've booked 2 weeks off in march—in fact,
haven't exactly booked them yet, but plan to. if still ok with you, will
join you in thailand.

no time to say more as v busy, but unless you say otherwise, will start
sorting it. hope festive season was good for you. Better than last year,
presumably. now I have time for a sachet of resolve before taking a
long lunch . . . what's work, anyway?

Cheers, love tom x

From: Amanda906@yahoo.com
To: Tansy
Subject: India

Dear Tans,

How is it all going? Hope you're still enjoying yourself and had a good Christmas and New Year. Do they celebrate either in Vietnam? Mine were awful, I have to say. I have so much news . . . It's all changed, you see, since I last wrote.

Here's the main thing: I'm not pregnant anymore. I lost the baby the week before Xmas. It was horrible—distressing and bloody and, I fear, brought on by my excesses—and yet for all that I was, and am, delighted. Which is not, of course, a straightforward or a socially acceptable way to feel.

Paul is devastated—I'd only told him about the pregnancy 10 days before, and now here it is, over. Things got worse for him, because now I've moved out. I can't really explain why. It just felt like the thing I had to do. I packed up and moved round to my cousin Maggie's (you've met her—you took the piss because she's so fond of feng shui) and I don't think I'll be going back. To be completely honest, I'm not 100% sure the baby was his. What a foul harlot I am.

So here I am. I haven't been back to work—this is my new email address. Maggie's about to go to India, to an ashram to do lots of yoga. My current thinking is that I'll join her. You'll be in India soon, won't you? Can we meet up?

Hope you're having a wonderful, free, and happy time. Also hope I'm coherent.

Much love,

Amanda

From: Will
To: Tansy
Subject: One year!

Hi Tans

Just a short message to remind you that we have now known each other for a year. Happy anniversary! I know it has also been a less happy anniversary and hope that's OK for you.

I have been thinking of you.

Love from your brother, Will

From: Kate
To: Tansy
Subject: happy new year!

Sweetheart—fuck! it's not so good to be back at work, is it? not that you'd know. hope you had a good one.

I looked in the mirror today to see dull skin, bloodshot eyes, and a double chin it's finally getting to me. am feeling sorry for self today.

and more impressed than ever with you no doubt you're slim, healthy and browner than me.

take care—love you

K xxxxx

ps amanda seems to have vanished from the office any news your end?

From: Tansy
To: Amanda
Subject: India

dear amanda,

my god, I hope you're all right. what a horrible shock. you mustn't be
worried about your reaction to losing the baby—whatever you feel is
fine, and nothing to do with anyone else. perhaps it's for the best.
just keep doing what feels like the right thing to you, and you'll end
up all right. I'm very sorry though, if your marriage is over. on the
purely selfish front, I'm delighted you're thinking of coming to India.

Pleeeaase do. I'd love to see you, and an ashram might be just the thing.

Keep in touch, and look after yourself.

lots of love

t x

From: Tansy
To: Tom
Subject: Re:

hello

yes, I think that should be fine. I should be in thailand by march. let
me know your flight details and I'll come to the airport.

I'll believe it when I see it!

had excellent xmas trekking, and spent a minimally excessive new
year on the train back to Hanoi. so I probably feel better than you do.

happy new year to you.

love, t x

BACKPACK

From: Tansy
To: Kate
Subject: Re: happy new year

oh my god, guess what? tom's coming to thailand! forgive my undignified excitement—I know I meant to be getting over him—but a familiar face is a precious commodity to me these days, and when it belongs to tom who gives a fuck about dignity and self-respect? hurrah.

had a v unusual xmas, walking by the chinese border with a random bunch of australian misfits. We looked into china at one point, but it didn't look very nice. then came back to hanoi and found your parcel at the post restante. thank you so much! it was pretty much the only present I got, and I love it. I will be the chicest backpacker (sorry, tourist) in asia, and the only one in agnès b. will save it for special occasions as most of my best clothes got ruined trekking. to be honest, it's a bit cold right now for a little sequinned top, but I'm catching the bus south tonight, and then west to laos, and it will be sunny there. it must be.

by the way, any symptoms of overindulgence on your part are only temporary, and you're probably imagining them anyway. you always look gorgeous and I can't imagine that's changed. and you won't get fat. your granny didn't go to the gym twice a week, did she? I have to confess to feeling rather smug now. I'm fit! and I'm almost enjoying myself, occasionally.

look after yourself, hon, and write soon.

masses of love

t xxx

CHAPTER
9

The sun is shining in Laos, and its sky is baby blue, and Tom is coming to Thailand. I am heading west, in Thailand's direction. I'm not in Vietnam anymore. At the risk of reminding myself of Carrie, I have done Vietnam. I unfold myself and straighten out. Standing up is a painful and weird thing. It involves lots of muscles that must have thought they'd been decommissioned for life, and had shut themselves down accordingly. I have been on the bus all night, but the moment I manage to drop off to sleep, to allow my exhaustion to overcome the massive hurdle of discomfort, we arrive at the border. I won't be sleeping at all. I wish I had a vodka Red Bull. A good coffee, at least.

I look out of the window, hoping for a border café selling Asian super-coffee to weary travellers. No chance. I couldn't drink it anyway. Not with this stomach. The very thought makes me spasm. The sunshine however immediately lightens my heart. I'm shallow, but, after two weeks of freezing rain, a blue sky suddenly makes me forget that I'm on my own, that I'm bunged up with Imodium, and I have to wait six weeks for Tom.

It briefly makes me forget that I left Ally, Andy, Mike, and Carrie in Hanoi, three days ago. Carrie's flying home from Saigon. Mike might catch up with me in Laos, and if I'm lucky I might see Ally and Andy in Thailand. Introduce them to Tom. Suddenly, I am enjoying the unlikely moment. Living in the moment, I vaguely remember, is something Ally talked about. It's a good thing, I'm sure of that.

Everyone pours off the bus before I have a chance to have a coherent thought. They tread on me when necessary in their haste to get into the real world. Even a woman with a broken leg scrambles for the exit with the best of them. This I understand. When I was little, I had a secret project to put myself in a parcel and post myself to France, just to see what it was like, and whether I could get there free, without a passport. My plan fell down on the practicals: if I was in there, how could I post myself? And if it was a secret, how could anyone else do it? I never worked it out. Now, however, I think I have my answer. The past hours must have borne similarities to being chucked around the postal system in an airtight container from which there is no escape. I posted myself to Laos, and in an hour or so I must get back into the parcel to arrive at the final destination.

Still, it's good to be on the move, even in a clapped-out old bus that is held together solely by the protection of the Lord Buddha (who is with us, beside the driver, in pictorial form with flashing coloured lights around him). Better to be here than still in Dong Ha, a grim, muddy little town that's situated right in the middle of Vietnam, and consequently suffered horribly during the war. I was the only westerner in the whole place, apart from two wild-eyed war vets from America who had come back, presumably, to overcome their post-traumatic stress. They didn't seem to notice my welcoming smiles.

I sat at a table in a café and waited two days for the bus, which eventually turned up six hours late. On the first evening, I absent-mindedly polished off a grey and smelly piece of fish. Half an hour later, my stomach registered its objection by evacuating its entire contents. That was thirty-six hours ago, and despite the fact that there cannot possibly be any fish, or anything else, left inside, it continues to spasm and complain. The Imodium is holding it together for now, but tenuously. I can't swallow anything, even water, for fear of having to stop the bus and shit in a ditch. This can't be happening to me. It's someone else's half-invented travel tale.

Thank God I'm not in Dong Ha anymore. Thank Christ I'm leaving Vietnam.

During one of the many stops that the bus makes, I enter a local café in search of water and a few minutes of peace from the constant jolting. Two girls at a corner table smile at me. They are six feet tall, at least. Both of them have creamy complexions and an extremely wholesome air. They look as if they have been fed on milk and honey all their lives.

I walk as steadily as I can to their table, and pull up a chair.

"Hello," I mutter. "Can I join you?"

I put my arms on the table, and my head on my arms, and everything goes black.

When I wake up, the girls are both sitting on the edge of my bed.

"Good," says one, when I open my eyes. I don't know whether it's night or morning, whether I'm in my room or theirs. "I am Anna."

"And I am Marguerita," says the other one. "We are concerned about you."

"I'm fine," I tell them. I don't like feeling dependent on strangers.

Anna puts a glass of cloudy liquid in my hand. "Drink," she orders. "It is rehydration salts."

I obey. I realise how thirsty I am. When I have finished it, Marguerita hands me a piece of bread.

"Eat," she commands. I nibble it nervously. I feel quite hungry. I notice my rucksack in the corner. This is my room.

"Where are you going to go from here?" asks Anna.

"I was going to go to Pakse," I falter. These girls scare me, and I don't want to say the wrong thing.

"Us, too." Marguerita is triumphant. "Then we will go tomorrow."

Pakse is hot and dusty, and I spend most of my time sitting in the hotel foyer, sipping rehydration drinks, while the Dutch girls explore the city. I have been thoroughly educated in the importance of keeping up a good fluid intake when one has diarrhoea. I won't dare to make that mistake again. At least Anna and Marguerita have scared my tummy back into a healthy state.

I am in such a quiet, semiconscious state of convalescence that I am only minimally surprised one afternoon when Mike strolls in, nods to me as if our meeting were entirely ordinary, and greets me with the words, "Hello there, mate. You looked fucked."

The four of us catch a boat down the Mekong for a couple of hours, and end up in a tiny town called Champasak. This seems like a worthy place to linger, and so we settle in for a holiday.

The one place in Asia that has offered everything I hoped for has been the shower. My ideal shower consists of cold water and a little plastic bucket. This one is perfect. Floor and walls are tiled with cracked white. A beam of sunlight comes through the tiny window. I stand, naked but for my jewellery, in the middle of the floor, take a bucket of water and chuck it all over myself. I feel like a woman in an Ingres painting. Like somebody's concubine. Rivers of dirt come off my body and hair. I scrape away at the stubborn bits, making sure I wash off all the sweat. I shave my armpits and legs, for there are concessions I will not make to the travelling lifestyle. Backpackers are hairy; I am not. The water I throw on myself runs across the floor to the outside world. In a strange way it is erotic.

My body is looking good, thanks to trekking and the now-vanquished diarrhoea. I can feel my leg muscles. My hair has grown longer and tanglier. I like my chinking cheap bracelets. I gave in to the sales patter and bought them from some beautiful tribal girls in Sapa. I try to convince myself that I'm not going soft. It's not as if they were begging. I was supporting local industry. I like everything. I like the change that Tom is going to see in me. I think of cuddling into his bulk, feeling his hands on my newly emerged ribs. Waking up under a mosquito net, next to him. I'll talk to him about Mum, because he knows me better than anyone does, and he knew her. He will help me exorcise her unexpected ghost.

She's with me, the opposite of an imaginary friend. It was bad enough having Tom in that role, let alone Mother. By the time she was my age, she'd had two children and was already on her downward spiral. I often wonder how a beautiful young woman from a rich, if nasty, family could transform herself, as soon as she hit adulthood, into an unrepentant alcoholic. An alcoholic so horrible that she spends twenty years drinking without coming close to admitting it. That's the kind of thing that happens to other people. Most alcoholics admit they've got a problem, sooner or later, and at least pretend they're going to get help. She never even got that far.

How could that woman, of all the people in the world, be my mother? There's not much comfort in the truism that she deceived herself more than anyone else. So what? I suffered more than she did, because she just sat drinking all day long without a care in the world, and I was the one with the job, and the life. I was the one making her eat something approximating real food, and trying to stop her drinking. I coped with her tantrums. I looked after someone who normally acted as though she hated me but occasionally veered into tearful sentimentality. But she deceived herself! So that's all right. Sometimes, I wonder whether I could have ended up like her if I hadn't come travelling. Perhaps I still could. As soon as I articulate the thought, I realise it has been at the back of my mind for weeks. Probably for months; in fact, for years. My main comfort through all those years was drink. Hers was too. I used drugs and alcohol to oil my social life, to smooth my relationships, to boost my confidence and to relax me. I wonder what her reasons were when she was my age. Since I've been travelling, I've been drinking all the time, owing to the absence of drugs. I've got quite fond of alcohol. I could get quite a nice little dependency going.

Perhaps I won't have any beer today, to demonstrate my self-control. Maybe I'll give it up for a while. If I can manage not to be an alcoholic, that means I can keep drinking for the rest of my life. Otherwise, sooner or later, I'd have to stop drinking completely, forever. I don't want that to happen. I like alcohol. I couldn't socialise without it.

Perhaps I should be able to socialise without it. Going out without drinking is the sort of thing I always dismissed as being something boring people do. I can't imagine doing it myself, not while I'm living this kind of life. Here I am in southern Laos, a phenomenally remote place, with three lovely people, and I still rely on alcohol. We drink beer all the time. Then again, I can't imagine abstaining under any kind of circumstances, particularly not back at home.

Suddenly, I am consumed with anxiety. I don't want to be an alcoholic! I feel as though someone's punched me in the stomach. I am looking it in the face. I can't do that. I can't become that. I'd better stop drinking. Soon, I'll stop drinking. Not just now; for now I'll enjoy it. But, in the near future, I'll give it up for a bit. I will detoxify. I will allow my liver to repair itself. I realise that I'm not very impressive. Deciding to stop drinking one day is as good as I can get, for now. It's not as if alcohol is my primary drug, even. But I've already been forced off coke. I need something to keep me going.

In my crisp, clean clothes I am ready for a long, languid lunch, and an afternoon's reading and strolling. I feel unsettled now, and I want everything to be easy. I feel fragrant, which is one good thing. The laundry here is one of the orient's inscrutable mysteries. I was astonished the first time I got my washing back. It was cleaner, crisper, and more lovely than it ever was at home, and yet they do their washing down at the river, with no apparent use of soap. They hit the clothes with rocks, and the rivers are filthy. They obviously have a different kind of science. I'm glad I ditched my London clothes. I know I look good in loose cotton. Some people, like Carrie, can't carry it off; whereas others, like me, can. Particularly now I have pronounced bones. Clothes hang better on me, now. I could almost take up modelling. Wearing the clothes doesn't make me a backpacker. Of course it doesn't.

As I step into my flip-flops, I listen vaguely to Mike's conversation with Mr. Somphavan, the genial owner of this little guesthouse, outside the door.

"In Australia," Mike is saying, "when you say 'football' it means Aussie Rules, OK? And when you say 'soccer,' that means soccer, which is the thing that *you* call football."

"Aussie rules?" says Mr. S. "What is different with that?"

"You don't need to know," says a new, northern English voice. "Football is football. Don't let any Australian or American tell you different. Have you got a room we could stay in?"

I know the voice. I open the door, my arms full of washing stuff, and step, fragrant, clean and damp-haired, into the communal room. Two men are standing with Mike and Mr. S. One is chunky and clean-shaven, with the straightforward confidence of an American. The other is a tall, thin man whose distinguishing features are his hair and bushy beard. He looks strange, perhaps Latvian. But he's not.

"Oh my God!" I exclaim, and put my things down on the table and rush over to him. I am about to hug him when, to my horror, I see him looking at me with bafflement. I pull up short. He still looks like a freaky Jesus, and if anything he's more hairy even than before.

"Don't knock it, man," says the American.

"You all right, Di?" smirks Mike at the same time. I can't think of a way to adapt my lunge at Max into a casual swatting of a huge fly, or a little dance, so I have to explain myself.

"We met in Saigon," I mutter, looking at my feet. I must paint my nails again. "You were nice to me in the nightclub."

He puts down his bag. "Are you Tansy? Bloody fuck, I didn't recognise you!" And he gives me a bony hug, during which our protruding bones crunch together. Cuddling's easier when at least one of you is fat, so I should still be OK with Tom.

He holds me at arm's length. "Christ!" he says. "You look so different." He turns to Mike. "Why did you call her Di?"

Mike shrugs. I catch him looking at me, laughing.

Max and his friend, Greg, are swiftly absorbed into our group. Greg is good-looking and blatantly, almost desperately, on the pull. As for Max, despite his strange appearance, he's charming company, just as he was in Saigon. In fact, he's his nicest at everyone. Things are looking up for the Dutch girls and me, and the Swedish girls from the other guesthouse are suddenly hanging around, wherever we go. I'd like it if Ally and Andy were here, but I'm sure I'll see them again, and I'm happy.

I wait as long as I can before tackling Max on how, exactly, I look so different. I don't want to seem self-obsessed by demanding details immediately. I smile to myself, because I know that the chief difference between me now and me when I met Max is weight. Fat. I am fat-free, and it won't last, so I want to hear him say it.

"So," I say, over my lunchtime papaya salad, "um, why do I look different from before?" I look at my forkful of papaya as though it is extremely interesting. I notice Greg checking out a passing Swede, who is clad in a tiny cotton dress that almost reveals her nipples. "Is it just that we only met once?" I add casually, giving Max a Diana look through my lashes.

"No. I remember you very well. You've just changed," he says, looking me over. He takes my chin in his hand, and moves it from side to side, studying me. It makes me laugh. "Your hair was all

gelled into place. Last time you were chic and elegant. You reminded me of Cindy Crawford, hence me being so anxious to buy
you a beer, but now you're just scruffy and normal like the rest of
us. And you're really skinny."

I have a vivid picture of Tom going home after his Thai break.
"How was Tansy?" asks everyone. "Oh, just scruffy and normal
like all the rest." This is not what I had in mind. Not at all. I suppose it serves me right for asking.

"But you look lovely," Max continues hastily and unconvinc-
ingly. "The biggest difference of all is that back then you were the
most miserable and homesick person in the world, and now you
look happy. And you still look pretty. Sorry, I should have said
that first. I'm not very good at this, am I?"

It's too late. I have become a backpacker, without even noticing. It's like putting on weight; it happens when you're not looking, and then you're stuck with it for months, or years, or forever.
I thought I was still chic, but I'm no different from Carrie or anyone else. I have lost my style, and I didn't even notice.

For a week, we relax in Champasak. It's a tiny place, and everything
in it is green. The trees have huge, tropical leaves. The air is still, and
smells of plants. I love it here. It's peaceful and laid back and quiet.
The guesthouse is on a sandy lane, opposite the river. We hire bikes
and drift around aimlessly. We eat and drink and play cards. We go
to the Wat, which is largely ruined but spectacularly atmospheric.
They used to make human sacrifices there. For the first time I can
remember, there's no one I'd like to sacrifice. No one is annoying
me. It feels weird. I know my life won't stay like this, but I know I
will always remember Champasak. I seem to spend most of my
time with Max. I can talk to him without really thinking about it,
like I can with Kate. We talk immense amounts of nonsense. One
afternoon we walk to the shops for soap and shampoo. On the way,
we pass a mossy old tree by the river.

"Did you know," says Max, "that you can tell which direction you're facing by which side of the tree the moss grows on? It always grows on the west side."

I look at the tree. "The river runs from north to south," I object, "so that moss is not on the west."

"Maybe it grows on the south, then." He studies the tree. "Or the east. I promise you, there is a kernel of truth in what I say."

"I believe you."

"And did you also know that moss contains a natural disinfectant? They used it on wounds in the First World War."

"Well, I'll tell you something else about moss. It has a supermodel named after it."

"Kate Moss. Do you know where moss goes to pray?"

"Nope."

"The mossque."

"Which part of the newspaper does it read first?"

He shrugs. "Don't know."

"The mossip column."

"Ahh yes, the mossip column. But what happens when a tree goes bankrupt?"

"Umm . . ."

"They call in the moss adjusters."

"What's that tree's favourite book?" I counter.

"Er . . . *Moss of the D'Urbervilles*?"

"I was actually thinking of *The Silence of the Moss*."

"Mine's a better pun."

"Well, mine's scarier."

We smile at each other, and get on with the shopping.

Before I came here, I hadn't ridden a bike for about ten years, unless you count exercise bikes, and I gather you don't. Anna and Marguerita were amazed to hear this. "In Holland it is very normal for everyone to travel by bicycle," Anna explained, "because it is an excellent form of transport, as it is cheap, healthy, and good for the environment."

"In London," I told her, "it's normal for everyone to travel by Tube, because it's inconvenient, unreliable, and it makes you aggressive before you even get to work. You don't cycle in London. You just don't."

The last time I rode a real bike was when I was sixteen. I started riding to school when I realised how good it was for toning the thighs. Unfortunately, Hampstead is hilly, so while going to school was a windy exhilarating rush, I usually walked home dragging it behind me (good for the arm muscles). The regime ended when I was stopped by the police after they noticed me zigzagging home from Lisa's house. Her parents were away and had hidden the key to the drinks cabinet under a flowerpot, the first place we looked. (I never invited my friends round to drink. It didn't seem so naughty.)

When the police car pulled me over, I had a flash of sobriety and recognised that I was unlikely to outcycle a police car. I braked reluctantly, and a woman got out.

"Over here, please," she said sharply.

"Why?" I demanded.

"Over here!" she repeated.

They made me lock my bike to a parking meter and ride home in the police car. Apart from last year's ambulance, it has been my sole experience of an emergency services vehicle, and it was similarly disappointing.

"Can you put the siren on, please?" I asked, but they didn't answer. They didn't even look at me, just at each other.

I knew they were expecting my mother to be a respectable posh woman who would be shocked and stern, and mortified at my behaviour. When I reluctantly led them into the sitting room, they looked as though they wanted to arrest her as well. She staggered up from her chair and offered the bloke her hand, palm down, plainly hoping he'd kiss it. I was dying inside.

"Morning, ossifer," she smiled. It was night. She was wearing her threadbare towelling dressing gown, exactly the way she'd been dressed when I left for school that morning. I tried to position myself in front of the whisky bottle on the floor, which had an inch left in it. Mum never had full bottles. By the time she let me see them, they were almost empty, so she could declare that she "might as well finish it now." Some days she got dressed all smartly and pretended to be sober. Some days she didn't bother. On the worst days, she didn't get dressed at all but still let herself believe she was an upstanding pillar of the community. Unfortunately, this was one of those days.

While the police were talking to her, I managed to move the bottle out of sight with my foot but I'm sure they clocked it.

"Good evening, madam," said the bloke, looking confused but reciting his lines anyway. "We've brought your daughter home to inform you that we stopped her for dangerous cycling without lights, and found her to be significantly over the legal alcohol limit."

"Did you, officer?"

"Yes we did, madam."

"Tansy, you shouldn't do that. I'm sorry, ossifer, she's at that age—what can you do?" She was trying to say the right things. Mum must have been thirty-seven then. She should still have been beautiful, and she thought she was. But her face was puffy, her eyes were desperate, and she was bloated. If ever anyone ended up with the face, and body, they deserved, it was my mother. The gap between reality and her perception of it was almost funny. She thought she was being seductive and conspiratorial with the policeman. She looked like a sad, uncontrollable old lady who thought she was a vamp.

On their way out, the policewoman took me aside.

"Do you need any help?" she asked, suddenly not treating me like a delinquent anymore. "I can arrange for a social worker to call."

I smiled a big, bright smile. "No thanks," I told her. "We're fine. She's not normally like this. Dad'll be home soon. She'll be fine."

"If you're sure. Give us a call if you ever need any help. And Tansy?"

"Yes?"

"There is absolutely no need for you to drink. If I see you drunk again I'm calling social services. Remember, many alcoholics are the children of alcoholics."

I smiled meekly, and they went. I hadn't lied exactly. I was sure Dad would, indeed, be home soon. He was probably home already. I never said where he lived.

I get to the little restaurant on the corner before anyone else, and I order a beer, put my feet up and open my book. This restaurant has become our favourite. The tables are outside, shaded from the sun by a straw roof, and the service is slow, which suits us fine. But I can't concentrate. I shouldn't be drinking. My internal voice is starting to nag.

Max wanders up, his joints springing. He sits opposite me, forcing me to move my feet. I put my book down and look at him.

"What's the tree's favourite TV detective programme?" he asks, by way of greeting.

I shrug.

"*Inspector Moss.*"

I laugh.

"Can I buy you a beer?" I offer. Alcohol is on my mind, and it feels like the natural thing to say.

"Yet more beer!" exclaims Max. "You're a shocking influence." I don't know what he's surprised about. It's the evening, after all, and we've exercised. "Don't you ever have a night off?" he continues. I glare, but he's not being nasty. He looks concerned. After a moment, he relents. "OK," he says. "Beer it is."

I shouldn't be drinking like this. One or two beers a night would be fine, but I'm pissed every night. This might be the perfect moment to give it up. I could attempt five clean weeks before

I meet Tom. I'd be a paragon after that, and I'd have earned some really excellent benders.

As we drink, we watch Greg, who is standing by the Swedes' table, chatting.

"Do you think he's finally going to make his move?" I wonder. "I think he'd be in there."

"You don't know Greg like I do. He's the fussiest bloke I've ever met. He's always looking out for someone special but no one ever meets his standards, and the ones who do will never talk to him."

"Do you think that's psychological? Maybe, subconsciously, he's too scared to get into a relationship. Does he ever shag anyone?"

"Why? Are you interested?"

"Yeah, right. Of course I'm not. I've got Tom. I'm just curious."

"Well, not since I've known him."

Greg gets up, flashes a last smile at the lithe Swedes, and comes over. We look at him expectantly.

"Not fiery enough for mc. Sadly bland."

I look at them. They are laughing together, wearing tiny handkerchief sarongs and bra-sized T-shirts. They are all limbs and hair.

"You are a hard man to please," I observe. "I fancy them myself, and I'm not even gay."

During dinner, I can't stop myself teasing Max. Anna, Marge, and I are campaigning to make him shave. We want to know what he looks like.

"I know who you remind me of!" I exclaim. "Cornelius! From *Planet of the Apes.*"

Greg agrees. "Are you the missing link?" he inquires.

"Shut it," orders Max. "I will not be shaving to satisfy anybody's curiosity. I'd rather be a monkey."

"But you must be hot," says Anna.

"No, I'm fine."

"Is it perhaps for you to hide behind?" presses Marge.

Max considers this. "Yes," he says finally. "It's partly for de-
fence. Often I don't really want to talk to people. I'd much rather
hang out on my own and have peace and quiet than put up with
some eighteen-year-old asking what A levels I did. You'd be
amazed at what a wide berth you get if you've got facial hair." He
looks straight at me. "I'd rather be beardy than a pisshead," he
smiles. Everyone looks at me and laughs.

That settles it. I look at them all. Greg is laughing. Mike is
laughing. Even Anna and Marguerita have forgotten about female
solidarity and are chuckling at my expense. This is it. I'm not
drinking. If they're laughing at my drinking, it means I stand out.
I never stood out as a heavy drinker in London because we all
drank as much as each other. Here, people are more moderate. It
is time for me to stop. It's a small step from being singled out as
a heavy drinker to drinking in secret, and that, I know, would be
the beginning of the end.

Someone changes the subject. They are discussing how often
their bags are searched at customs—Max, not surprisingly, comes
top of the poll. I think hard. I vow to myself that I will not touch
a drop of alcohol until I arrive in Bangkok, just to demonstrate to
myself that I am not turning into my mother.

"Tansy, are you OK?" asks Marge.

"Fine."

I'll tell them in the morning. I'd better stay up drinking as late
as I can tonight, and drink as much as I can, by way of a final
fling.

By half past midnight, Max and I are the only ones left, and
we are knocking it back in the communal room.

"I can barely keep up with you," Max observes, more than
once.

"It's great, isn't it? A renowned pisshead. Classy. It's all changing tomorrow."

It's a big room with a huge table. The door to the outside world remains open all night. A KLM blanket tacked up with nails cordons off the room I share with Anna and Marge. There's a huge fridge in the corner, stocked with beer and soft drinks, with a book on the top for you to write down what you've had. I can't believe everyone doesn't go travelling. Parkinson's Law states that work expands to fit the time available; Tansy's Law adds that leisure does, too.

Everyone hates backpackers because of their image, but some of us are all right. I correct myself. Some of *them*. Everyone hates journalists as well, but some of my best friends are journalists and I know they're good people. I'm a sometime journalist myself, and to the untrained observer I could also be mistaken for a backpacker. At least I'm not German.

As of tomorrow, my only drinking problem will be that I'm not going to do it. I hope I can manage. It'll be a test. I'll find out whether I'm physically dependent. When I stop and think about it, it terrifies me. Fuck knows if I'll manage. I've never had a period of sobriety in my adult life, and if this one doesn't work, I'll have to modify my travel plans and take in a Muslim country. Pakistan will be my drying-out clinic.

We're playing a stupid card game called stop the bus. It requires no skill at all, so I don't understand why Max keeps winning.

"Is your name Maximillian?" I ask. "Or is it Maxwell? It should be Jesus."

"I've always thought I'm more like one of the disciples," he says, slapping a five on the pile. "Not the main man himself, you know. Able to have outside interests. Still, I suppose Jesus beats Cornelius." He smiles at me. "Actually, I didn't want to admit this before, but I have been thinking about a change. It's hot in here."

"You mean going clean-shaven?"

"Yep. And the answer's neither. Just Max. Or, as I'm known amongst the tree community, Moss."

*   *   *

I cut his hair in the garden, by the light of a nearly full moon and a billion tiny stars. The night air is warm, and it smells of plants. I've never cut hair before, so I don't know why he's letting me do it. I try to concentrate but am amused by the huge chunks that keep falling away. They make me laugh.

As I stand behind him, scissors poised, I catch myself feeling something unusual. As soon as I notice it, it swamps me. I am astonished. My stomach does somersaults. How can this have happened? Am I pissed?

Max is sexy. I never noticed before.

"Going anywhere nice on your holidays this year?" I ask in a hairdresser voice. I must try to keep things light, keep this alarming revelation to myself. It's only the beer, I tell myself. I probably won't fancy him in the morning.

He thinks about it. "I suppose my holiday this year will be settling down. Staying in one place for a year or two. In that sense, I suppose it'll be a holiday from travelling."

"In India?"

"Yes. Pondicherry. Great name, fantastic place."

"That's really cool. When are you going? Can I come and visit?" Pondicherry. I don't think I could actually live in Asia, and I know I couldn't teach, but I admire anyone who can. Living in India, with all the poverty and begging, not to mention the murders, would take a stronger woman than I will ever be.

Max looks up and back at me. I almost cut off his eyebrow. "Tansy, I'd love it if you came to visit. Promise you really will. People always say that kind of thing but then they hardly ever follow it through."

"Hey, I'm going to. I'm going to India, aren't I? Of course I'm coming to see my friend in Pondicherry. As long as I don't get bumped off on the way. When do you get there?"

"Oh, I get there when I get there. By about September, I think."

"Are you ever going to go home, do you think?"

He is quiet. I am overcome with my new appreciation of this man. Even his beard doesn't put me off. His body is fabulous. I touch the nape of his neck, and it makes me shiver. He looks confused. I pretend to be brushing away some hair.

"I expect so, one day. I don't know. I can't really imagine settling back down in the Peak District, though."

"Are you from the Peak District? That's amazing—I went there on a geography field trip!" Another chunk falls to the ground. At the moment it is short at the front and long at the back, in a Michael Bolton cut. He has a mullet, and yet I can't keep my hands off him.

"That *is* amazing," he says, looking at the hair on the ground. "So did everyone else. Yes, my parents live in Bakewell, home of the Bakewell tart. Yum. In fact, I think I snogged her once."

"You snogged her?" I've never thought of Max snogging anyone before, I wonder why I never noticed his appeal. I must have been blinded by his excess hair. I am criminally shallow. It's not just his lithe body and his piercing eyes. Who, I ask myself, was kind to me on my first night in Asia, when I needed it most? Who has been my best friend and companion for the past week? Who would I most like to kiss in the entire world?

"So why did you leave Bakewell?" I try to keep my voice light but I feel his shoulders tense as he senses a change in mood. "Did the tart break your heart?"

"No, it wasn't the tart. Nor even the nice girl I went out with for years and years."

"What was it, then?"

"Something happened that made me want to see the world."

"What?"

For the first time, he seems a little bit cross with me.

"I don't want to be the topic of everyone's gossiping," he says abruptly.

"Well, you're not going to be. Do you really think I'd tell

everyone anything you told me? Fuck it, I've got enough hassles of my own at home. I'm not going to tell everyone your secrets. They can't be that fascinating anyway."

"You're probably right."

"So?"

"So?"

"You might as well tell me then."

"What if I don't want to?"

"Oh, but you do want to. I can tell."

"I'll tell you mine if you tell me yours."

"Maybe." I don't think so. I don't normally tell people about my home life until after I've seduced them. I can't see it helping much beforehand.

"OK, it's a deal. We'll keep each other's secrets. I trust you. So, you have to picture me. Just a normal bloke. You wouldn't have given me the time of day."

"I would!"

"You might have if I'd stopped you and asked you what it was, but you wouldn't have sought me out. If you'd needed the time of day, you'd have asked someone more intriguing."

"Did you have a beard?"

"No, I didn't. I was a very clean-cut young gentleman. The kind of boy people's mums like. You would have found me horrifyingly dull and unstylish, but your mother would have loved me. She would have welcomed me into her beautiful London home with open arms and a warm French laugh."

"I wouldn't be so sure about that."

"And I went to university, to Sheffield, so I was still close to home. I went out with a girl from my course, then I got a job as a trainee solicitor, at the firm I'd most wanted to work for. Things were smooth, you know? No hassles. Not great, certainly not bad, just fine. Normal. I started getting these headaches, and I always thought it was because I was hungover, or because it was sunny, or I had a cold, or whatever. Then, you know how things can change sometimes? You wake up one morning, and outwardly everything is exactly the way it has always been but you know something you didn't know before."

"I do know that." Like with me, and drinking.

"I remember the day it happened. I opened my eyes in the morning and I knew that there was something seriously wrong with me."

"And was there?" Of course there was. Otherwise he wouldn't be telling me.

"It was a tumour. Before I knew it, I was going into hospital for brain surgery."

"Fuck." I put the scissors down and sit on the ground. He gets off the stool and sits next to me. We lean against the wall of the building.

"And?" I ask.

"Well, that was it, really. It was benign. I'm fine. I go for scans from time to time just to be sure it hasn't come back, but that's not difficult. You can always find a posh hospital. I didn't know it was benign until after they'd operated."

"Fuck, that must have been . . . I mean for you and your family it must have been dreadful."

"It wasn't great." He pauses. "But then, when we found out, then it was great. I can tell you, there are not many more welcome pieces of news than the discovery that, in fact, you happen not to have brain cancer after all."

"And that made you want to travel."

"It made me realise how fragile we are, even though, as a young man, you tend to feel invincible. It was a huge jolt. If it had been malign, I'd have been deeply in the shit. It was like I suddenly had another chance. I'd been fully briefed up about chemo and radio-therapy, and all of a sudden I didn't have to have them. There was just no way I could carry on training as a solicitor after that. I wanted to see the world, and here I am." He looks around. "In the world. My mum wasn't too pleased with my plans, though."

"I bet."

"She knows she can't stop me. I just have to remember to keep in touch all the time. They got a computer, and email, specially for my missives." He looks at me closely. Our shoulders and arms are touching. All the little hairs are standing up. I casually move my leg so it's resting against his. I always forget that everyone else has a story too. Although the middle-class eighteen-year-olds are usually travelling because it's their "gap year," almost everyone of our age has a more complicated reason. Now I know Max's. I hate the thought of him in hospital. I want to protect him from an operation he's already had.

"Now it's your turn," he says.

I laugh, and take a glug of beer. "You don't want to know." I try to sound authoritative.

"We made a deal. What's your story?"

"You know it already."

"No I don't. There's got to be more to it than being disillusioned with London and let down by a bastard. I remember you in Ho Chi Minh. You were on the edge."

"Don't call Tom a bastard," I protest, half-heartedly, trying to keep him off the subject.

"*You* do."

"I do not. Anyway, I'm allowed to."

"So?"

"So nothing." Max's hair looks disastrous. "Trust me," I add. "You really don't want to know about me. You might also prefer not to look in a mirror ever again."

I look up at the stars. It is so clear, it's almost like daylight. Max puts an arm round my shoulders, and I lean on him. I am tingling. I know, now, what is going to happen, and I want to savour every moment of it. I don't want to talk about stupid old Mum.

"You have to tell me. It's not fair, otherwise. I only told you about me because I was curious about you. You're not allowed to trick me."

Then again, there's no point carrying my miserable life around with me as a secret, forever. I have always been ashamed of her; there's no need for that, not anymore. He's never going to meet her. Not many things in life are certain, but that one is.

"Do you really think I drink too much?" I ask. It's the first time I've spoken the fear aloud.

"You certainly knock them back. We all do. Why?"

"Do you really want to know?" He nods. I look away. His hair is too awful. I can't believe he let me do that to him. I lean further in towards him. Surprisingly, he is not spiky at all. He's soft.

In the warm night air, I try to think of a place to begin.

"My family is truly fucked up," I tell him. "Well, my mother is. She's not anymore."

Encouraged by the sound of my voice, I carry on. I tell him about my mother, and about my childhood, and about my brother, and, for the first time, it seemed to make sense.

"You're not proud of yourself," he says into my hair when I've finished outlining my life story. It isn't a question. It is a statement.

"No, I'm not." I am desperately holding one fact back from him. Even though I am pissed, I keep it to myself. Thank fuck.

"You, more than anybody I have ever met, and that is not an exaggeration, should be proud of yourself."

"That's sweet of you, but—"

"But nothing. Shut up. I haven't finished. You are funny, you're intelligent, you're brave. You don't let things overwhelm you when most people would be alcoholics themselves after what you've been through. You just picked yourself up, dusted yourself down, got to know your long-lost sibling, and got on with life. And," he leans in towards me, "you're gorgeous. You're beautiful, and you're sexy, and ever since the very first moment I saw you in Saigon, I've been desperate to do this to you."

He bends his head down to mine, and I turn mine up to meet his. His lips are soft, and I don't mind his beard at all. It is silky, and not at all bristly. In fact, I've been so wrong about it that I laugh. He pulls away, and looks at me.

"What?"

"Nothing. It's just your beard. I thought it would scratch me and be all painful, but it isn't at all."

"Does that mean I can keep it?"

" 'Fraid not."

"OK."

We stayed together, exploring each other, exciting each other, and talking to each other. Hours later, when we pull apart and go to our separate beds, exhausted, I lie still, listening to Anna and Marge breathing. My heart thumps, and I am exhilarated.

Max! I tell myself, amazed and still tingling. Max. Of all the people I've met travelling, I would never have expected it to be Max. I would be only half surprised to wake up, my head thumping, and to remember that I'd got off with Mike, or Greg. But hairy old Max has never featured in my speculation.

CHAPTER
10

From: Amanda
To: Tansy
Subject: Hello, Tans

Thanks for your message. This is just to let you know that I'm definitely going—I don't know when you'll get this, depending on how remote you are, but I might have left by the time you're reading it. I am, of course, nervous, but glad to get away. We fly on the 14th, Valentine's Day. Not the ideal Valentine's gift for my husband, I must admit.

I'll stay in touch whenever I can, and look forward v v much to seeing you and comparing notes. I can't tell you how much it comforts me to know I've got a friend out there.

Best love, Amanda x

From: Tansy
To: Amanda
Subject: Good luck!

that's wonderful news—have a fantastic time and let me know how you're getting on. am thoroughly enjoying myself in Laos. I am, unexpectedly, in the throes of a holiday romance, the joy of it is the lack of pressure—no question of it leading anywhere. however, valentine's day came and went without my noticing it. so you're in India. good luck.

x

From: Tansy
To: Kate
Subject: Surprise news

hiya, you'll never guess what? I'm having a fling. yes, me, the girl who waits forever for tom. somehow it crept up on me, and somehow I'm having a wonderful time. the guy in question, max, is someone I first met, briefly, in vietnam. then we ran into each other in champasak, a gorgeous little place in laos. he had big hair and a beard, but, under my influence, he got rid of it all. he's thin as well. It's quite bizarre, after tom's ample cushioning, to be able to feel someone's bones beneath their skin. I've always thought I couldn't fancy skinny men, on the grounds that they'd make me feel fat, but max has a fantastic body. All muscular. since I am, thankfully, bony as well for the time being, I don't feel blobby. as my current figure will not last, it could become a problem were we having a long-term relationship, but we're not. tom is the long term, and next to him I will always be slender.

the other good thing is, he's a completely lovely human being, and for some reason he seems to like me, too. obviously, then, this has no future. this fact in itself makes me relax with him. and plans to see tom in thailand are still v much in place.

must dash, as I'm in vientiane, the capital of laos, and the Internet connection is both pricey and slow. laos is wonderful, by the way. At last am genuinely having fun and not just pretending. hope all is cool there.

lots of love, t xxx

CHAPTER
11

My pace has changed. Everything has shifted. I feel as if I've become someone else. When I travel with Max, I have to do things differently. If we want to go somewhere, we go there. We don't plan a route and then stick to it. If the bus doesn't turn up, Max tries to stop me getting angry with it. He says it doesn't matter.

"This is completely different," I tell him as we stumble off a bus in Vang Vieng.

"What do you mean?" We look around, trying to get our bearings. A surprising number of backpackers were on the bus with us.

"I mean in Vietnam I was always hurrying to the next place, and then I dashed out of the country as quickly as I could so I wouldn't be a new person anymore, and so I wouldn't still be on my first country."

"I think you rushed it so you could get home sooner."

"Probably."

"If that's what you wanted to do . . ."

"I know. I should have got a plane."

We locate Greg and Mike in the crowd, and start walking. Everyone else is walking too, and the group pace progressively speeds up as we try to beat each other to the nearest hotel and get their best rooms. Our group has dwindled now, as Anna and

Marge have gone to Thailand. I've promised to visit them in Holland. I really will do it. The road is stony, and a few tuk-tuks judder by. We pass a café. It's open to the sunshine, and it's full of westerners.

"Christ!" I exclaim. "What is this? Is there some backpacking convention going on or something?" Vang Vieng is a small town near some mountains. I wouldn't have expected it to be particularly different from any other small town. We chose to come here because it said it was nice in the Lonely Planet.

"I think it's been discovered," says Greg.

Ever since I gave up drinking and started having a holiday romance, I have felt I'm living someone else's life. Sometimes I am moody about not being able to drink, particularly when we are in towns with wine shops. The French did leave some good relics behind, and I can't sample them. Other times I don't mind because I like to prove my willpower. I am not my mother. I will never be my mother. It's the best discovery I've ever made. Besides, my withdrawal from drinking is tempered by a rediscovery of sex. I am loving every moment of my fling with Max.

We get the last double room at the hotel. It's a big, new place. The woman who owns it tells us that there are now nineteen hotels in the town. "Too many," she smiles, but she doesn't seem to mind.

"You have many backpackers?" asks Mike.

"Many tourists," she confirms. A woman after my own heart. She proudly shows us a travellers' message board she installed at Christmas. We read the advice posted there by visitors. I try to appreciate their comedy but just end up alarmed. "Go to Tadlo," one instructs, "but don't fork out for a room as this is a real rip-off. Instead take your tent and camp in the garden." Someone else has written on the bottom, in pencil: "In fact there is no need to do this either as we met a local man, Tommy, and he took us to stay with his family. He lives by the river, in the second house on the right from where the boat lands. Knock on the door and he is glad to take you in at no cost." Appended is an unsurprising update: "We followed this suggestion but found Tommy not to be friendly at all."

"I don't get this place," I tell Max.

"Two words. Lonely Planet."

Mum has stopped intruding. She only comes into my head, now, when she's invited. It happened without me noticing. I realised, the other day, that she simply isn't there anymore. I only think about her when I need the impetus to stay sober. She isn't haunting me. When my thoughts do turn to her, I am forced to reassess our situation. I've always worked on the conviction that I had it worse than she did, but now I realise that I didn't, after all. Even when I was looking after her, at least I had a life. I had a job, and friends. Things could have been worse. It would have been worse to have been the one who'd given up on life, who was seeing life through the bottom of a bottle. The one who was waiting to die. My future is looking all right all of a sudden. I will travel with Max for a while, and then, when the time comes, we will go our separate ways. He will fly to Madras and make his way to Pondicherry to become a teacher, and I will go back to Tom. Max and I couldn't stay together even if we wanted to because we are ending up in different places.

We go to a café, late in the afternoon, and decide that, tomorrow, we'll hire bikes again and go to swim at the nearest waterhole. I've never been this active in my life, but I keep quiet about that because I am quite obviously alone in this. The thoughtless bastards are all drinking beer. Just because we're sitting by the river, watching local people wading and driving through the shallow water. Just because they're silhouetted against the mountains, and the sun is a huge ball of fire that disappears as you look at it. Just because the beer is cold and cheap. Maybe they're the ones with drinking problems.

"We'll get an early start, to avoid the heat," decides Greg. "There's no need to take much, is there? Just a daypack."

I seize on a focus for my frustration. If only I could consume some kind of drug, I'd be mellow. I can't stand having to be myself. It makes me petty.

"A what?" I ask him.

"A daypack."

"What if I haven't got a daypack?" I look jealously at his beer. One wouldn't do me any harm.

Mike and Max exchange amused glances.

"Yeah, but you have," says Greg. "You know. Your daypack. It's there, under the table. Your bag."

"Precisely!" This is part of my struggle to avoid becoming a backpacker. "It's a bag. Why does it have to have a new name? Why does it have to have a special backpacking name? Why don't backpackers have bags? They always have bloody daypacks and backpacks and sleeping sacks. I've used this same bag, this bag that has now apparently become a daypack, at home and no one would have called it anything but a bag there. It's from bloody Selfridges!"

Max and Mike are laughing at me now.

"Are you being a British eccentric?" asks Greg laconically. "Daypack is just a word. It has no deep significance."

"Yes it *does*. It's part of this wanky scene that is going on all around us." It's true: this bar is full of backpackers, each trying to look cooler, and to have more fun, than the next. They look very young. I'd say that we are all in the upper twenty percent of the age bracket, and none of us is even thirty.

"I know what you mean," says Max, remembering, at last, to support me. "It's a signifier of something. Every little world has its own language, and I suppose this one is no different."

"I mean, if it's my daypack, where's my nightpack? Does it go with my backpack? Should I have a frontpack? And while we're on that subject, the people who wear their so-called daypacks as frontpacks should be deported at once. No questions asked. Never allowed back."

"Sometimes it's just easier to do that?" Mike suggests.

"Well, you shouldn't. You need to sacrifice comfort from time to time in order to achieve some small residue of a semblance of style. It's not that much to ask."

"You are one angry lady," says Greg.

"Woman!" I snap, and smile.

Mike is pouring a large beer into two glasses. I eye them enviously. Greg takes his, and sips it.

"Ahhhh!" He turns to Max. "Does she have PMS or something?"

I have to distract myself or I'll down Max's beer before I even remember I'm not allowed to. "No I fucking don't. I'll have you know, this is the way I naturally am, whatever the time of month."

"Face it, lady, you're a backpacker." Greg has drunk half his beer now. "You've got a backpack, and you've got a daypack. We all have. It's the most striking thing about us."

"Us and all the other fuckers." And I call the waiter over, pause for a tense moment, and order a Coke. If only I could lay my hands on some real coke, then I'd be all right. But that, I know, is not the point.

We walk back to the hotel along a road which is lit by a few gas lamps outside shacks. Millions of insects buzz furiously in their beams. I am enjoying a phenomenon that manifests itself when everyone else is pissed. My head begins to spin. I become louder and lose inhibitions. I wouldn't trust myself to drive. I take on pissed characteristics, without even drinking a drop. And yet there is no chance of alcoholism. I wish I could have something, though. This is not the same. Not the same at all.

My yearning reverie is interrupted by a hoarse whisper from a man at the roadside.

"Opium?" he rasps. I stop.

"Did he say what I thought he said?" I ask Max.

He nods, amused at my wide-eyed excitement.

"He said opium?"

Greg stops too. "So let's do it!"

We all look at each other.

"Anyone tried it before?" asks Mike.

"Yep, I have." Max, the eternal traveller. "It's nice. Not earth-shattering, just pleasant. Tans, have I found the one drug you haven't sampled?"

"Is it the same as heroin?"

"No. It has to get refined and mixed with other stuff."

"In that case, you have pinpointed a gap in my education."

"Better rectify that one." Greg is happy. We troop into the hut. "So have you really tried heroin?"

"Not exactly. But I know people who have."

Mike waves his hand. "That's good enough."

The house is smoky and dimly lit, as seedy as an opium den should be. A woman with a dopey baby tucked under one arm ushers us into a back room with half its wall missing. The walls and the floor are wooden. A bulging moon shines right in. The man—her husband, the baby's father, presumably—is lying on his side, propped up on an elbow. He gazes at us, briefly, before attending to the task in hand.

We sit cross-legged, aware that our arrival changes the atmosphere.

All the clients are western. All of them are vaguely familiar from cafés and the waterhole. All look spaced out. Among them are three women we saw in the restaurant. Greg tries his luck with a beautiful woman in pink. I used to wish I was black, because colours look so wonderful next to dark skin, but even I realised, eventually, how flippant that was. I always envied Kate. She seemed to have the best of both worlds. Greg says something to the woman that I don't catch. She replies. Greg edges over to me.

"Tans, I need your help," he says urgently. "I need you to

translate. She's speaking French, and I don't know what she's saying."

"OK." I have almost forgotten that my French is GCSE standard, that I am not, in fact, bilingual. I shuffle over to the woman.

"*Bonjour*," I tell her. I have to take a chance that Greg doesn't understand at all. "*Il pense que je suis demi-française, parce que je lui ai dit ça, mais je ne suis pas, comme tu peux voir.*"

She nods, smiling. "*Evidement.*"

"*Qu'est-ce que tu veux lui dire?*"

She looks at him. "*Laisse-moi tranquille. Il y a quelqu'un qui tue les jeune femmes. Je ne veux pas parler pas aux hommes, et, en plus, je trouve qu'il est repugnant.*"

I turn back to Greg. "Sorry. She doesn't speak to strange men. She says it's nothing personal."

"Fair enough." He smiles at her, in case she changes her mind.

"She shoots—she scores," comments Max, when I return.

"I amaze myself with my own diplomacy."

I lie parallel to the man, as I've seen the others do, and take the pipe. My heart is pounding. It's not as if I haven't taken drugs before but I have never taken them in this sort of atmosphere, and not for ages. It's been two months and two weeks since I left home, and nothing illegal has entered my system in all that time. It must be a record. And this is an opium den in Laos; I don't feel as if I have much of a safety net. If I overdose this time, I'll die. He prods opium into the end of the pipe, and I inhale gingerly. There is a tickle in my throat, and I know I'm going to cough, but suppress it as much as possible because no one else coughed.

I float back to my place on the floor. At last! I feel wonderful. I am interested in textures. Max was right: it's not too strong, just fuzzy. I snuggle up to him. The room smells of lavender. This is a world away from a cocaine high. It is more like a Valium downer. It is comfy, and delicious. I stare at the moon.

"Do you think they took away that wall so we could look at the big moon?" I ask the world at large.

No one replies.

The opium woman comes in to take her turn. She walks over to me and puts her baby on my lap. It sits placidly, while its mother inhales her drug. I wonder whether it gets entrusted to spaced westerners on a regular basis. Probably. This probably happens every night of its life. It has pierced ears, and it looks quite sedated. She probably breast feeds, with opium milk. There is a rushing sound. Simultaneously, I feel my skirt going warm, and sticking wetly to my legs.

"No way!" I hold the opium baby in the air. My suspicions are correct. Lao babies don't wear nappies. Its mother plucks it from my arms, and laughs.

We lounge in bed, feeling strange and dizzy, for the whole of the next morning. "It's different, travelling with a girlfriend," Max says, holding me tight and snuggling close. "Don't you find that? With a boyfriend, I mean."

"Am I your girlfriend, then?" I don't like the sound of this.

"I think so. Aren't you?"

"I'd rather be your lover, or something."

I sense him looking at me.

"Is this because of that other bloke? The one I'm not allowed to criticise?"

"You only can't criticise him because you don't know him."

"You haven't answered the question."

I roll over, away from him.

"It doesn't matter, does it?" I say, curling up defensively. "I just think that girlfriend and boyfriend means something more permanent, and I like the way we're lovers, on holiday, in Indochina. Girlfriends and boyfriends cook pasta and watch *EastEnders*. We smoke opium and ride buses. That's all the difference is."

We change the subject. He won't call me his girlfriend again.

An awkward silence fills the room. Max rolls over and opens the newspaper we picked up when someone left it in the opium den. I get up and go to the bathroom. What I said to Max doesn't matter. Tom is my boyfriend. I stretch. I like this opium hangover. It makes me feel very fuzzy.

"Come here and look at this," Max calls.

"What?" I'm admiring my breasts in the mirror. They seem to have become shapelier, more perky, after enjoying his attentions. I lift my hands and pile up my hair, which makes my breasts look better still.

"A girl got murdered. Another one."

"No."

"Yes. It says here she'd been seen drinking with a white man. Eastern European, they think. Might or might not be the same guy as before."

"Was she British?"

"Uh-huh. She looks a bit like you, actually. Shorter hair. And she had a plastic tulip on her body."

The last girl, a third, had been found in India a week earlier. Something had been left near her body, too—a small teddy bear.

"Great. That's absolutely brilliant. People go travelling for years and years and years, from the Grand Tour or whatever, and everyone prances back home saying how it broadens their fucking horizons, and then the minute I go away, some nutter starts stalking us. Stalking us and killing us."

"You're being a bit hasty," suggests Max. "You don't even know where it happened."

"Where?"

"Strangely close. In an alleyway in Singapore."

"Singapore!" I am incredulous.

Max takes my hand. "It's OK. You'll be fine. You're with me. You're not alone."

"But I'm going to Singapore! I've got a flight from there to Delhi. I'll be there in three months. In a few months it would have been me."

"It would not have been you."

"You don't know that it wouldn't."

"And you certainly don't know that it would."

"I just have a creepy feeling. It's so close to us I know. It's not logical. When people at home are scared on my behalf I tell them not to be so stupid. I don't know. I guess that I kind of like not travelling on my own at the moment." I look at him, and he looks at me, and we seem to understand each other. I feel almost hysterical.

"How about going by a different route, then?" he says casually. "If you wanted to go to Dharamsala, you'd want to go to Tibet. We can go to China, and from there to Tibet. Drop in on Gabe. We could go overland into Nepal and India from there. You could even come all the way to Pondicherry if you wanted."

"But I've got a ticket from Singapore to Delhi."

"You can change the ticket, get a partial refund, can't you?"

Max looks so cute when he's smug.

"China? Tibet? Why not?" I say.

I feel a warm glow all evening.

CHAPTER
12

From: Roger Harris
To: Tansy Harris
Subject: MURDER IN SINGAPORE

TANSY:

ARE YOU SURE IT IS WISE TO BE TRAVELLING IN THE LIGHT OF
RECENT DEVELOPMENTS? NOW THAT THE DANGER HAS COME
SO CLOSE TO YOU, WE THINK YOU SHOULD CONSIDER COMING
HOME. YOU HAVE HAD ENOUGH ADVENTURES, I AM SURE.

LET US KNOW YOUR MOVEMENTS. WILL COLLECT YOU FROM
AIRPORT IF YOU FURNISH FLIGHT NUMBER, TIMES AND
TERMINAL.

BEST FROM US ALL

DAD

—PS ALSO NEED TO KNOW WHICH AIRPORT.

From: Tom
To: Tansy
Subject: see you soon!

all right, there? haven't heard from you in a while but just letting you
know about my holiday. I'm almost packed and looking forward to
seeing the sunshine and yourself. will you be different? which island
have you chosen for us? can you wait to see me? it's creepy about
the girl in singapore, specially for you I guess, but we won't be going
there, and anyway I'll protect you.

flight is BA105, arriving BKK at 2200 on wednesday. we'll just take a
taxi, yeah? before then I've got way too much work to do and don't
really believe I'm coming out somewhere so frivolous. I think it's funny
that I haven't been to thailand before and neither had you. everyone
else has. toby told me to go to ko samui. it sounds quite cool. what do
you reckon?

I suppose you want to know the gossip—well, toby and kate seem to
be back on which is unexpected. you probably know more about that
than I do thanks to the marvels of modern technology. work has been
stressful but enjoyable. I'm in the middle of a massive deal and it's
actually inconvenient that I'm coming away for a fortnight, but don't
worry, I'm not calling it off this time. as you know I thrive on stress and
I know that when I get back to work my desk will have vanished under
an everest of faxes, reports, letters etc. I dread to think what'll be in
my in-box. I'll try to keep up to date with emails at least while I'm
away.

tell me if there's anything you want me to bring, but be aware that I'm
not about to carry class-a drugs through customs and spend the rest
of my life In the bangkok hilton.

is there a real bangkok hilton, though? because I wouldn't mind
splashing out and staying there.

everyone says hi. can't wait for our first night together again. don't wear any knickers when you come to the airport. I have been having many carnal thoughts of you.

love

tom xx

To: Tansy Harris
From: Max
Subject: kisses

Just a few kisses from across the room. You look beautiful from this angle as from every angle there is.

xxxxxxxxxxxxxxxxxxxxxxxxxxxxxxxxxxx

PS How do trees communicate with each other?

To: Tansy Harris
From: features
Subject: backpacker murders

hi tans, how's it going? hope you well.

can you write us a piece about travelling and how these 4 murders are affecting the backpacking community, now that they've moved to s e asia. just your thoughts, fears, lack of fears, whatever. make it nice and colourful. about 1,000 wds would be great. asap. cheers.

jon x

To: Tansy Harris
From: William Marchmont
Subject: how is thailand?

Hi Tansy, it's me. How's it all going with you? Everyone seems to be quite worried, and I can see why. That is quite a big geographical shift in the killing. No one can decide if it's the same person or not. Are you sure you're all right out there? Of course you are, I shan't patronise you by suggesting otherwise. Go for it. Keep on having fun. How's your bloke? Hope he's treating you right. Take care in Singapore though.

One day I will travel. For now Scotland is quite enough. I had an email from your friend Kate the other day because she was in Edinburgh for a party, but unfortunately I was up in the north with my work. I gave her a call though (on my new mobile, after everything I said about them) and we had a nice chat. I'm glad you've got such good friends. I'd like you to meet mine, one in particular. I will say no more for now, but let's just say life is good.

It is pouring with rain here in a very unsurprising way, so please say hello to the sun for me. Glad to hear you so happy in your last mail. Carry on smiling and I'll see you whenever you've had enough of it all—with the new man in tow? Or is Tom a factor?

Much love

W xxx

To: Tansy Harris
From: aaontour@excite.com
Subject: Where are you?

hey, mate, how are you doing? we're in malaysia, in penang to be precise. We're really shocked about that girl killed in singapore—much scarier than when it was in india. the girl, shelley, was a friend of a friend of ours. she was a really lovely girl apparently, and very streetwise. they don't understand how it could have happened. not the type of girl to get into dodgy situations with strangers. her family are coming out for the body. so yes, we're hanging out with other brits once again, showing our colonial roots. we think you should come here. haven't heard from you for ages. has your bloke come to visit? is it true lurve? of course it is. we're going back to thailand after this. stay in touch and let's meet up. we can't have you travelling on your own. and we really mean that. cheers ally & andy.

To: fatface; mum&dad; groovygal@yahoo.com; wherethefucarewe@hotmail.com; beachbabe@excite.com; noelene; jan; raelene; charmain; clubbers4ever@northnet.com.au; blinky; bugsy; joelene; bondiboy@hotmail.com; jasonontour@yahoo.com; surfinmike@hotmail.com; dave24@compuserve.com; billyboy@uq.edu; tansyharris@hotmail.com; pissedashell@yahoo.co.uk; sheila@barbie.com.au; gibbo@yahoo.nz; ashleigh; auntie jill; brucegraham@aol.com
From: cariannejanegraham@hotmail.com
Subject: news from asia

Dear all,

Well as you will notice I have now left the safety of bussing it through europe and have arrived in asia, as some of you who I've met out here will particularly know. This newsletter is a belated happy christmas and new year to everyone as well. I hope you all had a good time. it seems a bit late to be saying that! but there you go.

Well, my christmas was certainly "different!" I can't say I particularly enjoyed myself but I think it was "character forming!" let me explain. I joined some new friends trekking in northern vietnam. You see it is their winter now, ie the opposite of australia, and it was a much, much colder winter than any australian winter I've ever known. In fact it was almost as bad as england! Those of you who have been to england will understand what that means. On the trip there was another ozzie, mike from queensland (hi mike!) who I hit it off with, shall we say, rather well. sadly he had to go to laos but I look forward to hooking up with when we get home (yes, you see, girls, you can go travelling and find romance!). There was an english girl, very posh, tamsin, I think she was related to princess diana so you see I am also mixing in high society!!!!!! We also had two further ozzies, ally and andy, so in a way it was like being back home! Quite an odd bunch I can tell you!

After the trek we returned to Hanoi—this was where mike and I finally got it "together" around the new year! sadly then we were going in separate directions.

I am now in saigon which I find to be very big and quite full-on. However, I am keeping my spirits up not least because this will be the penultimate time you hear from me!!!! yes, I will be coming home in 3 days. I will let everyone know whether the homecoming is weird or what, and then I will be just back at work like a normal person, I guess, and with no interesting stories to email to all my friends. I will make sure I keep in touch with all the people I've met on my travels and if anyone needs a bed in Dongdingalong then you are all welcome. Just not all at once please!

To everyone who's written to me individually, thanks, it's good to hear from you. I'll get back to everyone as soon as I can. Take care everyone and don't worry, I'm not with that nutter who keeps killing the girls! At least, not as far as I know! A good time to be going home!!

LOL, Carrie :-)

To: Tansy
From: Kate
Subject: take care

honey, are you sure you're ok out there? I mean I'm sure you are, like you say, the chances of being run over are far bigger, but it does seem alarming. and before you tell me, I DO know that singapore and thailand aren't (quite) next door, and I'm sure you're fine. just don't talk to any strange men, ok? you're much closer to singapore than you ever were to India, and you know it.

that doesn't include tom, strange as he is. how are you feeling about that reunion? how are things going with the thin man? he sounds like a sweetheart and absolutely unlike your previous lovers. well done. how does he feel about tom coming out? are you at the centre of a love triangle? please write back immediately with all answers.

toby and I split up again: there's a salutary warning for you re: tom. I remembered soon enough why our relationship was so short-lived the first time round. he really, really annoys me. it's not even his fault, it's just the stupid pathetic things he says, like "I don't mind, you decide." sometimes I want to do the planning and sometimes I don't. he thinks the fact that I don't like his wimpishness proves that women are evil snakes and want to be dominated after all. so I'm back to peering through the peephole before I leave my flat, and scampering across the hallway like a rabbit, which is fun. not. do not shag your neighbours.

I wish I was in thailand even though the daily mail & co. have provisionally decided that a woman travelling alone is asking for it. they seem a bit torn not knowing the nationality of this murderer. in the established hierarchy, foreign men are worse than lovely english roses, and as you know all the girls have been english (not to mention all blonde, creepily—DO take care). however, englishmen are better than any old slapper of a woman. so do they blame the women for stepping out provocatively alone, gagging for it? or is it a foreign psycho preying on our innocent little girls? there seems to be a shadowy western man lurking in the background each time. no one ever knows who he really is, and the nationality changes each time. passport details he gives to hotels turn out to be false, or otherwise they can't find him signed in anywhere. so we—the people—reckon it's him, but no one's even got much of a photofit yet, so who can tell, really? it could be coincidence. did jon ask you for a piece? could be refreshing, I think. the news is absolutely full of these murders, but it's mainly hysteria and doorstep interviews with grieving parents. terribly grim.

I'm going to my goddaughter's christening—you remember, Jane's baby des (she's called desdemona, quite why I can't imagine). don't know why people persist in going to church just for all the ceremonies. so hypocritical, but I can't really decline under these circumstances.

Just read through and realised it might sound like I'm talking about your mum but of course am not. funerals are different.

so, my petal, I have to go but look after yourself—a message not just from me but from all your friends back in dreary old safe little london. and for fuck's sake, change your itinerary. you don't really need to stay in asia, do you? what's wrong with fiji or home? good luck with t.

hugs & kisses

kxxx

From: Tansy Harris
To: Max
Subject: missing you

my love, you are too far away. come over here and caress me at once!

can't wait to get you back to the lodge. how about some naked yoga?

t xxxxxxxx

ps in moss code?

From: Tansy Harris
To: Roger Harris
Subject: I AM FINE

dad, I know it's all been blown out of all proportion over there, but there really is v. little to worry about. for one thing I feel way safer here than I ever did in london, for another I'm travelling with a strong man, and for a third I am leaving south east asia in a few weeks and going to china. I'll be surprised if he bothers to seek me out there, whoever he is. I know that what's been happening is grim and scary, but no way am I coming home just yet. I'm too busy having fun. hundreds of thousands of westerners travel in asia, and four have been murdered. statistically, nothing is going to happen to me. promise. thanks for the offer of the lift from the airport though. I'll take you up on it when the time comes.

am in bangkok which is drippingly hot but rather wonderful in a polluted, crowded, crazy way. we're staying near the khao san road which you might have heard of—it's a bizarre travellers' centre. life is cool. tom may be coming out next week, so if you want him to bring anything give him a call.

hope you're all well. the children must be different now. any more on the way? give everyone my love.

Tansy xxx

From: Tansy Harris
To: Will
Subject: another sunny bangkok morning . . .

my god, my brother's got a mobile phone! how the mighty have fallen, or risen, or perhaps both. glad things are going well for you. and it sounds like you might have some love interest in there as well. good work, bro.

the bloke is lovely, thanks (max) but I am currently confused. tom's coming out next week, as arranged and begged for by me ages ago, but I'm having such a great time with max that I don't know what I want anymore. of course I'm dying to see tom but I don't want it all to be over with max, not so soon. what's a girl to do? see what happens I suppose.

have made plans with max to go to china and tibet, and go that way to India, not least, after this latest death, to avoid singapore. just hope I can manage the thing with tom and hook up with max again afterwards . . . it's all turning into a bit of a nightmare. there is a constant sense of unease overshadowing all my trivial boy-problems.

shame you couldn't see kate. maybe next time. can't wait to meet all your new friends. meanwhile, look after yourself. thanks for not insisting I catch the next plane home like everyone else. we're the best.

lots of love

Sis xxxxxx

To: surfinmike@hotmall.com
From: tansy
Subject: hooking up with caz?

hey cobber, I think carrie just told me rather more than you wanted me to know. you dark old horse. when, exactly, did this "hooking up" take place? delighted to learn that you and she will be hookin' up again when you get home. you must be looking forward to it. was also gratified that after 10 days in my company she knows my name so well. obviously she has hidden depths. you'll have to tell me about them some time.

ha ha ha. where are you? max and me are in bangkok doing khao san road stuff etc. a little piece of the west—do we love it or hate it? I veer wildly between the 2. hope you're having as much fun as us. If you're about we're at the shanti lodge.

love, t xxx

To: Kate
From: Tansy Harris
Subject: Re: take care

my darling, so wonderful, as ever, to hear from you. I'm in bangkok
with max, and having far too lovely a time. we wander around the
streets, drink mango juice, ride on the boats, and eat pad thai. our
guesthouse is beautiful—all wicker and relaxed, a little oasis. they
do yoga on the roof as the sun is rising, and the food is the
greatest.

so I'm in the throes of a terrible and unexpected dilemma. I largely put
tom's holiday from my mind on the grounds that he'd probably cancel
again. when I did think of it I thought of it with joy, but joy that was
vague. I've been with max all this time because it's fun, and also
because I wanted to be less in thrall to tom, to approach it this time as
equals. now I discover that tom's coming next week and suddenly,
after all these months of hankering, I'm ambivalent to say the least.
what can I do? I'm so confused—just had an email from him with flight
no etc, which means I can't ignore his imminence any longer. the
trouble is, when max and I were first in laos I told him all about tom,
and I've mentioned him maybe once since we got together. manners
prevented me saying more, and anyway I forgot. in other words I don't
think max knows that I'm going to be spending two weeks with my
other love, as of next week. I've left it too late to be gracious about it,
haven't I, and he's bound to be upset. he's the sweetest, most
considerate and sexy man I've ever met. if I had to hurt one of them,
in some ways I'd prefer it to be tom, because he's done it to me. then
again I don't seriously doubt that tom is the one for me in the long
term. will keep you posted.

sorry that toby confirmed his wimpish status. he is nice, but so often
the nice ones just aren't exciting, are they? he's told tom to go to ko
samui, which I don't thank him for. endlessly tacky these days,
apparently. why don't you come away travelling as well? I'd love your
company and you know you want to laze on tropical beaches sipping

fruitshakes. you can choose a man for me. we'll find you a wonderful travelling man, too, and we won't go to ko samui.

now, I've been wondering if I dare confide in you about something. I don't think I do because all it would demonstrate was that the heat has affected my brain. I am going crazy, because, bravado aside, I see so much of myself in those poor girls. one minute you're travelling, perfectly normally, and the next some sadist is killing you. it's really quite unsettling. you remember ally and andy, the australians I travelled with at first? well they've been travelling with friends of the latest girl, shelley. apparently she had her head screwed on. not away with the fairies, not naive. there goes my last shred of hypothetical "it couldn't be me" comfort. she was just normal, just like us.

I don't plan to travel alone any more than I can help, now. max and I are constantly together, and we've booked flights to china early in april. I just hope it holds true after I've told him about tom. I know this is just a travelling fling, but I don't want it to be over just yet. fuck. what to do? now that I write it all down, I see that I'm up shit creek, sans paddle.

anyway, sweetie, stay in touch. and don't worry about me. I'm just being silly.

tons of love

me xxxxxx

To: Roger Harris
From: Tansy Harris
Subject: one more thing

hey dad, I forgot one more thing. can you look in my boxes of stuff and find the one with all the crappy little things in? there's a pack of cards with charles and diana on them, a few pens and notebooks, a teddy, and just trinkets really. it's in briony's room. cheers for looking. I need something from it so can you get back to me asap? thanks dad.

txxx

To: features
From: Tansy Harris
Subject: re:

hi jon—yes that would be fine. In fact the money would be handy (I'm joking—I haven't been away long enough to forget the vast largesse of your dept). 1,000 it is. should be with you tomorrow. bangkok wonderful & sunny & unscary (?).

cheers

tansy

To: Amanda
From: Tansy Harris
Subject: how are you?

hello amanda, how are you doing? Isn't it great to be away? promise you'll email me when you get the chance. do they have email in ashrams? I imagine not but you never know. are you sure you don't want to hook up straight away (probably not since that would involve one of us travelling 1,000 miles)? you're very brave: I don't mean, brave to go away alone, and I don't mean brave to leave your husband and pick yourself up and turn your life around after that horrible miscarriage, and I specially don't mean brave to go to india after what's happened there (she says from the "safety" of bangkok). no, I mean you're brave to go when, if the messages I'm getting are anything to go by, everyone is insisting you must stay at home. I know you're not even travelling alone at all, but to most untrained observers, travelling with another girl is pretty much the same thing. have a brilliant time. hope the ashram is turning out to be everything you need it to be. I'm sure it is. I've been doing some yoga out here in thailand, just the most dilettante kind, and I love it. I can't imagine how amazing the full-on stuff must be. carry on smiling, as my brother would say, and here's to our meeting in a couple of months.

much love

Tansy xxxxx

CHAPTER
13

Fuck. What am I going to do? I need to tell Max about Tom, but every instinct is begging me not to. I never imagined this dilemma. I look across at Max. He smiles and motions with his head. We both get up to leave the internet centre. I never believed Tom would actually come. It didn't occur to me that he would really travel all this way to see me. He'll probably pull out at the last minute, again. He probably won't. I wish he would. I hope he doesn't. I must be strong. I don't know what to do.

Max and I put our shoes on at the door, go down the stairs, and step out into the heat. We're at the end of the Khao San Road, just around the corner by the police station. There are people walking in all directions, people chattering loudly in strange languages. There are Thai people, black people, Japanese people. Mostly, however, these passers-by are white.

My aversion to other travellers has mellowed here. Bangkok is big enough to accommodate everyone. It's huge, and intimidating. We drew in on the train yesterday, after an uncomfortable night spent on seats, rather than berths, for misguided economic reasons. When I translate the money back into pounds, I can't think why we forfeited an entire night's sleep. Slums lined the side of the tracks as we came into the city. It occurred to me that we know nothing, really, of Asia. It is a mystery. We no more know the continent than rich Americans who go to Paris and London "know" Europe. No more than Carrie does, come to that.

The station was speckled with "falangs," as we're called. When we got out of the taxi on the Khao San Road, it was like being in Brighton. It was full of them, and in a way it was welcoming. It was like going home: the roads were tarmacked, the signs were in English, and the people were familiar. Thailand seems almost completely westernised, provided, I suppose, you stay on the obvious routes. This is how Laos will be in a few years. Besides, the travellers here aren't all fresh-faced show-offs. There are casualties and freaks, people who have been in Asia for years, people with drug and drink problems. Rumour has it that one middle-aged Frenchman has been around the Khao San Road for twelve years because he overstayed his visa in a drunken haze, and has never got the money or the energy to own up and pay the fine. From time to time, the story goes, travellers take pity on him and have a whip-round, and present him with the sum, and he buys drinks for everyone until it is gone. We saw him staggering around last night, grey-haired, red-faced and mellow. It's probably more pleasant being an alcoholic here than in a big chair in Hampstead. Perhaps by the time you're that far gone it doesn't matter where you are. Perhaps, in due course, he and Mum will share a whisky in purgatory. I wonder if I'm being a little sentimental. She won't end up in purgatory, she'll have taken the express escalator to hell. Or, if we're following *The Tibetan Book of Living and Dying*, she'll have been reborn into her next life. As what, I don't know. She certainly won't have accumulated enough "merit" in this one to move up a step next time. She'll come back as something pathetic, something horrible, something befitting a bad mother. I scratch myself. I'm covered in bites. It's probably her, in the form of a mosquito. It's the females that carry malaria, after all.

We drift along with the tide. It's too hot to be purposeful. Today it is more sunny than overcast. Around the corner, there's a billiards hall and an English-style pub. The street is lined with stalls selling the clothes that everyone, including us, wears. This is the first place I've been to in my few months away that has grown up specifically to service the needs of travellers, and I am interested and uncomfortable in equal measure. I look up at Max. We are in a completely new country, now, and yet we are still together, still happy. He puts a hand on my shoulder, and steers me towards a Thai man who has a big tray of pineapple, expertly peeled and shaped into pieces like Christmas trees.

"Two, please," he says, handing over the money. The man smiles. The fruit is sticky, all over my fingers. It's so sweet and juicy that it bears next to no resemblance to the pineapple we have at home.

"Yummy," I try to say, but the juice dribbles out of the corner of my mouth, and so I shut up.

Everything with Max has surprised me. I had assumed that, soon enough, I'd feel happy to move on and never see him again. Yet I feel more attached every day. I'm no longer waiting for him to turn around and shout at me, because he wouldn't do that. Our time together is emphatically not approaching a natural end. Quite the opposite. And anyway, we're going to China together, and I can't wait. Until now, I have not contemplated the logistics of, on the one hand, seeing Tom, and on the other, flying off with Max. Tom has been the distant future, Max the immediate one. Yesterday, we bought tickets from an agency round the corner, to fly just before our Thai visas run out, in a month. We read a guidebook at the lodge, and discovered an idyllic-sounding peaceful island, with no parties on it, and decided we'd go there. I'm surprised I don't want to go to a happening place with speed punch and dancing till dawn, but I don't. I want to go to Ko Jum. Maybe I could tell Tom not to come after all. But he's my love, and Max is just a fling. He's supposed to be just a fling.

"I don't feel special anymore," I tell him, sadly, trying to take my mind off it all. "You know, I left home reluctantly, I started off miserable, and then I began to have a fantastic time. I feel like

I've done something really exciting, really lucky and fairy tale. And then you realise everyone else is the same."

"They're not the same." He holds my hand. No one seems to mind, here. Both our hands are sticky. We grimace at each other and peel them apart. "For one thing, most of these people probably aren't travelling alone. It's going somewhere on your own that really does it, really makes you get yourself together and spend time with yourself. Makes you realise how possible it all is."

"Suppose. But look, we all wear the same clothes. I never thought I'd become a part of that." It is almost chilling. The street is lined with stalls, each bursting out of its allotted space, and each heaped with wavering piles of bright baggy cotton trousers. Some sell T-shirts with the Coke or Red Bull logo in Thai, while others purvey embroidered cotton blouses, for boys and girls alike. There are cheap fake-label sunglasses, cheap Walkmans, bootlegged tapes, fake student cards, fake press cards, and surprisingly authentic-looking "Prada" bags. You can finish off your backpacker outfit with a pair of brightly coloured espadrilles and an "Amazing Thailand" baseball cap, if the fancy takes you. Alternatively, perhaps you'd prefer leather strappy sandals from the shop over the road. That's been my choice and, without a doubt, they are the comfiest shoes I've ever owned.

Yes, these are practical clothes for the climate, but I still find it strange. The Thai people here seem to dress as westernly as possible, while we wear a strange hybrid of western and eastern clothes, imagining that we are making a statement of some sort. Sarongs with Coca-Cola T-shirts. Fringed and tie-dyed miniskirts. They are clothes that are designed to say, "I'm my own person. I'm beyond such western constructs as fashion. I like to stay cool and be comfy and stylish at the same time." And yet, for all the vaunted individuality, the only way not to conform, here, would be to dress in western clothes, like I did in Saigon. If the difference between tourists and backpackers is the type of bag they carry, the difference between travellers and tourists is in the wardrobe. I can deal with being a traveller. Never a backpacker.

It's ridiculously easy to spot the people who are new to Asia. We wander over to a café. Both extremes of traveller are present, in the forms of a jerking, grey-stubbled alcoholic in one corner, and a new boy sitting outside. We take the table next to him. He is white to the point of blueness, a bit spotty, and he looks scared. He is unmistakably British. He's still wearing his "holiday" clothes from home: a pair of shiny red shorts, a football shirt with "Beckham" on the back. He doesn't quite look old enough to be travelling on his own. He must be having a gap year before university. He's engrossed (or trying to look engrossed, a miserable activity that I recall only too clearly) in a brand new Lonely Planet book, and is occasionally trying, unassertively, to attract the attention of the waitress. When she comes over, he mutters, "Beer, please."

"Yes, darling, which beer?" she asks loudly. She's a strident middle-aged woman who calls everyone darling, whoever they are. She probably has a family of twenty-seven to feed from this one crappy job.

"Erm, I don't know, what have you got?"

Before she can answer, I lean my chair back. "Have a Tiger beer," I tell him. I make the claw. "Aaargh," I add. He smiles nervously, as if I were the tiger and he the prey.

"Do you have that?" he asks uncertainly.

"Of course, darling."

"And two here, cheers," I add. I am remembering my own introduction to Asia. This is my second day of drinking again, and I confirmed yesterday that I am a cheap date indeed, pissed after half a glass. I loved it, yesterday. I'd quite hoped I wouldn't, but going back to booze was like going home. Better than that.

"OK, darling," calls the waitress, over her shoulder, already halfway to the kitchen. She's back with our drinks in two minutes.

"Any good emails?" asks Max, pouring the beer into our glasses expertly.

"Just some news from home." I have to tell him that, against all the odds, Tom has booked a flight. I am about to do it. I really am. I am shaking in anticipation. Can I do it? Can I say, "You remember I told you about Tom . . . ?" Can I change our gorgeous fling, forever, with this fragment of a sentence? If I tell him that I am going to see Tom, I will not just change things between us, but destroy them. But if I want to see Tom again, I must tell him. And I do want to see Tom. If I was in a film, I'd contrive to juggle them both in neighbouring rooms of the same hotel, and after the hassles when they discovered each other, I'd still end up enjoying true love in the end. I'm not sure which of them would be the lucky beneficiary.

"What's wrong?" says Max, gently. "Was it bad news? Is everyone all right?"

Max is completely *au fait* with my family situation. He knows more about them than almost anyone. He doesn't treat me like a freak or a delicate china vase, but he's solicitous when he needs to be. I don't want to lose that.

I look at him, poised to speak. The boy at the next table scrapes his chair back and clears his throat. I have to say it.

"I had—"

"Excuse me?" says the boy, at the same time. "Sorry," he adds, as I look round. "Can you tell me, um, if there's any, like, places to watch films around here? I mean, not cinemas, just, I was reading . . ."

Max and I smile at each other. We've both been here. I put my frustration aside, calm my pounding heart, take deep breaths, and procrastinate enthusiastically.

By the time we're done answering his many questions, we leave him radiating relief through every clogged blue pore. As we stroll back up the road, in the direction of the lodge, I come no closer to mentioning Tom than I was yesterday, or last week, or any time since Max and I became lovers. Now it's urgent. I decide that I'll tell him when we get to the guesthouse. I'll join in the yoga class first, and that will give me the mental strength.

Suddenly, I'm not happy anymore. There are too many people in Bangkok. I'm just one of the crowd. No wonder people get murdered and no one ever gets caught. It's easy to vanish here. It's easy to be anyone. This place is full of people running away, people who aren't strong enough to stay at home. Coming here isn't brave, it's weak. It's not different, it's unimaginative and dangerous. Mine is not the most amazing experience anyone has ever had. The city is threatening. A huge, Asian city. Here we are, cowering in the white people's quarter, sticking with our own. And yet our own people are probably the most dangerous of all.

I wish I wanted to leave Max. I wish there was a chance that he'd be happy for us to separate for a few weeks and then meet up again to go to China. We'll sit down with another beer at the Shanti Lodge, and then I'll talk to him. I'll be properly pissed by then. It'll be easier. I'm staggering a bit as it is. Not much good for yoga, after all. I did it this morning. I'll do it tomorrow.

A little way up the road, a well-groomed white woman rushes over to us with a clipboard. She looks ridiculous, in a fake Chanel suit and inappropriate shoes.

"Excuse me," she says, looking at me piercingly. "I'm so sorry to bother you. DO YOU SPEAK ENGLISH??" She looks strangely out of place here. Perhaps she's a well-heeled tourist from one of the expensive hotels, come to look at the weirdos. But why the clipboard?

"Sure," says Max. "How can we help?"

"Oh, you are English!" She is making earnest eye contact with both of us. She seems to be looking me up and down, appraising me. "Fab. Right, if you could just come over here, I'll explain it to you." She turns to check we're following her, and walks backwards while she extends her hand towards us. I feel like I used to when cornered by a Hari Krishna on the street. I don't want to follow this woman. I want to walk slowly to the lodge and shag Max. And then get pissed and break some news to him.

"My name's Jennifer," says the intrusive woman, "and I'm a producer with an independent production company. We're making a little documentary about these dreadful murders that have been happening. You have heard about them, I suppose? I spoke to one girl who hadn't, would you believe it? And now it's so close at hand! It's irresponsible, really. What we're doing here is interviewing people, women mostly, I'm afraid," here she pauses for breath, and to smile flirtatiously at Max, "about what it's really like on the 'travel circuit' . . ." She makes quotation marks in the air. By now, we have reached a corner of the smartest café, where Jennifer's team are encamped with sound equipment and a camera.

"I suppose you're not travelling alone," she continues, wheeling round to face me, "but we'd still be interested in your perspective. Have you travelled on your own at any point?"

I have not uttered a single word since we were accosted. Jennifer, who is the owner of the shiniest hair I've ever seen, indicates that her people should set up their equipment around me. She must be the same age as me, yet she is patronising me down to the ground. I am deeply offended by her, and I know why she wants to talk to me. Did I bludgeon people into interviews like this when I was at the paper? I know I did. Could I have ended up being Jennifer, and she me? Easily.

"I appreciate being asked," I tell her firmly, "but I don't want to do this, I'm afraid."

She tuts understandingly. "But you must!" She speaks slowly, as if I were dense or foreign. "Come on, you'll be on telly! It'll be fun. You're blonde! And you're English—you're going to be perfect!"

"Why? So you've got me on tape if I'm the next victim?"

"God, it's not like that at all. How could you think that? We're not monsters, you know. We just want to make the story immediate for people, give them the background." I wonder how she manages to wear immaculate make-up and tights and stilettos, in this weather.

"Look," I tell her. "I was a journalist at home too, and I'm doing a piece for the *Herald* at the moment about all this, and the last thing I want is to be on telly. It would be a bit incestuous, don't you think?"

"No, I do not think. It's fantastic news that you're already media-savvy. You wouldn't believe how many people have no idea. We'll flag you up. You'll be a star." She motions to a man, whose leather jacket rests on the back of his chair (which implies that he's worn it at some point today, which seems implausible). He comes towards me with a clip-on mike. I back away.

Max joins in. "Excuse me, Jennifer? She is entitled to say no, isn't she?"

"Well, yes, she is, but frankly I don't know why she wants to . . . Oh, yes I do. I understand." She takes out her purse and looks me in the eye. "I can do a thousand baht," she offers, crossly. "God, you wouldn't believe how many times this has happened today. So much for renouncing all worldly wealth."

"I don't understand," Max says later. "I would have expected you to enjoy being on telly."

"It's so ghoulish. You know why she had an orgasm when she saw me and a multiple orgasm when she realised I was English. It's because I fit the exact profile of the victims. Precisely. She was hoping—and I know what journalists are like, so you have to believe me—she was actually hoping that I'll get murdered in the future, and then she'd have a great piece of footage on her hands. She must have come straight out here after the Singapore murder. Since he moved around in India, it's logical that his next step will be Malaysia and Thailand. There's nowhere else to go from Singapore. Ally's in Malaysia. And she's my friend."

"Tans, Tans, you're overreacting." He puts his hand on my arm.

There are tears in my eyes. "I am not overreacting. At least, I don't think I am."

He pulls me towards him. "Listen to me, you funny girl. You are not going to be the next victim. There probably won't even be a next victim. And all of this has nothing to do with you. Jennifer was just doing her job, the same as you. You're writing an article about this, aren't you? What's the difference between that and talking about it on telly?"

"The difference is that I have control over what I write in a fluffy little piece. That stupid woman can make the film of me look like anything she wants, and she can cut it how she wants, and if I do get killed, then—"

"Hold on a minute." He takes me by the shoulders. "You are not going to get killed. Where has this come from? I'm with you. I know that what happened in Singapore was a shock, but we're a long way away even from there. We're going to vanish into China and Tibet in three and a bit weeks. We can try to go sooner if you want. You've been the first to point out how silly the hysteria is. What's changed?" He looks me in the eye, and I look away from him.

"Promise you won't laugh at me?" I mumble. I'm stalling. I'm not really telling him about my primary concern, namely Tom.

"Promise."

I take a deep breath. "All those things he puts in their hands afterwards. The little things."

"Pens and shit?"

"Yes. They're my things. The first time it was a Virgin Atlantic pen. I've got one of them. The second time it was a royal family pack of cards. I've got one of them, too. The third time, it was a little teddy, which I've got, and in Singapore it was a plastic tulip, and I've got a load of them as well, at home. It's freaking me out."

He looks at me and successfully suppresses a smile. I see his eyes twitch; that's how I know.

"Come here," he says.

His shoulder is comfy, if bony. It smells of him. It smells of comfort and reassurance. I bury my face, and my tears soak through his T-shirt. He strokes my hair. I don't think anyone's stroked my hair for years. I wonder whether I could cry properly. I can't remember doing that before, not since I was a tiny child.

"Lots of people have those things," he says, into my hair, as my shoulders begin to shake. "He probably took them from the girls' bags. Airline pens and playing cards and teddies are what people have in their backpacks, aren't they? I promise you, my darling, it's just chance. There's no need for you to feel scared."

"But what if there is?" By now I am sobbing. I can't believe how ridiculous I sound. But I'm not crying about that. I'm not crying about my Virgin Atlantic pen, or my plastic tulips, or the coincidences, or anything I've read on the internet. I'm crying about my life. I'm about to lose this man.

"How could there be?"

"I don't know." The words barely come out. I am incoherent. Max knows. He cradles me in his arm and keeps stroking my hair until I come to a hiccupping halt.

"Sorry," I splutter. How pathetic. I must pull myself together.

"It's OK," he says. "Carry on. Cry. It's all right. I'm here."

I think about my mum, and the brother I never knew I had, and my hopeless dad, and the way I never got a chance to be a proper, annoying child, and the way I looked after her almost until the very end, and I cry, and cry, and cry. I don't think I'll ever stop, yet until I started, I never imagined I wanted to. My face goes red and swells up, my eyes must be bloodshot, my nose is running onto his T-shirt, and I don't know how I can ever leave him. But I know that I have to, and that makes me cry even more. The thing is, this travelling life isn't real. It won't last. Tom is from my real life, and I have to see him. I have to. It's my whole future.

CHAPTER
14

I end up at the airport, my bridges well and truly burnt; trying to convince myself that it doesn't matter.

When, at last, he walks through customs, with his familiar tubby shape and his floppy hair, my treacherous heart leaps in precisely its old manner. Tom, my eternal love, is here, and most of me wishes he wasn't. He has flown all this way, for me, and I largely wish he hadn't. He looks around, looks straight at me, sees a dishevelled, hesitant traveller with cheekbones, and carries on scanning the hall. The place is packed with eager people. I wave nervously. He looks again, does a double take followed by a second, exaggerated double take, and smiles and winks. I will my body to stop trembling as I edge behind the crowd. It really is Tom. He really is here. He has a red crease on his face from sleeping on the plane. He always sleeps on planes, because he carries a copious supply of melatonin. It drove me mad, on the few trips we took together, to discover that he was a non-conversationalist, a non-movie companion and, worst of all, after the initial Bloody Mary, a non-drinking partner. He just sleeps and dribbles.

He pulls me tightly into him. Max doesn't have all this padding. I'd forgotten how big and squishy Tom is. It is almost distasteful to be pressed into the fatty remnants of his expenses lunches and boozy evenings. Almost; but not quite.

Around us, reunions are taking place. A pink western man sweeps an exquisite Thai girl off her feet, twirling her around so her legs fly out and she squeals. I wonder if this man has come out to marry this girl or whether the arrangement is altogether more prosaic. Tom and I are more restrained than the other couple; in fact, in our demeanour, we are more like the uniformed driver to our right, who holds a card reading "Lotus Hotel Mr. Angus Fraser," and exchanges a formal handshake with his stranger (who, disappointingly, is not sporting red hair and a kilt).

After our hug, we look at each other, and turn and walk towards the taxis. Tom takes my hand. Even his hand is squashy.

"So," he says. "Ahh've ya bin?" I'd forgotten that he likes to talk like an Eastender, despite his impeccable breeding.

"I've been great," I smile, making sure I look as sincere as I can. I don't want him to think I've been missing him one little bit. As, in fact, I haven't. "Welcome to amazing Thailand," I add.

He slips his hand round my waist. "You've lost weight. You look really different. I don't think I've ever seen you out in public without make-up before. And what's all this?" He fingers my clothes. "Backpacker chic?"

"It's practical, really. Easy to stay cool. You can't wear make-up here because it would just slide down your face." Already, I am on the defensive.

But I think it's going to be all right. My head knows it is. It's just that my stomach is taking some time to get over the wrench of the last few days; the pain of Max walking out, leaving me to spend three days sitting at a table, playing with a cup of coffee, and watching other people being happy. The tears have constantly been in my eyes since the day he let me cry.

I told him the day after that, when we were sitting at our usual table at the Shanti Lodge. It was raining, hotly and gently, and we were sharing a Chang beer in the late afternoon. A slightly growly tape of Schubert's string quintet was playing quietly, and the room was open to the world on two sides.

161

"So," I said, "um, I suppose there's something we should discuss."

"What?" he asked. The rain pattered down, just a foot away from us. The sky was bearing down, grey and heavy, and I had a terrible feeling that everything was ending.

"You remember how that guy I used to see, Tom, you remember that there was a chance he was going to come to Thailand?"

"Yes," Max said slowly, putting down his glass. It rained for several minutes before I could carry on. Maybe I could tell Tom not to come after all, and Max need never know. I could do what they do on soaps, and change this sentence to something like, "Well, I haven't heard from him, but what I want to discuss is, er, where we're going for dinner tonight." No one would be suspicious of that, in a soap, but I think Max already had an idea of what was coming.

"I've had an email from him," I struggled on, "and I hadn't been in touch with him for ages, but he's sort of booked himself on a flight here, so I might have to see him, at least meet up, you know . . ." I tailed off pathetically.

Max, as I knew he would, immediately recognised that I had done nothing to cancel the romantic reunion, despite our five weeks together. Despite our tickets to China, and our plans for Ko Jum. He was surprised, furious, and hurt. As he stomped around the bedroom, later, packing his things, I tried to reason with him. He stopped, and looked at me, T-shirt in hand. I'd never seen him angry before.

"I just don't get it. You tell me weeks and weeks ago that he might come out to Thailand, you never mention it again, you plan to go to China and Tibet with me, we buy fucking tickets to China . . . Pardon me for not realising that all along you were intending to take time out to shag some arse-wipe from *London*." He said "London" in a sing-song, mocking voice, the way Greg would say it. I didn't know what to do.

"I don't want anything to happen between me and Tom," I struggle. "I'll tell him not to come after all."

Max sighed. "You'd already have done that if you'd meant half the things you've said to me. You'd have done it weeks ago. Were you just using me, all the time, to chaperone you until the next victim arrived?"

I'm still shaking a bit with the shock of Tom's presence as we drive through night-time Bangkok, past neon signs and people sleeping in the gutter, and endless pictures of the King and Queen. I am musing about how good the roads are, particularly after Laos, when Tom takes my hand.

"It's all a bit basic, isn't it?" He makes a gesture which takes in everything, from the interior of the thoroughly western cab to the office blocks, the people and the music which fills the car. This is a Thai pop song, our favourite. Mine and Max's. It goes, "Sha la la la la, sha la la la in the morning . . ." Hearing it makes my stomach lurch. Tom seems to take it in as I start humming, and he taps the driver on the shoulder.

" 'Scuse me, mate?" he says, in his mock-Cockney. "Can you turn the music down, yeah? Bit loud in the back here. Cheers, guv." Most London minicab drivers would struggle to understand that. Tom presses home his point by putting his finger to his lips. Then he reaches forward, and turns it down himself. He is folded up on the backseat, too tall for the space available. And he's definitely put on weight. That's good, I tell myself. It stops me feeling fat. Doesn't it?

On the inside of the windscreen is a pastel sticker with a picture of a smiling cartoon couple with a heart over their heads and the words "No life without wife" beneath them. I try to see the scene through Tom's eyes, straight from London. I discover that I can't. Bangkok is a world city, a financial centre, home to some very rich and very poor people, south east Asia's tourism hub. There's nothing challenging in what we can see from the taxi. Nothing essentially different from the west.

"Basic in what way?" I ask.

"You know, in a Third World way. All that poverty. I bet you can't get proper service, can you? When are we going to the beach?"

Max might be on Ko Jum by now. The book said there was a big long beach with two sets of huts. Nothing else; no nightlife beyond the huts' cafés. A few hammocks. No electricity after 9 p.m. On the other side of the island, there is a local community, without tourists. We both fell in love with the description of Ko Jum. I know he will have gone there now. Over the past few days, I have constantly been on the verge of getting up and going after him.

Tom yanks me closer and starts to kiss me. I close my mouth. My stomach is telling me to go after Max. If I found him and was sorry and sorry and sorry all over again, on a little island from which he couldn't escape for a day until the boat came back, I'm sure he would forgive me. He might, anyway. It would be worth a try. I couldn't run after him when he left that night. I just sat on the bed and looked at him as he picked up his rucksack.

"What about China?" I asked, knowing the answer.

"It was your choice," he said, and he walked out of the room, and was gone. He looked hurt, and wretched. He didn't look forgiving. I cannot bear the fact that I might never see him again.

After he left, I sat in our room for a bit, trying to accustom myself to the fact that it was now my room, not ours. The light was fading behind the blind. Suddenly, I couldn't stand it any longer. I went out, pausing at the door to put my shoes on, and walked slowly through the rain. I didn't care where I went. I was soaked within a couple of minutes, but I liked that. My clothes clung to me heavily, even though they were only cotton. I passed a 7-Eleven, and lots of other shops. I passed Thai people, who looked at me curiously, and westerners who mostly ignored me. One of them stared at me, and I recognised him as the bloke who insulted me in the nightclub on the second night of the trip. The one who wouldn't shag me if I was gagging for it. I glared at him, but I didn't really care. I ended up sitting by the river, looking across at some monks who were dressed in saffron robes and were waiting for the boat on the other side of the river. I didn't want to be in Thailand anymore. It wasn't the right place. I felt anxious about everything. The river was big and heavy and it smelt. The rain didn't stop.

In the cab, Tom is caressing me.

"Are you wearing knickers? I told you not to!" I have never before disobeyed him in matters sexual. "I'll get them off you soon enough. Are we nearly there?"

"Yes. Look, we should stop this. The driver won't like it. It's not what they do in Asia."

"Isn't it? I thought this was the land of ping-pong balls and vaginas! I didn't think anything we did could shock the natives of Bangkok." He looks at me cheekily. "Have I fallen victim to a media-propagated myth?"

"I'm afraid you have, my darling." I didn't mean to call him darling, but we smile at each other, and it's just like it used to be. I begin to relax. It's bound to be weird at first. It'll be all right in the end.

I have booked a big, expensive hotel, many miles away from the Shanti Lodge and the Khao San Road. When we arrive, I wonder if there's any way I can postpone having sex with him. It feels strange now, so soon after Max. I need a bit more time to get my head around the upheavals of this abrupt change of partner. The trouble is, I don't have the energy or the inclination to start telling him about Max. He'd realise how ambivalent I am, and what a struggle it has been to see him. I don't want him to feel like second best. I decide to go through the motions. I mean, this is the man I have fantasised about for months.

Sex with Tom has always been spectacular, but tonight it is rough, with too many bites and scratches. He holds me down and pulls my legs apart. I used to love this. I do my best to sink into the old familiar ecstasy, but it eludes me, and so I fake it so we can go to sleep. I feel like a whore, submitting to this rich man against my better judgement, in an expensive, anonymous hotel room.

I mustn't creep out in the night and wait for the next bus to Krabi, and the boat to Ko Jum. I have to give Tom a chance. He's lovely, really. It's me that's changed.

I slide across the giant bed, and slip out, disturbing the springs as little as I can. He is lying on his back, his mouth slightly open but, surprisingly, he is not snoring. The air conditioning makes it freezing in here, against all the odds, against the elements. I put on a fluffy bathrobe and stand by the window, but I can't see anything through it because it's so thickly glazed. You'd never guess that hot Bangkok was out there. The floor is deeply carpeted, and the television shows MTV and CNN. The minibar is stocked with Gordon's and Smirnoff and Budweiser. We could be anywhere. It is a little piece of the west, climatically controlled so the rich traveller doesn't have to confront anything at all different from what he is used to. Or she.

I wonder what I was like on the night I arrived in Asia. Was I like Tom is now? He is swaggeringly unsure of himself. He is, it seems to me, exercising the white man's right to be rude, because he doesn't know how else to be. He refused to eat in the restaurant or to come outside with me, citing the late hour as an excuse. Overruling my paeans of praise to Thai food, he ordered a burger and fries on room service, and then decided it was cold and sent it back, in loud, idiomatic English, while checking over the room service girl. When she'd gone he wondered aloud whether she was a prostitute. Was I that bad? I suspect I was. I was arrogant, rude, and closed-minded. I didn't venture outside my hotel room on the first night either. I had no idea, at the time, that it was because I was scared, and sad. I can't believe how different I feel now.

When I look at the outline of Tom, pampered and well fed,

cosseted in his enormous bed with his amenable girlfriend (as far as he is aware) by his side, then I feel the change in myself. When I think about all the nights I sat up with Max, and he drowsily listened to me talking about Mother, ten years' worth of talking, then I recognise the change. I'm not hiding anymore; at least, not so much. Part of me is still cowering, but there are things that should never see daylight, even with Max.

Max. I would never, two months ago, have considered it possible that I could get out of Tom's bed to face my anguish at not being with someone else, to feel soiled at having fucked Tom, my supposed true love. I try to imagine my reaction if, when I first saw Max, sitting in that cafe and looking all Latvian, someone had told me that I'd become so close to him that I'd prefer him to Tom. I'd have laughed in their faces. Max looked so funny. For God's sake, I even had to make him promise to shave before I could kiss him. No one has a beard in Soho, not even the tramps. But he liked it. It was his camouflage, and he'd had it for years; and yet he got rid of it, because I wanted him to. Tom would never do that. In fact, if I suggested he had his hair cut, he'd grow it longer, just to make his point.

I mustn't take my own anxieties out on Tom. It's not his fault. I look at him again, at his familiar, beloved outline, and I try to smile. I feel sick. I have to go after Max. I know I'm not being fair.

I take a miniature of Jack Daniel's from the fridge, and knock it back (I am still my mother's daughter when the chips are down). I was every bit as horrible, three months ago, as Tom is now. He's bound to be interested in my new perspective. Maybe he'll be interested in Thailand tomorrow. After all, he arrived at night, disoriented and tired. I haven't given him a chance. We'll go to Ko Chang together, as planned, in the morning. Then I won't be in Bangkok with all its recent associations. We'll both be somewhere new, and we'll be able to relax. We'll be nowhere near Max. And that'll be good.

And I'll talk to him about Mum, because he's the person I've been needing to talk to all along, and that, I hope, will staunch these bloody tears. I'm being pathetic, and I despise myself. I try to imagine a future with Tom, without Max. I come close to managing it. I don't sleep.

CHAPTER
15

Ko Chang means Elephant Island, but there aren't any elephants living here. The name comes from the big bulge in the middle, though it might equally be in homage to the favourite beer of the holidaymakers. This is a hedonistic place, with lots of drinking, and a tattoo artist to catch the uninhibited trade. There is, however, very little dope-smoking, owing to the fact that this island is a prime smuggling route from Cambodia into Thailand, and it swarms with police. Some people risk it. I probably would if cannabis delivered me any pleasure. I'd risk anything for a line of coke.

The accepted method of smoking is to stand ankle deep in the sea, and to face the beach. The beach is so huge that if anyone comes over to see what you're doing, you spot them miles off and simply drop the spliff and let the waves bear away the evidence. Tom has been practising this, in the company of assorted young dope-headed girls. I watch from my spot on the beach, or in one of the bars, with amusement.

I'm lying on the beach, and I'm drunk. I'd forgotten what a healer a good cocktail can be. I think I became quite sanctimonious while I was travelling. I am amazed that I went all that time without drinking. Tom thinks it's hilarious. "It just goes to show that nobody's safe!" he says. "If my Tansy can become an earnest serious travelling type, everyone's at risk."

If I tip my head back, I can see the tree-covered hill which would be the elephant's bum. If I tip it forward, I can see the flat sea. The air is warm and salty, and there's a slight breeze coming from the water. It's a pretty place, full of Britons on two-week breaks from work. The weather's perfect, and I'm finessing a golden tan. I am having a wonderful time. I was wrong to doubt Tom. I'm happy. I'm sure I am. We've been drinking a lot, talking, hanging out, and meeting people.

Tom and I are the best people on this island. Everybody adores us. They want to be us. This morning I had my first drink at precisely midday. If you don't drink in the morning, you haven't got a problem. And anyway, it was a vodka and orange, so it had vitamin C and was good for me. It doesn't count as a bad drink. The sun is just about to set. It's almost time for the evening drinking, the proper drinking, to begin.

Tom strolls over. I have done my best to readjust to him, physically, but it hasn't been easy. I like his rosy cheeks and his thick hair, but his body is so different from Max's. We haven't discussed any other relationships either of us might have had. I know that this means he's had a few. I wonder if he realises that, had I been saving myself for him, had I been celibate, I would have asked him straightaway.

I put that thought from my mind. Yes, Max was special. Shh. I mustn't remember that. Tom is my true love forever.

"Hey there." He offers me a hand and pulls me to my feet. "I said we'd get out there for sunset cocktails. I'm going to grab a shower."

While Tom gives himself a cursory going-over with my soap, I dress myself in a pink sarong and tiny white T-shirt. I add lipstick, and arrange my hair with his gel so it looks like I haven't tried at all. I spray my wrists, neck and hair with his CKOne. I am on familiar territory: I am City Tansy. I'd forgotten how much fun it could be. Admittedly, I recognise that I'm holding on. I'm waiting for the rest of me to catch up. I can live this hedonistic life. I can enjoy it. I need a drink. I need drugs. The one thing that has impressed Tom about my trip so far has been the fact that I smoked opium.

"I'll see you there!" I shout to Tom through the bathroom door. "You're certain you didn't do any accidental smuggling?"

"Check through the pockets if you want, doll. I don't think so."

Persistence pays off. In the breast pocket of one of his cotton shirts, I find a wrap of paper with a small amount of powder in it.

"Yay!" I shout. "You would have gone down if they'd searched you!"

"No way!" He emerges, naked and dripping, from our bathroom. "Fuck!" He looks impressed with his audacity. I dig out a Visa card, and form the powder into two lines. They're small lines: there's just enough.

"Can you believe it?" I am delighted. I know there are lots of reasons why coke is bad, but I can't recall them.

Tom is rolling up a five-hundred-baht note. He offers it to me first, and he rests a hand on the small of my back while I snort. I used to be embarrassed about doing this in front of people, but now it seems the most natural thing in the world. I feel the hit immediately, and I turn round and beam at Tom. This is going to be a good night.

I rest my feet, bare and beautifully painted, on the edge of the table, and I sip at a sticky cocktail as glamourously as I can. We are on wicker chairs on the beach. There is a huge crowd of holiday-makers around us. For the first time in months, I'm surrounded by people who admire me as soon as they meet me. They're impressed by the fact that I lived in Soho, and they're even more impressed that I worked for the *Herald*. They seem happy to overlook the fact that I wasn't exactly a famous investigative reporter. Not like Amanda. Being admired is seductive. If they knew I'd snorted cocaine this evening they would love me still more.

Tom and I hold court. We have both got lots to say. I love this feeling. I can relax completely after a line. I don't have to try to be likeable: I am likeable. We are entertaining them with our recent history.

"So, Tans wanted to go travelling. We both did, for a while, but you know what it's like. Work calls, it's hard to take a year off just to doss like this. I mean, it would be pleasant, but most of us couldn't do it, you know what I mean?"

The onlookers laugh and nod. There is a massive group of girls, all on holiday together, and I think most of them fancy Tom.

"You can do it if you really want to," I tell them, "but only if you really want to."

"I suppose it came down to the fact that she's braver than me, more willing to chuck it all in."

I look at him. "I had less to chuck in than you did, that's why. I couldn't wait to get away."

"She'd been having a bit of a shit time at home. So in the end she went without me." He holds up his hands to forestall protest. "I deserved it. So there I was, still in London, still working all the hours God sent, and all of a sudden my girlfriend is off in the sunshine, hanging out with beardy backpackers, and I'm worried she'll forget me."

"I didn't forget him."

"So I booked two weeks off, and here we are."

A girl sitting at Tom's feet looks at him with adoration. "That's so romantic!"

There is a general consensus that she's right. It's news to me.

"If I was really romantic, I'd stay out here with her, but unfortunately that's where real life intervenes."

"Maybe you should propose," suggests a woman who has, unwisely, had her hair plaited into rows. Her face is too chubby to carry the Bo Derek look.

Tom looks over at me and smiles. "You never know. If I did, it wouldn't be in public." he says. There is a soppy chorus of *"Ahhh."*

It's like a blow to the stomach, with a baseball bat. My head starts to spin. I pull my legs down from the table, and stand up, shakily.

"My round," I mutter, and go to the bar and order ten margaritas. I start telling the barman my troubles, but I don't think he understands. I knock one drink back, and start on the next. I can't see any way round this apart from drinking myself into oblivion. I don't stop to think who I remind myself of. I can barely articulate anything.

"Don't want to marry Tom," I manage to mutter, "Can't deal with this."

I am on the third cocktail when someone grabs me round the waist. "Hey," says Tom. "Only joking. You should have seen your face!"

I wake up early in the early morning, feeling dizzy and disoriented and, suddenly, overwhelmingly miserable. I search my memory for a reason. When I look at Tom, sleeping in the gloom of the hut, it floods back. The thought of Tom proposing to me jolts me afresh. Although it's a ludicrous idea, and he'd never do it, I should still have liked the principle. If Tom is my true love forever, and, even when I was with Max, I have never doubted it, then I should have welcomed the suggestion. Marrying my true love, eventually, shouldn't upset me this much. I have no interest in the institution of marriage in itself, but a future with Tom would be the summation of all my desires, the proof of my success. So why can I only think of Max?

I get up, without disturbing Tom. I've papered over the cracks, but—I try to follow the metaphor—now the house has subsided and the cracks are tearing the paper apart. I'm beginning to be ashamed of the ease with which I've slipped into being with Tom, the way we used to be. It's easy to spend every day on this beautiful island, chilling on a sandy beach. Being pissed all the time is comfortably familiar. The cocaine was nice and normal. I can, without moral objections, make my contribution to the misery of the Colombian people. I can, often, come close to writing Max off as a holiday romance, a temporary lover who built my confidence.

The words "Maybe you should propose" have made my carefully balanced world collapse. I am repulsed by the idea. I don't want him. I chose the wrong one.

The beach is deserted. There are some plastic cups and the blackened remains of a fire on the sand. I kick off my flip-flops and untie my sarong. I walk into the sea. My bikini rested in a screwed-up bundle at the bottom of my backpack until recently. I'd forgotten it was there. Now I wear it every day. I should get a new one.

A small internal voice raises an objection: I don't want a new bikini. I don't want to spend the rest of my year off on beaches.

I wade out and lie on my back. The morning sky is perfectly clear. I can smell the trees and the flowers. In the cool of the morning, I recognise that I am a pale shadow of the person I was when I was with Max. The facts come thick and fast. My house is falling down. If Tom proposed to me, I would say no. Absolutely not. I don't like myself when I'm with him. I shouldn't need to show off to shallow people, and I shouldn't need coke. The people here don't like me. They like what I stand for, which, they think, is success. They don't know me at all. I remember Max growing a big beard to avoid that kind of interaction.

I haven't challenged Tom at all. He knew I'd welcome him with open arms, whatever my situation. I don't know how I slipped back so effortlessly. I don't know who I am. I don't know which person is me.

I stand up. The water only comes up to my waist. I want to throw myself around in the waves, and wail. I got it wrong. I've thrown away everything I achieved. I have relapsed. I should have guessed that I can't sustain life as a sober, proper person the moment temptation crosses my path. But I liked it. I shouldn't have given up so easily. I barely even looked over my shoulder to see what I was leaving behind.

"I got it wrong," I say, testing out the sentiment. There's no one to be seen, anywhere. I have no idea what the time is, but it can't be any later than six thirty. I shout as loudly as I can. *"I got it wrong!"* I yell. I tell the waves, the beach, and the little heap of clothes. I tell the bulging island and the clear blue sky, and the sun. I cry and I scream. I tell the rows of huts. The girl with the Bo Derek hair pokes her head out, looks around, and fails to see me. Tom must be sleeping. It takes a lot to wake him up.

I should leave this island. I love Max. This is not something that has occurred to me before, but it isn't a surprise. Of course I love Max. He's gorgeous, sexy and funny, and he'd do anything for me. I can say anything to him. I could, that is. Before I dumped him.

I am second in line when the tattooist comes on duty. I need to do something self-destructive. Getting pissed isn't dramatic enough, because I'd do that anyway. I need to hurt myself. I want to show the world that I don't care about the future, and that I am nothing more than a scummy old backpacker.

The tattooist works in a café which is decorated with psychedelic swirls, and populated by chattering girls.

"What are you getting done?" they ask, eagerly, glad to see me here. I wonder whether they'd copy my design, on the grounds that I am "cool."

"I thought a swastika," I tell the fifty-ninth questioner, sourly. She is the would-be Bo Derek.

"Yeah? Cool," she says absently. "I'm getting an eagle. Did you hear that shouting this morning? Some nutter."

"Oh, that was me."

She laughs, and continues flicking through the tattoo book.

My design isn't in the book. It's the first thing that comes into my head, the thing that has shaped my life. I am more interested in the act of being marked, indelibly, with an Asian needle than in the picture it draws. I have no interest in knowing whether it is a new or a clean needle. I want it to hurt.

I show the tattooist the picture I've sketched on a napkin. I wonder, briefly, what he makes of the hordes of middle-class Britons availing themselves of his services.

"OK?" he says. He doesn't react to my drawing.

"OK," I confirm. I've decided to have it at the base of my back, almost on my bottom, so that I won't be able to see it, but if I ever have sex with anyone again, they will have no choice but to notice.

I hitch up my T-shirt and spend half an hour sitting awkwardly on my ankles, leaning forward on my hands, and enduring the agony of a hand-held needle in bamboo repeatedly penetrating my skin.

Before too long, the quiet man announces, "Finish!"

"Thanks." A bottle of vodka is emblazoned on my back, and it will stay there forever. So there.

I watch Tom's face closely. There is something in his eyes that I've never seen before. He is almost scared of me.

"You just got someone to draw that on with pen, yeah?" he says quietly. "This is a joke, right?"

I am glad to be shocking him. "Nope, it's real. Look." I lick my finger and rub at where I think it is. It doesn't hurt at all, so I've lost track of its exact location.

"You mean you've got a bottle of vodka tattooed on you, forever?"

"I've been scarred by alcoholism, haven't I? Now the evidence is before you!" I leave him gaping and walk away. When I look back, he is finishing my breakfast.

I lie on the beach. Tom is giving me a wide berth, for which I am grateful. I am struggling with myself. At some moments, this life with Tom looks attractive. I'm young, quite young, and there is no reason why I shouldn't be carefree. My Walkman and shades are providing a barrier between me and the world. Behind them, I try to work out what to do. I can clench my teeth, tense my muscles, and shut it all out for a few hours, and no one knows, because I look like everyone else. A tear is dribbling down my cheek, looking, I hope, like an innocuous bead of sweat. I can't be carefree when I love Max and I've lost him.

Max is the best person I've ever met. He was a wonderful man and I dumped him. I have to find him and beg him. I can't spend the rest of my life knowing that I loved someone and drove him away. I have nothing against Tom. He's just Tom, the same as he's always been. I've managed to have sex with him by being pissed every night, and I've tried not to think about Max.

I was going to talk to Tom about Mum, but it never really happened. I felt silly as soon as I tried, on the boat over here, so I barely mentioned her again.

"I've been a bit more screwed up than I'd realised," I told him, casually. We stood, in the spray, looking at the hunched elephant island approaching.

"Yeah?" He was distracted. "By what?"

"By Mum. By the way I had to look after her. I shouldn't have lived like that. I should have taken her to rehab even if she didn't want to go."

"You used to say you wouldn't do that."

"And I didn't, did I? I'm just saying that I should have. I kind of missed out on having a childhood because of it."

He smiled. We were nearly there. "Childhood's overrated if you ask me. You did fine."

"But that's the point. I didn't do fine. I've been trying to sort myself out. And when I think about how much I used to drink, and how many drugs I used to take, it's, well, I suppose it's a bit frightening. I could so nearly have ended up like her."

Tom sighed. "Tans, there's the world of difference between you and your mum, for Christ's sake. That woman was monstrous. One of the things I liked about you was the way you were up for

177

anything. You didn't used to be neurotic. Take a chill pill. We're on holiday."

I weakened. He might have been right.

A sudden gust of wind covers me in sand, which sticks to my sun lotion. Max might be on Ko Jum. There's no point hanging around thinking about it. I love him, and it's time to be strong. I have to collect my courage, and my bags, and leave, right now. It was cowardice that made me let Max go in the first place. I should have followed my instincts then, and I'm going to follow them now.

It's not that there's anything intrinsically evil about Tom. He's not nasty on purpose. I used to enjoy living his way. I have nothing in common with him anymore. They were only surface things to start with. We would have been disastrous together. Fuck it, we were. We are.

I remember exactly when I fell in love with Tom, and now I'm not sure it was love at all. It happened when I took him home for the first time. I knew it was a risk, but I couldn't spend another night away. Mum needed me.

Late on Saturday night we staggered in as quietly as we could manage, and I left him in my room while I went to check that everything was all right. He was intrigued, and tiptoed after me. I don't know what he was expecting. Perhaps he thought I secretly had a child, or a coven of dwarfs employed to provide sexual services. He certainly wasn't expecting to see me undressing a crazy middle-aged woman and tucking her up in bed while she kept up a string of random invective like a drunk on the Tube.

I looked up and saw him standing in the doorway.

"Hey, what the fuck . . . ?" he asked.

"Nothing. Go to my room. I'll tell you in a minute." I was so firm that he obeyed. I put a glass of water where she could easily reach it, had a look around for hidden bottles, muttered goodnight (I hadn't kissed her since I was eleven), and switched the light out.

"So you've met my mother," I told him afterwards, smiling tightly.

He didn't know what to say. No one ever knew what to say. When I told them about her, and she wasn't actually there, she was just abstract, they'd mutter something like, "Oh God, how awful, poor you." However, if anyone met her, or saw her, that was inadequate in the face of the smell she gave off and the look in her eyes. People who met her said as little as possible. They couldn't say, what a disgusting woman, let's cross the road, like they would if they saw her in public, because she was my mother. But there was nothing else to say. Tom hugged me tight, enfolding me in his big, reassuring body, and kissed the top of my head. He looked at me tenderly for a while.

"How long's it been?" he asked.

"Forever," I told him.

"Does anyone else look after her?"

"No, just me."

He was sweet and loving for weeks after that. He treated me as though I was part Florence Nightingale and part delicate Fabergé egg. He met me from work, took me to restaurants close to home, even occasionally helped me look after her. At his instigation, we made improving trips to the cinema and the theatre, to give me a life away from my responsibilities. I fell in love with him in no time at all.

One Sunday lunchtime, I went out to buy the papers and left them watching *EastEnders* together. When I came back he'd made each of them a large gin and tonic. He was furious at my anger. We had our first screaming match, and Mum joined in, just for the hell of it. "I can't deal with this!" she yelled. "I can't deal with this!" The spell was broken, and the pattern was set; but I never got over my gratitude for the fact that he'd been willing to deal with her at all.

That's it. I can't lie here rationalising, when, wherever he is, Max thinks I'm happy without him. I'd better go and tell him the truth.

I tie my sarong, making sure the tattoo's showing. Tom waves. He's in the sea. I wave back in what I hope is a dismissive manner. He starts to walk in. I speed up. By the time he reaches the hut, I have crushed all my stuff into my rucksack and am in the process of changing into some proper clothes. The hut is wooden, and although a light bulb swings in the middle of the ceiling, there's no electricity during the day. The windows are too small to let in any serious light, so when Tom stands in the doorway, the whole place goes dark. I take advantage of this to complete my changing.

"All right?" he says. "What are you up to?" He squints as his eyes become accustomed to the darkness. He has developed a proud swagger, which is perfectly judged for his favoured activity of strolling along the beach in his trunks while thin girls simper, "Hi, Tom." He dominates the beach. He dominates everything.

"I'm packing."

"Yeah, it is a bit messy. Look, we're going for lunch at Thor's. Come on. Take your mind off that fucking tattoo. That must be some fucker of a comedown you're on."

"Sorry."

"What?"

"Sorry for everything. Can you come in? I want to talk to you."

"You haven't gone and got another one, have you? It's not easy to get them off, you know. I don't know what the fuck you were thinking."

I shake my head, and look at him until he sits on the edge of the bed. I sit next to him, and take a deep breath.

"There isn't any nice way to say this, so I'll just come out with it. Look, I woke up this morning feeling completely different. Feeling real. You laugh at me for being a backpacker, but since I've been travelling I've changed, in a good way I think. I'm proud of what I've done. I stopped drinking, I made friends where I didn't know anyone. I had a relationship. I met the most amazing man.

He couldn't be more different from London people. I left him so I could see you, and I shouldn't have. I don't love you anymore. I don't think I ever did love you, properly. You don't love me, either. I've got to go and find Max. I'm packing my stuff because I'm leaving." I pause. "I don't expect you to understand."

"You're what?"

"I'm leaving. I'm going to get the boat this afternoon. Without you."

"And where will you go, on the boat this afternoon?"

I'm glad I can't see his face properly.

"I'll go back to Bangkok, and then I'll try to get a night bus down south. That doesn't matter anyway. The important thing is, I'm really sorry, Tom, but I don't want to be the person I become when I'm with you. I like you, a lot, but I don't think I'm strong enough to resist changing into the person you expect me to be. So I can't stay with you. I don't want to be the centre of beach life. I don't want to be pissed every day and snorting coke. Did you know twenty thousand people die every year in Colombia because of people like us, taking coke?" I'd like to keep talking, but I have to stop and let him have his say.

"So? We don't care about crap like that, do we? It's not our fault. If it wasn't us who bought it, it would be someone else. Tans, I know it hasn't been easy for you. You were a bit odd when you came to the airport, but if you've been seeing someone that would explain it. I've been going out with a girl too—I still am. I told her I was coming here to see a school friend. Because this was never going to be about a serious relationship, was it? We're not in a position to have one. This was about having fun. We're never going to get married. I was *joking*. Don't take yourself so bloody seriously. You're not a backpacker. You're always the first to say that."

"Actually, I think I am a backpacker. I know this is a crap thing to do since you came out to visit me, but I've got to go, before it's too late. I love Max and I've got to go after him."

"Love Max, my arse. You love Max but you don't seem to mind shagging me."

"We haven't exactly been at it like rabbits, have we? And I've been pissed every time, you may have noticed. Look, Tom, I don't want to be mean to you. I like you, and you haven't changed."

" 'It's not you, it's me.' Is that what you're saying?"

"It isn't you. It is me. I thought I'd feel the same way I used to feel, and I tried to force myself to feel like that, but I've changed. I thought the thing with Max was just a fling, but it's not. I love him. I really, really love him, more than anything in the world. I adore him. I'd do anything to get him back. This afternoon is when I take control of myself." I gesture to my bags which, Tom can now see, are neatly leaning against each other.

Now that he believes me, he is furious.

"Take control of yourself? That I would like to see. I can see right through you, you know. I don't know if there is a Max, and if there is, I don't think you give a fuck about him any more than you do about me or your mother or your brother, or anyone except yourself. You're trying to get back at me for not coming travelling with you. I didn't expect that, so well done, you've caught me out. You've lured me all the way to practically bloody Cambodia, and now you're going to dump me here. Nice one, Tans."

We are on ground so familiar it makes me sick.

"You don't understand anything," I tell him. "You've never understood anything. You've never really cared about me at all."

"So flying all the way out here to fucking see you doesn't count as caring?"

"You didn't come here because you care about me. You wanted a holiday, and a shag. You wanted to check that I was still there for you, as your fallback position."

He snorts. "You don't know me at all."

"I know you better than you'd like. And I feel sorry for you, because you're completely blind to the rest of the world. I mean, you come to fucking Thailand and you eat burgers? Please! You have absolutely no fucking idea what it's like, not living in London."

"And I suppose you know it all now, now you're a *backpacker,* do you? I'll tell you what I know. You are completely fucking mental. You're so like your lovely mother."

I can almost hear illusions being shattered all around us. Everyone must be able to hear every word we shout. The golden couple hate each other. Pass it on. Neither of us gives a fuck what they think. We don't really care about each other, either. We're fighting like animals, like we always have done. I've never noticed it before, but it's suddenly clear as daylight. Tom doesn't care about me, and I don't care about him either. I just craved approval, all along.

I grab my bags, dodge past him, and run through the eaves-droppers, up the sandy hill. "I'd rather be mad like me than sane like you," I shout over my shoulder, and run as fast as I can, with Tom in hot pursuit. I sit by the road and pray for a tuk-tuk to come along. He rushes up, sweating.

"Are you really doing this?" he demands.

"Yes."

A big tuk-tuk comes round the corner. A man clad in a pair of shiny mauve Speedos and flip-flops saunters along and waits for it to stop. He helps me shift my things onto the roof, and I climb aboard. I am breaking away from Tom. I have nearly done it. I will be gone in a few seconds. My heart is pounding.

As my foot is on the step, Tom grabs my wrist and holds it so tight, it hurts. He pulls me back onto the ground. I stagger, and almost fall over. His bulk scares me. His handsome face is completely distorted.

"You fucking bitch," he says in a deadly quiet voice. "You've lost it. Don't you dare come crawling back to me later. It's over. We won't be friends. We won't be anything. You're going to end up rotting in hell like your mother, and I can't wait to see it. Like mother, like daughter. You're just the same." He lets me go. The man, who is near enough to hear, frowns and shifts as far away from me as he can. As we start moving, I lean towards Tom.

"No I'm not." I smile as sweetly as I can. "I'm going to be fine." I wave until we round the corner. With any luck, these might be the last words I ever say to him.

CHAPTER

16

There are hordes of westerners on the quay. A few Thai people are shepherding them about. The Thais have a look in their eyes that conveys both disdain and only-doing-it-for-the-money. The westerners, meanwhile, are older than the tattooed masses on Ko Chang, and smarter than anyone I met in Bangkok, apart from that woman Jennifer. She'd belong here. These are the sort of people you might meet in the Caribbean. They are on their way to Ko Phi Phi, on what appears to be two group tours, one American, the other French. They stand apart from each other. The Americans ignore the French because they're not American, while the French are disdainful in return because the Americans are. They will all, I imagine, stay in smart hotels and join organised scuba diving trips. The less fit might go out in glass-bottomed boats and look at the coral and the pretty fish. Like the fish, the people are dressed in the brightest colours they could find, and like the fish they have no concept of what's stylish. The fish, however, seem to get it right by instinct.

My boat is leaving at one o'clock. Forty minutes after that, I'll be on Ko Jum. I pray he's there. I was so sure he would be, but now I don't know. What will I do if I can't find him? It's more than possible that he has gone somewhere else. It's probable. He could have gone straight to Pondicherry. He might have hurried home to Bakewell. He might have gone to lose himself in China, but I doubt it. He could be in Indonesia or New Zealand, Mongolia or Timbuktu. I'll begin my search on Ko Jum, but I think it will be fruitless. He'll only be here if he wants to be found. I have blown it for good.

I blink rapidly, and cross the road, pass the deserted market, and sit at a wicker table in a café. There's a football match on the telly. I don't give a fuck who's playing. Tom would care. Max wouldn't. I've got an hour to wait, and nothing to do. The journey here passed in a blur. For the first time in my life, I was certain I was doing the right thing, but I knew I was doing it too late. I caught the boat to the mainland, standing on the deck and looking backwards all the way, in case Tom came after me in a speedboat to hurl more abuse. Feeling safer, I joined a community tuk-tuk to Trat, and caught the next bus to Bangkok. Then I got a taxi from the bus station to the Khao San Road, bought the last seat on the night bus to Krabi, had a gin and tonic to keep me going, and set off on the overnight journey. All the time, I was thinking of Max. Tom was nothing. He is not important; he has no place in my life. The weeks with Max mean something. The years of fighting with Tom are nothing at all. They are gone. They might as well never have happened.

On the bus I became aware that I'm travelling on my own now. I'm back to square one. It's just like when I arrived in Saigon. Once again, I have no companion, only this time there's a killer on the loose. Even though I wobble sometimes, I can't really take that seriously. Whatever Ally might have heard, second-hand, about that fourth girl, she must have been naive up to a point. She must have gone somewhere with a stranger. Now that I've got over my hysteria at having the same common old items as those girls, I know my chances of meeting him are minute. I'm too sensible to wander off with anyone. I think I'd recognise someone that evil.

In fact, I'm almost enjoying the excitement. It seems unconnected to me. It's something to worry about, something that could go horribly wrong, and it's not my fault at all. It's got nothing to do with the wrong choices and stupid decisions I've made. If I got killed, no one would be able to blame me. Everyone would feel sorry for me. I'd be an uncomplicated victim, and the thought is quite refreshing. If I can't find Max, I don't think I'd mind dying a violent and early death. It might make me an icon of sorts. I'd be following in the footsteps of Diana, Marilyn, Jayne Mansfield, Grace Kelly.

I know that, theoretically, any man I see could be the murderer. He must have been a bit like everyone else, superficially, or those girls wouldn't have let him close enough. On one of the buses, a small, bespectacled bloke who looked about twenty came and sat next to me. We were among the first to get on, so bus etiquette dictated that he should have taken an empty seat, put his bag firmly next to him and looked out of the window to deter fellow passengers from joining him. Instead, he stood over me until I grudgingly moved my bag. He smiled a weird smile and started asking me all about myself.

"Don't you mind travelling on your own then?" His voice was high-pitched and feminine, and he had to look up to make eye contact with me.

"I'm not travelling on my own," I told him firmly. I almost felt I could crush him under my thumb. Instead, I looked away until he took out a well-thumbed copy of *The Hitchhiker's Guide to the Galaxy* and started giggling to himself periodically. Occasionally I'd sense him looking at me sideways, as if he wanted to share a gem of wit from his book, but I was the Ice Maiden and he didn't dare. Wanker, I thought at the time, but it could just as easily have been "killer." It wouldn't really have been him, though. He was too obvious.

I wish Dad would hurry up and write back to tell me that the box is still there. Just to reassure me. It's bound to be. He hasn't been burgled—he would have said. And I don't know any serial killers. When I consider the logistics, I know it's in my mind. I'm OK, on my own. I can do it. All the same, if I can't find Max, I am tempted to go home for a while. I haven't got a home to go to, but I have got friends, and some bits of family. I could make a pilgrimage to Bakewell, to really annoy Max. I've still got money, although it won't last long in England. One thing's certain: I can't carry on with the journey we were going to make. I thought I'd be fine going to China and Tibet and Nepal and India with him, but there's no way I'm going to those places on my own. The newspapers would say I was stupid, and for once they'd be right.

The sun is particularly bright today. The colours are washed out by the intense light. I can't bear the thought of the unreliable spring at home. I'd still go back if Max was going to be there. Maybe Greg or Mike could tell me where to find him. Perhaps I could meet up with them again, see if the Dutch girls Marge and Anna are still around. I could find Ally and Andy, who must be nearby. Maybe I could go to Australia for a bit. I think I'd feel safe there. It's never appealed before. Things have come to a sorry state when I find myself considering, even just for a moment, taking Carrie up on her invitation to Dongdingalong.

I could fly to India and join Amanda at her ashram. If I can't find Max, those things will seem dull and second best. But I might do them anyway, and email him every day until he decides that seeing me again would be less hassle than having me filling his email account with undignified pleading.

On the other hand, I might see him in an hour. I had a perfect speech worked out last night, but I've forgotten it all. My mission is simple: to capture the attention of someone who never wants to see me again. To make him listen to me, and to convince him that, although I effectively dumped him in favour of someone I had previously considered my great love, I now realise that the "great love" is a tosser who is not worthy to lick the ground Max walks upon. Max must believe that he is now the great love, and also that I am not fickle. It's going to be a tough one.

I can see my boat. Several have docked, and I can confidently identify mine as the least shiny one. No scuba trips on this boat. No suitcases. It's the backpackers' express, to Ko Lanta via Ko Jum. He won't be there. I suppose I'll stay a night and come back and try to piece myself back together. Piece myself together. I don't think there is a "back."

I find a spot on the roof of the boat, and get my book out, and make sure I don't talk to anyone. The only people I've spoken to since I left Tom have been ticket vendors, the creepy man, and, once I got to Krabi, hotel people. The bus arrived too late for me to catch yesterday's boat, so I spent the night in a guesthouse that offered a terrace of wicker huts. I sat out under the stars for a while, indulging my misery, and finally crawled into my sheet sleeping bag at two in the morning. An hour later, I woke up when the man next door, with whom I shared a wicker wall, arrived home from a bar. Within seconds, it became clear that he'd brought a friend. There were western grunts, and Thai giggles. I could hear every word of their conversation. It went like this:

Her: Do you love me?

Him: Yes, of course.

Her: But why did you choose me in the bar?

Him: Because you were so beautiful.

Her: Would you like to be naughty boy?

Sounds of fumbling and giggling.

Her: Oh.

Him: I'm a bit tired, all right?

Her: No want to play?

Him: Yes, of course I want to play, only I had a lot to drink and I'm tired. Perhaps if you suck . . .

Her: Oh no, I go.

Despite my conspicuous coughing through the wall, neither of them lowered their voices. The woman duly left, and within ten seconds he was snoring. I didn't go back to sleep till five o'clock, and woke up at half past ten.

189

The man—middle-aged, pot-bellied, pink, exactly the way he sounded—was drinking a pot of tea outside. I glowered. He smiled conspiratorially, and winked at me. I suspect he's one of a large community of sad western losers who've failed with women at home and kid themselves that paying for sex in Thailand elevates them to the highest echelon of romantic success. This one is in a class of his own, as he can't even manage it with a prostitute. I rolled my eyes at him, and shook my head firmly. I didn't smile. He looked away.

I am burning, but I can't be bothered to get my cream out. I have a thumping head from the sun, but I don't start looking for my hat. I'm being hard on myself, I think, in the hope it will increase the chances that Max won't be. I have been successfully giving off "do not, under any circumstances, talk to me" vibes to all the stupid, smiling morons on this boat. Everyone's trying to look so happy. I notice that there are hardly any women on their own.

The island is much bigger than I expected. It's covered in trees, and there's a long, sandy beach. I can't see any people. I start preparing to get up and get off, when I begin to see them. There are people lying on the beach, swimming in the sea, rocking in hammocks where the trees meet the sand. There appear to be a couple of people wearing white robes, meditating on the rocks. Lots of people look a little bit like Max, but only for a couple of seconds. A long wooden boat has come out to meet us. I jump up, shift bags onto shoulders, and am the first down the ladder. A smiling couple and two monks follow.

The breeze is salty. The wooden boat bumps around, undramatically, on the waves. I am scanning the beach, but I can't see him. I leap out in the shallow water, not caring about my leather sandals, and someone passes me my bags. I rush into the first set of huts. I know he won't be here, but I'm going to look everywhere.

He isn't there. I leave my stuff with some smiling Germans and run to the next place, scanning everyone I pass on the way. I peer into hammocks, veer towards the sea to check out the people who are swimming. He isn't there.

At the other set of bungalows, I check out the café. He's not there. I run around. I don't know why it's so urgent; if he's on the island, he won't be leaving till tomorrow. He's not around the huts. I can't look in all of them. I don't know where he is. He might be a couple of metres or five thousand miles away. I start asking people. No one knows what I'm talking about. I go back to the first huts, and sit with the Germans and tell them my garbled story. They are mildly amused, in a kind way, and buy me a fruitshake. I describe him to them. Tall, thin, tanned, handsome, blue-eyed, brown-haired. Probably stubbly.

"Have you seen him?"

"This sounds like me, I think," says a man who, indeed, fits the description but who is emphatically not the man I love. My energy suddenly deserts me. Of course he isn't here. We found this place together. It'd be the last place he would come to. My only hope is the fact that he asked whether I was coming here with Tom, and I said of course I wasn't. That means he could have come here to make voodoo models of me and stick pins in them and throw them out to sea. It doesn't feel like a place for anger.

I book myself a cheap bungalow, for a couple of pounds, and leave my things in it. I locate my cleanest, loveliest clothes. The likelihood of seeing Max today is diminishing, but if it happens, I want to look nice. I must try to look pretty, but sensible. I haven't washed since the morning I left Ko Chang. It didn't even occur to me to have a shower in Krabi. I think it was part of my self-punishment programme. The sand is still sticking to me in places, and I've sweated buckets since I last cleaned myself.

The communal showers are remarkable, in that they have three walls, but no door (a hung-up towel does the job) and no ceiling. They are built from sturdy concrete, which makes the fact that they are missing vital elements all the more surreal. They are situated on the grass by the trees, and open to the deep blue sky.

As I shower in deliciously cold water, I feel that I'm in an art film. I expect a dwarf and a woman in a black hood to come around the corner at any moment.

I see a pair of feet walk past as someone goes into the shower next door. Boy's feet. I must stop thinking everyone is Max. Most boys have feet. His feet have no distinguishing characteristics that I can recall. I scrub at myself a bit more. The shower starts running next door. He has, however, got a pair of sandals like that. So has everyone else. They're normal Reef ones. I wonder whether I could hoist myself up and look over the dividing wall without being noticed, just to check. Probably not. Whoever is in there would misinterpret my action completely. It would be better to time my exit to coincide with his.

He switches his shower off, and I am only half done. Boys know nothing about hygiene. I get shampoo in my eye and grab the corner of my towel to rub it ferociously. As I do so, the bloke from next door is hurrying past with a towel round his waist. I stare at him.

I was right. It wasn't Max.

"Greg?" I ask.

He looks up and gasps. "Holy shit! Tansy! Maybe you could put some clothes on."

"Fuck. Sorry. Look away." I rinse my hair. Then I whip the towel down and wrap myself in it. "You can look. Are you with Max?"

"Why? Are you with your London guy?"

"Christ, no. I'm never seeing him again. Is Max here?"

"Do you want to see Max?"

"Greg, of course I want to see Max. I've spent two days getting here from the Cambodian border because I want to see him. I'm dying to see him. But I don't expect he wants to see me."

"He's too late if he doesn't. Look, ask him yourself."

Greg is looking towards the trees. A figure is coming out of a bungalow which is almost in the woods. He turns back, and locks the door. Then he comes down the couple of stairs, his joints doing their loping, springing thing. Greg waves to catch his attention. He walks towards us. I can't identify the moment when he sees me because his face betrays nothing. When he gets close enough to speak, he looks at me and doesn't smile.

"Wasn't expecting to see you here," he says.

CHAPTER
17

I'm in China, and I'm on my own, and I'm almost enjoying myself. The few westerners I've met have told me knowledgeably that Kunming is an easy part of China in which to start your trip, because it's so close to the Lao border, and it gets the southern sunshine, and the people are friendly. For the first time, I genuinely feel safer among the natives than I do with western fellow travellers. I'd be delighted to talk to western women, if there were any, but they all seem to have been scared off. Even though I know I'm being silly, I am reluctant to risk talking to white men. I feel vulnerable on my own. I don't like hanging out in backpacker places—which, here, means the hotel lobby, or anywhere with an English menu—because I am compelled to glare at all the blokes and cultivate an air of "he's just coming, actually." Occasionally, if they show any interest in talking to me, I might wave to an imaginary friend outside a window, gather up stuff, and disappear. Just to be safe.

I'm scared, and wary. This new one brings the murder tally to five. It happened in Kathmandu and the girl was blonde and Scottish. She had a pink silk scarf in her hand. Just like mine. She'd been strangled, like the others. Just when I thought I'd taken the heat off myself by shimmying through the iron curtain, I find myself surrounded. They say Singapore might have been a "copycat" killing by another demented nutter, but an unimaginative one this time (I am comforted by the idea of an omniscient "they"; in fact, of course, no one knows anything). In other words, there are either two of them on the loose, or one who is extraordinarily clever and elusive.

So far the murders have gone in a straight line from Bombay, the very last planned stop of my trip, via Delhi and Dharamsala, both of which I was planning on visiting, to Singapore, which was to have been my last stop before flying to India. Then, when I changed my plans, someone was killed in Kathmandu. I know these are all exceedingly common destinations, but it's as if he's coming to get me. I know how stupid that is. How solipsistic. I shouldn't see things in terms of how they relate to myself, but that's the way I've always seen everything.

I hate being away from Max, in case he changes his mind about meeting me in Chengdu in three days. It took me so long to win him round that I feel I should be with him, consolidating my position. I worked on him for twenty-two and a half hours on Ko Jum.

I used every method I could think of. I made endless protestations of love, first and foremost. Surely, I thought, no one can chuck away the offer of eternal love without at least giving it a try. I refused to leave him alone. I threatened to stalk him around the world until he gave me a chance. I told him some moss jokes. I threatened to move to Pondicherry and get a job as an English teacher. I reminded him that, without him, I'd be a lone blonde female with a killer on the loose (all is fair in love), and I apologised again and again and again. I was single-minded, and I was not going to give in, however long it took. It was the most important thing I've ever done.

At midday, the next day, he had had enough. "Just leave me for a bit," he ordered. He was flustered by then. I could tell I was getting to him. I gave him ten minutes, and went after him. He was easy to find, staring at his book in a hammock, and rocking himself with his foot. He looked away quickly when he saw me coming, and pretended to be absorbed even though his book was upside down. I knew, then, that I was on the homeward stretch. I squatted next to him, the sand hot between my toes.

"Hey, I mean it," I reminded him. "I really really mean it, I'm never going to let you go again, and you don't have any choice."

He looked at me, sighed, and threw down his book. He swung his feet round. "OK, then. We'll give it another go. Anything for a quiet life. You get one chance." He held up one finger, sternly, but he was smiling. I jumped onto his lap, and the hammock touched the sand with our combined weight. I tried out a kiss, and he kissed me back.

"I will never, ever do anything like that again, so you've really got nothing to worry about."

"Let's just see how we go, shall we?"

Greg was swinging in a nearby hammock, and at the sudden and obvious reinstatement of the status quo, he came bounding over.

"Yay!" he shouted. "Thank God. Now we're all friends again, yeah? I don't have to take sides?"

"You were on my side, I could tell," I told him. "Otherwise you wouldn't have swapped bungalows."

"*Au contraire,* I wasn't on anyone's side. I just wanted to sleep and I quite plainly wasn't going to get any with you around. Unlike my motherland I have always been strictly neutral."

"Well, I don't want to know what the pair of you were saying about me before." They looked at each other and smiled and opened their mouths, and I cut them off. "I said, *I don't want to know,* thank you very much all the same."

"Fair enough," said Max. "You're right, you don't." But then he smiled and squeezed me, and I forbade myself from imagining it.

In no time at all, I began to forget that we hadn't been together all along. Being friends again felt right, and everything else was a

bad dream. The three of us had a large and early lunch, to celebrate. Thai food used to be my favourite in London. It's certainly
my best in Asia. I ordered pad thai, and it was the nicest I've ever
had. I love the crunchy peanuts. I love the tangy lime.

"Do you think they'd mind if I ordered another one?" I wondered aloud when I finished, wiping my mouth with the back of
my hand.

"I'm sure they'd be delighted." I was a bit nervous that Max
seemed so happy. I felt it wasn't natural. His mood was bound to
swing back the other way. Plus he hadn't seen my tattoo yet. I'd
made sure my sarong covered it for the duration of the delicate
negotiations.

"But they'd think I was greedy," I pointed out.

"They would," Greg confirmed, "but do you care?"

"No, I don't." And so I had lunch all over again. The sun was
shining, and I was in my best mood ever.

Greg was cheerful as well. He had met an aristocratic French-
woman named Juliette in Laos, and he was very smitten with her.

Max did his best to throw himself wholeheartedly into our re-
vived relationship. Occasionally I felt Tom's ghostly presence peering over our shoulders, and at other times Max would walk away
on his own and shake me off. I saw how much I'd hurt him, and
how presumptuous it was to come back and expect to pick things
up again. I did everything I could to make things easier. I told
him I loved him, day and night, until he asked me to stop.

"Let's not pressure it," he said.

"Oh. OK."

Most of the time, we were fine. We were even fine when, after
lunch on that first day, I took my sarong off on the beach, and
rolled over onto my stomach.

"Um," I began. "There's something you might notice that's
different about me."

"What the *fuck* is that about?" demanded Max, touching the
tattoo. He said it gently.

"A moment of madness, I suppose. You can see what my state of mind was like."

"You must have been desperate. It looks very odd on you. Are you going to keep it?"

"No. But I'll have to for now. Do you mind?"

"I can live with it. It proves you right, you know. Shows that you really were as crazy and miserable as you say. Shit, it's dreadful. Get rid of it as soon as you can."

Later, in the evening, we went back to the beach and lay still, alone.

"So we'll go to China and meet up with Greg and Juliette?" I asked, looking up at the stars. About a hundred metres away, there was a bonfire. One of the Germans who had been kind to me earlier was playing "American Pie" on a guitar.

"Um, yes, that would be good . . ." he said hesitantly.

"But?"

"I cashed my ticket in. I could see if I can get another one. Tans, I feel really weird about this."

"Where are you going to go, otherwise?"

"To be honest, part of me was hoping you'd come back." He started to falter. "I mean, I know it was a problematic concept, and it wasn't by any means an assumption I was making, but I think that was what made me come here, because I knew you'd guess I was here, and that was what was keeping me here, maybe against my better judgement. I hoped you'd realise how completely and utterly stupid you'd been."

I smiled at his stumbling. He'd cared about me all along. The night was a perfect temperature, and perfectly still, and the sound of the waves and the distant voices floated through the warm air.

"What if I hadn't come back? Or if I hadn't been sorry enough, or begged you enough, or threatened you or whatever it was that did the trick?"

"I was going to get a flight to India. I'd have shown up early. I'm sure they'd have been glad to have me. I would have emailed you when I got there. Even if you'd still been with him, I'd have emailed you to make sure you weren't doing anything stupid. I didn't want the next time I saw you to be on the news."

"I've kind of got over thinking someone's out to get me. Don't you think I was quite brave, coming all the way here on my own?"

"You had no choice, did you? I don't think I'd have felt very good if anything had happened to you on your way to find me. But—"

"I know," I interrupted him. "The chances are so slim."

Back in Krabi, we discovered that my plane to Kunming was full, so Max booked onto the next flight, a week later, and we pooled our money and bought him a connecting flight to Chengdu. I'll get the train tomorrow, and a couple of days after I get there, Max will turn up. I really hope he will, anyway. He never managed to give one hundred percent to our new relationship, like he did before.

We're going to meet at the Traffic Hotel. They really know how to sell things here. I can't wait. All I have to do is to stay alive until then. All I have to do is travel on a Chinese train, by myself, for twenty-one hours. I won Max back, even though it's still tentative. I came to China on my own. I should be able to manage sitting on a train for a day, without too much difficulty.

Tonight, I am going to attempt to eat at a restaurant where the local people go. I've copied the characters for "I'm vegetarian" out of the guidebook, as well as "fried rice and vegetables," and "tofu." I'm going to find an anonymous Chinese restaurant where I can smile around at anyone who fancies gawping at me, and read my book, and fill myself up. I've been so shocked by the fact that I'm in China, and on my own, and that someone is out, if not to get me, then to get someone like me, that I've hardly remembered to eat. This is not an affliction from which I have ever previously suffered. However bad things were at home, I always filled myself up. On the night Mum died, I needed something in my stomach to stop me throwing up (from alcohol, I insisted to myself, rather than anything else). So, after I drank to her good health—her good death—with her own vodka, I left her on the floor and went into the kitchen, to get myself a bowl of crunchy nut cornflakes. I hitched myself onto the Formica worktop, and dangled my legs, and ate as slowly as I could. Perhaps I hoped that, while I was crunching the nuts, she'd pick herself up, take herself to the undertakers, and climb into a coffin. I wanted her to save everyone the bother. I never wanted her to wake up and be alive again. It would have been the last thing I wanted.

Now I'm hungry. Mum has vanished from my head again. She's predictable. I like that. So has Tom, needless to say. It's just me, now, and I'm starving. Intermittently, over the course of the day, my first full day in China, I have had stupid cravings. At one point I found myself imagining a tray of chunky chips drenched in vinegar and coated in salt. I longed for it so much that I could smell it and taste it. Later on, I couldn't get the vision of white toast with butter and honey out of my mind. I bought a mango cornetto this afternoon, a delicacy I have never seen at home. It gave me the sugar boost I needed to get through the confusing streets. I never wanted to come here on my own, but here I am, and I don't mind so much. The key fact, I constantly remind myself, is not that I am alone but that I'm in China. All the people are Chinese. The buildings are grey and communist-style. The air has a different smell. The receptionist at the hotel has a number, rather than her name, on her badge. She is number 025. People look at me as if I were a strange, fascinating and slightly distasteful creature. Then, when I return the gaze, they stare back with equanimity, checking me over.

In some ways it's almost as if I've returned to the west. The girls wear the tiniest of miniskirts, and couples hold hands in the street. That's not like south east Asia. Capitalism is surprisingly rampant. There is advertising everywhere. Every little detail is fascinating. Things you wouldn't normally remark on, at home or in Thailand, make you stop and stare; and stopping and staring is a favourite activity.

I take a deep breath, tell myself to be brave, and walk into the crowded restaurant. The noise of people shouting, scraping plates, and clanking dishes and pots in the kitchen goes down by about three hundred decibels as I stand on the threshold, and all the faces turn to stare at me. I pretend none of this is happening, and look around for a spare seat as if I were in the station café at Waterloo at rush hour, and things were perfectly normal. There is one tiny empty table, across the room. With so many sets of eyes upon me, I am conscious of every little movement I make. I am clumsy, gigantic, ungainly. I can feel the disapproval. I stumble between tables, edge between one seatback and another, and only just avoid walking straight into a waitress, who has stopped, her hands full of dishes, to look at me. I almost feel dizzy. I know I have gone beetroot red. When I reach my destination, I want to take a bow, but I resist the temptation, remembering that I am representing a skin colour, a continent, and an entire economic system. Best behaviour is called for. I am Tansy, the west's Ambassador to the Random Restaurant of Kunming.

The noise starts up slowly when I sit down and it becomes clear that I'm not going to do anything else outrageously interesting. There are still lots of stares, but they begin talking among themselves, probably discussing my gallumph across the room. I wonder whether they think I'm a strange kind of animal. Not quite a human being. More like a performing monkey. I would really like some company, now. I never did meet that female soulmate I used to assume was waiting for me in Asia. I've met a reasonable number of women travelling alone (in the early days, that is, before they were all scared into little groups), but none of them has been at all like me. I wonder whether that's because very few people like I was make the effort to go travelling. If they do, they go with their boyfriends and stay in nice hotels, just like I was going to do. If Tom hadn't bailed out on me, he and I would have sneered our way around Asia, never come to China, and gone back to our affluent lives and the same old jobs. We would have taken back some social cachet, some souvenirs, and nice suntans. I would definitely never have been desperate enough to speak to a man who looked like a Latvian chimpanzee. I would, therefore, have missed out on love.

I feel quite safe, but I still wish I could see the news. If the killer has come to China, then I want to know about it. What if he's already murdered someone? What if he's in Kunming? I tell myself sternly that to go from either Singapore or Kathmandu to southern China would be a huge and illogical leap. Backpackers don't go to China in the same way that they go to Nepal or Malaysia. He'd be hard pushed to find a lone blonde in China. In fact, I could be the only one. It's far more likely that he's gone back to India, or stayed in Nepal, or vanished, undetected, forever. Perhaps he's even been caught.

I realise that this has been the hopeful refrain of everyone I've spoken to over the past few months. "He's probably been caught," we always say. "Maybe he's died." The truth is, he almost certainly hasn't been caught. He's almost certainly alive, and hunting.

The waitress comes to my table, and smiles warily. She's about seventeen. I have the pieces of paper in my hand, in an attempt to avoid further entertaining the proletariat by searching my handbag when I should be ordering food. I hold out the first one to her. I'm vegetarian. She takes it and studies it, her head on one side. She holds it further away from herself, then brings it in close. She nods. Then I give her the follow-up sheet. Fried rice with vegetables and tofu, please. She understands this one almost at once, and laughs and nods. Unable to contain his curiosity a moment longer, an old man in a Mao suit gets up from a nearby table and peers over her shoulder. He, too, studies my efforts hard. Then he turns to the rest of the diners and announces something in Chinese. There is a small buzz. I hope he's just told them what I'm going to eat, rather than commented on the quality of my calligraphy. I smile tensely at him. He beams back. His face is lined and he looks a hundred and three.

"No speak Chinese?" he says.

I shake my head.

He points to himself. "No speak English!"

We smile at each other's hopelessness, and he takes his seat. This man must have witnessed the foundation of the People's Republic of China, the Great Leap Forward, the Cultural Revolution, the Tiananmen massacre, and everything that happened in between. He was born around the time of the fall of the Qing dynasty (a little later unless he really is as old as he looks), and now he's ending his days in a communist country that is shakily embracing capitalism. I try to imagine his life, but I can't. I can't even imagine his house, or where he will go from the restaurant, or what he does all day long. And I don't expect he can imagine mine, if it would occur to him to try.

While I eat, the waitress sits opposite me. She has decided that this is a good moment for her to learn the English language, and I cannot fault her enthusiasm. As soon as I realise what she wants, I get out my phrasebook. She gasps with delight and flicks through it. Soon, she is pointing to a phrase. What is your name?

"My name is Tansy," I tell her as clearly as I can through a mouthful of vegetables. Fried rice with vegetables appears to mean fried rice with a few green bits in. I'm glad I can use chopsticks with the minimum level of skill, or I really would be a laughing stock.

"My name is Tansy," she repeats. "My name is Tansy."

"No," I say, realising that I've answered the question, when she just wanted to know how to say it. "What is your name?" I say.

"My name is Tansy," she answers.

"No, *my* name is Tansy. Never mind. What is your name?"

"What is your name?"

"That's right. Very good. And what is your name?" I try to

convey that I am actually asking her, by an exaggerated raising of my eyebrows and pointing at her.

She understands. "Cheng," she says.

"My name is Cheng," I say slowly, and gesture to her.

"My name is Cheng," she repeats, then she gestures to me.

"My name is Tansy," I tell her. She understands. "Hello, Cheng," I say.

"Hello, Tansy?" She is hesitant.

"Yes!" We are both delighted. I make her teach me the same in Chinese.

"Wo xing Tansy," I falter. She applauds, as do the people at the next table.

I realise I am missing something, so I take the phrasebook and flick to a different section. I show her the phrase, "One beer, please."

"Yi pijiu," I stutter. She thinks this is the best joke she's ever heard, tells someone nearby, and dashes off to the kitchen. No one seems to mind her laxness in taking their orders. I think they'd all be up close and staring if they were in her place.

CHAPTER
18

From: Amanda
To: Tansy
Subject: heading north

hi Tansy, how are you? and where? I've left the ashram and have just arrived in Delhi and am having a brilliant time. I feel so much calmer and happier than when I left, because the ashram was fab, exactly what I needed. Maggie and I are travelling with a bloke we met there, Pierre, so that's ideal as we now feel safe. now, do reassure me that what Tom's saying about you isn't true. I know it isn't, but I am a little concerned. I must check. the version I heard ended up with you sailing away saying you were going to find Max. this seems encouraging. he sounds a darling. Tom is spitting chips. apparently he's claiming you've completely flipped. I don't think anyone would buy that one (but what is all this about a vodka tattoo? he's making it up, yes?). game set and match to you, my dear. however, do confirm that my interpretation is correct. thanks.

India continues to be tiring and exciting in equal measures. Delhi is big, hot and smelly, and a humungous culture shock after all the peace and quiet of the past month. we're staying in a little guesthouse off Connaught Place, in the centre, and are sharing our room with a mouse. the heat and the stench are extraordinary. clouds of pollution, and hordes of men trying to sell us holidays in Kashmir. now, I may not be an experienced traveller, but even I know better than that. tomorrow we're going to Agra to see the Taj Mahal. someone at our guesthouse told us cafes in agra poison you to make you stay longer. ho hum.

I seem to have got over the worst of the traumas, thanks to one month of daily meditation (as opposed to daily medication, which did the job before). thank goodness, it wasn't one of those dodgy ashrams—when I say the word people seem to think I was having tantric sex with a scheming guru, but it wasn't like that at all. It was just very peaceful, very calming. I had a few emails from Paul. he's completely baffled by me. one day, in his eyes, we were a happily married couple, comfortably off and with lots of friends, and the next I tell him I'm pregnant and burst into tears, which he writes off as a) tears of joy and b) hormonal and he is delighted, and then the week after that I have a miscarriage and feel nothing but huge relief, like I must have done something good in my past life after all. and then I leave him and go travelling with Mags, emulating my good friend Tans. poor guy is in a hell of a state. It's not quite fair but he partly blames you. for being my inspiration.

but a guy at the ashram told me that if all my instincts were against the pregnancy it was because the baby wasn't ready to come into the world yet, and because I wasn't destined to be a mother, perhaps yet, and perhaps ever. he seemed very certain that nature, or god, or the plural gods, or whoever, were looking after me. and I do find that a comfort. I think I had a narrow escape. imagine having a baby and no instincts to look after it.

so, where are we meeting, and when? I can't wait to see you. our plan is, when we get back from Agra in a few days, to go to Nepal and do some trekking, and escape the heat. we're going to the Langtang Valley, right up by the Tibetan border. then we'll come back to India—I like the idea of the monsoon. When do you think you'll arrive in Kathmandu? perhaps we'll coincide after our trek? keep in touch, anyway.

take care. obviously stay away from strange men, as I will. is all that still going on? I'd forgotten about it until now. with any luck he's dead of malaria or given up on it all. I'm so out of date. looking forward to seeing you more than I can say.

Big kisses

Amanda XXXX

To: Tansy
From: Kate
Subject: are you ok?

darling, are you all right? I don't know what to think, as have had tom on the phone 3 times sounding off about you. He says you're having a nervous breakdown, and while on the one hand it could be his injured pride talking, on the other I thought I should check up on you as I haven't heard from you for a while. please tell what happened. He says you took him to an incredibly remote place, where you got some kind of bizarre tattoo, and then you ran away laughing, saying you were getting your revenge on him for not going travelling with you. given your previous emails this seems unlikely, but I'm so far away I don't know. he also claims to have had sex with five different women after you left him (including one from the faroe islands!!), but this could be more information than you need to know.

I take it, anyway, that you decided Max was a better option. are you with him, or was it too late? update, please. come to that, which country are you in?

I was so upset about the murder in singapore. that's really near where you are, I think. and then the other one in nepal. it all seems to be dangerous. am trying to remember how far singapore/nepal feature in your plans. typical of you not to go travelling like normal people do but to put your friends through these kind of horrors. I don't think I'm going to have a proper night's sleep till I've met you at the airport.

it's nice and sunny here, for once, and the days are long again which is always cheering. After work today we sat outside the eagle, and emma (who's new since you were here, and has to fill the "friend" spot in my working life) and I thought we'd have just one glass of wine before we went home, then we decided that if we were going to struggle all the way to the bar it might as well be a bottle, and then before we knew it it was 11:20 and we'd had four bottles and nothing to eat, and we were being thrown out. It's hardly worth going home, some days.

must go as loads to do, but please write back as soon as you get this, just so I know for sure you're ok. and where you are.

much love

K xxx

From: Roger Harris
To: Tansy Harris
Subject: Message from Internet

TANSY

HOPE ALL IS WELL WITH YOU. WE ARE FINE. WEATHER IS GOOD. WE CONTINUE TO WORRY ABOUT YOUR SAFETY AND REITERATE THAT YOU SHOULD CONSIDER COMING HOME. YOU HAVE PLENTY OF TIME LEFT FOR TRAVELLING IN YOUR LIFE AND CAN GO AWAY AGAIN ONCE THE MURDERER HAS BEEN CAUGHT.

RE: YOUR BOX. WAS UNABLE TO LOCATE THE ONE YOU DESCRIBE. IS IT URGENT? JESSICA AND I DID A THOROUGH SEARCH. PERHAPS IT IS IN SOHO.

KEEP US UP TO DATE WITH YOUR MOVEMENTS.

LOVE, DAD

Hello tansy this is jessica. are you in tieland? I had to do a talk at
school the other day and so I took the antlas and did a talk about the
places where you are travelling too. me and mummy drew it on in red
pencil crayon and mrs. garrett said it was very good. daddy says you
will come home soon. will you bring presents. I hope so. do you like
cristina.

You and me are better at emale than daddy arent we, because he
does it LIKE THIS.

with love from jessXXX

To: Tansy
From: Max
Subject: where's my posh chick?

honey, you'll probably be in chengdu by the time you get this, and that
means i'll be on my way. can't wait to see you. Just wanted to
reassure you that I am NOT going to change my mind, because I
know the thought will have occurred to you. I'm glad we're back
together, I really am. If I seem a little distant sometimes, it's because
it's all been such a shock. Also I don't know about the future. We must
talk about southern India & other plans.

Am at the shanti lodge whiling away the days till my flight. They're all
asking after you. they were concerned that last time they saw you you
were miserable. I reassure them that you are sad no longer. see you
at the traffic hotel. look after yourself and speak to no men
whatsoever, on safety grounds and for my sake.

Lots of love, me x

To: Tansy
From: Will
Subject: where are you?

Hi there, Tans

Haven't heard from you in a while—how are you doing? And which exotic country are you in now? Lucky old you. Mind you even in Edinburgh it is now warmer than it was, which is pleasant. Did you change your plans in the light of what has happened? I've always thought China would be a fascinating place to visit and if you are there or are going there (or have been there) please tell me all about what it is like. Not to mention Tibet. Give my love to the Dalai Lama!

I have booked two weeks off work in the summer, and I think I will probably see if I can find a cheap flight to somewhere in Europe for me and Mary, who is my girlfriend. I have not told you about her before, because I didn't want to rush things. But now I can say that she is very friendly and kind and I think you will like her. She works in the same office as me and we have had an "office romance" which I never thought would happen to me in my life!!! So far it has lasted 7 weeks and 3 days. The other day we were having a little argument, nothing serious, and I called her "Bloody Mary"! Then I remembered that it was what you like to drink so it made me laugh and she asked what I was laughing at, so I told her and she laughed too. With your help the situation was resolved! So I owe you some thanks I think.

Make sure you are safe. Look after yourself, sis, and stay in touch with E-mails which are a wonderful thing you must agree.

Love from your big brother, William x

From: Tom
To: Tansy
Subject: [none]

I feel sorry for you more than anything else. Had a great time after you went, anyway.

To: tansy
From: aaontour@excite.com
Subject: china girl

hi lans, you and max must be in chengdu by now. it was great to see you in krabi. we couldn't believe it when we ran into you on the street like that—and we were on our way to the email place, to see if you were around! I am so glad you stopped me talking when you did—I would never have recognised max as the hairy guy in saigon. I just assumed it was your bloke from home. and I was just about to say so. thanks for jumping in.

your reunion sounded so romantic. good on you, girl, he's great. and handsome! what a story to tell your children. he's obviously much nicer than your london bloke.

andy says I must say we were "well chuffed" to meet up again. he's got heaps of english phrases on the go now and he uses them all the time. we will have to come over and visit you so he can see if he can blag his way as an englishman this time.

guess where we are? kunming! we really would be stoked to come to tibet with you—we talked about it and decided it's the best thing for us to do right now. we will turn up in chengdu before long and hook up with you there. so we're not far behind you. be careful and have heaps of fun.

"cheers" as you would say.

ally

To: Tansy
From: Stuart Higgins
Subject: worried about you

Hi tans, it's from me really, Guy. Remember me? Sorry, I haven't been very good at keeping in touch. I just wanted to drop you a quick line to say that tom told me about your illness and I'm really sorry to hear it. It's nothing to be ashamed of—mental illness is no different from physical illness—and you really must get some help. I remember before you left you didn't know whether you could travel on your own. Now perhaps your question has been answered. So promise me you'll see a doctor wherever you are, or better still come home? Go on. You'll feel so much better. Being violent towards your friends when they're trying to help you really is a problem (don't worry, tom told me everything, and I don't think any the less of you) you must also see that mutilating yourself is a signal of your troubled soul.

Life here is the same as ever. Soho busy. Lots of drunks bumbling around. Your bedroom is empty, so there's always a place for you. I chucked Mo out after she took a load of my clothes to oxfam without asking on the grounds that they were so crappy she assumed I couldn't object. Grrrrrr.

Chin up, and come home soon. You have plenty of friends to look after you. Maybe not tom, but all the rest of us will help however we can.

Love, guy xxxx

From: Tansy
To: Max
Subject: I'm waiting!

hey there, I'm writing this in the "business centre" at the traffic hotel. the hotel is perfectly nice and warm and cosy and has barely any traffic passing as it's right by the river. god knows where they plucked the name from. I'm staying in a dorm until you get here, but I've already got us a double room booked for then. for now I'm sharing with two women, both friendly.

got here this morning, after a 21 hour train journey. It was crazy! I got a taxi to kunming station, after getting the hotel receptionist (no. 018: don't you love communism) to write "station" down for me. I was a million years early, so sat around on my bag for a while and allowed passing folk to have a good look. then I started asking where the train was, but no one would tell me. at the info desk they shooed me away to the ticket hall, but at the ticket hall they waved me back to information. I had visions of me returning to the hotel and never being able to leave kunming because no one would tell me where to catch the bloody train. finally with about 15 minutes before it left, I went to a ticket gate which was closed and showed my ticket to a man in uniform, who reluctantly gestured towards a darkened corner. they x-rayed my bag and let me through, but was only allowed to get on the train at the correct door for my carriage. I located the carriage with 4 minutes to go. hauled myself on, and wished I was chinese because then at least I wouldn't get the staring brigade all the time. you know what it's like.

I read my book for most of the journey, didn't see another westerner, and made it with no mishaps at all. The taxi man at the other end even understood my shaky "traffic hotel" hieroglyphics and brought me here: I had a sudden fear I might have written something that looks similar but has entirely different meaning, eg "sell me to a brothel please."

chengdu seems interesting: not exactly stunning. hired a bike this afternoon and saw some sights. going to try to cycle to a vegetarian buddhist monastery tomorrow. can't wait to see you, I'll be the one waiting in the foyer.

hugs, kisses and love forever.

Tans xxxx

ps ally and andy decided to join us! they're on their way. will probably get here just after you.

To: Kate
From: Tansy
Subject: greetings from china

hi my darling, guess where I am? china. ie very far from singapore
and nepal. and guess what else? Tom was making it up (er, except for
the tattoo. I was feeling crazy, and it's only small, and I'll get it lasered
off as soon as I'm back in the 1st world . . .) I'm fine. in fact I'm
overwhelmingly happy. had a horrible time with him, entirely my own
fault I realise, for labouring under the weird belief that he, and not
max, was the one for me. but I ran away and located max again, and
won him round eventually. since then, things have got better and
better. I'm kind of on my guard at the moment, as I'm on my own till
the day after tomorrow when max will get here, but have found a few
other lone women sheltering at this hotel in chengdu, which is kind of
in the middle of china depending whether you count tibet or not. I
think not. it's a big town full of massive grey buildings. there's a mao
statue in the square up the road which is the main landmark. china's
so different I wouldn't know where to begin. In fact I can't begin. every
single thing is different, but some things are kind of familiar. so you get
lulled by the big adverts everywhere, and coca-cola in every shop,
and even kentucky fried chicken apparently though I've yet to see one.
and then something so strange will happen to shock you. I went out
on a bike this afternoon—I hired a big rattly black one from the hotel.
the entire cycle traffic, which is enlightenedly on separate roads to the
cars most of the time, is controlled by women with whistles. they are
petrifying. they tell you when you can go and when you can't, and I
watched a man commit a minor offence like cycle over the line and a
woman marched straight up to him and fined him. aarrgggh. who
knows what infringements I've been accidentally committing? I live in
terror. then I got lost, and kept cycling around in the hope that sooner
or later I'd turn up back at mao. I asked one of the scary women the
way, but she wouldn't speak to me (asking the way consists of looking
around helplessly and saying "mao?"). she acted as if I wasn't there,
just like you would if a nutter came up to you on the tube, smelling of
booze. so I found him on my own, in the end. I've never been so glad

to see anyone in my life. all is strange. I'm not talking to western men at all, just in case.

take care, and keep writing. we should be flying to tibet later in the week, but apparently there's even email in lhasa (what a travesty) so will mail you when I get there.

tons of love

T xxx

From: Tansy
To: Tom
Subject: yeah, right

glad you had fun. me too.

have a nice life.

ps 5 people is impressive, but remember not to spread yourself too thinly or you won't be "special" anymore.

From: Tansy
To: William
Subject: china

hi William, I'm in china! I haven't got over the novelty of it yet. you must come here one day, it's absolutely amazing. I never realised how fascinating I was until I came here. now I know I am the most interesting girl in the whole wide world & have been stared at very much indeed.

I'm in a place called chengdu, a big city with lots of concrete in it. the only reason to come here really, rather than anywhere else in china, is because it's the only place with flights to tibet. Max and I made friends again and he's coming to join me tomorrow, which is excellent. our 2 friends, ally and andy, are coming too. I'm off to book our flights now. you nominally have to be part of an organised tour to go to tibet, but we're hoping it won't be too organised and we'll be able to do our own thing a bit.

from there we'll go overland to kathmandu, stopping at everest base camp on the way (I'm extremely excited about that), and I will never leave max's side in case there's a killer lurking. I must admit to being a bit scared by the whole thing, particularly now he seems to be in nepal after all, and that's exactly where we're headed. when all of this started, it seemed like an interesting diversion that had nothing to do with me, and now here I am heading into the danger zone. also, all those objects—I don't know how closely you've read the news reports, but there was always an object with the body—were just like things that I had. they're all in a box together at home, and now dad can't find it. clearly it's a coincidence, and I am obviously going mad but am feeling v. uncomfortable and paranoid. I think it's to do with all the other working out of things that I've been doing while I've been travelling. I'll talk to you about it all when I see you.

meanwhile, the sooner max gets here the better. you see, first you discover that your mother's an alcoholic, and then it turns out your sister's a ranting lunatic.

talking of mum, I'm sorry I was so dismissive all the times you tried to ask me about her. when I get back we'll talk about her properly. I've only realised in the past few months how hard it is coming to terms with a death like that. we're all that's left of her.

fantastic news about mary. good work, bro. can't wait to meet her, and for you to meet max.

much love

Tansy x

From: Tansy
To: Roger Harris
Subject: message for jess

hi jessie

thanks for your email. lovely to hear from you. I'm flattered that you did your talk about my travelling. now you know where I've been on the map. I have a new place for you to put on: China. it's very, very different from england, as the political system is called communism, which means everyone is meant to have the same amount of money (but it doesn't work out quite like it's meant to). also, the people here are only allowed to have one child. all the babies are very fat, fatter than archie, because they get all the attention. they're always dressed in lovely new clothes because there are no other children needing things. I think they must be quite lonely.

I don't even know who cristina is! sorry to be so useless. I expect I like her.

I won't be back very soon, but when I am I will definitely bring presents.

lots of love

tansy xxx

PS dad: I'm not coming back just yet. I'll be fine and will keep in touch, promise.

To: Amanda
From: Tansy
Subject: kathmandu rendezvous

hi there, you sound great. so glad it's all working out for you. I would never have imagined that out of everybody I knew, you'd be the one going to the ashram to find yourself. we must definitely meet up in nepal and compare notes. I can't wait to see the new you.

have to dash now because people waiting for me to go out to dinner. am in china by the way. make sure you stick with people at all times. you do know that someone else got killed in nepal, don't you? but you'll be fine with Maggie and Pierre. see you in a few weeks!

masses of love

T xxx

ps in a moment of madness I did get a tattoo. will show you when i see you.

CHAPTER
19

"You know what this is?" says Andy, eventually. "Pants. As the English would say." Andy's grasp of what the English would say is perhaps not always as firm as he likes to think.

We all put down our chopsticks.

"You are so right," Max admits.

"Disgusting," I agree. "What are we going to do?"

"I can't eat this crap anymore. Does anyone want to get anything else?"

"You kind of lose your appetite." I'm not hungry at all now. I feel sick. I can't believe I've eaten so much, when it tastes of shit.

"Shall we just have another beer and savour the atmosphere?" asks Max. I look around, and am startled, as usual, by the difference in Ally's appearance. She's always startled, too, at the change in mine. Brown hair suits us both. We tell each other so several times a day, but I don't think we're convinced yet.

There is an atmosphere of sorts—not least, there is an atmosphere between Ally and Andy—but, on balance, I'd rather savour our hotel room. We are sitting in an alley off a Chengdu back street, on red plastic stools. These are almost the right size for Ally and Andy, but they barely come past my ankles when I'm standing up. My knees, and Max's knees, are so hunched up that we have to lean around or between them to eat. We've been optimistically trying to devour a "Chengdu hotpot" which is, apparently, a famous delicacy. On the little table in front of us is a pot divided into two sections, over a bunsen burner. In one section is warm, heavy meat fat, and in the other is warm, heavy chilli oil. On a plate nearby we have various pieces of raw meat and vegetables on sticks, ready to be held in the fat or oil until cooked, like a foul fondue. We really wanted to like it.

Max calls the waiter over and asks for more beers. The beers are huge and cheap, and we are well on the way to drunkenness. I don't mind. I have proved to myself I can do without it. As people finish their meals, with no obvious expression of disgust, the tables and chairs are taken away. Thus, while we began the evening in a sea of people, we are now virtually stranded in the alley having a perverse night-time picnic.

Three chubby children are playing nearby, daring each other to come closer to us. A family of rats is doing something oddly similar. The oldest and biggest child, a girl of about nine, finally runs up and says, "Hello," and runs away to a safe distance to watch our reactions. Six human and eight rat eyes are upon us. Max jumps to his feet and goes to talk to the children, who look both thrilled and scared. They are all immaculately dressed. Each of them, no doubt, is a cosseted only child.

Now I've got Max back, my moods veer between absolute happiness and vague terror. Max is being almost completely like he used to be now, so happiness usually wins out in the end. The only source of tension between us is the question of what to do when we get to Pondicherry. Max wants me to stay there. He says we can't have a relationship unless I do, because he won't go back to Britain. The trouble is, I've only been away for four months, but I know that, sooner or later, I'll want to go home. I don't want to be forced to live in India. We avoid the issue, most of the time.

I can summon London if I concentrate really hard. It makes me dizzy, and I'm sure the beer doesn't help in that department. It's a weekday. It's about 2 p.m. at home. I try to dredge up a clear picture of the *Herald* newsroom, and eventually it all comes back. The water coolers, the fax machine, the big plants, the lack of natural light. I strike Amanda from my picture and replace her with a stranger called Emma. I then transport the Amanda figure to India, dress her in white robes, and place her in the lotus position at the feet of a kindly guru. Then I move her to a dirty, mouse-infested bedroom in Delhi. I can believe in that. I cannot, however, make myself believe that the newsroom is actually there, and functioning, now. Hundreds of people are working there at this very moment, getting excited about some story or other, rewriting agency copy, or making arrangements for dinner. All of those usual things are happening now, in the very same minute in which I'm sitting between Max and Ally and waving reassuringly at the children. I used to belong in the other world. I'm not really sure how I ended up in this one. I'm not sure how anyone does.

The only thing here that I would change—apart from the foul food, of course, and the fact that people like me keep getting killed—is the way things are between Ally and Andy. Neither of them has said what's wrong, but I can't bear the look in her eyes. I hope it's an external event, rather than the agony of a relationship going wrong.

They've been with me, in the flesh or electronically, for the whole time I've been in Asia. When Max and I bumped into them in Krabi, they happily accepted the fact that I was not with Tom but with the hairy man we'd met in Saigon. I interrupted Ally when I realised she hadn't recognised him.

"Hi," she smiled. "You must be—"

"You remember Max," I said loudly, before she uttered the word "Tom." We were all relieved.

They've looked after me when I needed it, they came away with me for the anniversary, and now they're coming to Tibet with us. I was delighted at their appearance at our hotel. They're like my funny little parents. I want to stamp my feet and tell them to be happy. They have to be happy. I am. It's not fair.

When they arrived, I had just stormed away from an argument with the woman in the tour office about when we could fly to Tibet.

"It seems impossible to get anything done round here," I complained when the greetings were over. "I know they don't particularly want us in Tibet, but you'd think that, since we'd got this far, they'd relent. I tried to book us on tomorrow's flight, but she wouldn't let us go. First of all she said it would be fine, and then when I went back with all the money, she pretended she'd never said that. I tried all the other agencies but they all said the same thing."

"What was their excuse?" Andy shifted from foot to foot. He didn't have his usual upbeat energy.

"Fog in Lhasa."

Ally smiled. "You can't argue with fog in Lhasa."

"So I discovered."

We're all going on Monday, the day after tomorrow. Meanwhile, Ally and Andy are trying very hard to give the impression of being the happy, comfortable couple they always were.

The day they got here, Ally knocked on the door and came into our bedroom. "Forgot!' she chirped. "I got you a present!" She handed me a plastic bag.

"Why?"

"Can't I get you a present if I want to? Look in the bag, you'll like it. Maybe we can try it out."

I opened the bag, unable to imagine what it might be. Backpackers don't buy presents for each other. I'm sure they don't. Inside, there was a heavy cardboard box with a picture of a white woman with glossy chestnut hair on it.

"Is it hair dye?"

She leaped on the bed beside me. "Yes! Isn't it great? We can dye our hair brown, and then we'll be safe! Because every single woman who's been murdered has been blonde."

"They've all been English too. You don't need to change your lovely hair. Yours is almost white. It'd be a shame."

"Bugger that. Come on." She set off, extra-cheerily, for the bathroom. I hung back, and she turned round.

"Ally? Is everything OK?"

"Course," she said breezily. She was too cheerful. I knew at once that it wasn't. She hesitated, about to say something else, but at that moment Max came in, and the moment was lost. Still, we laughed at ourselves as brunettes. I feel like a sexy librarian, with an air of mystery that a blonde will never attain. I should be safe now. I finish off my new look with a shiny pink hairclip. It is an immense relief.

Now that we have decided not to eat the hotpot, I am amazed at the amount we consumed before we gave up. The guidebooks gave it such a tasty write-up that we were all expecting to like it, and ploughed on hopefully, assuming the others were enjoying it, until Andy stated the obvious. No doubt if you ordered it in a posh restaurant or a hotel, it might be edible. But this street houses at least ten hotpot restaurants, which means there must be a brisk trade in the crappy version.

"Do you think it's a cultural difference?" I ask.

"What?"

"They like hotpot and we don't."

"I like Lancashire hotpot," corrects Max.

"Yes," I agree, "but we are not talking about Lancashire hotpot."

"We can manage most Chinese food," muses Ally. "I think we're just unlucky. But it is strange, isn't it, that Szechuan food is so famous, and here we are in the middle of the capital of the Szechuan province, and their food is so vile that it would make us ill if we ate another mouthful."

"It makes me realise," I say, "how good the food has been on this trip so far. It's been wonderful, until now."

"Just wait till you get to India," Max promises. "You'll be in heaven. Mmm. A vegetarian in Pondicherry. Have you got a treat in store or what?"

I remember how the main thing I wanted from travelling was a soulmate. It turns out that the best girlfriend I've made on the trip has been the very first person I spoke to when I arrived. I dismissed her out of hand as a possible friend, because she was Australian, she was short and bespectacled, and she didn't know that Ghost was a shop. Perhaps optimistically, I picture Ally and Andy coming to Britain to visit us, years from now. Ally and I will go for a girls' night out. We sit elegantly in a bar, sipping, in the most restrained and controlled manner imaginable, from glasses of red wine. We're older, more sophisticated, and I'm thinner. We are lifelong friends, like women in a schmaltzy Hollywood movie.

"How did you ladies meet?" someone (the barman?) asks us.

"We met in Vietnam," one of us explains. "Then we travelled in Asia with our boyfriends."

We laugh together and reminisce. We tell him about this very evening, with the hotpots and the rats. Then, I suppose, we take a taxi home from this imaginary bar to a little house (its location hazy) where I live with Max.

We, too, have a good story. We met in Vietnam, and then we met all over again, in Laos. The Max part of the reverie is less straightforward than the Ally part. To get to the cottage stage of our relationship, we have to navigate the medium-term future. I scrutinise the people in my daydream. Do they look like they lived in Pondicherry for a few years, teaching English and becoming the sort of people who spend lots of time in India? Or did we re-enter the industrialised west?

I do want to go home, I realise. I want to ground myself, remind myself that I have a base. I want to see my friends, and my brother. I can't just go and live in India. I need to go back to where I came from first. There's no reason, however, why I should stay in London. I haven't even been to India. How can I tell whether I want to spend years there, with Max? I couldn't even teach. I'd be mean to everyone and make them cry.

I thought that once we were back together again, we'd be fine.

I didn't realise it was going to be difficult. I never thought I'd have to compromise.

The others are looking at me.

"You OK?" says Andy. He has never stopped being protective of me, since he upset me in Apocalypse Now.

"Yes. Of course." I smile at Max. We'll have to work it out, somehow. The most important thing is that I must have my Max, forever.

"Were you listening?" Max asks. "Do you think we should get some biscuits?"

"What? Biscuits? Mmm, yes. Do you think they have them?" If I went out to visit Max in the south of India, I could stay for as long as I wanted. We could take it as it came and it would soon be obvious where I wanted to be.

"No." Ally looks at Max, a "what can we do with her?" look. "We were saying, one of us should go down to the shop there."

"Get some materials for soaking up this beer," Andy clarifies.

I stand up. "I'll go. I want to go to the loo anyway."

Ally jumps up. "Me too."

I stretch my legs as much as I can while I walk, to try to relieve them of the aches from the past hour's crouching. I'm happy to be here. I'm not scared anymore, because I've got a boyfriend and mates, and I came to China on my own. I changed my appearance. I can visualise a future in which, whatever happens, I will be all right. We have even got someone to visit in Lhasa (admittedly, it's someone his own mate declares to be "really quite weird"). At last, I am getting over my madness.

When Max arrived, I was overwhelmed with relief. Finally, I felt that I had earned him. I'd been sitting in the foyer for hours, reading a borrowed copy of *Midnight's Children* and looking up hopefully every few minutes. Mentally, I was moving on from "his plane must have been delayed" and "he must have got in trouble with customs," to "I knew he wouldn't come." I was wondering what I'd do without him. Go anyway, with the others. Go sadly. Be mournful in Tibet. I wouldn't be the only one.

Then, suddenly, he was in front of me, looking as handsome and as kind and as sexy as he'd ever done. He stared at me, grinning. His hair was beginning to go springy again, but he'd shaved that morning, just for me. I leapt up, and he lifted me off the ground and swirled me round, just like the couple at Bangkok airport. Max was in China, we were in our fourth country together, and yet we've never been home.

"Ally," I say, looking down at her as we walk to the toilets. "Tell me what's wrong."

She stops pretending to be fine and shakes her head. Her shoulders droop a little. "You don't want to know. I don't really want to talk about it at the moment."

"You'll feel better if you do. Take it from an expert."

"It's nothing that bad. Promise. I'll be fine."

"And Andy?"

"Oh, he'll be fine for sure. I will tell you. Later. Can we talk about something else?"

I give up.

I wonder what I would have made of the loos here if China had been my first port of call. It's bad enough as it is, and I am extremely hardened to the Asian squat toilet. I even prefer them, now, to western ones, because no part of you has to touch a hole in the ground. Communal weeing, however, is a facet of communism that I wouldn't seek to bring back to the west.

The building is tiled, inside and out, with white. We walk, giggling, past a glaring attendant, give her a couple of notes, and each choose a secluded corner. I straddle the stream between two tiled posts. I'm wearing my jeans, fake CK ones that I bought in Bangkok. I don't feel so glamorous with them round my ankles. The trouble is, I don't mind getting on with it and having a piss, and Ally and I have certainly lost all inhibitions with each other, but the staring brigade have a field day if they see me in the loos.

They call each other over. They want to see if I wee like them, I suppose. To check whether I have the same bits. It's the same in the showers, except that observers there have the unexpected benefit of noticing my tattoo. They love that. I must get rid of it as soon as I get home.

Luckily the hotel has proper loos with doors on, so there's no need for me to join in with communal shitting. As I am rejoicing at this happy fact, a poo floats merrily past, below me, on the stream that runs round the room.

The street is dark and the restaurants are beginning to close as we walk back to the boys, arm in arm. A lone man walks past, and says "Hello" when he is too nearly gone for us to reply. A few shopkeepers look in our direction. I steer Ally into the corner shop, feeling extra clumsy because of the beer. The proprietor looks alarmed. I pick up a packet of biscuits with cartoon cows grazing on the side, and offer him a sizeable note. He smiles, relieved, and gives me a massive amount of change. I mumble an approximation of the word for thank you—*sheshe*—and we are gone.

I'm glad that, even with my brown hair, I look weird to them. At least no one expects me to understand. It's touching that people are pleasantly surprised that I am familiar with the basic mechanics of shopping. Their expectations must be low indeed.

We return with the biscuits, and cram as many into our mouths as we can. The inedible hotpot has been taken away, and more beer has arrived. Max is running up and down the alley with the children, making them shriek. Andy has pushed his stool up against the wall and is beginning to snore. The young waiter is hovering. We offer the biscuits to him, and to the children (could you do that at home? I wonder. Reject a restaurant's fare, buy junk instead, and share it with the staff?) and decide that it's time to go. The fat girl's parents materialise, looking horrified to see her playing with westerners. They appear just as she is accepting a biscuit. Her mother says something sharp to her, and she turns back to me.

"Sank you," she says.

"You're welcome," I tell her, and then I turn to the parents, who are well dressed, young, and affluent looking. "She's very clever," I tell them. Her mother, again, says something sharp to her, and once again the girl turns to address me.

"Sank you," she says again.

I can't think of anything else to say, so I repeat that she is welcome, and nudge Ally. "Time to get the bill?"

We look at Andy. He looks as though he could happily spend the entire night there, upright, on his little stool. A rat runs over his foot, and the fat girl looks longingly at it, desperate to chase it away, but her mother takes her hand and leads her off. She leaves us backwards, waving. She is dressed, from head to toe, in pink. From her hairclips to her shoelaces, all is fuchsia. She doesn't seem like a girl who would appreciate that but, looking at her mother, I can see she has no choice.

On the way back to the hotel, Max leans on me and hiccups. Together, we swerve around the pavement. We stumble and laugh. Andy and Ally have a little distance between them but they are both staggering. I try to see whether they're talking.

"Don't," says Max. "Up to them."

"Hey, I decided something," I tell him. "Would this work? What if I went home for a while and then came out to India, and we took it from there?"

"Serious?"

I nod.

"We'll think about it. How long would you go home for? Would you turn back into the cokehead London girl?"

"No I fucking would not. If you despised me that much, why did we get together in the first place?"

"I'm not always sure."

I look at him. The corners of his mouth are twitching a little. He's laughing at me. That's annoying.

*   *   *

228

I wake up with a strange feeling. This is my first hangover since I left Tom. My head thumps. My mouth has been wallpapered in rough mucus. I can barely move. My stomach is churning. Surely I must be ill. It can only be the hotpot. I snuggle further into Max's arms, and catch a faceful of his morning breath. I realise mine must smell the same. I'm thirsty, and I need a piss. Mainly, I'm thirsty. I lie still for fifteen minutes, trying to force the need for more sleep to subsume the thirst. It doesn't work. Wearily, I roll out of bed.

"Hmnnnh?" says Max.

"Nothing, honey," I tell him, stroking his hair. It pings up in between my fingers. Did we argue again last night? My head is really bad now. I put on his T-shirt and my jeans, and head for the bathroom.

I examine myself in the mirror. As ever, my non-blondeness is surprising. I am distressed to note that I look every bit as bad as I feel. Knotted inky hair is sticking up all over the place, in every direction at once. Sparrows could raise families in there. The skin around my eyes is so puffy that I can barely squint out. The red blotches on my face are masked by my tan, but I know they're there in spirit. I shake my head, and my brain rattles.

I used to wake up like this every morning, and I used to call it fun, and I used to call myself happy. I brush my teeth, gulping down as much water as possible in the process. On the way back to the room, the floor attendant asks me a question. Every morning, she asks us the same thing, even though she knows we don't speak Chinese. "Yes," I tell her. I nod, and my head hurts. She wants to know if we are staying tonight. If I said no, she'd chuck us out of our room as soon as she could.

I go back to bed. As I'm climbing in, I look over at the alarm clock. It's five to five, but I'm not sleepy anymore. I cuddle up, and wonder why on earth I used to think drinking to excess was worth the hassle.

CHAPTER
20

"You will *so* not be allowed to take that into England," Ally points out.

"I don't care. I'll carry it with me for now, and then I'll leave it in Bombay when I get the plane home. I'll have it for seven months. I like it. It's cool."

"It's fantastic."

"And it's small enough. I can keep it in my pocket and feel hard. I've never had a knife before. I feel like a revolutionary."

"You look like a Mafia hit woman."

The metal shines in the sunlight. It's a classic dagger, with a long and surprisingly sharp blade, and a crossbar like a miniature sword. A circle of turquoise on the hilt makes it irresistibly sexy. The turquoise is surrounded by small, inset pieces of coral. The stallholder is eager to cement the purchase. He needn't worry. I've got my heart set on it.

"OK. Good price," he begins.

"What's your price?"

"My price, one hundred."

I am tempted just to agree and pay it, as this is about seven pounds, but I haggle a bit for form's sake.

"Sixty?"

"Oh no. Eighty."

"Seventy."

He beams. "Seventy-five. OK." I nod, and he packages it up in newspaper. When I hand him the notes, he touches all his other wares with them, for luck. I sheath my purchase, and tuck it into my pocket. I feel hard. I have brown hair and a boyfriend, and I'm armed.

The morning is sunny and cold, and Ally and I are shopping at the stalls around the Barkhor, Lhasa's inner pilgrimage circuit. The outer one, the Lingkor, has been largely lost but this one survives: a wide paved walkway with a glorious temple at its centre. Everyone is walking clockwise round the circuit. Some people prostrate themselves on the ground at every step. It is lined with traders, who sell everything from multicoloured prayer flags to fake designer fleeces. Mostly, the stalls are piled high with jewellery, buddhas, carpets, and daggers. Everyone seems to sell silver bracelets bearing the same Tibetan writing.

"What does that mean?" I asked a man this morning when I was contemplating buying one. I am always nervous of foreign writing. It might look impressive, but I feel it is important to know what message one is imparting. Some of the English slogans I've seen in Asia bear witness to this: I was particularly charmed by an old woman on the boat to Champasak, whose T-shirt asked the urgent question: "Is it hot in here or is it just me?"

"Buddha," the salesman tried to explain. He held his hands out in a meditation pose. "Ommmm . . . mani padmay hommmmmm," he intoned.

At that moment, Ally walked over. "It's a mantra," she explained. "The most famous one there is. I think it means the jewel in the heart of the lotus, something like that."

He nodded and smiled at her. "Yes, a mantra. Cheaper!"

I was reassured, and bought it. I have also acquired a huge woollen jumper, because I did not come to Asia prepared for this kind of cold, and a turquoise necklace, a fat little buddha, and, now, my wickedly sharp dagger.

We walk on. The buildings around here are whitewashed and small, with coloured, or washed-out, prayer flags. They are a world away from the modern, tiled box-buildings that fill not only every part of China I've seen, but also most of Lhasa. We are now, in fact, in the only quarter of the city that retains a Tibetan atmosphere. The rest of it is full of karaoke bars, shopping malls, and windows that are glazed, unaccountably, in blue glass. I knew that China had invaded Tibet, and that this was a tragedy for the country, but I hadn't realised just how obvious it was going to be. I wonder whether this is why the Tibetan people—instantly distinguishable from their occupiers, not only by their features but also by their flowing, brightly coloured clothes—invariably seem so happy to see us. No western tourists are interested in Chinese Lhasa because its only interest is in its perversity. It's terrible and horrible.

"Do the Chinese keep this bit of the city Tibetan so that we'll come here and spend our money?" I hazard.

"I guess so. They love tourism, as long as they can control it." Ally knows about these things, and so she should, after all the Dalai Lama books I've seen her reading. It is undeniably true that wherever we go, we are greeted with Tibetan smiles and welcomed. Everyone greets us on the street. *"Tashi dele!"* they call, and we call it back. There aren't many Han Chinese around here. The few there are glare at us. It is all I can do to stop Ally marching up and telling them a few truths.

"They don't know, do they?" I remind her. "They only know what they're told. They probably genuinely believe they've liberated this country."

"That's true, but you'd think they'd just look at what's going on around them. Think for themselves just for once in their lives."

"You and I would probably be the same."

"We wouldn't!"

"We might. Why should these people care about Buddhism

when they grow up knowing that all religion is evil? Why should they be interested in the Dalai Lama when he's supposedly a tyrannical, anti-revolutionary despot?"

"They get massive incentives for moving up here, you know. It's disgusting. The one-child policy gets waived, I think, so the Tibetans will become a minority in their own country. Once that's happened—and it probably already has—the Chinese can do anything. They can relax. Just keep a few picturesque monasteries going for the likes of us. Sorted."

Lhasa is the most wonderful, and the most dreadful, place I've ever been to. I love being here, and I hate it. I feel much calmer in myself. Other people are in danger here, if they're Tibetan, if they talk about the Dalai Lama or rebel against the authorities. I'm not in danger. I'm a prized tourist. I legitimise the regime, and I keep Tibetan culture going to a small extent. I am complicit, I know. But, despite that, I'm glad I'm here. I remember telling that arsey man on the plane to Vietnam that I was going to Tibet. I thought I was lying, but it turns out I wasn't.

We've been here a couple of days now and we can't string it out much longer before we have to join the overland trip to Kathmandu. That should take about a week. I don't want to leave Lhasa but at the same time I can't wait to see the rest of Tibet, specially Everest base camp. Ally and Andy are rallying a little, but neither of them will tell us what has upset them. Max says that all we can do is to let them know that they can tell us if they want to.

I feel different in Tibet. The differences come in so many different forms that I don't know which is affecting me the most. As well as the mental stress of being in a country so ruthlessly occupied, there are strange physical symptoms. The air, up on this plateau, is thin. I noticed it straightaway. As we walked down the steps of the aeroplane, the exhilaration hit me like an ecstasy rush. There were mountains around the landing strip, and everything looked stony and dusty. The joy was unexpected; I never feel like that, getting off a plane. Apparently, this is what the lack of oxygen does for you, at first. I wonder, now, whether this effect of altitude is the origin of some of our figures of speech. I was getting high. Coming up.

We've been drinking vast amounts of water, because, apparently, it combats altitude sickness (my metaphor works, you see; it is exactly like clubbing). None of us has been sleeping well. It is an unfamiliar and unpleasant sensation to wake yourself in the night by gasping for oxygen. For some reason, the lack of any meaningful sleep doesn't seem to affect us at all. On our first afternoon, we walked from the hotel, through the Muslim quarter and, in a roundabout way, to the Barkhor and the Jokhang temple at its centre. Our heads were dizzy, thumping. The intense colours added to the strangeness of it all. The prayer flags come in bright shades of blue, red, yellow, orange, and green. The inside of the temple was decorated in similar vivid colours. As we went into the temple, we smelt the yak butter candles. They are so pungent, and so distinctive, that I know their smell will remain with me forever, as the aroma of Tibet.

And then, suddenly, all four of us began to wind down, simultaneously, like clockwork dolls. My limbs became heavy. I couldn't walk anymore. I looked to Max on one side of me, and Andy and Ally on the other, and I recognised that we were all feeling the same. We had to sit on a step for ten minutes before we gathered the energy to get back to the hotel. Gabe was triumphant when we met him later. Gabe is Max's famous weird friend. He has dreadlocks, and appears to dress only in purple. I have hated him from the moment we met him. He claims to have been bumming around this city for months, but I don't believe him. He's just trying to impress us.

"I knew that'd happen," he crowed. "It always does! Always, with new people. Ha! You wanna be an old-timer, like me."

We are tired now, and walk straight to the café where we're meeting Max and Gabe for lunch. Andy, meanwhile, is asleep at the guesthouse, as he has been since we've been here.

"He isn't ill, is he?" I asked Ally.

"Ill? No, of course not."

So that's one possible reason for the sadness crossed off the list.

Much as I love to see Max all the time, I could do without Gabe's company. He's worse than weird. He's horrible. He's smarmy and creepy and nasty. He has an elaborate backpacker's tale about how he came to Tibet by road, outwitting all the Chinese police at all the checkpoints, breaking all the laws, and making lorry drivers risk their lives and liberty to help him.

"And the meaning of this," he explained, "is that I'm not officially here. Therefore, I am not subject to any of the little rules and regulations that govern your stay. I am the only free man in Tibet!"

Ally and I hate him, and Andy really hates him, but Max says we're being drama queens. ("Oh, c'mon mate!" Andy protested. "At least award me the accolade of drama *king*. Be fair.") Max can tell that we want to conspire to conclude that Gabe is the sick killer, and we know that we're not allowed to say it, because of course he isn't. He's just a normal, annoying bloke. But I don't believe he's been in Tibet for as long as he says he has, all the same. He could have been anywhere.

The café looks out over the corner of the Barkhor. We go up the stairs and into the open room. It's got the atmosphere of a massively trendy place in London. The floor is wooden, the place is almost empty, and we sink down into a huge, comfy sofa. The menu is printed on rough, handmade paper, dyed purple and mustard.

The outside of the building, according to the menu, is painted orange because it was the house of a mistress of the extremely naughty sixth Dalai Lama. The fifth was the great one. The sixth was a shagger by all accounts, and the fourteenth seems pretty cool to me, although you can't say anything like that very loudly. The food is Tibetan, with the addition of a few dishes from the other side of the Himalayas.

"Dahl baht, please," says Ally. She still hasn't told me what's wrong.

"Fried vegetable momos for me," I tell him, and we order a big flask of sweet, milky tea. We have consumed gallons of this in the past three days. Outside, down on the ground, three pilgrims are prostrating themselves around the pilgrimage circuit. These people have wooden blocks on their hands, to aid their progress. They fling themselves down on their stomachs, draw their knees up, and stand up, and do it again. Three Chinese policemen, sitting on rickety plastic chairs by a stall, watch them without interest.

"Tans?" says Ally, in a small voice. "Can I ask you something?"

"Of course."

"If, say, you'd met Max in England, and you'd gone away travelling together, and got on so well, and been just so happy, and you'd been away from home for years and years, and you thought you knew him better than anyone else . . ."

"Yes?"

"Then what would you say if you discovered that, all along, he'd been married and he'd never told you?"

"Max isn't married, is he?" I am suddenly scared. For all I know, he could be.

"No, don't be stupid. Not Max."

"Andy?"

She nods. "What would you do?"

"Do you mean, he's been married in the past but he never mentioned it, or he still is?"

"Still."

"They're not together, though."

"No. He said they got married and then she left him, and that was when he met me, and we came travelling. I wouldn't have minded if he'd told me straightaway, although of course I'd've been dubious about being with a married bloody man. But he never bloody mentioned it. Three years—two years in England

and a year in Asia—and he never told me a thing like that. I'm just his rebound person." She is tearing a napkin to shreds, and trying to hold herself together. I put my arms around her. She's so small that I feel I could break her. She sobs.

"You're not his rebound person. How did you find out?"

"We were doing email in Krabi, just after you'd gone. His screen froze. He was trying to shield it from me, but he couldn't stop me reading it. It was from someone who said she was his wife."

"So you asked him what she was on about?"

"Fucking right. I asked him more than that. It's stupid, isn't it? It's like something from a soap. Fucking Andy, of all people! We've done everything together, everything, for the past three years, and he's a bastard with a wife."

"Did he explain why he didn't tell you?"

"Says I'd have been scared off at first. Then he was just too pathetic, I think. Never even bothered to get divorced. He thought I'd see the legal papers." She shudders in my arms. "He makes me feel sick. I've been trying to get over it, but I just can't. I can't stand the sight of him."

We are interrupted by the arrival of Max and Gabe.

"Shall we go?" Max asks quietly when he sees Ally. I nod.

"What's the problem here?" demands Gabe.

"Nothing," I tell him.

"We'll see you later," Max says firmly. I do love Max.

Ally looks up. "It's OK. Sit down. It's fine." She tries to smile. "I feel like this all the time. Nothing's different. I'll just go to the loo and I'll be OK."

When she's gone, I ask Max if he had any idea.

"No. Andy hasn't said a word to me. I'm not bloody surprised."

"Should be ashamed of himself," agrees Gabe.

Ally returns looking normal. She points out a young western man. "Look," she says. "The paper." We've all been dying to check the news, and although we found a cybercafé opposite our hotel, it was closed. We haven't had the energy to walk around Lhasa in search of an internet terminal; it seems all wrong. While we are here, it seems better to visit the temples.

The man in the corner is reading a paper. "It's the *Kathmandu Post*," says Ally, who got a good look in passing. The man looks like a monk. He has a shaved head, but in a gentle, Buddhist way, rather than skinhead style. He has a calm manner. I would have no qualms about asking him for his paper. He's not scary. He's not the one.

He's got it folded back to the sports page, so we can't see the headlines. We don't care about the sport; nor do we want a full round-up of the international news. We just want to know if anyone's died, in Singapore, Malaysia, Nepal, India, or indeed, Tibet. Naturally, people have died in all those countries, but the person we are interested in is fair-haired, from our own country, and travelling, and she will have something with a spooky similarity to something of mine in her hand or on her body. She might have been seen with a white man shortly before her death. His paper's probably too old to be useful anyway. But I'm dying to know. In the end, I can't stand lingering anymore, and go over to him. He looks up.

"Hi!" I say. I feel silly.

"Hello." He has a European accent of some sort, I don't quite know which. Maybe, like Tintin, he's a Belgian in Tibet.

"Er, we were just wondering, would we be able to have a look at your paper after you?"

"Of course. I will bring it to you in one moment."

"Is it recent?"

"Yes, four days old. A guy at my hotel arrived from Nepal this morning. By road, straight here. He handed it to me."

I want to ask him what the main news is but he doesn't look as if he wants to be kept from the football pages.

"He's bringing it over," I say as I sit down. Ally is taking photos out of the window.

"He looks like a nutter. You should stay away from him. We all know how *scared* you girls are."

"Gabe, shut up. He's nice."

He turns to Max. "Hear that? I'd be worried if I were you."

"Oh, I'm not worried."

I catch Max's eye and widen my own eyes. How, I try to ask him, silently, could he have inflicted this person on us? He squeezes my hand.

"I'm not worried at all," he repeats.

I squeeze him back. "You want to watch what you say to me," I tell Gabe. "I'm armed and dangerous." I pull my knife out of my pocket and unsheath it.

"You bought that?" Max exclaims. "What for?"

"Because I like it."

"Andy better watch out," laughs Gabe. "Revenge of the sisterhood."

I look at Ally. She smiles weakly.

After a few minutes, the Belgian floats over and hands me the paper, still folded back at the sports page. He must be a Buddhist monk who lives in India, I decide, come to see the origins of his religion. He doesn't stop to chat but drifts straight back to his table and takes a book out of his bag. It makes me laugh. I haven't seen the familiar red, green, and gold cover of *The Tibetan Book of Living and Dying* for months. I wonder whether I should read it myself.

Max leans in next to me, and I try to straighten the paper out. I've never been any good with broadsheets. I should have worked for a tabloid. It folds backwards, and develops some persistent creases. Eventually, we have a front page, with old-fashioned typeface; I am about to comment on the archaic layout when I see the picture.

The photo must have been taken before she left home. She's got the same glossy, perfect hair. The subtle but technically perfect make-up. The PR-style smile, even though it's just a snapshot.

She's blonde. The picture has the slightly fuzzy quality that photographs of dead people always have. This shot was never intended to be in the papers. I don't have to read the words to know what's happened to her. The room contracts. There is a high-pitched ringing in my ears. I can feel Max's breath on my neck. She must have been in Nepal. Nepal, where we had planned to meet in three weeks. I wonder what she really looked like, by now. Less glossy, more like a real person. If I used to be Cindy Crawford (and, let's face it, I didn't; Max was just on the pull), then she was Claudia Schiffer. My breaths are short and shallow, and I feel dizzy. I can't put the paper down. I can't look away from her face.

"What?" says Ally. Her voice echoes. Eventually Max answers, across the void.

"Another girl." He tries to take the paper out of my hands to pass it across the table, but I hold on. He prises my fingers apart and takes it away. He puts his arm around my shoulders and pulls me in towards him. "It's horrible, I know, honey, but you're going to be OK. We'll be with you." He kisses my forehead.

"I don't care about that." I don't like speaking, because I don't want to say the words. When I open my mouth I fear that vomit, not speech, is going to come out. "I know her." I hear myself speaking. I know her. I said it, so it must be true.

"You know her?" I am aware that Ally and Gabe are looking at me.

"Yes. It's Amanda. I'm meeting up with her in Nepal." I smile at Max. "I told you about her. She can't wait to meet you."

"Amanda Evans," says Ally, reading out of the paper. "Twenty-nine years old, from London. Her battered body was found in the village of Langtang, near Nepal's Tibetan border. Fuck. Tans, are you OK? Shall we go back to the hotel?"

I don't know what I want to do, so I nod. "I worked with her," I say as we walk clockwise round the square and into a back street. We pass vendors of carpets, food, clothes, everything. One stall seems to specialise in Leonardo DiCaprio and Princess Diana memorabilia. "We never particularly liked each other then, but since I've been travelling we've become really good friends. Email friends. I've been so looking forward to seeing her."

"She had some dramatic events in her personal life, didn't she?" says Max. He has his arm round my shoulder and is steering me towards the hotel. "I remember you talking about her."

I nod. "When I went away, she was married to this really nice guy, but she'd been getting off with a friend of mine. Then she found she was pregnant, and instead of being pleased she was devastated. She hated the idea of it. She hated the baby, and she hated her husband. She says she had a miscarriage but I had a feeling it might have been self-induced in some way. So then she felt she'd had a narrow escape, and she needed to get away from everyone who was gossiping about her, and she needed to get away from her life, and her job, and she had a bit of a breakdown, I suppose. That was when her best mate, Maggie, invited her to India, because she was about to go to an ashram. She had a fantastic time there. God. Poor Maggie."

"Which ashram?" This, I suppose, is the kind of thing that travellers say. I know Ally has been to one before.

"No idea. It wasn't a dodgy one. When she came out, she sounded like a different person, in her emails, anyway. She had a new lease of life. Not for long, though. That bastard. What a fucking waste. She should have stayed at home."

I can say these words, but I can't believe Amanda is dead. The last time I saw her was at my leaving party, and now she's dead. Apart from a girl in the year above me at school who had leukaemia, I've never known anyone of my own age who's died. Dying is for the old and the old-in-spirit. There's no sense in this. It's the height of trite to look at the deep blue sky and roar "Why?" and I don't do it, but it's what I'm doing inside. If we were in Nepal, I'd go to where it happened and leave a piece of cardboard with "WHY?" scrawled on it (despite the fact that I know those are traditionally made by photographers). I'd write her a little poem. Leave her flowers. Do all the things we used to laugh at when I worked in the newsroom. Try to make some impression on the world, to remind it, in some way, that Amanda was here. Keep a part of her here for a little while longer, because sooner or later, people will forget. The world will move on, without her.

I sit on my little bed in the room we share. Max sits on one side of me, Ally on the other, and a drowsy Andy is lounging on the floor. Ally seems to be ignoring him. Gabe has gone back to his hotel, down the road, and I'm glad about that. I don't want him here, observing. I only want my friends. I want to keep them with me all the time. I am holding an enamel mug of hot water, but I'm not drinking it. It's a tiny bit comforting to have it in my hands. My travelling adventures are over. They have to be.

"Shall I go home now?" I wonder aloud.

"If you want to go home," says Max, "then you can. Of course you can. But we have to get you from here to Kathmandu first."

"Can't I fly?"

"The flights over the Himalayas don't start until next month."

"Can I go back to Chengdu?"

"Maybe. Perhaps you could fly to Chengdu, and then to Beijing, and home from there."

Ally takes my arm. "You have to do whatever you want, darl. But if we all went to Kathmandu, as quickly as we could, from here, then you could have your friends around you, and fly back from there. It's much cheaper. We'll look after you."

"Too bloody right we will," confirms Andy with a curt nod.

"We could go tomorrow, couldn't we?" She looks to Max, and addresses her next remark to him. "I'll go out to the travel office now with our passports and sort it out."

"We can leave a letter for your other mates," adds Andy. "Reckon they'd understand."

"Greg and I calculated that they'll be here today anyway," says

Max. "If they're not, yes, we'll go without them." He turns back to me. "We'll go straight there. Should be able to do it in four days if we don't stop at Everest, and then we'll get you a flight home."

"Will you come to London?"

"Of course I will."

"What about Pondicherry?"

"Shhh. Never mind Pondicherry. Plenty of time for that in years to come. Only if you want to, though. I'm not going anywhere without you."

I cuddle into his shoulder. "Thank you. I feel like I should have gone to her funeral, but there's nothing I can do about that. Funerals are overrated, anyway."

"It's probably already happened," says Andy, picking up the paper and scanning it. "Either that or it'll be postponed until they've done all the tests on the body. It doesn't say."

It's grim to hear my friends talking in the way they talk on the television. Suddenly we have slipped into a particularly exotic episode of *Law and Order*. I should be screaming, "There's been some mistake! It isn't true!" But I know it is true. I don't doubt it for a moment. I don't know what this is about, or who is doing it, and why, but it has become real. I don't have the energy to reconsider what the things by the body might mean. They are my things, and this is now real. I file it away to think about later.

"Did Amanda have something with her? You know, like the other . . . the other women." I was about to say the other ones. The other bodies. The other news stories.

Ally and Andy sit together, awkwardly, to peruse the story.

"Sure thing," says Andy. "Listen to this: 'Miss Evans was holding in her hand a silver locket containing within it a picture of a baby. Interpol officers are investigating the possible significance of this item of jewellery.' "

"What kind of journalism's that?" I ask, baffled.

243

"Nepalese journalism," explains Ally. "He should have read it like this." She reads it again, in an Indian subcontinent accent.

Max is looking at me, questioningly. A silver locket. There wasn't one in my lost box of trinkets, but there was one in Mum's stuff. I found it after she died. An old silver locket with a baby photo in it. I assumed, at the time, that the baby was me, but in fact it could just as easily have been William. That never occurred to me. I can't remember what I did with the locket. Put it with all her valuable stuff, I suppose, vaguely thinking that I'd sell it one day. It would have been at Dad's house, because that's where I dumped everything. Storing it all was the least he could do.

"There was one," I tell Max.

"Lots of people have silver lockets," he points out.

"And lots of people have all the other things."

"Yes."

I know, we both know, that not a lot of people have every single one of these things, all together in a missing box, but I don't want to think about it. We don't say it. There's no point.

I can't eat in the evening. Gabe clearly isn't coming back, Greg and Juliette haven't appeared, and Max and the others are, understandably, hungry. I'm curled up on the bed. Max lies next to me and strokes my hair.

"Are you sleepy?"

"No."

I know I won't sleep tonight, even if I can breathe; even if there are no dogs outside the window. I can't eat anything. All the normal functions that never suffered after Mother's death have suddenly been shot to pieces.

"Come to the restaurant with us," Max instructs me. "We'll just go down the road, to Tashi's. You don't have to eat, although you should force down a little bit." He looks to Ally to back him up, and she nods emphatically.

"No," I tell him. "I don't want to. You guys go. I'll be OK. I'll lock the door and just lie here for a bit. Please. I need some time."

After they've left, I drift. The room is so pretty. There are four single beds, each with an embroidered duvet. The walls are stencilled with flowers, and the windowsill is big enough to sit on. I wonder if this is all in my head. Maybe the whole trip has been a dream. My subconscious could be making this up. Perhaps I'll come round in a minute, and I'll be in the hospital after Mum's funeral, having my stomach pumped, back in love with Tom. Never having met Max. I know these murders have nothing to do with me, logically. But my friend is dead, and so now I am involved. I shouldn't be away from Max for a moment. I won't be safe. If Amanda wasn't safe, then I won't be. I'm like her. I shouldn't see this in terms of how it relates to me. I should be thinking of Amanda.

Suddenly, I realise that, if the newspaper with Amanda's story in it has reached Lhasa from Kathmandu, by land, then the murderer could have done the same thing. It's unlikely, but it's possible. He could be in this very city. And I am on my own. My brown hair doesn't seem like much protection anymore. I check that the door is locked, and lie, curled up, waiting for the others to come back for what feels like hours. Sometimes I hear footsteps outside, but they carry on past.

After about an hour, there is a loud rap at the door. I don't answer. Whoever it is tries the handle, and knocks again.

"Who is it?" I ask quietly.

"Tansy! Boy, are we glad to hear that voice!"

"Hello Tansy! We are here!"

"So, open up! It's us. Greg and Jules. They said this was your room. Aren't you going to let us in? Are you decent? You wouldn't believe the journey we've had."

I struggle to my feet, and open the door. They are glowing with happiness. Juliette is more beautiful than ever. I motion to them to come in, and I try to smile. At least I'm not on my own

245

anymore. I listen to their tumbled stories, most of which seem to concern being very sick on a falling-apart bus on appalling roads for two days. I keep opening my mouth to tell them, but I can't do it.

I don't want to say it again. Sooner or later, they'll ask.

CHAPTER
21

The moment I drift into full consciousness, in my narrow single bed, I know I'm not going back to sleep. This happens every night now. It is a weird kind of wakefulness; an absolute, crystal consciousness that I never achieve during the day. Because I don't sleep at night, the days end up feeling like the dream times, and the nights take on a terrifying clarity. I'm in the opposite world; the world of the negative. It makes me wonder about sleep, which I always assumed was universal to all humans. I never questioned my ability to sleep, any more than I questioned my ability to eat. Are there people everywhere who lie awake every single night, feeling like outcasts? Have I joined a secret, non-sleeping fraternity? By the very nature of the affliction, I suppose there is no fraternity here. This is one for individuals. It's lonely.

I am experiencing the world differently from the other three people in the room. I go to sleep when they do, and every night, I am adamant that it will be different. "Right," I tell myself sternly. "Tonight I'm so exhausted and drained that I'm not going to wake up. This is the night when, finally, it all catches up with me, and I sleep through till morning." I think about myself in the same way people talk about babies. *If only she'd sleep right through. Let's get her tired today to make her sleep.* I would love to regress to babyhood. I long to lie back and wail until someone feeds me warm milk, sings a lullaby, and rocks me back to sleep on their shoulder. But I don't want to alarm Max any more than I already have.

I always drift off, comfortably, when they do, and I always wake up again within a few hours. On previous nights, I have lain still, ferociously trying all the mind-emptying techniques I can think of, wishing I'd read enough of the *Living and Dying* book to know some proper meditation techniques, and crying with frustration when nothing works. Then I drop back to sleep an hour or so before we're meant to wake up, and see everything underwater when I get up.

Tonight I'm going to try a new approach. As soon as I realise I'm awake, I get up as quietly as I can, cursing the fact that even between the six of us we don't have a torch that works. I'm already wearing my clothes for warmth, so I just pick up my boots and go outside as quietly as I can. I sit down, do up my laces, and walk across the courtyard.

It is lit up like daytime. Maybe that's what's confusing my body (I wish it were so simple). The moon is almost full, and there are a million trillion stars. I'll miss the stars when I'm home. I never regretted the fact that I couldn't see them when I lived in London. I barely even remembered they were meant to be there. I'll remember them when I get back. I breathe the cold, clean air. I'll miss that too.

London. Home. This is one issue that preys on my mind during these long and empty nights. I don't want to go home. London doesn't even feel like home anymore. It isn't my home; it just isn't. You can't see the stars, and you have to have a job. If London isn't home, however, I don't know where is. Nowhere is.

It must be about two in the morning; the dead time between night and the very early morning. Two o'clock is a time to go to bed, not to wake up. No one gets up at two, except me. Lhatse is almost totally silent. In the distance, a dog barks. Nothing is happening. It's a small but significant town, an overnight stop for tourists and lorry drivers between Kathmandu and Lhasa, and everyone in it, apart from me and a dog, is asleep. I wish I knew exactly what was wrong with me. One night I'll leave some paper by the bed and I will use my insomnia to make a list of my problems, and try to work out which of them is waking me up. Perhaps if I'm scientific, the world will order itself and become explicable.

I can't take in the fact that someone wilfully put an end to Amanda's life, although, of all people, I really should be able to absorb the news. I can't get used to the idea that I will never see her again, just as I will never see Mother again. I still don't think I mind about Mum, but it is hard to believe that I will never again see the words "Amanda Evans" in my in-box. I am trying to alter my expectations of Kathmandu from meeting up with her and having a fabulous girly time to getting the next flight home. It's a difficult change to make. Consciously I know that I won't see her again; I just wish I didn't keep bloody forgetting. I often catch myself speculating about how different she's going to be, or where we'll go together, or whether she'll get on with Max. Then I remember. I did the same thing with Mum for a while. It was exactly the same feeling, apart from the fact that it was the polar opposite. The negative. I'd come in from work and look at her chair, register vague surprise that she wasn't in it, and suddenly remember that she wasn't going to be sitting in it ever again. I would be swamped with the most glorious relief. I'd pour myself a glass of wine, and sit down, in the comfy armchair, and kick my feet, and I'd laugh at her. I used to hope her ghost was watching, and I'd give it the finger just in case.

When I sold the house and moved in with Guy I felt I'd left her behind (I didn't realise she was planning to follow me to Asia). I don't believe in ghosts, but if ever there was an unquiet spirit, it would have been Mum, looking back on the fucked-up mess she made of her life. Her physical absence has been the best thing that ever happened to me, and I don't regret it for a moment. The fact that, now, she really is absent from my psyche, almost all the time, is the icing on the cake. The extra measure in the G&T.

But no one will be dancing on Amanda's grave, except, perhaps, the person who killed her. I have the strangest feeling of unreality. A part of me is convinced that she's alive, really. I haven't spoken to anyone who knew her, to confirm that she's not. In Lhasa, I had a shocked exchange of emails with Kate and other people at home, all of whom implored me to come back as soon as I could, but emails aren't real. They're not like speech. I am basing my grief on an article in the *Kathmandu Post,* and some writing on a computer in Tibet. Perhaps it's a joke. Either that or it's all in my head. I wouldn't be at all surprised if she walked across the courtyard and came to sit down with me, now, and explained that it was a mistimed April fool.

The thing that, infuriatingly, I can't ignore at night is the involvement of all my things in these murders. It must be coincidence, it simply must, but how come? "What are the chances of that happening?" I say aloud, in a Harry Hill voice.

My voice sounds alien and self-conscious in the empty courtyard, like when you hear yourself in a tape recording. Tears fill my eyes, and I try to blink them away. I just can't work it out. I can't decide whether I'm being paranoid, or whether I really am involved. It has even occurred to me, in the night, that I might be doing the killing myself. I might be completely crazy. I might have a split personality. I can't imagine how I would have been able to enjoy a murder spree in India at the same time as struggling through Vietnam, Laos, and Thailand. I don't have any "lost" days, as far as I am aware. I might be much cleverer than I think. Maybe I did the one in Singapore. I decide to look through all my things, every single piece of paper in my bag, just to see if there are any old, strange boarding passes. I'll do that in the morning.

What I really hate is how pathetic I'm being. Since we read about Amanda, the slightest stupid thing makes me cry. I had to blink back the tears, earlier, when I wanted a wee before bed and the loo was too dark and I was scared of falling down the hole. Tibetan loos are drop toilets, with perfectly preserved matter underneath, should you care to look, and they don't even smell because of the cold. I knew I wouldn't really fall down the hole because I'm too big, but one of my legs might have slipped through. The courtyard was lit up like it is now, by the moon and stars, so everyone could see me if I crouched down out there. All I had to do was find a dark corner, but for some reason it all got too much for me, and I had to run back into the room and make Max hug me. He took control of the situation, found me a dark spot, and even guarded me while I emptied my bladder. I can't do anything for myself anymore. I'm useless. I don't understand myself. I've always prided myself on being strong, and here I am, weak.

It is so quiet. I can't really be the only person in Lhatse who is awake. I stand up, and wander through the archway onto the street. The light from the sky is better than any streetlamp, which is just as well. There's no chance of any street lighting here, largely because there's no electricity.

It is completely still. I walk a little way down the street. I can see the mountains in front of me. We climbed onto a hillside when we arrived yesterday, and sat under a deep blue sky, warm in the sun, and looked at the bleached landscape. It stretched on and on, all the same. Below us, an entire Tibetan family was ploughing a field with a couple of yaks. The children brought a shaky little lamb over for us to stroke, and asked a hundred times over for a pen, or some coins from our country, or some sweets. I wonder how they know. The children in every Asian country I've visited, apart from China, demand exactly the same items. How does word travel? How do the street urchins in Hanoi and the farming children in Tibet come to associate westerners with pens, chocolate, and coins? I suppose the only connection is people like us. Some people must actually be handing these things out. It makes me think of Max and me, shaking hands with the village children in Laos, inadvertently spreading the word.

251

I stop to listen to the silence. There is no noise at all. Where there is no electricity, there really is nothing to do after dark. I wonder how it used to be in the west, before the lights went on. Housework must have been a lot easier. I imagine a moment when homes all over Britain were illuminated by the first, unforgiving, electric light bulbs. Suddenly, the dust and dirt in the corners were revealed to all. A nation of women saw the future, and it needed a good scrubbing.

The great myth of technology has always been that it cuts down on labour, but it seems to me that it does so only in the ways in which the male bosses want it to. People are laid off from jobs because computers can do things quicker, but women still have to labour at home, even though they have dishwashers and washing machines. They just have extra machinery to dust as well. They have to look after their jobless husbands, have babies, and go out to work. I wonder whether I'm being sexist, whether the modern world isn't like that anymore. Certainly, I am far messier than any man I've ever been out with, and I've always assumed that was my prerogative; that, although men had many grounds for rejecting me, my untidiness was not among them. It was just, I thought, a part of me, and rather endearing. Am I going to need to brush up on my polishing skills in order to snare my man?

No. My man is Max, and he seems fairly snared already. He'd no more expect me to become a diligent housewife than I'd expect him to support me financially, or provide me with a monthly housekeeping budget.

There are so many stars, and they are so bright. I can't believe I never used to notice they were missing. I only ever saw them on holiday, and they startled me. The rest of the time, I was too busy being stressed to recall that they would be there if they weren't banished by electricity and cloud.

I despair, not for the first time, of the western cult of stress. It seems so alien here. The Great Leisure predicted in the fifties certainly never happened. Quite the opposite. I am certain, now, that westerners, and Londoners in particular, rush around madly all the time to give themselves some sense of validity, to cover the fact that their lives are miserable and empty. People are scared of being alone and at leisure. I know I was. When I worked in London, I'd have felt a failure if I hadn't been able to say "Stressed" in response to "How are you?" Stress equalled success. Even when my primary source of stress was taken away, when the coffin was lowered into the ground, I kept myself artificially on the edge, ignoring my subconscious as it grappled with the real problems. I would routinely go out all night, and then go into the office and do the minimum work possible, before repairing for a carbohydrate-ridden lunch and a Bloody Mary. Thus I was always clasping my head, and claiming to be tired and overworked like everyone else.

I wonder, now, what the really overworked women made of me. These women would vanish for a few weeks to have their babies and come back to work looking pale and exhausted. They must have observed Kate and Amanda and me living our hedonistic lives, and they must have felt a twinge of bitterness. We regarded them as slightly sad and very boring, as the people we didn't want to turn into. They must have seen silly, deluded girls who thought they knew it all, but knew nothing. We reserved quiet nights in for the occasional Sunday, with a pizza and a bottle of red. Anything else would have suggested we didn't have enough friends. It would have meant we were losers. With hindsight, we were running as fast as we could from ourselves. It's funny that I had to run away physically from London before I caught up with myself. And so did Amanda.

As usual, I am beset by the dull thud of realisation.

The clumping of my boots seems to be amplified. I don't know where I'm going, but I think a bit of aimless wandering might tire me out and send me back to sleep. I don't want to go too far. I step carefully over a ditch full of stagnant liquid waste, and sit down by the side of the road, on someone's doorstep, to look around. There are mountains in all directions. I love places with mountains all around; places you can see out of. You can never see out of London, not even from Hampstead Heath. I'm not quite sure if these count as mountains or hills but since we're on a plateau higher than anything the British Isles can produce, I'm giving them the benefit of the doubt.

Nothing is stirring. I feel better for sitting here, for being out in Tibet. I lean back and look up at the sky. We have strung the journey out for longer than I'd intended, precisely because it is such an astonishing country. Part of me wants to stay here. We've been on the road for four days, and every moment of the trip has surprised me. When we set off in our smart jeep, along "Beijing Lu" and past the huge red and white Potala Palace—the Dalai Lama's rightful home, and the symbol of Holy Lhasa—I thought I was just taking the best route home. I was shocked that it was suddenly all over. I knew I had gone back to the other kind of travelling, the sensible, western kind, when the journey doesn't matter, when it's the destination and how quickly you get there that counts. Yet, time and time again, I have been proved wrong. This journey matters, more than ever. I want to be in Tibet. I want to be in a danger zone. I want to be where Amanda was: she was just across the border. If it happened to her, I want to see whether it happens to me.

After two days, I asked everybody whether we could expand the trip to take in the rest of Tibet after all. I want to be here. When, otherwise, will any of us see Everest Base Camp? Lingering keeps reality at bay for a while longer. Our mandatory guide, Dawa, and driver, Soto, were happy to take the extra money. Dawa is young, wiry, and melancholy, while Soto is round and cheerful. He learnt his English from songs. "Because I love you more than I can say," he croons, oblivious to meaning, as he drives. He wears his baseball cap sideways.

I want to push myself. I deserve it more than she did. In a contrary way, though, Tibet seems to have healing qualities, despite my insomnia. We had a bizarre encounter in Shigatse, two days ago, which I can't get out of my head. Two monks in a ramshackle café invited us back after dark. I went with Juliette, Greg, and Max. We'd lost Gabe, and Ally and Andy were having a serious discussion. I haven't discussed Andy's marriage with him. I don't trust myself not to get violent.

We were the only people in there, earlier in the day, and from the dust on the chairs I'd surmised that no one had partaken of our hostess's tea for quite some time. She was an elegant woman with two small, round children. All three of them had wind-blasted, rosy cheeks.

As we were beginning to drink, there was a small commotion at the back of the room, and two monks appeared. The woman nervously shut the front door and fastened it. Monks in their flapping red robes are a common sight, and we smiled at them without thinking anything of it, and went back to our conversation.

"But is it true there was a love story when the boat sank?" Juliette was asking. "I think it was invented for the film, yes?"

"Oh, yeah," said Greg. "Sure, because the real story of the real *Titanic* wasn't tragic enough so that they had to invent this bloody floppy-haired kid . . ."

One of the monks approached us. "Hello," he said quietly, bowing his head towards us.

"Hello, how are you?" asked Max.

"Fine, thank you. Your country?"

I pointed to myself and to Max. "England," I said.

He nodded.

Greg pointed to himself. "America," he said.

The monk looked excited. "America!" he echoed, and he looked at Juliette.

"Laos," she said.

This amazed him. "Laos! Very . . ." he didn't know the word, so he mimed rubbing his fingers together, for money.

"Very poor people in Laos," she agreed. "I'm very lucky."

His friend was hovering in the background, looking nervous.

"Do you go to Tashilhunpo?" the monk asked. This was the name of the huge local monastery.

"Yes," said Greg. "We're going there now. Do you live there?"

The monk put his head to one side. "Yes," he conceded, "but I think, no. Very bad things, there. Chinese, very bad, Tashilhunpo."

No one followed us when we went back to the house later. We checked all the way, amazed that the monks trusted us to be vigilant, even though they didn't know who we were, or anything about us. They were trusting us with their freedom, their lives. The stars were shining brightly. Before we could knock, the woman opened the door looking terrified, and shooed us in nervously.

As soon as the door was shut, the first monk appeared, and beamed. He shook our hands ceremoniously and ushered us through the back of the café into a dark passageway and through another door. We walked into a room which was lit by lanterns.

"Fuck me," said Greg.

An entire wall was taken up with the biggest poster I have ever seen. It was a hallucinatory vision of blues, oranges, pinks, reds, yellows and greens. The Dalai Lama sat, serene, in the lotus position in the middle of a rainbow. All around him, Buddhist things were going on in the brightest, most joyful colours imaginable. We had not dared speak his name in Tibet unless we knew we were alone in an enclosed space, and yet here were Tibetan monks bringing us—strangers—into a room over which he presided.

"You're very brave," Max told our host, pointing to the picture.

"Dalai Lama!" said the monk, proudly.

"The Chinese don't see?" I said, hoping that speaking pidgin English wasn't insulting.

"No!"

We looked around the room. As well as the quieter monk from

before, there was another man, sitting at a table, wearing normal clothes. He saw us looking at him, and smiled.

"Hello," he said. "I have come to translate, because I speak English."

"Nice to meet you," I told him.

"Thank you for coming," said Max. We sat down at the table, with the woman hovering worriedly in the background. No one quite knew where to start. I didn't really know why they'd taken the risk of inviting us back.

"Tea!" said the first monk, and picked up a huge Chinese thermos and poured it out into tiny cups.

"Why are you here?" Ally asked when the pleasantries were, once again, out of the way.

The chatty monk said something to the translator, and he turned to us. "We want to tell you a story, so you can tell it in your country," he said.

A pair of eyes glints at me, and I jump up. The eyes are a long way down the road, but they are shining unnaturally. Perhaps they are a spirit, but they're more likely to belong to a dog. These two would be almost interchangeable, in Tibetan Buddhism. The last thing I want is any kind of interaction with a horrible Tibetan wolf, a reincarnation of a bad monk, so I start walking hastily back to the hotel. I try not to look over my shoulder. I know that lots of these dogs have rabies, and a frothing crazy death is not the end I have planned for myself. I don't have an alternative in mind, admittedly, and I don't suppose dying of rabies is any worse than being murdered by a stranger, or dying an alcohol-induced death over the course of twenty years. I don't think, however, that I want to die just yet.

We never got to hear the monks' story. We won't be taking it back to our country. The translator began. He got as far as, "He say his brother is in a very bad situation in prison, please tell it in your

257

country," when he was interrupted by a loud rap at the front door. Everyone stiffened. One of the monks held his finger to his lips but we didn't need telling. Whoever it was rapped again, louder this time. We sat in terrified silence. I reached for Max's hand. There was a loud shout, in Chinese. At this, the Tibetans leapt to their feet. The woman bundled us into the café section, sat us down and put our cups of tea in front of us. We sat, shaking with fear, and tried to pretend to be normal. She left the room for a moment and came back dragging her children, who were rubbing their eyes and looking drowsy. They climbed onto Ally's and my laps, and the woman gave us all a last appraising look, and opened the door. Three Chinese policemen came in, shouting, and remonstrating with the woman. She answered back, and they yelled at her. Then they came over to us.

"What you do?" asked one.

I was scared. We were all scared. Max, as the most level-headed person the world has ever known, was silently elected our spokesman.

"We came back to have a cup of tea at this café, and to see the children, and to bring them some chocolate and pens," he said calmly.

"Why the door is locked?"

He shrugged, and Juliette and I made elaborate "don't know" faces, turning down the corners of our mouths and raising our shoulders. He turned to the woman and we hoped she was saying the same as us.

"Why she no open the door?" he asked Max.

"I asked her not to," said Max. "In the west, it can be dangerous for someone to come to the door at night. For security, it is best not to answer."

He nodded suspiciously. "In China, is not."

"OK."

"In China, no crime."

"OK."

We were all smiling desperately. We were almost friends, when another policeman decided to search the house. He headed straight to the door and went through into the passageway. There were sounds of doors opening. We knew he was walking into the Dalai Lama's room.

We were braced for the shouting, the arrests, and our own arrest and torture as well. I squeezed Max's hand until my knuckles were white. But there was nothing. Just feet walking around the house. After about five tense minutes, he came back.

The English-speaking policeman instructed us to go back to our hotel and not to visit private houses again.

"Sorry," I told him. "We just thought it was a café." To prove it, I got out my purse and gave the woman money for the three teas. She beckoned to me to follow her for change. The policeman asked something brusquely, and she answered. He gave a nod.

We walked into the room which had been adorned by a picture of the spiritual leader and which had held the rebel monks. It was a normal, drab, empty room. The only remarkable aspect of it was the enormous poster of Chairman Mao on the wall, exactly where the Dalai Lama had been. This was not a rebellious house. Not a place for dangerous counter-revolution. In fact, it was exemplary. She tipped some change into my hand, gestured to the room, and smiled broadly. She put her hand to her chest and breathed deeply.

"Lucky," I said. We smiled at each other, and then we all left as quickly as we could. I wish I knew the brother's story. We will never, ever know it now.

The dog isn't barking, and that must be a good sign. I speed up into a run and go back into the courtyard. The dog trots on past. Either I've given him the slip or he wasn't interested in me in the first place.

There is a figure sitting on the step. It's someone fully dressed. I stop, and wonder whether it can see me. It could be Amanda. It could be the killer. It could be me, or a ghost. It's between me and the bed-room door, and I don't know what to do. I hear myself taking shallow breaths, and I try to edge round the courtyard in the dark.

The person looks up and as soon as it sees me, it stands up. I recognise the funny skinny outline, and run headlong into Max's arms.

"Hello you!" I tell him happily. "I was scared when I saw someone out there but I should have known it was you. Who else would it be? I'm mad."

"You can't have been as worried as I was when I woke up and saw you gone. Tans! You should have woken me. You know, with everything that's been happening . . ." His voice trails off. "With what happened to Amanda . . ." he tries again. "I was worried."

"I'm sorry," I tell him. "I just came outside because I couldn't sleep, and then I went for a walk. I haven't been far."

"You should have woken me."

"I'm awake every night. You don't need to be too."

We sit together, and I rest my head on his shoulder. I'm beginning to feel a little bit tired. "I do think I'm mad, I really do," I tell him.

"Of course you are. My little crazy girl." He kisses me, and I turn my face towards him to receive it.

"No, but really." He doesn't understand. "I honestly think I'm losing the plot. By the time we get home, at this rate, you'll have to put me in solitary confinement."

"Would you let me do that?"

"Isn't the whole point that I wouldn't have a choice? I looked into it once, because I thought I could maybe do it to Mum, and they'll only put an alcoholic in solitary if they're a danger to themselves or anyone else. And I'm not even an alcoholic yet."

"Well, would you let me confine you, or would you shout and scream and bite and kick until the orderlies got scared and ran off? A process by which you would prove to everyone's satisfaction that you were a danger to the world."

"That, probably. Look at the stars."

We sit, holding each other, and look at the countless diamonds in the sky. How I wonder what they are.

"Do trillions come straight after billions?" I ask.

"Yes. What's after that? Do you know?"

"Squillions come after trillions. Then it's gazillions, I think."

"That's right. After that it's bazillions, then krillions, and by then you have reached the mighty famillion."

We invent ever higher numbers, and five minutes later we still haven't got a number high enough for the stars in the sky.

"How about infinitillions?" I try.

"I think that's it. You, my darling, are looking at one infinitillion of stars."

"Why only one?"

"OK, infinite infinitillions."

"I am, too."

Max sits up. I can tell that he wants us both to go back to bed, now we've had a little interlude together. He wants to bring me in, and tuck me up, and let us both return to the acceptable night-time activity of sleeping. For Max, this was a one-off, a romantic half-hour under the stars. Now things can be normal again, or as normal as possible when you're in Tibet and there's a serial killer across the Himalayas, and you've got to get home as soon as possible, and all you really want to do is concentrate on the remarkable country you're in. I don't want to go to bed. I want to stay out, in Tibet. I want to be vulnerable.

"Stay a little bit longer," I say, and pull him back down. "We never have any time for ourselves. I'm always with Ally, you're often with Andy, and there's Greg and Juliette, not to mention your lovely friend."

"You're really not impressed by Gabe, are you?"

"It might be a bit easier if he didn't keep on and on about Amanda all the time." I had been fully expecting to like Gabe more as the journey wore on, but instead I like him less. This is largely because he has a morbid curiosity about my friend, an attitude that would not be out of place on the pages of a tabloid newspaper or a gossip magazine but which I find incredible in our current situation. He knows he can't ask me for all the sick details because I know no more than he does, so instead he seems to say anything that comes into his head.

"You know your friend," he shouted over his shoulder in the jeep yesterday. He was wearing purple jeans and a purple woolly jumper.

"Which friend?" I shouted back, to stall him.

"The dead one."

"I do know her, yes."

"What do you think her husband'll make of it?"

I stared hard at him, but he always appears impervious. "I imagine he's devastated."

"It kind of proves that he was right, doesn't it? What if she'd had the baby? She'd have been all right then, wouldn't she? Or maybe she wouldn't. Maybe she'd have died in childbirth."

"Shut up, Gabe." I wished he hadn't heard me telling the others her story.

"Do you think she got an obituary in that newspaper you worked for? Is that one of the perks of the job? Would you get one if you were the next to go?"

"Shut the fuck up." I looked round for some back-up, but Max was kneeling up, facing backwards and talking to Greg and Juliette who were squashed into the back with Andy. Ally, sitting on my other side, had her Walkman on. Gabe looked wounded.

"Pardon me, I was only interested. You know, interested in your friend. Concerned."

"That's a funny kind of concern. Anyway, you're not concerned. You're ghoulish."

"Isn't that a Hungarian dish?"

I can't bear the sight of him. Losing Gabe will be the one good thing about leaving Tibet and not travelling anymore. Once again, I have to confront the idea of home. At least it's Gabeless.

"How are you feeling about going home?" I demand, forcibly holding Max down.

He sighs. "Mixed feelings. I mean, I want to go because I want to be with you, and it's clearly right for you to go back at the moment, and I don't have any regrets about coming with you. We've got the rest of our lives to go back to India and teach English. But I've been away from home so long. I can't imagine it. Can you? The orderly streets with traffic jams, the houses, everything all British and normal. Pavements and supermarkets. Clouds and drizzle and big red buses. No big red buses in Bakewell, of course. Just coaches full of schoolchildren."

"I can't imagine any of it. I can't imagine that it's just carried on like before. It used to be my place, and now it's not. I almost feel affronted that it's carried on without me."

"I know what you mean. It's scary, going home. Because you wonder if it really is your home anymore. I mean, I love my family and I really know how lucky I am to have them, compared with you and Greg and half the people in Tibet, but I don't feel like I belong with them so much as I used to."

"That's exactly it. I feel like I've moved away from my old home, because I really can't imagine being happy in London again. Not that I was ever that happy there to start with. I just thought I was. But I haven't got anywhere else to live, not at home."

"You could try Bakewell."

"But you don't want to be there. Unless you're trying to tell me something, that doesn't sound like a good idea."

"So we try something else. Somewhere else. Where would you like to live?"

"I'd live in India with you. It'd be cool. Anywhere. Ireland. Laos. Tibet. I don't know."

"So we'll go to Ireland. We'll go back to Laos. They always

need people like us in India, or anywhere. We can live wherever we want. There aren't any limits on us, Tans. No one's forcing us to live where we were born. Give it a little time, and we'll go away again. Best give Asia a wide berth for now, that's all."

"Someone's forcing us to go home now."

"Yes, but they'll catch him. They might even have caught him by now. That's not going to affect us anymore. We'll be on the plane before you know it, and we'll be saying, that night under the Tibetan stars, doesn't it seems a million years ago?"

"Infinitillions of years ago." I am caught by something he said. "So are we over the Pondicherry argument then?"

We smile shyly at each other. Max speaks carefully. "What happened to Amanda throws it all into perspective, doesn't it? I shouldn't force you to live abroad if you don't want to. We'll work something out. We'll compromise. If you'd like to live with me, that is. Christ, I haven't even made the leap from lover to boyfriend yet."

I punch his arm. "You *so* have."

"Lucky me."

"And I'd love to live with you, even in Pondicherry, if I'm invited." I snuggle up. We grin at each other, and Max suddenly seems not to want to go back to bed anymore. He slips his hand under my many layers, and whispers something, so close to my ear that it brings up goosebumps on my arm.

I nod. We get up and move out of the courtyard, to find somewhere less visible; and, even though it's cold, we clear a path through each other's clothes, just enough to make love under the stars.

CHAPTER
22

The road to Rongbuk Monastery is the worst so far. It is barely a road at all. The jeep crashes around, throwing us all about. Max and I are taking our turn on the backseat, so we suffer most of all. My lip is bleeding because we tried to kiss earlier, at the same moment that Soto drove over a boulder. I'm surprised that neither of us got a black eye from the other one's nose.

It's like the moon here. The ground is dusty and covered in stones. There are a few scrubby plants. We are higher than ever. The landscape is lunar in every way except for one. That is, at the head of the valley, with a wisp of cloud attached to its summit, and gleaming in the afternoon sun, is a mountain. It doesn't seem right, here, to call it Everest, to name it after a member of the British survey team. It would, however, be unbearably pretentious to call it by its Tibetan name, which is spelt Qomolangma and pronounced something like Chumbawumba. I can just imagine going home and saying we spent a night at Chumbawumba Base Camp. I would deserve a punch in the mouth. I would probably get one.

It doesn't even matter that it's the tallest mountain in the world, now that we see it. That kind of competition means nothing. It's beautiful. It doesn't even look huge, from here, because we're already five thousand metres above sea level, and considerably closer to its summit than we are to anything else. All of us, even Gabe, are silenced.

"That is the highest piece of land on this planet," says Max, looking to the summit.

Gabe recovers himself quickly. "Actually, it arguably isn't. The peak of Chimborazo in Ecuador is the furthest from the centre of the earth."

"Fuck you, Gabe." Ally speaks for us all.

"Please. Any time you want."

Ally and Andy exchange glances.

"It is so very beautiful," says Juliette. "Does it not seem strange that the western man looks at this gorgeous mountain, as we do, and sees something to be climbed, to be conquered?" Juliette has picked up the word "gorgeous" from me, and sprinkles it liberally into her conversation.

"The local people must have thought they were mad when the British arrived in their plus fours," I say.

Greg attempts a British accent. "I say, Jeeves, pack me a slice of roast beef and a flagon of mead. I don't like the way this old bastard mountain is looking at me. I'm going to show it who's the boss. I shall take my spare tweed jacket in case of dire emergency."

"Never to be seen again," adds Max, darkly.

"It does seem like the grossest violation of nature," I say to Juliette. "Looking at it, it makes me realise why people used to think the gods lived up the mountains. We're not meant to be there. Our bodies stop working. We can't breathe here. We can't sleep. We're not in our place. It would never occur to a Tibetan or a Nepalese that they needed to climb that mountain, would it?"

"Only if they were a sherpa," adds Andy, "and they were getting paid for it. More money than they could imagine."

The air here is crystal clear. When we reach the monastery, we find it nestling into the side of the valley. Its buildings are white-washed stone. At the front is a huge stupa—a big onion-shaped Buddhist structure that has deep meditative significance. It emits peace and love, according to Ally. Just what's needed. It is surrounded by prayer wheels, and with prayer flags streaming from its summit. I may not quite understand stupas, but I know that you walk round them clockwise, turning the prayer wheels as you go, and that this makes you calm. Even me. Even now.

The monastery is an odd place, as befits its setting. It is quiet, but I sense, or I imagine, some underlying tension. The atmosphere is charged, hostile. No expense is made to make the accommodation comfortable, and I'm glad. I want this, the last place I actually visit before going home, to be as rough and ready, as different from anywhere else, as possible. We are, of course, used to privations and would have been astonished to find running water or electricity here. There is no shop, no food (we were alerted to this fact by Soto, and have brought some lurid plastic pots of noodles, with Chinese writing and pictures of beef on the side), and a fantastic row of loos. From the end one you can look at Everest as you shit.

The "guesthouse"—a row of ten bedrooms—is presided over by a weird young monk who blows tunelessly on a plastic recorder as he goes about his duties. He allocates four rooms to our party, despite the fact that there is no one else staying tonight. We collectively engineer Gabe into the Tibetans' room. Soto and Dawa shrug, and don't appear to mind. At least they can talk about him to his face without his taking offence.

We set out our sleeping bags on the bare beds. Max pulls two beds together so we can cuddle under his sleeping bag, because I didn't bring anything that stands up to the temperatures of Tibet at night. Every other guesthouse we've visited has provided heaps of old blankets, and I've nested under them in my sheet sleeping bag. Here, we get nothing. The recorder-blowing monk gives us a thermos of water, and a candle. This is it. It will be dark in an hour or so, and we go out to wander around.

Max and I walk towards Mount Everest and sit on a rock. In the strong sun, it is warm enough to wear shirt sleeves. The sky is so deep, and so perfectly blue (apart from that wisp at the summit) that my sensation of no longer being on earth is heightened. I lie with my head on his stomach.

"I can't believe we're here," I tell him. "I can't believe we nearly didn't come. It's magical."

"It is," he says, stroking my hair.

We stay together, not speaking, for a while. Then Max goes to make sure we've got some hot water for our noodles, and I climb up to a rock on the valley wall. The buildings are behind me. I can only see the mountain. It feels like a dangerous place but, logically, I know that I couldn't be any safer than I am here, for the simple reason that there's only us. Us and some Tibetan monks who, even if the one we've met isn't exactly normal, are not an immediate danger. It is so still. I watch the mountain go pink in the sunset. The folly of looking at it and seeing a personal challenge is so great it almost makes me smile. It would make me laugh, if it wasn't the deluded westerners who rule the world. It doesn't seem so funny when I remember that. We are not the comical outsiders. We are in charge. Buddhists are the outsiders in world power terms. Ally, I maintain, is no more a proper Buddhist than I am.

This is a retreat. It is the calm before the storm. I feel more scared at the idea of going home than I did about leaving it. My priorities have been completely altered since I've been travelling. I can't believe I can go to China on my own and be happy, if a little shaky, but I am deeply ambiguous about the idea of going home. Home, where everything is familiar. Soho, or "my darling Soho" as I used to think of it, where the streets are crowded with all sorts of people, from the homeless boy I used to abuse to the innocently sightseeing tourists, to the less innocent men who drop in to see the sex shows, or to visit the "top Models." The streets were busy all the time, even in the middle of the night, and there was no room. There was no space; nothing to breathe. And here I am sitting by the biggest mountain in the world, breathing air that is contaminated by perhaps one vehicle a day braving the horrible non-road. It doesn't smell of anything. It smells crystal clear. It's like the world used to be. I wouldn't be surprised to see pterodactyls swooping overhead.

I hate the thought of leaving all this behind, of not seeing Nepal, and not going to India at all. I wonder, again, why I'm going. Because I'm scared. Because, rightly or wrongly, I think someone wants to kill me. Because someone has my box of things, and is leaving them with the bodies. Because Amanda's dead. I'm terrified, and I'm fleeing. If it wasn't for what happened to Amanda, I would not feel the slightest inclination to go to London. Max has been telling me about the south of India, and I long to go there with him. I want him to take his job in Pondicherry. Perversely, I want to go and work there too, now. I know that I'm the reason he's not going. Sometimes I wonder whether he's sticking with me now out of duty, and because he's so lovely. I wonder whether he'd be better off without me. I know he would; but does he realise it?

If, if, if. The thoughts in my head make me wonder about my sanity, but I can't stop them coming. If I sat out here until I died, then Max would be free to live in the balmy south of India forever. If I wandered off and was never seen again, then he wouldn't have to spend all his money on escorting me to London. If I'd been killed instead of Amanda, then it would all have been neat, and tidy, and right. I've done bad things. Amanda was just becoming happy. Max doesn't realise what I'm really like. There is one more thing to do. This thing has been niggling at me for months. It has been the last thing I held back when everything else came out. I have to tell Max about it, and only then will I be ready to face west again.

As soon as the sun tips behind the valley wall, I start shivering. The mountain, ahead of me, is glowing pink in the last of the light. I look at it for a while. I'm getting really cold now. It's time to see the others. I get up, and hear a voice from below.

"Are ya cold?" it says. I am startled, and look down to the valley floor.

"Christ, Gabe. You scared me shitless."

"Sorry. Just admiring the view. I was coming to tell you to come in. It's going to get shit-cold any . . . second . . . NOW." As he speaks, the last of the rays disappear, and I realise we are racing against time. We have to do everything that needs any light, and we have to do it now.

"Cheers." I make an effort and smile at him as I climb down, dislodging large numbers of stones as I go. They rain down upon him but for once he doesn't complain. We walk towards the monastery together. It's not far.

"Hey." He holds me back for a moment by taking my elbow. "I'm sorry if I upset you by asking about your friend. I didn't mean to. It's just kinda hard to think of the right thing to say, and I didn't want to say nothing, y'know? Although perhaps that might have been the better idea."

I smile again. "It's OK." I force myself to overcome my revulsion and accept his apology. I try to do what a Buddhist would do. The Dalai Lama would let it go. "It wasn't your fault. Anything would have upset me. It's an upsetting time. When my mum died people didn't know what to say either. Come to that, they didn't know what to say when she was alive."

"Why's that?"

This is a small but important moment. "She was an alcoholic. That's why she died." I've never before been able to tell anyone that while I've been sober.

I leave Gabe gaping and wondering what to say, and go into our room. Max is pouring water from a thermos into three noodle pots. I am strangely cheerful.

"All right there? Mmm, what shall we have tonight? I think I'll go for the smoked salmon on brown bread to start, and then the vegetable and Gruyère bake, with a side order of new potatoes, and an insalata tricolore." I haven't thought about that sort of food lately. It makes me hungry, with a hunger that will never be satisfied by what we've got on hand.

"Sadly that's off, madam. The last of those dishes were served to another satisfied customer just moments ago. I can offer you some very fine noodles. Served in the original plastic shell. Furthermore, I can offer them with or without the contents of several sachets."

"Mmm, it's my lucky day. Do we have to eat really quickly so we can get to the loo before it's dark?"

"You should go now, just to be on the safe side."

"But I don't want to."

After we've eaten, we realise we haven't got enough water left for the next day. There's just a tiny bit left, just enough to brush our teeth, and a small amount for the morning. Not enough for an Everest expedition. We know that the monks live their lives by the sun, and that we can't wake the recorder-squanker to make him boil us up some more. Their fire won't even be lit now. It'll be embers. So, to conserve what we've got, we brush our teeth in what's left of the noodle soup. It feels entirely counter-productive, and I am left with half my mouth feeling refreshed and minty, and the other half hot with stock.

It is pitch dark. When I venture out, with the candle, to tip the toothy water onto the ground, I nip round the corner to see if the mountain is glowing, or visible in any way. It isn't. It would be against all known laws of physics if it was phosphorescent, as I half expected. You'd never know it was there; perhaps it isn't.

Before we go to bed, we need to adjust our clothing. We get out our backpacks and take out all our jumpers. We put on as many as we can, add gloves and scarves, and all our socks. It's freezing. Worse than freezing. Viciously, bitingly cold. I don't know how people sleep out on Everest. No wonder so many of them die.

I can't sleep. I am psyching myself up to talk about what I did.

Max can't sleep. At least, for once, I'm not alone. We are five thousand metres high, at the top of the world.

"You're wide awake," Max notes about an hour after we started concentrating on closing our eyes and shutting down our brains.

"So are you," I point out. He is holding me round the waist. I like that. I feel safe, guarded. "How are we going to get to Everest in the morning if we haven't slept?" I add.

"We'll be all right. We're going to feel like shit anyway. It won't make any difference. What shall we do now?"

"I can think of something."

Sex with Max, at all altitudes, gets better and better. We peel back as few layers of clothing as possible to allow access. Max has cheekily left a condom within easy reach. I feel him, hard, through his jeans, and pop his buttons open, allowing him to ping out. It hasn't become familiar yet. He's always surprising me. I believe that sex in Tibet entitles us to membership of the mile-high club.

Afterwards, we're more alert than ever. I know I need to talk to Max now, and I start rambling just to put off the moment.

"It's primitive, isn't it?" I say. The thought of the inhospitable terrain outside makes me shiver. "We're just sheltering from the night. We couldn't survive out there, and even in here it's the barest minimum."

"Not quite the *barest* minimum," corrects Max, smoothing my tummy. "When I went to get the water, I saw where the monks sleep. Some of them are on ledges around a courtyard, open to the air on one side. They must have to summon up all their powers of meditation to drop off to sleep."

"Fucking hell. How hardy. And it's not a one-off for them, is it? It's every single night. They actually live here."

We try to imagine what it would be like if your address was Rongbuk Monastery, Everest Region, Tibet. I don't suppose you'd get many letters.

"I don't expect the Chinese get up here often," says Max. "They probably have quite a lot of freedom."

"But everyone who comes and goes would be monitored at the checkpost."

"True."

I think Max is in danger of dropping off to sleep. I need to speak quickly. This is the moment. I know it is.

"Can I tell you something?" My heart is pounding, and I don't wait for an answer. The words are coming fast. "You know my mother? Well, you know that she died over a year ago. I didn't tell you exactly how she died. I haven't told anyone—well, only one person—and I'd like to tell you now. Is that OK?"

He sounds surprised. "You know it is. You can tell me anything. In fact I'm very honoured that you'd want to. Tell me whatever you need to tell me. Anything you want to say, say it."

"I know. Thank you. Well, this is quite a big thing. I hope you'll still mean that when you've heard it. You might not want to know me anymore."

"I will."

"Well, the thing is, as you already know I nursed her through her alcoholism my whole life. I tipped it down the sink. She had tantrums. She threw the glass or the bottle at me. I generally ducked, apart from one time when she got me on the forehead. When I went to school the next day they made me go to casualty for stitches. She shouted and screamed and trembled and stole my money, and shat in her pants, and I was the only person looking after her, all the time."

Max doesn't say anything. He just holds me tighter.

"It took me a while to work out that everyone didn't live like that. I was amazed when I worked out that we were different. Sometimes I'd leave her for a night and go to Dad's for the weekend, but then I always got handed a baby to look after. It was a piece of piss, holding a baby, compared to looking after her, but I resented them like fuck, because they were so bloody cosseted. They were my brothers and sisters. Why did they get everything? I don't much like Lola, but at least she made sure her kids had everything, and even if she didn't spend much time with them herself, she employed people to look after them.

"So," I continue, in a dangerously shaky voice, "in the end it was too much for me and I couldn't do it anymore. I hated her. I'd just come out of a really bad relationship, you know all about that. More than you'd like to know, I'm sure. I couldn't see any future for myself that didn't involve me checking on bloody Mum all the time. The only time she went out was to get money and go to the liquor store. I should have just rung up the social services and got her taken away like people get their old fridges taken away, but I was in too deep for that. I felt too tied to her. My whole life had revolved completely around her and I didn't have the strength for what she'd say when she realised she was being carted off. So I saw she was getting ill. She was yellow and she could hardly speak anymore. She was in pain, but it didn't stop her drinking. I should have got the doctor round, but I didn't. And she was getting worse and worse. She stank, even though I made her get in the bath most days. She wouldn't speak to me anymore. She'd glare at me and I'd glare at her. You know, they'd stopped serving her in the liquor store by then because, finally, she couldn't pretend she was a normal woman bulk buying for a party. I saw her once asking some schoolchildren to buy her some whisky. You should have seen them laughing. I was so ashamed. She looked like a bag lady.

"Anyway, she was getting iller and iller, and nastier and nastier, and I felt like I didn't have a mother anymore, that I hadn't for years. I could tell, just from looking at her, that she was on the way out. She was dying. When you see someone who's dying, you know it. She could hardly move anymore. She was on her last legs. She wasn't on her legs at all. Her doctor told me an excessive quantity of liquor would kill her. I was waiting for her to die. Then I couldn't wait anymore. It was agony for both of us.

"It was Christmas Eve." My voice sounds weird as I get to the crucial part. I don't want to say it. "I made up my mind that our

Christmas present would be freedom, so I bought an oversize bottle and left it on the counter. I knew she'd drink it all, so I went out. When I got home, it was over, and I was free. And if I hadn't done that I wouldn't have met you. But just because good came of it doesn't change the fact that I killed her."

There is absolute silence. There isn't even a dog barking. The wind isn't blowing. We're on the plateau, and I have confessed, and nothing is happening.

"Christ," says Max, in the end. He is holding me tight. "Poor baby."

"Do you think I'm a terrible person? Do you think I could go to prison?"

"No, I don't. Oh Tans, I tend to forget exactly how shit things were before, because you're so balanced now. My poor, poor girl. Of course I don't think you're bad. You found a way out of an insupportable situation. You won't go to prison, because what you did was justified. Also, and more importantly, because we're not going to tell anyone else, ever."

"No, we're not." I feel drained, and suddenly sleepy. We don't say anything else, and I drift off, reflecting that I now understand the Catholic Church's penchant for confession. It's a wonderful feeling. I'm ready to go back, now.

CHAPTER
23

We have set the alarm for seven o'clock, thinking how virtuous and hardy we will feel when we get an early start towards the mountain. Unfortunately, we overlooked the fact that it doesn't get light until nine, because Tibet is on Beijing time. I suppose the Chinese don't want to risk setting Tibet on a dangerous path to independence by letting it have its own time zone. It's lucky the British weren't that cautious with the empire; half the world would have been working all night and sleeping in the daylight hours, like me. Mind you, look what happened to the empire.

We both issue a groggy murmur, and I reach out and switch the alarm off. We lie there for a bit. The room is pitch dark. I can see a krillion twinkling stars through the window, and not even the first glimmer of dawn.

"Fuck," says Max, and there is a long, long period when two people fail to get back to sleep. Once you're awake, here, with all its attendant frailties, it's an uphill struggle to lose consciousness. No wonder they developed the practice of meditation. My efforts at sleeping collapse entirely the moment I remember that I told him my secret last night. Fuck. Fuck fuck fuck. The thing that I haven't even allowed myself to think about. The thing I swore to myself that I'd never tell anyone. What shall I do? Shall I pretend it never happened, let him think it was a dream? Shall I jump straight in and remind him, seek reassurance? Shall I pretend to be asleep and avoid the issue a little longer?

"Do you want a painkiller?" I say in the end.

Max squeezes me. "You're angelic, you know that?"

I know I've got some aspirin in my bag, but I can't see a thing.

"Where's the candle?" I demand.

"On the floor, but there aren't any matches," says Max.

I manage, eventually, to locate what I think are my painkillers by holding down the light on the alarm clock. I pour the very last of our tepid water into an old noodle pot, and we swallow them, suffering. The water is fouler than anything I've ever tasted, even yak butter tea. I feel intensely vulnerable, and want to do everything for Max, in the hope that he'll carry on liking me.

"Honey," he mutters, swallowing. "I still love you, all right? I'd like to spell that out. You don't have to wait on me. We'll talk later. I don't think anything bad about you. Promise."

We don't set off until the middle of the morning because the recorder player declines to boil us any water. Greg and Juliette have enough left, but Ally, Andy, Max, and I are denied it. We wait and wait, assuming that the monk is attending to it, but it never comes. Eventually, Ally takes me by the hand and we go into the monastery to seek him out. I am glad of the distraction. Anything that stops me thinking about my confession is worth doing.

The first thing we see are the shelves where they sleep. A couple of monks are dozing on them, nesting in their robes. Inside, we edge around nervously, seeing no one. The corridors are dark. The ceilings are low. It smells of yak butter, incense, and old dirt. After five minutes of stumbling, we emerge into a big room that looks like a kitchen. A couple of monks are in there, doing things, but they both ignore us. At the centre of the room is a huge hearth. In it, yesterday's ashes sit blackly.

Distantly, a recorder is being blown randomly. It gets closer. He appears a few seconds later, and stops, and looks at us looking

277

at him. I feel we have intruded horribly, that we are not welcome here. After a few seconds, he gestures to the black hearth.

"No fire," he says.

Thus we are perhaps the first Everest expedition to carry no water whatsoever. Greg and Juliette have gone on ahead but promise they will wait for us at base camp. It is the coldest I can imagine it ever being, anywhere. It must be a long, long way below freezing. The journey is straightforward—we look at the mountain, and walk towards it—and it's flat. Two dogs from the monastery come with us, bounding ahead, and making doubly sure we get there. It's the hardest piece of exercise I've ever done. I feel there must be lumps of metal in my boots, and magnets just under the earth. It's impossible to lift my feet. I am wearing everything. All we have are a few cans of Red Bull that we bought at a tiny, implausible shop in Lhatse, and a packet of tasteless glucose biscuits.

The path is on the side of the valley that doesn't get the morning sun, and my toes, my nose, my fingers are numb. The mountain is in the light, and I envy it. A pack of strange animals runs across our path. There is no sign of the others up ahead. Normally, I slow my pace to walk with Ally, whose little legs won't carry her as fast as Max goes. Andy takes quick strides, so he can be manly and keep up with the boys.

After twenty minutes, however, I have to walk with Max.

"Do you mind?" I ask her. "Max and I really need to sort something out."

"Sure. You go ahead. Tell you what, when you catch them, you can send Andy back if you like, tell him I need to talk to him. I do. I've decided what to do."

"Which is?"

"I'll talk to him first. Then I'll tell you. Just point him in this direction."

I could kiss her. "You are such a mate. We have to keep in touch forever."

"Course we will."

"Hey," says Max. "I was hoping you'd catch up."

I turn to Andy. "Ally says can you wait for her. She needs you for something."

"Well, when the little lady calls, the bloke had better listen!"

I glare at him. He sits on a rock, and looks back, nervously, at Ally's tiny figure, struggling under the weight of all her clothing.

"Be honest," I tell Max, as soon as we are out of earshot. "Do you find anything difficult in what I told you? I won't believe you if you say no. You are a human being."

"It is a little strange, but to be honest it didn't completely surprise me. I'd never consciously thought about it, but you'd told me enough before about the way you used to live, so that I guess it did figure. Look, no one should have to live like that."

I feel he's being slightly evasive. "What do you feel? Really? I hate to be one of those girls who say what are you thinking all the time, but what *are* you thinking? I mean, one of the things I find weird is that, with this killer on the loose, he's only doing what I did to my own mother, and yet we feel completely unambiguous about him. We condemn him utterly. Everyone does. What makes me different?"

"Circumstances. You didn't kill anyone in cold blood. You were provoked beyond endurance. You were entirely justified. And she was dying anyway. For fuck's sake, Tans, you must never, *ever* equate yourself with the man who killed Amanda and the others. Never. Have you been doing that all along?"

"Yes, I suppose I have."

"Well, stop that right now. OK?"

"All right. So what are you thinking?"

"How fragile people are. The same thing I realised when I thought I was going to die. You feel so alive, but then you can be dead the next day. Or you can have something in your head that's been secretly killing you for months or years. And your mother seems to be the opposite of that. She'd been killing herself slowly,

all that time, and yet her body had remained alive. Stop me if you
don't like me talking like this."

"No, carry on."

"It seems horribly banal that, just by mixing up two things
that she probably consumed daily—did she take Valium?"

"Mmm, usually at night. Never in the quantities I gave her."

"Well, that just by combining them, she died. Just like that.
Twenty years too late, in a sense. Tans, who was the other person
you've told?"

"My brother. When I was drunk. I was off my face."

"No one else."

"No one."

We walk on in silence. A few minutes later, we come upon a
building and a big tent. A Tibetan man is unpacking boxes by the
tent's entrance. *"Tashi dele!"* we call. He looks round, and returns
our greeting. So this is Everest Base Camp. In the popular imagination—or at least in my imagination—it has long been strewn
with rubbish. I thought we'd be ankle deep in used loo paper and
discarded oxygen canisters, with a few Coke cans and Mars Bar
wrappers chucked around for good measure. In fact, the whole
area is pristine. The bright sun reflects off each grey or white
stone, and the effect is one of blinding, unsullied perfection.

"Do you have any water?" I ask the man hopefully. He spreads
his hands and shakes his head. I don't believe him, but I don't
blame him, either. Everest survival is not helped by the handing-
out of essential supplies to amateur freeloaders.

"Is there an expedition?" Max asks.

The man nods, and points to the mountain, which is looking
huge and proud in the sunlight.

"American," he explains.

A little way further on, on a small rocky hill, we find Greg and
Juliette. They look extremely happy. Lunar rubble stretches in
front of them to the base of the mountain itself. Some sun-
bleached prayer flags flutter from a large stone nearby.

"Apparently, the next base camp is over there," says Greg, pointing to the foot of the mountain. "There's an American and British group there. We met one of them. He says they're looking for Mallory's body."

"They just want an excuse to climb the mountain." I am cynical.

"Probably," agrees Max. "It's not as if no one's looked for Mallory's body before. Have you got some water?"

Juliette passes it to him. "Mallory is a mountain climber, yes?"

"He's the guy that said 'because it's there,'" says Greg. "Great quote. 'Why do you want to climb Everest?' 'Because it's there.'"

She surveys the mountain towering in the distance.

"It's still there. And where is he?"

"We'll probably never know," says Max, handing me the water. It is warm, and it tastes of plastic. It's perfect.

Ally and Andy arrive just as we are leaving. They look more comfortable together, but I don't know how to interpret this development. Ally returns my smile, but says nothing. We leave them to look at the mountain, and turn our backs on it, and walk back to the monastery. Now it really is time to go home.

Soto is trying to repair the jeep. "Sheet," he mutters when we come close enough to hear. "Sheet!" he says again, and roars with laughter.

We laugh with him. We only have one more night in Tibet now, and I will miss Soto's rendition of the English language.

"What's wrong?" says Greg. "This does not look encouraging."

"I'm sure he's got it under control," I tell him. There is another jeep parked nearby. I look around, and see a Japanese couple emerge from one of the bedrooms, looking cold. I wave at them, and they wave back.

"I think one hour," says Soto.

We mooch around and discover that there is nothing to do in Rongbuk. The only way to keep warm is to walk, and yet walking is exhausting beyond belief, and we're not allowed to go far away in case the car starts. The problems with the jeep seem to be taxing Soto's technical knowledge, and we consider stealing the newcomers' vehicle and leaving them our crappy one.

"It's been fine all the time," says Max as we sit on a rock for a while. "Just our bloody luck to break down here."

"Where's the nearest garage?" says Gabe, who has been very quiet.

"Only in bloody Nepal," suggests Andy. "And how do we get to Nepal? By car."

"I don't suppose the AA comes out here," I say to Max.

"Alcoholics Anonymous?" says Greg. "Chance would be a bloody fine thing. Not even a bottle of beer to keep us going! We can't stay another night because we haven't got any damned food."

"I'm sure the new people will share with us."

"I expect nothing would please them more," Ally agrees, sarcastically, and I can imagine that an extra six people demanding shares in our noodles last night wouldn't have thrilled us. I look at our little group.

"Is anyone a mechanic? Has anyone even done a car maintenance course?"

"I have." It is Juliette. Of course it is. She knows everything. "But I think Soto knows what he does."

Greg beams. He is so proud of her. I don't know what they're going to do when they get to Nepal. Juliette wants to go back to Phonsavanh, and even if she didn't, it would be difficult for her to go and live with Greg in America. What would she do with herself? I can't imagine her in Connecticut, or even multicultural Manhattan. I laugh at myself when I remember how keen I was to go to America rather than Asia. I suppose I have Tom to thank for forcing me here. Here I am, broken down at Everest. One of my friends is dead, I am unburdened of a secret, and I am ready to get on with life. Without Tom sending me here in the first place, that couldn't have happened. He's never going to appreciate his role in my future well-being.

Juliette goes to see if she can lend a hand. The rest of us go for a little walk. We tell her where we're going so she can run after us when she gets the car going.

"Has anyone met the other group?" asks Ally.

"I did," said Gabe. "They seemed quite nice. There were only four of them. Two guys and two gals. Travelling the other way from us."

"Isn't it funny how you get into little groups?" I muse. "I mean, we're all random people just meeting here by chance, but we're still a little bit resentful of them coming to our place when we were here first."

"We won't be resentful if we end up eating half their food," Gabe points out. "We'll like them a lot more than they like us."

"What nationalities were they?" asks Max. "Which would be the most generous, do you think?"

"There was a Japanese couple, a Brit guy and a girl. I'm not sure where she was from because she didn't say anything. White. European, I'd guess. The guy was friendly enough—I think they were a couple. But I don't know who's generous. I guess we could have a word with the Japs. Try to part them from their seal meat and whale blubber. Fuck it, I could stomach anything."

Ally narrows her eyes at him. "Gabe, you push it sometimes."

Later, Juliette seeks us out. We are starving.

"I am sorry, it is not good," she says. "I do not know why it does not go. It is too difficult for me. Soto says now is too late. We stay the night."

It's the middle of the afternoon. "It's not that late," I tell her.

"It is not safe to drive in the dark on this road," Juliette points out, and she is absolutely right. We need to arrive in daylight, as well as to leave in it.

"Fuck." Andy speaks for us all. "Another fucking freezing night. Bloody marvellous, that is."

"So we won't be in Nepal tomorrow."

"It makes you see how basic life is here," says Max. "There's no phone, no spare parts, obviously, no food. Maybe the monks'll have some food for us. Or we could shoot an animal."

"No we couldn't," Ally corrects him. "Even though they've always had to eat meat here to survive, they're still Buddhists. The people who do the actual killing are outcasts."

"As I'm leaving the country tomorrow, or at least as soon as I can, I could cope with that." It's really, really cold. "How are we going to manage?" I ask. "I'm cold already. Shall we just go back to the rooms and read our books and get some water off that awkward bastard . . ."

"That cunt," corrects Gabe.

"Yep, him. And snuggle in our sleeping bags?"

"What you're saying," deduces Ally, "is, shall we go to bed. If we go now we won't get up till morning."

"There's nothing else to do." I notice Greg and Juliette looking at each other.

"We'll see y'all later," says Greg, and they trot off in the direction of their bedroom.

I decide to watch the sunset again, because I'm bored of lying in our freezing room, looking at the ceiling and thinking. I killed my mother. Now I have said it. I know it, and Max knows it. I feared it would destroy our relationship, and yet Max supports me completely and unquestioningly. He has put aside any scruples he may feel. I won't tell anyone else, ever. I just have to accept that I did it, and forgive myself, and carry on living. The best legacy that Mum can leave me is this: I will do everything it takes to be as unlike her as possible.

I kiss Max. "I'm going to see the sunset," I tell him. "Back before dark."

"You'd better be," he says.

I feel peaceful now. I am finally beginning to be able to live with myself. I climb back up onto my perch, above the valley floor, and cross my legs, and imagine that I'm a Buddhist. Sometimes I think I might investigate Buddhism when I get home, but really I know I won't. I will find a yoga class to go to. Meanwhile, I'm spending another night up here in the sky. It's not so bad, really. I look at the top of the mountain which, again, has a wisp of cloud hanging from its summit, the only blemish on a clear sky. That peak has been the cause of hundreds of deaths, but it's western human nature that is at fault, not the peak itself. People talk about it as an "angry" mountain, but I don't think it is. I think it's people's fault for going somewhere they're not meant to be. When they're at the top, they are literally dying. Just time to take a photo before you have to hurry down to breathe again. I'd much rather live among mountains than assault them. Mallory will never be my hero.

Someone scrambles up behind me. It must be Max.

"Hiya," I say, without turning round.

"Hello, Tansy," says a familiar voice. Not Max. I look round. "Oh, hello," I say calmly. "What are you doing here?"

CHAPTER
24

He sits down next to me. I know he's not really here. My mind has, obviously, conjured him up because I told my secret. I pushed it away for almost eighteen months, and now I've faced it. I can't deny, any longer, that I did it. I was completely, and directly, responsible for my mother's death. And I told Will straightaway; I told him that dizzy New Year's Eve when I ended up in hospital. I know I told him, although I could never articulate the thought. Neither of us ever mentioned it again.

I am impressed with my mind, and its ability to force me to confront issues with the inspired use of hallucination.

I smile at him. "So?" I say.

"You don't seem very surprised to see me, *sis*. I'm disappointed. It took an awful lot of planning to meet you here. I even had to sabotage your van to make sure we'd have this opportunity."

That's funny. It makes me smile. "I suppose you did. How did you get here?"

"I've been all over the place. But I got here the same way you did, by paying a handsome sum to the Chinese government and joining an overland tour. Mine was from Kathmandu."

"Are we meant to be talking about Mum?"

"You're sharp, aren't you? Yes, we are."

I look at him. He seems extraordinarily real, and I wonder if I have gone quite mad. He is thinner than he was, tanned, a bit younger looking. He has a handsome face which is oddly like mine. We look like twins, and we don't even have the same father. We don't even know who his father is. Will's wearing a fleece, a windproof jacket, a pair of jeans, gloves, and some sturdy boots. I would have expected my brain to summon him dressed as I last saw him, in a crumpled checked shirt and combat trousers, just before I left England.

"How's life in Scotland?" I ask him.

"Scotland? I expect it's fine. I haven't been there for years."

"Are you sure you're Will? Because you live in Scotland. I mean, I kind of know I'm imagining you, but do try to get it right."

"Sorry. I'll have to try harder. You really think you're imagining me?"

I laugh. "This is so weird. Yes, of course I am, because I was just thinking about you, and I just told Max the thing I told you on New Year's Eve."

"What thing was that?"

I look at him. His eyes are hard, and he's not smiling anymore. "You know."

"Say it."

"Do I have to?"

"Yes."

"I killed my mother."

"Whose mother?"

I can only manage a very small voice. "Our mother."

"Say the whole thing."

"I killed our mother."

"You murdered her."

"It was euthanasia."

He throws a rock as far as he can, with huge force. It hits the ground below us, and splits open.

"It was not fucking euthanasia, you stupid bitch, because euthanasia happens with the victim's consent. What you did was murder. Cowardly murder, as well. Not even proper murder."

I'm scared now. The shadow comes across us. It's getting dark. I want to make this apparition go away.

"Time for you to leave now," I tell him.

He laughs. "You really don't think I'm here, do you? Well, I've got some news for you, *sis*. I am." He pinches my arm.

I shout, "Ow!" It really hurts.

"Real enough for you?" he says calmly. "If I wasn't real, I wouldn't have hurt you. Look, I'll show you something else. I'd like to bite you, but that would be stupid, they'd identify me like a shot when they found the body. But look at this." He takes a clump of my hair in his gloved hand and pulls it. I roar with pain. It is a burning pain. I feel it rip out altogether, and my head flies away from his hand.

"Look!" He's smiling gently, and holding it out to me. "Here is your hair. Now, if I was a figment of your imagination, I wouldn't be able to pull your hair out, would I?"

"William?"

"You know what my favourite invention of the modem age is? Email. Isn't it brilliant? Because with a hotmail address, you can be anywhere you want. People believe you when you say you live in Scotland. But in fact you can be writing from Bombay, or Delhi, or, I don't know, let's say Dharamsala, where I must say there are a lot of fucking *stupid*, annoying travellers just crying out to be put out of their misery. Some of them are nearly as annoying and as deserving of death as you, my own flesh and blood. My next of kin."

"Will, what are you saying?"

"You know what I'm saying. Come on, you're a clever girl, you've been to university. It's staring you in the face. Everything in the emails was made up. A girlfriend called Mary! Yeah, right. I just needed to keep tabs on where you were."

"You're saying you've been killing the women. You mean you

killed my friend! You murdered Amanda. No, you can't have. I'm still dreaming. Go away."

The last rays of sunlight have vanished. It's going to be very dark very soon, and I know that, when it is, Max will be out to look for me. I have to keep him talking.

"Oh yes, sorry about your friend. I meant to say. Imagine my delight when I ran into her again! The last time I saw her was at your leaving party. I shagged her in the loos, did she ever tell you? Murder must run in our family, don't you think? And now, without further ado, I'm going to do that deed before that nice young man comes to look for you. I'm doing him a favour. In fact I'm making the world a better place." He has his hands round my neck. "I've been looking forward to this. My final victim. It's you I've wanted to kill all along, in case you need it spelled out. You may have noticed that I've been to all the places you were going to go to. I knew you weren't going to see them, you see, so I thought I'd do you a favour and see them for you. You confused me a little by going to China when you were meant to be in Malaysia—please, Tansy, you could have given me a little more notice—but then I realised we could meet in Tibet and that might be more fun. When you mentioned Everest, I knew it was the right place. After this I will vanish into the night and become someone else."

"You've been the Canadian guy? The Eastern European?"

He nods. "Not difficult. I'm Rocky," he says, in a Canadian voice. "And I am Yevgeny," he adds, sounding Russian. I am shocked by how good he is. Then I am terrified.

"Why do you have to kill me? Where did you get my things from?" I have the knife in my fleece pocket. I cough vigorously so he looks hard at me, wondering whether it's genuine. While his attention is on my face, I reach my hand into my pocket, slip off my glove, and take hold of the handle.

"Two questions. I'll take the second one first. It was extraordinarily easy. I broke into your father's house while they were away. Not difficult. I covered my tracks and they never even knew they'd been burgled. I'm a pro. I wanted to scare you. I wanted you to wonder whether this was about you. It worked, didn't it? It cast a shadow over your whole trip. You said so yourself.

"As for why you have to die, I think that should be obvious. Because you deserve to. You don't know what it's like to grow up with no one. The only thing I ever wanted was to meet my mother. I just wanted to know where I came from, why everyone else has parents but not me. Even the fucking psychiatrist said it might 'ground' me, if I handled it right. I wrote to her for years. She reckoned she couldn't deal with it and she wouldn't see me because she said she didn't want to upset you. Now, that's a badly misplaced loyalty, if you ask me. She wrote me letters, and in November, she said she'd see me at Christmas. She fucking invited me to come to the house on Boxing Day. Said she'd tell you about me before. And then what happens when I call? I was so scared about ringing her, and she's only fucking dead!" He tightens his gloved grip round my neck. I can hardly breathe now. "And then the fucking spoilt brat herself, the golden girl who would be so upset if she knew about me, she gets pissed, takes a noseful of coke, says she's glad that my mother is dead . . ." I can feel his fingers shaking. "She was my mother before she was yours, and then this brat, that's you, you tell me you murdered her! You ruined my life. And then you expect us to be friends. You're evil. I hated you from the moment I met you and I hate you even more today, and that is why you have to die, now."

"You killed more people than me." That's what I try to say, but it comes out rasping and barely audible.

"I did, but you started it."

"No!"

"Oh yes."

He tightens his fingers. I am dying. I am dying right now. Will is killing me. I have the dagger in my hand, but I don't know how, or when, to use it. I need to get it straight in, somewhere where it'll do the maximum damage. My brother is murdering me, and my only hope is to murder him first. We've both killed before. It doesn't feel like a hallucination anymore. I gasp and force a tiny amount of air into my lungs. He is so big and tall. He's much stronger than me. I don't want to die.

It's nearly dark. We are hidden by a rock from the view of the monastery.

I hear Max's voice. "Tans! Where are you?"

I struggle to make a sound, and force out a pathetic cry, before Will tightens his grip and I have no breath at all. I feel the coldness of the knife in my hand, and a warm circle where the turquoise is. I try to hold on to it. I feel limp, and I try to keep some strength back. Will is on his guard, but at my limpness I feel him relax a tiny bit. I think my eyes are open, but I can only see black. I whip my arm out, and plunge it into a random part of Will. He hardly flinches. Useless. He grabs me tighter in retaliation. I push it in up to the hilt, and twist it. I feel it hitting a bone.

"Tansy!" Max is very close. Will lets go, and feels my pulse. Bugger. I must still have a pulse if I'm thinking. I seize every ounce of strength I have, and roll away.

"Max!" I shout. It comes out as a breathy "aaa." I hope he heard it. I roll off the rock. At least this way I get away from William, however I land. I feel myself flying through the air. I hear Will swearing, and Max says my name. And that is all.

CHAPTER
25

On the day I am due to leave hospital I realise I have finally slept through the night. When I wake up, expecting it to be grey and everyone else to be asleep, I am surprised to see the sun edging through the windows, and to hear the sound of activity on the ward.

The sun is apologetic and feeble. "Excuse me," it mutters. "Sorry to trouble you, just wanted to let everyone know there's a new day. Got that? Then I'll get back behind the cloud." It's not the Tibetan sun, blasting down into the magical kingdom. It is the English version, but it is daylight nonetheless. I am back in toned-down England, and back in hospital at that. It's an all-female ward this time, as the omnipotent "they" decreed that I would be too traumatised to sleep if there were strange men in the room.

I dimly remember that I used to utter the word "insomnia" when my heart was thumping because I'd snorted too much charlie. I'd lie in my bed in Hampstead, listening to the birds, and I'd groan. "Poor me!" I'd rage. "I've got insomnia! It's *not my fault.*" I'd take one or two of Mum's downers, and eventually I'd drop off, as, eventually, did she.

Then I thought I had insomnia in Tibet, and I suppose I did. From here, though, it looks like easy insomnia. Innocent insomnia. The situation was the same—I was involved, it was my fault, and those were my things, however unlikely that seemed—but I didn't know about it. I hadn't come anywhere near suspecting that it could have been Will. I was sad about Amanda, but I didn't know the truth. I was ignorant, and it was bliss.

This kind of insomnia makes me lie hopelessly awake in the darkness, all night long, listening to all the other women breathing and snoring. I used to be miserable about an external event, about Amanda being murdered, not about the internal knowledge that I was responsible. Now, day and night, my head is always filled with my brother; I desperately try to recall everything I said to him in those pathetic, please-like-me emails. It makes no difference, now, but I can't stop thinking about it. I made it easy for him because I wanted him and me to be a nuclear family unit. Indeed, we now look like a nuclear family—an explosive one. All he had to do was to send emails asking where I was going, and I happily reeled off a list. Every time I mentioned a place, I condemned someone to die there: I know I should be dead, and I would be dead if Max hadn't been in exactly the right place; if he hadn't picked me up and run to the monastery with me.

I only know what happened because Max fills in the blanks for me. I get him to tell me the story again and again, hoping that, in becoming familiar, it might become banal.

He saw it get dark, he says, and he went out to look for me. He wasn't worried at all, at first; he just assumed I was talking to Ally, or one of the others. When I wasn't anywhere around the guesthouse and no one had seen me, he took a candle, because none of us had a working torch, and he set out across the valley, in the direction he'd last seen me heading.

"Where did you get the matches?" I asked him once.

He looked down. "I'd actually borrowed them earlier. From Will. I didn't know it was him. Obviously. But I blew the candle out," he added hastily, as if using Will's matches had been an act of treachery. "I could see more from the moon."

He could see enough to know that he couldn't see me, so he headed for the rock that he knew I'd sat on the day before. He was calling my name, increasingly concerned, yet unable to imagine what might have befallen me. Then, to his amazement, I flew off the rock and landed at his feet.

"I didn't want to pick you up," he explained, "in case you had a back injury. I wasn't going to—I was almost going to run and get help instead—but then I realised there was someone else up there. I could hear him going 'Fuck, fuck, fuck,' and so I picked you up and ran back with you. I didn't know who it was, but I knew it was bad. And for all I knew you were dead."

As he was running, as fast as he could with such a burden, he heard Will climbing down. "He was trying to follow, but he couldn't really run. He sounded really uneven. I could hear that he was limping."

From this, we and the police guess that I stabbed him in the leg. They found my bloody knife on the rock, and carted it off for DNA analysis. Thank God I bought that knife.

"After a while, I heard him stop. I think he went off in the other direction. By then I was practically back at the buildings."

"What happened next?" I always ask him, although I know the answer.

"As soon as I looked at you, I knew it was him. The psycho. Your instincts just take over in a situation like that. I didn't know what I was doing, but things just happened. I took you to our room, and yelled for help. I have to say, Gabe was fantastic. So were Ally and Andy and Greg and Juliette. So was everyone, in fact, apart from this girl from the other group, who'd been travelling with Will. His girlfriend—he was using her as cover, they reckon, because people were only looking out for a solitary nutter. She completely refused to believe it was him. But we knew it had to be because I'd heard him speaking English, and there was definitely no one else about.

"We all decided to leave, then and there. We had to get you

out of there—you looked terrible—and no one else fancied trying to sleep with him out and about. You looked completely fucked. Your neck was red all the way round, and it was going yellow and black before our eyes. Juliette was in charge of looking after you because she knows about first aid. She thought you were physically OK, but until you came round no one could know what head injuries you had. So we all piled into the other jeep, even Will's girlfriend, in the end. She went to pieces and Gabe had to shut her up. You were spread out over our laps. Everyone was sitting on each other and crammed in the back. The lights were on full beam. Soto drove quite slowly, until we got to the police checkpost. I don't think any of us had ever been grateful to arrive at one of them before."

"And then you brought me home."

"And then we did. We took you to Tingri, and we all slept for a few hours, and then we drove out of China, and into Nepal, and the day after that we took you on a plane."

"Thank you." My eyes, invariably, fill with tears at this point.

I know William is still out there, somewhere. I think of all the women who died because of me, because they looked a bit like me, because they were travelling, like me. All the families who are grieving, forever, because of me. There's no chance of sleeping. I don't even deserve to sleep.

But last night the nurse, Pamela, found me an extra strong sleeping pill, claiming she was sick of my complaining. It knocked me out entirely. I slept right through the night. I can't even remember my dreams. There was no visitation by Will, clambering up the rock and smiling coldly. This makes me, if not happy, then hopeful. I thought I'd never get a full night's sleep again, and now I have. Even though it was drug-induced, it is a start. I feel groggy this morning, but I feel equally groggy when I haven't slept.

I may have renounced recreational drugs, but being in a hospital context seems the perfect excuse. I asked, with alacrity, for morphine the moment I got here. The doctor laughed at me. "We don't normally give morphine for broken legs," he explained.

"I've got an arm as well," I complained. "Concussion. And my bruising is extensive. You said so yourself."

"And I grazed my knee," mocked Pamela.

"Shut up," I told her. She's the same nurse who was on duty on New Year's Day, the year before last. Unfortunately, she remembered me. We glowered at each other for a while but then she relented because, after all, I have been in the papers. Now we are almost friends; not that this makes her nice.

I can hear the sounds of the ward. I don't know why they get going so early in hospitals. It's not as if anyone's going anywhere. I wish I could get up and wander around, but the only journey I ever make is in a wheelchair to therapy. Sometimes patients come and sit with me, and I appreciate that, because I have no compunction about telling them to go away if I want to be alone. I quite like a bit of interaction because it distracts me from what's going on inside. My psychiatrist Penny pointed out that I've probably always been able to act happy and feel sad. I just never knew I was doing it before; and, even though things at home were much worse than I ever acknowledged, I've never been quite as unhappy as I am now. It was my brother; all along, it was my brother.

My best hospital friend is Megan, a sulky sixteen-year-old, who's just had her appendix out. She mooches around, hunched over, pulling her drip behind her like a reluctant dog. We met soon after her entertaining induction into hospital life, which I watched with interest. She snarled at everyone, including her mother who looked exactly like her. She looked at the hospital gown and said, "I'm not putting that on!" so loudly that the whole ward laughed. She glared at all of us. It was a 180-degree glare.

"They're all old!" she said loudly. Then her eyes rested on me for a moment, and she looked away. I knew she'd clocked me.

Sure enough, she trundled over later, almost doubled over with pain.

"Hello," she smiled, through gritted teeth.

"When's your operation?" I asked her.

"Two hours. I feel like fucking crap." She looked at me sideways, to see if her language shocked me. I must be a grown-up, in her eyes.

"You look like it. You'll feel better when it's over."

"That's what they say. I hope so. What are you in for?" She looked a bit sly.

"I think you know the answer already."

She giggled. "I saw you in the paper. I was going to see if I could have your autograph."

"Well." I had to consider the logistics of this unexpected request. "You could, but it would have to be with my left hand because . . ." I looked at the heavy cast on my right arm. She followed my gaze.

"Are you right-handed?"

"Yes. But you can have my special left-handed signature. It'll be a collectors' item."

"Cool."

"Just bring me something to sign, and a pen."

The next morning she was confined to bed and sent Pamela over with a copy of the *Daily Mirror* open at a story which was headlined: "Brave Tansy on the mend, say docs." I looked at my face, which stared back at me with a shocked expression. It was in sharp focus, taken as I arrived at the hospital. I wasn't blurred, because I wasn't dead. I scrawled "To Megan, love from Tansy Harris" in baby writing beside the article, and gave it to Pamela to take back. Megan waved at me across the room. I have never been asked for my autograph before.

"Enjoy it," said Pamela. "Your first and last."

Today I'm leaving the safety of the hospital and going home. The only physical home I've ever had has been the house in

Hampstead, and that's long been sold to a late thirties couple who hope to have a baby to fill up one of the rooms. It was their money that got me to Asia in the first place. The same money got Will there, come to that. There's been so much publicity that they must know, now, what they funded. I bet that woman Jennifer's kicking herself for not filming me.

I wouldn't go back to the Hampstead house even if I still had it. Today, I'm going to Dad and Lola's, which is suddenly the most stable place there is. Max is coming, too. He's been staying in my old room at Guy's. But now he's coming to be my moral support at Dad's. Max says he'll take me to Bakewell when I'm a bit better. I'd like to be there, away from London, and not in the very place where Will knows he can find me.

It took the police ages to work out who he was. It turned out they did have his details on file, but they'd never known him as William Marchmont. After he was adopted, his name was Peter Bond, which is nice and anonymous. Peter had spent time in Broadmoor, of all places. They tracked down his birth certificate when I told them everything I knew about him. My mother, Anne Marchmont, was on there, and there was a blank space for his father. The big surprise was that Mum hadn't really called him Will. She'd named him Ringo, just as teenage girls today call their babies Leo and Britney. She was only sixteen when she had him. She was a child. She was the same age as Megan.

"What would you call a baby if you had one?" I asked Meg, curious.

"As if!" she exclaimed, offended. When coaxed to be hypothetical, she came up with Kian for a boy, and Geri for a girl. "Or Tansy," she added. I was honoured.

"Why Kian?" I asked.

"Hello? He's in N'Sync?"

"Don't have one yet though," I told her hastily. I didn't want to be a pernicious influence on the younger generation.

"Yeah, right," she said. "I'm really going to rush out and have a baby, just because I know its name." I was glad she was in for her appendix and not an abortion.

Baby Ringo, it seemed, had been through several incarnations before that psychiatrist fatally suggested he track down his birth mother. They think he got obsessed by the idea, which was when he re-adopted his original surname and tracked his mother down. I always thought Will's sense of dislocation came from having grown up in children's homes and lived rough since his teens, abandoned by everyone. In fact, he was adopted by a couple, the Bonds, in Guildford, but he went off the rails at a young age. I wonder what would have happened if Mum had kept him. If she'd met Dad, and had me, and we'd grown up together. I wonder what kind of a brother he would have been, when I would have realised how different he was. I feel certain that he would have killed her before I did.

Now he's still out there. Every night that I've been here, in hospital, I've sweated my way through till dawn, knowing that he'll be back. I think I'm safe here, sharing a room with eleven other women. I also know that I will never be completely safe when I leave.

The police say they are confident of catching him. "Interpol are on the case," one of them told me, self-importantly.

"Interpol are on the case," I repeated to Max. It is a good phrase to say. An unlikely one, for real life. Even he looked impressed. The Met have offered a huge reward for information. Apparently that's the standard way of making the underworld people come forward (and a lot of cranks as well, no doubt). He must, for instance, have bought several passports, and if the police know the names, they'll nab him within days. They claim. I'll believe it when I see it. I think if they were going to get him they'd have done it straightaway when he was limping towards Mount Everest, on a frozen night, with no shelter and nowhere to go. It is, of course, most likely that he's dead. If he veered away from the valley floor, it could take a while to find his body. Until they find it, I won't get any natural sleep.

William is a clever man. He killed at least six people without being caught. He planned to kill me, and disappear. He must have had a plan. He had a bag. It probably had a tent in it, and some food. He knew what he was doing. He's still out there. I know he is.

I'm torn between my instinct to block him out of my head altogether and the knowledge, as Penny tells me, that if I don't work through it now, it'll come to get me later, even if he doesn't. When they couldn't find any police records of a William Marchmont, I hoped and prayed that I didn't have a brother at all, that I'd been randomly targeted by a madman who had, somehow, hit upon me as a target when Mum died. That would make me as much of a victim as any of the other women. It would put me into the innocent category, and I would have been able to join in the general sympathy for myself. But it didn't turn out that way. He really was my half-brother (the half element seems important now), and he really was after me. He wanted to kill me, because I killed our mother.

I haven't mentioned that part to the police. Max has drummed it into me that I mustn't, and I'm glad he did. No one has asked. They're not expecting me to be a criminal. I have told one person, but Penny won't tell anyone.

When I discovered her sitting by my bed one day, I was irritated. When she wouldn't go away, I worked myself up into a state of fury. She kept trying to talk to me. How dare she, I thought, when I'm feeling so much pain. My neck was, and is, so sore that breathing, and swallowing, are major achievements. The bruises are healing, but my whole body is tender. My leg is broken in two places from when I crashed to the ground, and my arm, which, apparently, I reached out to break my fall, is comprehensively smashed. I couldn't turn away from her because I couldn't move, but I shut my eyes and willed her away.

"Hello, Tansy," she said when she came the second time.

"Grrrmmmnn," I said, frowning.

"I know it's difficult for you, but you'd feel better if we talked about it."

"Don't wanna."

"I know you've got to get your body better, but remember that that's not all. You need to work through everything that's happened to you as well."

"Not now."

She kept appearing when I least wanted to see her. She'd sit there, all quiet and understanding. I raged against her, internally. She looked so bloody nice, with her immaculate grey hair touching her shoulders, her impeccable lipstick, and her Armani glasses. I scrunched my eyes tight shut because I didn't want to see how nice she looked. I wanted to try to get on with having a life. The only way forward I could see was to put this all behind me and never talk about it again.

After ten minutes, on her third visit, I worked myself up until I was livid. I wanted to see Megan but she wasn't coming over because this woman was there. Every time I opened my eyes a fraction and turned my head to see if she was still there, she was smiling and looking bloody understanding again.

"For Christ's sake," I said in a loud whisper. I didn't want any of the others to hear. "Does the National Health pay you just to sit there and look that *look* at me? I can't believe you really haven't got anything better to do. You're slacking, aren't you? Why don't you go away and do some proper work? How come the National Health pays for Armani glasses, anyway? Leave me alone!"

"I'll leave you for today, if that's really what you want," she said calmly.

"Yes it fucking well is. Fuck off." I looked at her in the same way Megan looked at me when she swore. I wanted to shock her because she looked so genteel, but she didn't bat an eyelid. Then I had to feel guilty about being mean to her.

The next day, Max turned up while she was sitting there. He handed me a sheaf of emails and leant down to kiss me.

"How are you feeling?" he said.

"I'd be better if she wasn't there," I whispered. "Can you make her leave?"

He turned to her. I lay back, closed my eyes, and listened.

"Hello," Max said politely. "Er, I'm Max, Tansy's boyfriend."

"Hello, Max," she said in that warm, trust-me voice. "My name's Penny. I'm a psychiatrist and I'm hoping Tansy will talk to me, but she's finding it a bit difficult."

I turned my head. My neck hurt.

"I am not finding it difficult," I told her. "It's easy. I don't want to talk to you. Full stop."

"I'll leave you two alone then," she said mildly, and off she went.

"Thank God!" I said. He sat down next to me, and took my left hand.

"You've got to talk to her." His voice was firm. "You have to. This is the one thing I'm going to force you to do even though you don't want to."

"It's up to me."

"Remember when you were travelling. Remember the state you were in, when we met, when we were in Laos? You had no inkling then that this was connected to you. Or, at least, you had an inkling but we couldn't believe it was possible. Even before there was Will to worry about, remember the things you had to deal with? The ghost you had? Your mother? Remember how you felt when she died?"

"I was glad. I kind of made myself be glad."

"And?"

"And I had to come to terms with it all, I suppose, and I had to stop drinking, and all that." I look at him accusingly. I can see where he's taking me.

"What if someone had offered you counselling when she died? Or, even better, before? What if someone had interrupted your media life to offer you support and help? You know what you'd have said. Exactly what you're saying now, except more forcefully. But you would have benefited from it tremendously. And you still will. This woman seems perfect, not to mention tolerant. She doesn't have to keep trying, you know, but she is. And you know why I care so much? Because this is absolutely crucial to us. The only way we're going to get on with having a life together is if you work through it all now. Forget all the hassles about where to live. This is the thing that will make or break us. I don't want it to overshadow us forever. You have to, darling. Do it for me. Do it for us. Be brave."

He had firmly got me into a position where I couldn't refuse. "S'pose I could try," I muttered.

They wheeled me off in a squeaky wheelchair to see Penny's little room. I liked seeing new scenery, but I was nervous. I'm scared that, once I start talking about it, I'll get bogged down in this forever. In fact, I can't imagine not getting bogged down forever. Mum did. Will did. Why should I be different?

"Tell me what happened," said Penny, smiling and being all friendly. She seemed quite calm at having enticed me into her room. I'd expected triumphalism.

"You know what happened," I said. "Read the bloody papers."

"I want to hear it from you."

Stumblingly, I told her the story, missing things out, going back over them, and trying to make a shaky kind of sense of it. On the second session, she asked why Will hated me. I told her what I'd told the police, that, first of all, he was a nutter and not susceptible to normal rules of rationality, and secondly, he thought I'd had the stable, loving childhood he'd missed out on, and, incidentally, he was wrong. He hadn't known, or believed me when I told him, what Mum was like. If he'd known, he wouldn't have hated me. He'd have hated her.

"But there must have been a trigger for all this. Had you done something to upset him particularly, to set him off? I'm not saying it was your fault, quite the opposite in fact, but I do wonder if there's another issue in there." She was looking at me shrewdly. She wouldn't let go. She knew I was keeping something back.

Eventually, she wore me down. I asked whether the things I said were completely confidential. She tripped over her words in her haste to assure me that it was.

"Only if you absolutely promise not to tell anyone. Specially the police."

She promised with alacrity. I'd never heard her sounding keen before. I was interested to hear how it would come out.

"I'd told him something that I'd done," I said carefully. "I only told him because I was drunk after the funeral. He was asking me all about Mum and I didn't want him to, so in the end I told him the truth, which was that, well, first you have to understand about Mum . . ."

She already knew about Mum, but I told her all over again to emphasise that I was not a cold-blooded murderer. "I poisoned my mother with alcohol," I told her.

"And the police don't know."

"I'd appreciate it if they never did. I don't think they need to. There was lots of alcohol in her blood when she died, but no one questioned that."

"We'll leave it that way. Now, what do you suppose made you tell your brother?"

The relief was immense. Now I can actually have therapy that helps me. I don't have to keep anything back. I've seen Penny every day, and I like her more and more. It turns out that we talk about my childhood far more than we talk about Will. I'm beginning to realise, now, that most people would have cracked a long time before I did. That it really wasn't my fault. Or rather, what was my fault was that I never asked for help, even as an adult. I just carried on nursing her, and holding the outside world at bay, almost all the way through my twenties. If I'd just asked, I would have got help.

I'm also realising that, despite it all, I did love her in a funny kind of a way. And that I'm not a bad person. And, finally, that I need to establish as good a relationship as I can with my father. I've always overlooked him because he bailed out and left me behind.

Penny's middle-aged, and she's got a lovely face. She's the mother I would have wanted to have. When I told her that, she got alarmed and insisted I wasn't meant to form any kind of attachment, that she was just a neutral observer. But today I go home, which means I am "better," and the NHS decrees that I can see her for an hour a week.

"I really need to see her every day," I complained to Dad. "It's part of my recovery. Otherwise I could end up mad, like Mum."

He was trapped. "Go on then." He's paying, so I'm about to become one of her posh patients who, she says, pay for her agnès b wardrobe, her Armani glasses, and her holidays. Sometimes we just sit and talk about clothes. She says there are some gorgeous things in Ghost this summer. I can't wait to have the necessary functioning limbs to try them on. I've asked her to take me there (retail therapy is, after all, a well-known offshoot of boring old normal therapy), but she says it wouldn't be professional. Kate'll oblige.

My curtains are swept aside.

"Horrible morning," says Pamela, who is almost smiling. She plonks the breakfast tray in front of me and I haul myself up to a sitting position. "Looks like it's going to rain. So, today we see the back of you at last."

"No more hospital food. No more paper knickers. Poor me."

"Don't get too cocky, missy. You'll still be struggling to wipe your bum."

"Cheers." I'm going to be wheelchair-bound for a while because my right arm is too fucked to hold a crutch and, try as I might, I can't propel myself along without two. The attendant indignities are of a magnitude I had never contemplated before. It took me ages to get used to the bedpan and the bedbath. Being a patient, it seems, isn't all about lying back prettily, sighing, and being a poor little glamorous victim. I've always known I wasn't one of them anyway, but I liked the image.

"Eat that up, and we'll get you dressed. Your friend Kate brought some new clothes in for you to wear home."

"Did she? Where are they?"

"You can have them later."

"What does it say on the bag?"

She glares at me. "Go on, eat."

The last clothes I wore were my cold weather Mount Everest clothes. I was wearing jeans, tights, socks, boots, T-shirts, jumpers, a fleece, jacket, gloves, a scarf and a woolly hat when Max picked me up. Since I got back to London, I've been sporting the familiar hospital nightie, still the most undignified garment ever invented. It gapes open at the back, for no reason I can fathom except to remind the patients that they're at the mercy of other people's whims. It is teamed with paper knickers. I like watching people walking around the ward, trying to hold it shut behind them. I haven't had to do that because I haven't done much walking. I only managed one attempt at hopping along, with one crutch, and while I was trying, the fact that everyone could see my knickers didn't bother me. I was more worried about them all seeing my tattoo. I asked the doctor to remove it, but he said it wasn't his area of expertise. He agreed to refer me to the right person. As soon as I can move properly, it's coming off.

Max is going to have the task of taking me to the loo when we get to Dad's. I am appointing him Overseer of the Bodily Functions. Of course I would prefer not to. I'd quite like to retain just a little mystique, and I cringe at the things he's going to have to do for me. Despite everything, however, Max still seems to be Max, and I still seem to be me. Our relationship doesn't seem to have suffered from the revelation that the serial killer was my brother, and being back in Britain isn't entirely awful. In fact, it's comforting.

I wish we weren't staying at Dad's. It's the first place Will'll look for me. Even though Max will be staying there, he can't be with me all the time, and anyway, I can't rely on a man. I need to be able to look after myself. Will broke into the house before, and if they don't catch him he'll do it again. This time he'll really get me. I won't have a chance, because I won't be able to run. The police have installed a panic button, just in case (or "in the highly unlikely event of the suspect returning," as they invariably put it), but I'm still scared. I imagine the panic button being repeatedly pummelled by the toddlers, and the police ceasing to respond. I got Max to bring me a copy of *The Tibetan Book of Living and Dying*, so I can try to keep myself calm. I think of the monks in Tibet, living peacefully even though they're in constant danger. That's what I need to be like. I haven't started reading it yet. I will, though.

On the positive side, I'm interested in the idea of spending time with the remains of my family. Jessica seems like she's going to be a worthy sister. She's brought me all kinds of presents, from a homemade card she got all her class to sign, to chocolate, and a copy of *Harpers* she stole from Lola's bag. Even Lola seems to have lost her wary streak. I suppose she doesn't need to compete with Mum anymore, since first of all Mum's dead, but, more important, Mum spawned a psychopath. Grim as the children can be, none of them is likely to grow up to be Will. Max has made it his business to charm her, and consequently she professes delight that we're taking up residence for the foreseeable future.

Just as I am thinking of Max, he arrives. He is bearing a bouquet of flowers, and another sheaf of emails.

"Morning!" he says chirpily. "I've come to take you away."

"I've finished my breakfast," I tell him, upturning my face for a kiss. "I have served my sentence and I'm free to go. Pamela's got my clothes. Get me out of here."

"Roger and Jessica'll be here in a minute. Jess and I have been fighting over who gets to sit in the back with you."

"And who does?"

"Me. She was too tempted by the idea of the front seat."

I'd always had some notion that the act of coming home, to a country in which we were both brought up but had never been to together, would change me. Part of me feared I would revert to the party girl I used to be (I am, of course, now appreciating that chance would be a fine thing indeed). Max would be chilling out in India, and suddenly all we had would evaporate. I know we'd never have got on if we'd met before we left, if we hadn't stumbled upon each other in smelly old Ho Chi Minh City.

But now we're on home turf, in a place where we're going to have to live for a while at least, and it feels like a permanent relationship. Kate and Guy have been looking after Max—giving him food and drink, explaining how the Tube works, and bringing him to the hospital—and they profess to think he's wonderful. I love him more than I ever imagined loving anyone, and the strange thing is, he seems to feel the same way about me, despite all the danger, despite my unworthiness, and despite the fact that I'm smashed up and complaining heartily. He's a solid foundation, a rock. I don't quite know what I did to end up with him, but I am determined to keep him this time.

"Who are the flowers from?"

"They're from the Evans family. Amanda's parents. Look, read the card."

"They don't blame me? Really?"

"They certainly don't. Not at all."

"They must be heartbroken that I was the one that got away, not her. I wish it had been her. Shall I write and tell them?"

"Write to them, yes. There's no need to say that, though."

"OK."

"Here's the paper. Look, read this article. It's OK, it's not about you."

I take it. "No way!" I exclaim. "Those guys found Mallory? We certainly underestimated them."

"We certainly did." He smiles.

"Greg called this morning," he says, stroking my hair off my face. The colour of it is all over the place by now. It must be quite rare to have dark hair and blonde roots.

"How is he? Where are they?"

"India. Trying to work out where they can go, together. He reckons he'll go back to Laos for a bit and see what happens. They both send their love. You've got loads more emails, here. There's another one from Marge and Anna. There's a long one from someone called Carrie. Ally's written again. They've split up. Not surprising, and she sounds very upbeat. She's decided to get a working visa and come back here for a while."

"Brilliant."

"Andy's gone back to get divorced, she says. Bit slow off the mark. Poor guy. I had an email from him, and he's devastated. Mike's home too. He's applying for weekend custody of his little boy, at last. Kate says she'll drop by in the evening." Since I've been here, I've been amazed at the number of people I met travelling who've been in touch. Max monitors my email account for me. I seem to have more friends than I realised.

"Greg could just go and live in Phonsavanh, couldn't he, with all his money?"

"Can you imagine living out the rest of your days there?"

"Nope. Not here, either. When are we going home?"

"Now, it looks like. Here's Roger."

I look up and see my father and my half-sister—my sister—at the end of the ward. All eyes are upon them. Jessica runs over to my bed, skidding to a halt. She looks like a perfect little girl with her long dark hair and freckled button nose.

"Do you mind!" snaps Pamela as she passes. "No running, thank you."

Jessica wrinkles her nose. "She's not very friendly, is she?"

"Oh, she's all right," I tell her. "She's got a heart of gold."

"How can you have a *heart* of *gold*?" she demands.

I'm not an orphan, after all. I've got a family, and I've got friends. I've got a whole parent, who I hardly know at all. And I've got Max, holding my hand. Perhaps things are going to be all right.

I could really do with a drink.